WHERE THE LIONS ROAM

ALBERT SIUTA

Bob,
You Have Miles To Go
before you Sleep!

Albert Siuta (signature)

gatekeeper press™

Columbus, Ohio

Where The Lions Roam

Published by Gatekeeper Press
2167 Stringtown Rd, Suite 109
Columbus, OH 43123-2989
www.GatekeeperPress.com

Library of Congress Control Number: 2021937237

ISBN (paperback): 9781662906817
eISBN: 9781662910272

Dedicated to my mother and father.
This work brought you together again,
if only for a brief moment.

Rozelle Catholic High School

From the Desk of Bro. Owen Oakley

Principal

July 11, 2004

PJ:

Don't back out on me now! Taylor says you are having second thoughts about attending the cross country camp next month. She indicated that you think "it is a waste of the school's money." I assure you it is not! I am getting a lot of pressure from the archdiocese to increase our enrollment, and improving our sports program is one of the many improvements we are undertaking. We really need your help and expertise. I remember hearing stories about the teams we had during the mid-'60s to late '70s. Everyone wanted to run for RC!

The Xtreme Running Camp is the perfect opportunity to meet coaches and runners from other schools and find out what makes them tick. Even though we will not have any of our own runners at the camp, it is a good idea for you to attend and meet some of the coaches from the neighboring schools. More importantly, we want you to learn how to attract more kids to the sport! Last year only two people signed up for the team. Besides, with your love of the sport, I am sure you will enjoy the experience. Have fun.

Bro. Owen

P.S. How's the job search going? I see Mifflin Chemicals is going out of business. I guess they made a mistake last month when they let you go. Have faith. Endure!

Chapter 1

Xtreme Running Camp

At age thirty-seven, it had been nearly twenty years since PJ Irwin last attended a runners' camp as a high school student. Today, PJ as a high school coach arrived at the Xtreme Running Camp a little late on what was turning out to be a beautiful mid-August evening. As the other runners and coaches watched a training film on hill running, he slipped inconspicuously into the back of the room. PJ felt uncomfortable attending the training camp, because he didn't have a single runner of his own attending. But hey, it was an all-expense-paid trip to the Poconos, and a week of hill running. A week to consider the full-time job offer he had just received from Parker Engineering.

"Hi," came a voice from the shadows. "The name is Lebwink, Wayne Lebwink."

"Hi. I'm PJ Irwin."

"Where are you from?" asked Wayne, glancing toward the projection screen to check out a shot of Alberto Salazar winning the New York Marathon.

"Rozelle Catholic," PJ replied. "We're in—"

"New Jersey," Wayne interrupted. "Anyone who's been around as long as I have knows RC. They were a powerhouse in the '60s and '70s."

"So I've heard," PJ quipped, judging Wayne to be in his early sixties.

"They had this kid – Savage, Joel Savage – who held the state record in the mile at 4:11. From 1968 to 1972, they fielded nationally acclaimed teams in the distance medley and the two-mile and four-mile relays."

"They must have had a hell of a coach."

"A genius," Wayne said, displaying a thoughtful grin. "Gag was a former football player with no experience coaching distance runners when he took the helm as coach at RC."

"Gag?" asked PJ.

"You know, Frank Gagliardo. He coaches at Georgetown now," Wayne said in obvious disbelief that there was a cross country coach on the east coast who didn't know of the legendary Frank Gagliardo.

"Oh, Gagliardo," PJ answered, pretending to recognize the name.

"Yeah, he had amazing control over his kids," Wayne said. "But then again, Gag was one big, tough son of a gun who could probably wrestle King Kong to a draw. They were probably afraid to cross him."

"Really? Tell me more."

"Actually, the kids loved Gag. He studied thousands of articles and books on running and carefully applied what he learned. The kids really respected him. He bred discipline, fostered a seriousness. You know, discipline is the name of the game in this sport – in life too."

PJ glanced up at Wayne and noted his intense expression. Wayne looked toward the screen again, this time viewing an image of Abebe Bikila running hills in his heyday. Then without making eye contact with PJ, he said, "It's been twenty years since we saw the long green line!"

PJ wondered what Wayne meant, and while he waited to question him about it, he overheard him and another coach discussing a problem with one of the teams that hadn't arrived yet. Something about the bus breaking down and that they would be arriving very early the next morning.

On the way back to the cabin to turn in for the evening, PJ hurried after Wayne and caught him just before he entered his cabin. "Mr. Lebwink?" PJ prompted.

"Yes?" Wayne asked, reaching toward the screen door without looking back at PJ.

"What did you mean, 'the long green line?'"

"You know, green. RC's team color. They would run as a pack in races and come across the finish line single file, creating a long green line," Wayne said. "See you tomorrow, Irwin," he added, then slipped into the cabin for the night.

It turned out to be a long evening for PJ, as he grew tired of answering the question "Who are you?" and coming up with excuses as to why he didn't have a team with him at camp. Finally, after one fine coach snickered when PJ told him he was coaching at RC, he decided to head back to the cabin he was sharing with six runners from St. Joseph's High School in Metuchen, New Jersey.

Along the way, he thought of his wife Taylor, who had gotten him the coaching position at RC where she worked as the assistant to the principal. Getting PJ this job was a way of getting him back on his feet after the layoff. More importantly, Taylor couldn't stand having PJ at home during the layoff. He was driving her crazy, and he knew it. Lacking a job to keep him occupied, PJ had reverted to re-engineering their home and lives. He thought there was a better way to do everything, and usually he was right. He couldn't rest if there was a leaky faucet, a broken hinge, or an overgrown lawn. He was a product of his upbringing.

PJ's mother raised him on her own after his father was killed in Vietnam while he was still an infant. The only picture he had ever seen of his father was a blurred black-and-white image showing him with a few other eventual war casualties.

PJ's mother made up for the lack of a father figure by enrolling him in Cub Scouts, Boy Scouts, Little League, the Polish Falcons, and an all-boys parochial school. She provided most of the discipline he needed, and made most of his decisions for him until about ten years ago when she started to deteriorate from Alzheimer's. Shortly after the diagnosis, he met Taylor, and they eventually married. He still took care of his mother, who at times didn't even know who he was.

It was his mother who instilled the discipline that was intrinsic to him becoming one of the top runners in New Jersey. PJ could still run a 10K in less than thirty minutes, and was considering one final run at making the Olympic trials. With a little bit of serious training, he thought he just might be able to do it; and now that he didn't have to travel on engineering assignments every week, he might have the opportunity to train better and get his times down to Olympic standards. The only thing that could possibly stand in his way was this temporary job coaching cross country at RC this year.

PJ wasn't very fond of teenagers, and only took the assignment because Taylor had begged him. She had him wrapped around her finger, and had convinced PJ that this experience would prepare him for when their eight-year-old son David reached that age. As a result, now here he was at running camp, somewhere in South Sterling, Pennsylvania – bug-ridden, manure-scented, horse-and-buggy-infested Pennsylvania.

As PJ prepared for bed, he decided he would get up extra early and go running before the rest of the coaches and runners got up for their morning workout. Then he would dedicate his morning to helping the kitchen crew serve breakfast to the other runners and coaches, putting off another round of introductions and questions such as "Where's your team?"

As he lowered himself into bed, he heard a radio in a neighboring cabin playing "Jamaica Say You Will" by Jackson Browne, a song he remembered from one of his mother's albums. She used to say his lyrics reminded her of Paul, her late husband and PJ's dad.

She didn't say much of anything anymore.

A cool breeze wafting in through an open window washed across PJ's face as he waited to drift off into sleep, and he smiled and thought of his father, wondering what he was like. He imagined how different their lives would have been if the helicopter carrying his father hadn't been shot down in Vietnam in 1969 when Paul Senior was only twenty-eight. He wondered what it would have been like to really know the man.

As a second breeze washed across his face and slightly chilled the tears that had formed in his eyes, PJ turned and gazed out the cabin window toward the moon, sighed deeply, and shut his eyes.

Chapter 2

Warming Up

"Huh? Is it morning already? It's still dark!" asked one of the young runners who was sharing his room from inside a nearby sleeping bag.

"No, son. Not yet. Go back to sleep," PJ said as he slipped through the screen door out into the cool morning air.

Sitting down on the front porch steps, PJ put on his Asics running shoes, the brand he had been loyal to since his high school days in the early '80s. Back then the company was known as Tiger, and their shoes were hard to find. The running boom that started in the late '70s, though, put the company on the map. Prior to that, PJ purchased his Tiger Montreals from a guy who ran a shoe distributorship out of an old garage, located behind a funeral home in Massachusetts.

PJ was also loyal to his pre-run stretching routine: toe touches, followed by Achilles stretches, thigh stretches and groin stretches. He did them slowly, holding them while he counted to fifteen; and while he stretched, he thought about almost anything – his family, his friends, his job, his latest bowel movement…just about anything. Today he thought about Parker Engineering.

An outfit that designed and built chemical plants, Parker Engineering would hire project engineers like PJ in large numbers, and release them in a like manner when the workload dropped. Normally, PJ wouldn't even consider interviewing with an engineering firm; but it had been nearly a year since the layoff, and he was beginning to dip into his post-severance package savings.

Parker Engineering was a local firm with good community ties. They held a 15K race every September, and many runners planning to run the New York Marathon ran Parker's race as a final tune-up for the marathon. Parker also designed and built the football stadium for Abraham Clark, the local public high school, and called the stadium Elliot Field in memory of Elliot Parker, who founded the company in 1948. A self-made millionaire, he contributed millions to both the school and town until he died of a stroke in 1988. The company was now owned and operated by his son, Victor, who shared much of his father's devotion to the community, though Victor had become a recluse since his seventeen-year-old daughter committed suicide in 1984.

Thirteen, fourteen, fifteen, PJ thought as he did one final groin stretch.

Sliding his hands across his calf muscle, he felt it twitch as he played with the stretch, bringing back the memory of the time his mother tried to teach him how to wrestle. PJ had been bullied by Ralph Barracks, a neighborhood kid, and PJ's mother Rose took it upon herself to teach him to defend himself. She came from Irish stock and knew how to handle herself. PJ recalled trying to get away from one of her wrestling moves, and as he grabbed her leg he realized how muscular she was. As hard as he tried, her speed and strength were just too much for ten-year-old PJ. Regardless, her lessons had formed the foundation of PJ's strength through his life, and he smiled as he gave the stretch one final pull before jumping to his feet to start his run.

PJ descended from the porch and jogged toward the camp exit, stopping in front of the main lodge to review a map of the running loops laid out by the coaching staff. One seven-mile loop exited the camp in an eastward direction and traveled a half mile up a steep hill, then wound along a beautiful, partially paved mountain path known as Cliffside Road. He thought this would be a nice run since the sun would rise in about twenty minutes, and he had overheard the night before that the views from Cliffside Road were supposed to be stunning.

The second option for running this morning was the easier downhill loop into town, which would be much more forgiving on his legs at this early hour.

After taking a quick sip of water from the fountain, PJ was on his way. As he approached the exit of the campground, PJ was still wrestling with which way to go. His legs were tight, and the cool morning fog made it more difficult to loosen up. Would it be left for the steep uphill, or right for the easy run into town?

Which way would mom go? PJ thought to himself.

Chapter 3

Fog Running

Taking off to the left, PJ headed uphill toward Cliffside Road. *Never waste a hill*, he thought as he battled the ascent and tried to wake up his sleeping legs.

Normally, PJ worked out twice a day, six days per week. Six months earlier, he had increased the intensity of his training routine after reading about Umar Sayed, a rival from his high school running days, who was tearing up the New Jersey road racing circuit. In 1978, Umar and PJ ran first and second in the New Jersey Meet of Champions at Holmdel Park, Umar edging PJ over the last twenty yards of the 5K race to win in 15:53, even though a week earlier PJ had run 15:40 unchallenged on the same course at the group meet.

A local reporter, Grant Edwins, who had been covering the sport for the last forty years, reported after the championship meet that "Sayed had risen to the occasion" and that the finish "proved too intense for Irwin." Crushed by the article, PJ went out four days later and ran 15:35 during a practice run on the same course.

PJ was currently entertaining a fantasy that he would train incognito until he was ready to race again, and then face Sayed on the road race circuit. He had improved his training program during the first part of the year and won two races during the last two months. (Well, he didn't exactly win, but he would have had he entered.) In June he jumped into the 10K run sponsored by the city of Elizabeth and ran unofficially without entering. During the last mile of the race, he unleashed a final kick that put him thirty to forty seconds ahead of the second runner. At the final cross street, PJ turned abruptly and ran in the opposite direction without completing the race. As he passed the runner-up, Rufino Mendosa, he congratulated him on a nice race and headed off toward Warinanco Park.

He had done what he set out to do – test the waters. Mendosa eventually won the race, and during a post-race interview he referred to the "Elizabeth Phantom" who had led most of the race, then turned around and ran off into oblivion. PJ framed the article and hung it in the basement next to his weightlifting set.

A few minutes after he passed through the totem poles that bordered the camp entrance, PJ completed the initial hill climb and was into a rhythmic pace, lengthening each stride as he loosened up on a flat section of road.

As PJ passed a mailbox bearing the name "Zimmer," a dog barked in the distance. PJ could barely see the house through the thick fog that enveloped the area. *I hope it's not a goddamned chihuahua on the loose*, thought PJ. When he was twelve, a chihuahua put him in the hospital when it bit him in the Achilles.

"Ugly damn rodent dogs!" he scoffed under his breath, picking up his pace a bit until he was convinced he was not being followed.

Approximately three quarters of a mile into the run, the road veered to the left and began to rise sharply in another uphill grade that was heavily shrouded in fog. PJ did his best to stay on the dirt road by looking straight down for signs of tire tracks. Shortening his stride, he leaned into the hill as he tried to maintain his pace. To the right, the terrain began to drop off as he continued to ascend the hill that seemed to spiral in a never-ending curve to the left. His legs were beginning to burn, and he started to use his arms more to gain momentum as he fought the hill.

With sunrise still ten minutes away and a heavy fog covering the area, PJ made his way to what appeared to be the centerline of the road as it straightened out for a brief spell. Off to the right was a sharp drop-off with a view that was still hidden by the lack of daylight – and heavy fog – making PJ unaware of the beautiful vista he was missing. Cliffside Road was four miles long, though, and there would be plenty of views to take in after sunrise.

Just then, the road began to spiral to the left and slightly downhill, just enough to rest his legs and provide the setting he needed for a brief burst of speed.

I'll cut a tangent and run as close as possible to the corner jutting out of this mountain, PJ strategized. *Then I'll carry the pace for another four hundred yards and ease off.*

Suddenly, PJ felt a pain across his forehead, chin, chest and thigh, then found himself crashing to the ground.

"Oh shit," he muttered. "What the hell was that?" PJ peered behind him as he staggered to his feet in the middle of the road, his head reeling with pain as he tried to focus on the surroundings.

At first he couldn't see the obstacle he had run into; but then through the fog, he made out a metal utility pole support cable. "What friggin' hick puts a cable like that so close to the road!" he lamented, rubbing his sore forehead. "Who the hell would put—"

He felt the sting of blood dripping into his eye, and began to remove his shirt to wrap it around his head, which ached so severely that he started to think he may have to turn around and go back to the camp.

As he pulled his shirt over his head, he saw a flash of light around the corner of the mountain. At first, he thought he was beginning to pass out, but then through the fog and darkness, he watched as the light divided into two round orbs. At the same time, he noticed the sound of a diesel engine growing louder. *What the hell?* PJ thought as he looked toward the orbs.

Suddenly, the source of the light became clear to him. A vehicle was heading through the fog straight toward him, the noise of the engine growing louder as the fog-enveloped mass took shape. It was a truck of some sort…no…it was a bus! A school bus full of children was bearing down on him; and for some reason, through all the fog, PJ was able to make out the horrified look on the bus driver's face as he tried to avoid the runner.

To avoid the bus, PJ ran to the right side of the road, which was blanketed in fog that disguised the sharp drop-off only a couple feet beyond the edge. The bus driver slammed on the brakes, and the bus veered in the same direction.

As PJ left the roadway, he felt the ground give way beneath his feet. In a flash he was airborne, and then tumbling down the side of the mountain. Despite the chaos of the fall, PJ recognized the loud noise the bus made as it impacted the side of the mountain and began to cartwheel down the slope, following closely behind PJ.

Despite the fog, it was light enough now for PJ to see the rear door of the bus fly open as it careened down the hill. He watched in horror as one of the occupants was ejected and the bus bounced completely over him, coming to rest about twenty yards below him.

Clinging to the root of an evergreen, PJ heard the moan of fire erupting under bus. He tried to get up to check on the bus occupants, but his own pain was too intense. A few seconds later, there was a tremendous explosion, and PJ knew the spilled fuel surrounding the bus had ignited the fuel tank. What was left of the bus was engulfed in flames.

There were a few screams, followed by an eerie silence. PJ grimaced and sobbed, giving into the feeling of helplessness that overtook him. He couldn't move. He couldn't help those kids.

When his head dropped wearily to his left, he caught sight of another set of eyes staring directly into his. *Lifeless eyes*, he thought. *The eyes of a young boy. Can't be more than sixteen.* The boy wore an old, worn-out gray and green sweatsuit.

Just then, the boy's eyes focused on PJ. He coughed and then muttered something that PJ did not quite hear.

"Whaaat?" PJ groaned.

Once again, the boy peered into PJ's eyes, but this time an eerie feeling came over PJ. He listened hard to the words the boy uttered.

"We have to…win the…Easterns this…year," the boy gurgled in a low, barely audible voice.

Win the Easterns? PJ thought. *Damn, this bus must be the group of high school runners that didn't make it to camp last night.* Only bona fide runners would know that the "Easterns" were the East Coast Championship Cross Country Meet held every year at Van Cortlandt Park in the Bronx, New York, or at Warinanco Park, in Rozelle, New Jersey.

PJ looked at the boy and noticed blood flowing from where his left ear used to be. The boy reached out his hand and touched PJ's face just before his head slumped, and very soon after his hand grew cold. The only sign of life from the twisted wreckage had succumbed to his injuries. Only PJ remained.

He closed his eyes and drifted off.

Chapter 4

Alzheimer's

"Let's go, Dave! It's time to go!" Taylor called out across the yard to her son. The eight-year-old sprang from the swing set and broke into a sprint, headed for the Tahoe.

"Looks just like his ol' man!" called their neighbor, Fred Biff, the head basketball coach at RC. Fred grew up with PJ's mother; they had been part of the same parish since they were children.

"Tell me about it!" Taylor answered. "I can't keep up with either of them."

"Heading out to see Rose?" Fred asked.

"Yes," answered Taylor. "The home just called and said she started talking briefly this morning."

"Really? That's great."

"Yeah, who knows? They said she seemed alert and coherent," Taylor answered, her voice breaking slightly. "I just thought I'd go and see if David could get a glimpse of the 'old' Rose Irwin."

"I hope he can," said Fred. "She was something, that Rose. I remember the day she got the news of Paul Senior's death. She was so strong…so very strong! She's been through so much."

PJ had been named "Paul James" after his father, Paul Senior; but ever since she received that telegram in August 1969, telling her that Paul Senior had been killed, Rose had been PJ's source of strength. Taylor knew that Rose was the person who molded him, and that PJ couldn't imagine not having her around. She feared that soon, though, he would have to face this reality.

Rosemont Nursing Home was located in West Orange, New Jersey, in a beautifully serene setting, surrounded by a stone wall that revealed little of the grounds inside. Inside the entrance gate, the driveway wound for about a half mile, bordered on both sides by dense evergreens. Regardless of the idyllic setting, Taylor was always uncomfortable when she visited, and as the main building broke into view, she immediately noticed a myriad of lonely eyes peering through windows of rooms occupied by guests of the nursing home.

Sad, she thought.

As she pulled in to park the car, she glanced up toward Rose's window. For a moment she thought she saw someone looking out at them, but she wasn't sure. Bringing the car to a halt in the visitor lot, she looked back again toward Rose's window, but this time there didn't appear to be anyone there.

Wishful thinking. I'd love to be able to tell PJ I spoke with his mother today, she thought.

As Taylor and David entered the lobby, two of the female residents noticed David and smiled at him. Shy by nature, David moved behind his mother. Taylor smiled at the women and said, "Hello, this is David. He's a little shy."

The women, both appearing to be in their eighties, giggled and craned their necks to get another look at David.

Blushing, David rolled his eyes and said, "C'mon, Mom, let's go see Grammy!"

Chuckling, Taylor said, "Okay, let's go! See you gals later!"

As they entered Rose's room, they found her sitting on the edge of her bed. When Rose looked toward them, they noticed that her eyes were wide open and red and that her cheeks were tearstained, as if she had been crying.

Just then, Dr. Mass entered the room. "I'm so glad you were able to make it, Taylor," he said. "She seems to be very upset today. More flashbacks to Paul Senior's last moments in Vietnam. I thought you might be able to help comfort her." With that, Dr. Mass patted David on the head and left to continue with the rest of his rounds.

"Hello, Rose," Taylor said. "How are you today?"

Rose slowly raised her head and gazed out the window for a few moments. As she turned back toward Taylor, her shoulders slumped, and her eyes welled up with tears. She reached out for Taylor, and the two embraced.

"Paul has been in a terrible accident," she said. "He's been hurt very badly. His head is bleeding," she added as she started to cry a little harder. "Lots of twisted wreckage…" she said, groaning softly.

Taylor's eyes filled with tears as she hugged Rose. *How tough it must be to lose the only man she ever loved*, Taylor thought. *For the last thirty years these nightmares have been haunting her. Reliving the helicopter crash…the notification of her husband's death…the funeral she attended with PJ – or "little Paul," as she liked to refer to him.*

Taylor wished she could find the right words to console her mother-in-law, but they just wouldn't come. Instead, she simply held Rose in her arms until the older woman grew too weary to sit up any longer. As she helped Rose into bed, David continued to play with a ball he had smuggled into the nursing home. Taylor wiped the tears from Rose's cheeks and kissed her.

"Come on, Dave," Taylor said. "Grammy needs her rest."

As they headed down the hallway toward the lobby, David turned back when he realized he had forgotten his ball. "I'll be right back, Mom," he said. He sped off down the hall and disappeared inside Rose's room.

While Taylor waited near the lobby, David slowly tiptoed toward the table next to Grammy's bed, where his ball sat just as he left it. As he reached for the ball, David was startled by the sound of his grandmother's voice.

"My Paul…my little Paul…he's been hurt," she groaned. "Please tell your mommy to go to him," she added.

David stared at her for a moment and then ran out of the room and back down the hall. "Mommy, Mommy!" he called out.

"Shush!" she replied. "Some people are trying to rest right now!"

As they drove home, Taylor tried to explain to David what had just taken place, telling him about his grandfather and how he lost his life in the war in a helicopter crash. She explained that his grandmother had flashbacks and dreams about the tragedy.

"Was Grandpa short?" David asked.

Surprised by the question, Taylor fought back giggles as she turned and looked at the boy. "Why no, I don't think so. Why do you ask?"

"Because when I went back to her room to get the ball, she said 'little Paul' had been hurt," he remarked.

"Hmm, I don't know, David. I don't think he was short," she replied as a strange uneasiness fell upon her. "Come on, let's get home and wait for Daddy to call us from camp."

Chapter 5

Blowing in the Wind

When they returned home, Taylor noticed the red light flashing on the answering machine. Three messages were waiting. "I'm going to play Nintendo!" David shouted as he ran into the family room.

Taylor pressed the playback button on the answering machine. The first message was from her friend, Bea Strong, who had just gotten tickets to see Jackson Browne at the Garden State Arts Center and wanted to know if she and PJ were interested in going.

"Well, that's a dumb question," Taylor giggled. "PJ owns every Jackson Browne album ever made, including a few bootleg albums. He would *never* miss an opportunity to see Jackson Browne!"

The second message was apparently a wrong number. It sounded like a young boy, perhaps a teenager. "The long green line," he whispered. "It'll be beautiful, man, beautiful!" He added, "And you won't regret it, we promise!" Then there was silence.

As she was entering David's room to collect a load of clothes for the wash, the third message caught Taylor off guard. "Hello, Taylor. This is Dr. Alonso with the South Sterling Medical Center," the caller opened as Taylor rushed into the den to hear the rest of the message. "This call concerns your husband, PJ. No reason to be alarmed. However, it would be best if you could call me at 717-555-8956 when you receive this message."

Taylor immediately dialed the number and impatiently waited for the phone to be answered. *I hope it's not another bout with kidney stones*, Taylor thought. Ever since PJ eliminated caffeine from his diet, he hadn't had any more problems with them. However, the stress of unemployment could be a trigger.

"Good afternoon, South Sterling Medical Center. How may I direct your call?" a hurried operator squawked from the other end.

"Yes, I'd like to speak with Dr. Alonso, please," Taylor said.

"Hold on while I page him," the operator responded.

The silence was deafening, and Taylor's palms began to sweat. She loved PJ to pieces. Some years earlier he had been diagnosed with high blood pressure and high cholesterol. He had briefly given up running in his mid-twenties, and his weight had ballooned. After his friend Kevin died of a heart attack at thirty-seven, PJ decided to change his lifestyle and take up running again. Ever since, he had been the picture of health... except for the kidney stones.

"Hello, this is Dr. Alonso," a voice bellowed from the receiver.

"Hello, Dr. Alonso, my name is Taylor Irwin. I'm returning your call regarding my husband, PJ." She started to add, "You called earlier about—"

"Oh yes, our runner friend," the doctor responded briskly. "Well, he took a bad fall and he's a little cut up. Nothing severe, but he has suffered a minor concussion. It would be best if someone could come and take him home. I don't think he should be behind the wheel of a car."

"You're sure he's okay?" Taylor asked, her worry evident in her tone.

"He's fine," the doctor answered. "When can we expect someone to pick him up?"

"I can be there in about three hours," Taylor said.

"Good. I'll forward you to the courtesy desk and they can provide you with directions," Dr. Alonso said, transferring the call to the operator.

Courtesy desk? Taylor thought. *I hope they can help me with directions!*

After retrieving David from the family room, the two of them set out in the Tahoe to bring PJ home. Along the way, Taylor realized that she probably should've called PJ's room to talk to him. Recounting what the doctor had said to her, she realized that she didn't know the nature of PJ's "cuts and bruises."

"Mom?" David asked.

"What, hon?" Taylor answered, glancing over at him.

"Do you think Nike will get into Fred's garbage while we're gone?" he asked with a grin.

"Oh shi—!" Taylor quipped. Nike was their six-year-old, sixty-five-pound springer spaniel who was hyper beyond belief. A week ago, he got into the neighbor's garbage and left a trail of it leading directly to their house. It took Taylor two hours to clean up the mess before Fred returned home.

The dog seemed to be acting up quite a bit lately. First the garbage, then he went off into the woods and rolled around in a dead deer carcass. Taylor grinned as she recalled PJ running up and playfully tackling the dog, only to realize the dog smelled like decaying flesh. Nike kept jumping on PJ until PJ was finally able to snag some soap and the hose and clean the dog up. The whole time PJ kept complaining about what a "smelly bastard" Nike was. It was comical watching the two of them.

"If he does," Taylor said, turning her attention back to David, "then we'll just have to ask Daddy to clean it up this time."

"If he isn't hurt too bad," David added.

Taylor noticed the concern in David's expression and assured him that the doctor said it was minor. In her own mind, though, she wondered.

As Taylor continued her drive up Route 206, she remembered another Nike incident that PJ witnessed two weeks earlier. It was about six in the evening, and PJ had left for a run at Warinanco Park. He had just passed a group of local runners who were in various stages of warming up, when suddenly from out of nowhere Nike came running across the football field directly toward the runners, stopping and eagerly accepting the petting from the group. Then as he turned to leave, Nike took hold of one of the runner's shoes lying loose on the ground and ran off. As he sped out of sight with the irate runner's shoe, PJ laid low, not letting on that the dog was his. Later that evening when PJ returned home, he came across the shoe lying on his front porch. The shoe was a Nike Oregon Waffle model, popular in the '70s, and still in pretty decent condition.

"Nike probably did this guy a favor," PJ told Taylor that evening. "They have much better shoes nowadays."

At about 5:30 that afternoon, Taylor crossed over the Delaware River into Milford, Pennsylvania. David was squirming a bit, so she knew she'd better stop soon. She pulled the Tahoe over at a Getty station in Milford, across the street from the Hoagies and Grinders Hut where she and PJ had their first lunch together. Back when they first started dating, they used to go camping in the Poconos during the summer. PJ loved running in the mountains, and Taylor just loved the quiet times together with him.

A bell rang as Taylor entered the station and pulled up to the pump. An elderly attendant with a handlebar mustache approached the car. "What'll it be, young lady?" he asked with a smile.

"Uh, fill it up, please," Taylor answered. "And may we use your restroom?" she asked, nodding toward David as he emerged from the car.

"Oh yes, go right ahead," the attendant responded with a slight laugh. "The key's in the office on the counter."

Taylor nodded and headed toward the office with David at her side. Upon entering, Taylor immediately picked up the scent of the attendant's half-eaten Italian sub that was sitting next to the keys.

"I'm hungry, Mom," David said, also noticing the sandwich on the counter.

"Me too, Dave," Taylor replied as she reached for the keys. "But we're in a hurry to pick up Daddy. We'll just grab some snacks when we leave." She pointed to a display case with chips, pretzels and other junk food.

David's eyes widened when he noticed a box of his favorite cookies. "Great, Mom!" he cheered. "They have Mallomars!"

"Wonderful," Taylor mumbled as she led him out and around the side of the building.

Taylor waited outside as David went into the vacant restroom. "Make sure you wash your hands," she told him.

"Yes, Mom," he answered, closing the door behind him.

David had recently graduated from toilet to urinal, but this was the first time he would use the urinal without his dad being nearby. As he fumbled with his fly, he glanced around the room, taking in the array of graffiti that had been deposited over the ages. He noticed one that said "Milford High School Sucks!"

I hope I don't ever go to that school, he thought, as if the graffiti had been written to inform him personally of important news.

Above the mirror he noticed a poem that some scholar from yesteryear had left. "Here I sit, brokenhearted / tried to shit but only farted," it read in thick black ink. David giggled. He could never swear at home, and reading it in the privacy of the Getty station restroom made him feel as if he was getting away with something.

"David! Are you almost done in there?" Taylor's voice emerged from outside the restroom.

"I'll be done in a second, Mom," David said as he hurriedly finished unzipping and started to relieve himself. As David methodically wet down the entire backside of the urinal, his eyes moved toward some tiny graffiti written on the grout between some ceramic tiles bordering the urinal. When he finished peeing, he moved closer to the tile so that he could read it. Squinting, he read the words written in faded blue ink. "David, always remember, the answer is blowing in the wind." David angled his head so that he could read the remaining few words that ran vertically down the tile grout. "And help your mom feed Nike every once in a while!"

David dashed out of the restroom, eyes wide with eagerness to share what he had just read with his mom. As he glanced around, looking for her, he noticed she was holding a chocolate ice cream cone. She motioned for him to come and take it while she continued to pay at the cash register. A few moments later he was face-deep in Hershey's best, and he had completely forgotten about what he had read on the men's room wall.

Chapter 6

Just Something He Ate

The rest of the trip to South Sterling, Pennsylvania, was uneventful. David had fallen asleep shortly after finishing the ice cream cone, so Taylor entertained herself by flipping through the radio stations in search of something that was not country music or news.

The South Sterling Medical Center was a ragtag collection of buildings of different shapes and sizes, the majority of which were red brick and most likely from the early 1900s. The largest building had a more modern glass solarium section, which appeared to be the main entrance. Taylor parked in the visitor's lot located immediately in front of the building.

"C'mon, David, let's get up. We're here," Taylor whispered as she gently shook her son awake.

David smiled as he focused on Taylor and then realized where he was. "Let's go get Daddy!" he exclaimed as he grabbed for the door handle.

Taylor quickly exited her side of the Tahoe and ran around to grab David's hand. He tried to pull free, but to no avail.

As they entered the building, Taylor noticed how busy the place – which appeared to be in the middle of nowhere – actually was. Spying what looked like an information desk, she headed toward it; but just then the emergency room entrance door flew open. Two paramedics rushed in with a patient on a stretcher.

"Mary, we've got another one from Paintball Express!" the lead paramedic shouted.

"Okay, Tom," a nurse in the emergency treatment area responded. "Put him in Room 4."

"That's the fourth one today," the receptionist behind the counter said to Taylor as their eyes met. "That paintball place should have been closed down months ago!" she added. "Anyway, how can I help you?"

"I'm here to pick up my husband, PJ Irwin," Taylor answered.

"Oh yes, the runner with the concussion," the receptionist answered. "He's in Room 327. I think the doctor wants to speak with him before he leaves. I'll let the doctor know you're here. Meanwhile, you can take the elevator to the third floor and meet him in his room."

David smiled, thinking, *Oh boy, I love elevator rides!*

As Taylor exited the elevator on the third floor, she again noticed how busy the hospital appeared to be. She walked slowly down the corridor until she came to Room 327. Poking her head inside, she saw PJ sleeping in a bed near the window. He was the only one in the room. As she drew closer, she noticed a slight abrasion on his forehead in the shape of a diagonal line running down through his eyebrow and continuing across his lower lip. She also noticed a similar long scratch in his chest, as if something had slashed across his forehead, lip and chest in one swoop.

"Is he asleep, Mommy?" David asked.

"Taylor?" PJ muttered.

"Yes, honey, it's me," she replied. "How are you feeling?"

"Oh Taylor," he moaned. "It was all my fault."

"What was all your fault?" she asked, surprised.

"I caused the accident. I killed them!" he said and started to cry.

"What?!" Taylor asked. "What accident?"

PJ looked at David and then back to Taylor. "The bus accident…the runners who were killed…I walked out in front of their bus early this morning and caused the bus to drive off the road to miss me." He tried to control his sobs.

"What?" Taylor gasped. She had been told nothing of this on the phone.

"I've asked for an update on their condition. I asked if anyone survived," PJ added. "But no one will give me a straight answer. I've got to know. My friggin' head is killing me!"

Taylor dashed from the room and grabbed an intern walking past the nurses' station. "What happened to the kids on the bus?" Taylor demanded.

"You must be Mr. Irwin's wife," the intern said, a grin appearing on his face. "I told your husband at least three times that there was *no bus accident.*"

"What do you mean?" Taylor asked. "He said he caused a bus accident—"

"I know, Mrs. Irwin," the intern interrupted politely, "but it never really happened. Your husband was running before dawn – in the fog, I might add – and ran into a steel utility-pole support cable."

"Is that why he has the racing stripe on his forehead and chest?" Taylor asked.

"Exactly," the intern answered with a chuckle. "He's going to be alright. Luckily for him, my neighbor likes to walk his chihuahua in the early morning. He found your husband unconscious in the middle of the road, above the campground. In a way, your husband owes his life to my neighbor's chihuahua, because that little rascal was up barking and wanting to go for a walk early this morning."

He paused, then added more seriously, "When people suffer a blow to the forehead like he did, they often wake up with memory loss or speaking of visions and dreams. It's usually only a short-term issue and nothing to worry about. Trust me, he'll be alright."

Relieved, Taylor turned to go back to PJ's room. "Can he go home with us tonight?" she asked.

"Of course, but he can't drive. He's on some pretty strong painkillers right now."

"So what did you find out?" PJ asked as Taylor re-entered the room.

"I found out the bus accident was just a dream that resulted from the blow to your forehead," Taylor answered with a laugh.

"That's what the doctor said, but I was there. I saw it all!" PJ barked.

"PJ, relax," Taylor answered. "You whacked your head pretty hard and were out cold for a while. A local found you lying on the road above the campground. You apparently ran into a steel utility cable and knocked yourself out," she added.

Pulling out a compact from her purse and holding the mirror out to him, she asked, "Don't you remember any of this?" She held the mirror so that PJ could see the cut on his forehead, eyebrow and lip. "These cuts match the slice on your chest."

PJ studied the image in the mirror and the cut on his chest. "I see," he said, sounding relieved. "So there was no bus accident?"

"Nope! Just a downed marathoner."

"I may be down, but not for long. I've got Sayed and the Open 5K Championship to prepare for." With that, PJ jumped out of bed, grabbed his head for a moment, then looked at David and ruffled his son's hair. "C'mon, champ," PJ said to David. "Let's blow this popsicle joint!" David smiled and helped his dad gather his things for the ride home.

As they exited the hospital, PJ looked back at the building, stopping briefly to hug Taylor. "It was just so real. I...I'm so relieved," he whispered into her ear, his voice cracking.

Taylor could feel his weight shift and his knees buckle slightly. She helped him to the car, and they were soon on the way home. Along the way, she mentioned the hero chihuahua to PJ. He just moaned and shook his head.

Chapter 7

Baldpate Mountain

The ride home was a quiet one, with both PJ and David sleeping most of the way. Taylor passed the time by listening to the latest Stephen King novel on cassette. She was an avid fan of the great horror writer.

As she turned onto Delaware Avenue near Rosedale Park, the cassette tape came to the end and automatically ejected, and the radio started to play "Band on the Run" by Paul McCartney and Wings. PJ always kept the radio station in the Tahoe set at 103.5, a '70s station. Taylor looked over at her sleeping husband, smiled, and switched to 98.5 in time to hear the tail end of Sting's latest ballad.

As Taylor pulled into their driveway, she stopped to get the mail from the box on the other side of the road. When she started to cross back across the roadway, she noticed a group of young men running down the street. As they passed, she was impressed by how fit – and how extremely quiet – they were. She couldn't even hear their footsteps as they passed by. Her eyes met the lead runner's as they passed.

"Hello, Mrs. Irwin," he said, taking Taylor by surprise.

"Huh? Uh, hi," she returned as she watched them go by. *Cute-looking bunch*, she thought. *And how quiet they run, like Kenyans.*

As Taylor hopped back into the Tahoe, PJ woke up from his nap. "How ya feeling?" Taylor asked.

"Ugh," he groaned.

"Do you know those runners?" she asked him, motioning behind her toward the road winding past their house.

PJ looked but saw no one. "What runners?"

Taylor looked back in the mirror and could see no one either. "They must've already passed over the rise in front of Weidel's house."

"Were they that local group of master runners?" PJ asked. "That's what I need, a little more age-group competition."

"No," Taylor answered. "They looked like high school or college age. Kind of cute, nice form."

"Nice form," PJ teased. "From the rear view, I bet!" he added with a raised brow.

"Oh, hush," Taylor snapped back playfully. As she continued up the driveway, she spied the western edge of their property, which was an open field with a view of Pleasant Valley Road, approximately 1,200 meters from the driveway. She knew this because PJ used this stretch of road to do threshold-level repeats of 1,200 meters. Slowly she inched the car toward the house, trying to catch one last glimpse of the runners. *C'mon, show yourselves*, she thought.

"Hey, how about parking this thing? I gotta piss!" PJ blurted out.

"Strangest thing," Taylor remarked.

"What's that?"

"Those runners. I thought we'd see them over there by now," she said, pointing past Weidel's place.

"They were probably trail runners and entered the woods at the Baldpate Trail."

"Oh yeah, I forgot about that," Taylor said as she came to a stop and put the car in park.

The Baldpate Trail was a beautiful path through the old Kyzer estate. The Kyzers had donated the land to the township with the stipulation that it remain undeveloped. The entrance to the trail was about 400 meters up the road from the Irwin house, and Taylor enjoyed running this trail with Nike. Approximately a mile and a half into the trail was a small clearing with some abandoned buildings and a pond. Nike loved to take a dip in the water while Taylor stopped and stretched. On occasion, Taylor would invite PJ for a "run in the woods," and these dashes would always end up with an escapade inside one of the abandoned buildings. On one occasion, a bare-assed PJ nearly got to meet the groundskeeper for the place. Fortunately, a scantily clad Taylor ran interference while PJ finished dressing, slinked out the back of the building, and dashed off into the woods.

Chapter 8

Time for an Ass Whoopin'

August 15th had finally arrived, the first official day of "unofficial practice." With most cross country teams, the first organized practices took place during the summer before school began, and the better schools like Brothers Christian Academy and Pope James would usually meet "unofficially" as early as mid-June. Based on his recent running camp fiasco, PJ was not that eager to start, and decided August 15th was soon enough.

To help PJ, Taylor sent letters to all the students enrolled at RC, informing them when the first day of practice would be. In the letter she took the liberty of declaring this team "the most exciting new addition to RC athletics in years." In addition, the letter introduced PJ as the new coach.

RC was a basketball powerhouse and routinely attracted talent from around the world. Most recently they had landed Ulysses Sousa, a highly touted freshman from Brazil who perfected the twirling dunk in grammar school. However, in cross country they had no such luck.

Over the last few years they hadn't even been able to attract a full squad of runners, and three years ago the cross country team was demoted to the rank of "club," receiving very little funding compared to the other sports teams at RC. PJ's management experience and practical common sense told him that the "club" status had to change, and the first step to making this happen was to attract enough kids to the sport. Taylor's letter was a good head start; but no matter what, the most important thing to do was to get the kids enthused about running and being on the team – a difficult task, because cross country was a grueling sport. Any runner knew that what they did on a daily basis was what other sports did for punishment.

As PJ sat down to breakfast, he picked up a copy of *The Ledger*, the local newspaper. He quickly turned to the third page of the sports section and found the local running-scene article by Jim Lamba.

"Sayed won the Union Center 10K yesterday," he told Taylor as he continued to read. "That son of a bitch! Listen to this! 'I felt good today and I feel on schedule to run well at the Stillwater Stampede in December,' declared Sayed. 'I look forward to racing PJ Irwin again. I heard he wants to get another chance at me! Maybe this time he'll do better – assuming he shows up. And he knows what I mean by that.'"

Taylor looked at PJ with a grin. "I already read it," she said, returning to the dishes. Taylor knew that Sayed was referring to the much-hyped River to Sea Run some five years earlier, when both PJ and Sayed got caught up in a barrage of attacks on each other on the internet and in letters to the editor in the local papers.

PJ had not missed a day of running in the nineteen years leading up to the River to Sea race that year; but three weeks before the race, PJ began to experience pain in his knee. Two days later he underwent arthroscopic surgery to repair a torn meniscus, and he started physical therapy the very next day. Even though he was told not to run in the race, PJ got up early and tried to sneak out of the house to race against Sayed. It was a matter of pride. To Taylor, though, it was a matter of sanity, and she hid his running shoes – all of them – the night before. He never made it to the race, and for some time he blamed her for it.

"So?" Taylor said with her back to PJ.

"So...what?" PJ asked, looking bewildered.

"I think you know what time it is," she said as she glanced toward the clock and then back at him.

Studying her expression, PJ noticed her grin took on a different, more provocative nature. "It's time for a 'run in the woods?'" PJ joked.

"No, it's time for an ass whoopin'," she responded.

PJ agreed and walked out onto the back porch to stretch before his morning run.

Chapter 9

Legends

Jim Lamba, the newest addition to the staff at *The Ledger*, started out his career at the now defunct *Daily Journal*, a newspaper that primarily served Union County. Prior to his arrival at *The Ledger*, the local running scene was covered by the legendary Grant Edwins.

Grant had been writing for *The Ledger* ever since he graduated from Seton Hall in 1962. Now, at the age of sixty-two, he was gradually being put out to pasture by a management team interested in changing the "complexion of the workforce."

At one time Grant covered every race run in New Jersey, including all the high school meets. In fact, he had developed the first database of results and records, which he continued to maintain for the NJSAA, the New Jersey State Athletic Association. He also used to have his own newsletter; however, his new management team made him close up shop when they found out. What had once been a perk for him for doing such a fine job for *The Ledger* was now considered taboo.

"Good morning, Grant," said Jim as he poured coffee into his New Jersey Devils cup.

"Hi, Jim," Grant replied, peering over his reading glasses and taking in the spectacle of Jim juggling the coffeepot while eating a donut. "Are you scouting any of the cross country teams this week? This is about the time of the summer when I would start—"

"Nah," Jim interrupted him. "I'd rather cover some of the big-money races in the area. Besides, nobody wants to read about high school cross country anyway."

"I think it's exciting to interview the kids and watch them grow up during their high school years," Grant remarked. He had watched kids grow up in the cross country scene for decades. He knew the current runners, parents who were runners, and even a couple grandparents who were runners. He never forgot a name, and he was proud of it.

"I think it's exciting to sell newspapers," Jim chuckled, "and cross country does not sell papers." He turned to leave.

"I hear RC has a new coach," Grant said, pouring the last of the coffee into a mug that had *Rozelle Catholic High School* printed on it, a gift to him from a runner named John Hoffman. Grant had taken a personal interest in him and his brother Bobby when they ran in grammar school, eventually both becoming youth All Americans. Bobby went on to win the prestigious Eastern States High School Championship. After that, they attended Penn State on full athletic scholarships, and John became a successful brain surgeon. All of this success had been triggered by Grant Edwins' simple act.

Jim turned and, with an incredulous look, said, "RC has never even fielded a full team! Not in the three years since I arrived at *The Ledger*. They need more than a coach!"

"Back in the day they were great!" Grant argued, his voice rising slightly.

"Back in whose day? Yours, maybe, but you're living in the past. They have no chance! Not one. No chance!"

"If it wasn't—" started Grant.

"If it wasn't for you, I'd be enjoying this donut while catching a glimpse of the new gal in Classifieds," Jim said, cutting Grant off again. "See ya!" he sang as left the break room.

"Young know-it-all," lamented Grant. "He couldn't write his way out of a paper bag, and now he's replacing me more and more!" His blood started to boil.

As Jim hovered around in the classifieds area, Grant grabbed his steno pad and headed for the door. It was August 15th. Time for a trip to Warinanco Park.

Chapter 10

Voices

PJ left the porch at 8:00 a.m. sharp. Warinanco Park was only four miles away, and he was supposed to meet the team at 8:30. Leaving at eight gave him plenty of time to run there and cool down.

As PJ sailed down Chestnut Street to 3rd Avenue, he checked out his form reflected in the window of Yeung's Kitchen and the Rozelle Pharmacy, a habit most distance runners developed – a quick check of their arm carry and posture to ensure proper form for the remainder of the run, or until the next set of storefront windows.

At 8:23 PJ reached the park to find it empty, except for a woman in an orange tank top jogging around the track. As PJ passed her, he noticed the logo of the Boilermaker Run printed on the front of her shirt. He remembered the year he ran that race. He had been head-to-head with his idol, Frank Shorter, who had won the Olympic marathon in 1972.

Walking slowly around the track, PJ scanned the horizon for signs of high school-aged runners. After about five minutes, a Ford Fairlane station wagon rolled up next to the track, and out jumped three boys in running shorts. PJ watched as the car drove off and the three boys started walking in his direction, stopping briefly to let the woman in the orange tank top run past them. The tallest of the three must have known her because he said, "Hello, Ann Marie," as she passed, and she smiled back.

"Coach Irwin?" asked the Irish-looking kid as they approached.

"Yes, hello," answered PJ, affecting a macho tone. "And who do we have here?"

"I'm Teddy Dohne, and this is Rod O'Leary and Andrew Cartolano," Teddy answered as he glanced over at Rod, who was snickering.

"What's so funny?" asked PJ, fighting back the urge to laugh himself.

"Don't waste your time with them," snapped Andrew, the smallest of the three kids. "They're brain damaged, that's all." He glanced over at them and gave Teddy a shove.

"So, do you guys know if anyone else is planning on showing up?" PJ asked as he scanned the area.

Rod looked at Teddy, and they both chuckled. "I don't think so, Coach!" Rod laughed. "But wait until next week when some of the teachers start handing out detentions. Then we'll have some victims – er, uh, I mean runners," Rod added with a hint of sarcasm.

"Oh, that's right. I forgot. The detention class is actually the running club!" PJ wisecracked.

"That's right!" all three of them answered in unison and then started to laugh.

"That's why Ted and I are here!" Rod boasted proudly, pretending to pull on his invisible suspenders. "We were both taking summer classes and last week Brother Owen gave us detention for the rest of the summer."

"What for?" PJ asked with a laugh.

"We're not sure," Teddy answered. "One minute we're deep-freezing bananas with liquid nitrogen in the back of Mr. Plank's chemistry lab, and the next thing you know we have detention!" He sounded incredulous.

"Oh, come on, Ted!" Rod laughed. "We were supposed to freeze the banana until it was rock solid and then hit it with a hammer and shatter it. This knucklehead smashed the wrong banana and sent goop all over the lab!"

PJ fought back the urge to laugh as long as he could, but eventually he gave in. As he did, the three kids gave each other a nod of approval. "And why did you get detention?" he asked Andrew.

"He didn't," interrupted Teddy. "He actually likes to run."

"Is this true?" PJ asked, noticing for the first time Andrew's muscles and the definition in his calves and thighs.

"My dad got me into it when I was in middle school," Andrew explained. "He used to take me to youth cross country races somewhere in Randolph, at Brundage Park, and I'd run on a team called the Stillwater Bears."

"How'd you do?" PJ asked. He had heard of this team at camp. The camp founders, Laura and Gurn Gordon, had been coaching this team for a number of years. In fact, rumor had it that every year, half the kids in the Meet of Champions got their start running via the Stillwater Bears.

"I used to get my ass kicked," Andrew answered with a hint of frustration as he looked away.

"So why do you stick with it?" PJ asked.

The silence was deafening as Andrew gathered an answer. Teddy and Rod were both staring at him as if discovering something new about their longtime buddy. "I do it because…" Andrew struggled with the words as he turned his gaze toward PJ and locked onto his eyes. "Because I hear voices when I run."

"And I see dead people," Rod joked.

"Yeah, at the end of a race," Teddy chuckled.

"And they're usually kicking your butt, Teddy!" Rod snapped back.

PJ sensed something deep in what Andrew was trying to describe. "Andrew, what do you mean, you 'hear voices?'"

"When I raced in middle school, I'd hear this voice inside me telling me to keep it up, to keep going," Andrew explained. "And every time I gave in and slowed down, the voice would vanish, as if it had abandoned me for letting it down. I haven't heard that voice in quite a while. I miss it in a way."

PJ nodded as if he understood and jumped to his feet. "Well, let's get started, and see if we can find that voice again," he said. As he began to stretch, he couldn't help but notice the concentration on Andrew's face. *This kid's got game*, he thought.

PJ knew the voice Andrew described. Every runner knew it. Every runner heard it. It was every runner's fiercest competitor. It was themselves. Andrew needed to meet this person. He needed to discover the runner in himself. PJ was haunted in his youth by the same voice, and it was his coach that helped him discover his own limits. His coach; his mom; Rose.

"We'll start with an easy three miles today," PJ told the trio. "I'll tag along and we'll get to know each other a little better."

"Do you know the course?" Teddy asked.

"No, not all of it. Why don't you lead the way?"

"You hear that, Andrew? I'm leading the way!" Teddy said as he broke into a stride in front of the rest of them.

PJ noticed a gesture and a nod between Rod and Andrew. A few moments later they stepped up the pace until they were right behind Teddy. Suddenly Rod leaned forward – as if he had stumbled slightly – then without warning, he reached out in front of him and grabbed the bottom of Teddy's shorts. As soon as Teddy's shorts dropped around his ankles, Andrew gave him a shoulder-level push.

Teddy tumbled bare-assed to the ground about 200 meters into the cross country course. Rod and Andrew fell to the ground, laughing, as they watched Teddy spring to his feet and continue running, his shorts still around his ankles. "Kiss my ass!" he shouted back at his two buddies.

And then it happened. Teddy pulled up his shorts and broke into a sprint out to the 600-meter pole, which was a slight uphill run most of the way. His stride and arm carry were efficient – actually perfect. He had a slight lean, and his arms didn't swing from side to side like so many young runners. Instead, his arms moved gracefully from front to back.

Andrew and Rod took off after him, but Teddy owned this hill. They would never catch him. As he rounded the 600-meter pole, he eased up and allowed the other two to catch up with him. As a group they looked back and adjusted their pace even more to allow PJ to catch them. At first, PJ thought of going with them in their mad dash up the hill, but these dogs were marking their territory, and PJ was going to respect that…for the time being.

As they neared the course's three-quarter-mile mark, the group rounded a cement structure in the middle of the park. "This is the Alamo," Rod said, pointing toward the steps leading up to a garden hidden within the structure. "Kids from Cranford usually fill the place up on race days. It's a good place to cheer from. You pass it again at the two-and-a-half-mile mark."

"So where do the RC fans hang out on race day?" PJ asked.

"At home," Rod and Andrew said in tandem and then laughed.

"The mile mark is just up ahead near that left-field foul post," Andrew added as he pointed toward the baseball field directly in front of them.

Warinanco Park contained numerous baseball and softball fields. In addition, there were soccer fields, cricket fields, a lake, tennis courts, and a beautiful all-weather track.

As they passed the mile mark, Teddy again took the lead. They had just completed the first loop of the course and were now heading back toward the white post they passed three quarters of a mile earlier.

"You know, if Teddy put in more miles, he'd be awesome," Andrew said to PJ matter-of-factly. "He didn't train much last year because his father was sick and he had to help his mom out at their store. He's a natural athlete, though. He played soccer recreationally for one of the city teams. Every year the RC soccer coach tries to recruit him, and every year Teddy turns him down, saying he's too busy. This year's different, though, because Teddy's father sold the store and retired. Now Teddy has the time to train and play."

As they passed the white pole near an area known as Lovers' Lane for the second time, the pace quickened and they descended a slight hill, heading toward a bridge that took them to a trail on the other side of the lake.

"The two-mile mark is right at the end of the lake," Rod said, motioning toward the end of the lake near the main entrance to the park before he inched forward and got next to Teddy. He patted him briefly on the back, and they exchanged a few words.

Rod and Teddy had been friends since first grade, and had played PAL football in sixth and seventh grades where Rod was a star running back. Unfortunately, RC did not have a football team, so Rod decided to run track instead. Though he was a fairly decent intermediate hurdler and 800-meter runner, this would be his first attempt at cross country. He was a straight-A student and well-known for his sense of humor, and for giving 110 percent to whatever he did.

"They're pushing the pace," Andrew said in a low voice as he and

PJ headed toward the Alamo near the two-and-a-half-mile mark. Andrew seemed restless as he watched, and they fell farther behind the leaders.

"So what's that voice inside your head telling you, Andrew?" PJ asked as they started to climb the next hill.

"I think we should go get them."

"I'm game if you are," PJ responded, and together they picked up the pace. As they strode up the final hill on the course, they had closed the gap to within twenty meters. PJ matched Andrew's stride as they passed Teddy and Rod.

"Drop the hammer on him, Andrew!" Teddy yelled as all four of them started to kick across the street toward the final lap on the all-weather track.

"We love this part of the race, Coach," said Andrew. "It's like we're entering the Olympic stadium during the marathon!"

Suddenly, the friendly banter stopped, and nothing could be heard but the sound of feet hitting loose gravel and heavy breathing. Andrew shot to the lead with Rod and Teddy close behind. PJ strode quietly behind them, adjusting his pace and gathering himself for what lay ahead. As they drew closer to the track, the group sped along a line of trees known to New Jersey cross country runners as "the Nursery." It was along this tree line that many a race was decided, many a kick was launched, many a hope dashed. And it would be here that quiet Andrew was going to spank his two buddies for pushing the second half of the run. It was here that Andrew was going to remind his coach who the runner was and who the coach was. And it was here that PJ would gain three disciples.

His next move would win them over. His adjustment, as subtle as it appeared, surprised the other three. PJ blew by Andrew about halfway through the tree line. Andrew shifted into another gear, but PJ was still gapping him. As PJ hit the track with 450 meters to go, he himself hit another gear, and all Andrew could do was watch.

PJ glanced at his watch as he reached the white line across the track. He had 400 meters to go and was feeling strong. He picked it up a little as he entered the first turn. Glancing back over his shoulder, he saw Andrew about thirty meters behind him. PJ drove his arms and increased his leg turnover as he raced down the back straightaway. When he glanced back one more time as he entered the final turn, he saw Andrew driving his arms wildly. Striding down the final straightaway, PJ decelerated slightly. Andrew continued to kick, and caught PJ just as they crossed the finish line. PJ's time for the last lap was a fast sixty-two seconds.

"Did you just hear that?" PJ asked.

"Hear what?" Andrew answered.

"That voice in your head? I believe it just said, 'Nice job!'" PJ said as he turned and started to cheer for Teddy and Rod as they sprinted toward the finish.

Andrew smiled at PJ, then walked over and high-fived Rod and Teddy.

"The old man's got legs," Rod said to Andrew as he nodded at PJ.

"Did he beat you?" Teddy asked.

"No, he caught me," PJ interrupted. "But I'll get him next time. Nice workout, you guys."

PJ stared at the three boys as they stood near the finish line, bent over and panting, trying to recover from the run. *They have potential, but we need more bodies*, PJ thought.

Just then, PJ noticed the same station wagon that dropped the boys off at the park waiting for them at the end of the track. Rod looked over his shoulder and said, "Coach, our ride's here. Are we done?"

"Yeah," he answered. "Same time tomorrow, gentlemen?"

They nodded in agreement and walked slowly toward the car.

"If any of you know any other runners, please try to get them to come out. We need numbers!" PJ shouted to them.

As they drove off and PJ was jogging toward the park exit to begin his run home, he noticed a group of runners crossing the road and headed toward "the Nursery." They were running at a nice clip in perfect unison, and as they drew closer, PJ couldn't help but notice that, although they had to be running a six-minute pace, they were hardly breathing. As they passed, the lead runner glanced over at PJ, nodded, and then appeared to pick it up. The other six runners went right with the leader. As they reached the track, PJ remembered his watch and quickly reset it so that he could time their last lap.

PJ's eyes widened as he saw the group surge into the first turn. They were flying! At the 200-meter mark, PJ stared in disbelief. They had passed the mark in thirty seconds flat! *Unbelievable*, he thought. As they rounded the last turn, the runners in the back of the pack increased the pace, and soon all seven of them were spread across the track in a straight line. They all crossed the finish together…in sixty seconds!

As PJ continued to stare in their direction, he noticed that they didn't stop running completely. They simply slowed and did a recovery lap on the track before taking off into the woods.

We'll never be able to compete with them! PJ thought. The run home was agonizing as PJ realized how far behind the other teams RC must be. Hell, he didn't even have a full squad yet. They were going to need a miracle.

Chapter 11

Back to School

The next morning Taylor called PJ from the school parking lot when she heard a hissing noise coming from the rear tire on the Tahoe. She wanted PJ to come down and fix it; after all, she had been after him for weeks to buy new tires, because these were looking pretty bald.

Rozelle Catholic was situated on approximately twenty acres on the edge of the town. A small stream meandered through the middle of the property, making for a peaceful, scenic setting. The school, the baseball field, and the main parking lot were located on the south side of the stream, while to the north was a soccer field surrounded by a cinder track.

As PJ entered the driveway to the school, he noticed a tall, slender gentleman with graying hair and a neatly groomed beard operating a backhoe near the bridge leading across the stream to the track. He appeared to be planting a series of new evergreen trees.

Suddenly, PJ slammed on his brakes to avoid a kid coming around the corner of the school building, pushing a wheelbarrow full of topsoil. This kid was literally sprinting with it toward the man on the backhoe. As PJ watched this boy, who appeared to be about seventeen years old, sprint behind the wheelbarrow, he noticed the muscles in the kid's arms and calves as he struggled to keep the wheelbarrow from tipping. PJ continued to watch as the boy approached the planting area, and the gentleman jumped down from the backhoe to give him a hand. Looking up briefly, the gentleman smiled at PJ as he passed the two of them. PJ smiled back and pulled into a parking spot next to Taylor's car.

PJ jumped out and surveyed the damaged tire. Moments later he had the trunk open and was removing the spare and the jack. When he closed the trunk, he found himself face-to-face with the bearded backhoe operator.

"Need any help?" the man asked, extending his hand. "I'm Ed Kinney."

"No, I should be able to handle it," PJ replied as he shook the man's hand.

"Hey, Dad, do you need any more topsoil?" came a voice from across the driveway.

"No, I think that'll be enough," Ed replied as he turned and winked at PJ. "That must've been his twentieth wheelbarrow load!"

"Did he run like that while pushing the wheelbarrow for all twenty loads?" PJ quipped with a sarcastic laugh.

"Yep," replied Ed matter-of-factly as he snatched up the jack and started to position it under the car.

For a moment PJ's heart skipped a beat. His eyes returned to the boy as he watched him jog back toward the work area and pick up a shovel.

"What's your son's name?" PJ asked.

"Mike," Ed said as he picked up the wrench and began loosening the lug nuts on the wheel. "He's a senior here and he helps me with the landscaping."

"He looks like he's in pretty good shape," PJ remarked.

"Oh yeah. When he's not working, he's usually out riding his bike around, or hiking and running."

"Running?" PJ said. "Does he run on the school's team?"

"No," Ed answered with a chuckle. "He just…he just runs!"

"My name's PJ Irwin. My wife Taylor works here."

"Yes, I know Taylor," Ed answered. "She helped us with Mike's registration this year."

Ed had the tire off the car in record time, and PJ rolled the spare into position. Ed snatched the tire from PJ, lifted it onto the hub, and started to tighten it up.

"Hey! You're not making him do all the work, are you?!" PJ heard

Taylor's voice as she exited the school building and approached the two of them.

"I…uh…" PJ felt a little awkward as Ed tightened the last nut. "She's right, Ed. Why don't you let me finish this?"

"Sure thing," Ed answered as he lowered the jack and jumped to his feet in one graceful motion. "It was nice to meet you," he added as he turned to head back toward the backhoe.

"Hey, Ed, I'm coaching cross country here this year, and I wonder if Mike might be interested," PJ said before Ed got very far.

Ed turned and smiled. "I'll ask him."

PJ thanked Ed for the help and proceeded into the school with Taylor. Brother Owen wanted to meet with him briefly.

Chapter 12

Detention = Run

Rozelle Catholic High School was built in the mid-'60s and had changed very little since then. The U-shaped, two-story building consisted of twenty-six classrooms, a chapel, a gymnasium that could be separated into three sections, and a cafeteria. The enrollment had wavered between 600 and 850 over the years. Originally founded as an all-boys school, girls were admitted in the mid-'80s when the schools in the Newark archdiocese were consolidated.

As PJ walked through the main hallway to Brother Owen's office, he passed the gymnasium. Fred Biff, PJ's neighbor, was supervising a pre-season basketball practice. PJ's attention was drawn to Sousa, the new Brazilian recruit, as he soared through the air and gracefully delivered the ball to the hoop in a Jordan-esque layup.

Continuing down the hallway, PJ passed a hundred-foot-long display case containing memoirs and sports trophies collected over the years at RC, among which were numerous basketball and baseball trophies and a retired basketball jersey once worn by a kid named Gomez. As PJ walked farther down the aisle, he passed some recently won volleyball trophies, along with some photos of past athletes and their coaches.

A few feet farther down the hall, PJ came upon a large collection of slightly tarnished – but very impressive – cross country and track and field awards from the late '60s and early '70s, the most impressive of which was the Penn Relays two-mile relay and distance-medley plaques won in 1969 and 1970. During this period, RC had seven runners capable of running the 880-yard dash in under two minutes!

As PJ surveyed the collection, his eyes fell upon a tall, dust-covered trophy that read "Eastern States Cross Country Champions – 1969." This was one of the best-known races on the East Coast. Briefly touching his head where he had injured himself at the cross country camp, he mused, *Famous enough to dream about after a hard blow to the head.*

Taylor reached Brother Owen's office well ahead of PJ, who was still carefully studying the collection of track and field trophies, which seemed to drop off sharply after 1971, with none after 1976. "C'mon, PJ! Don't keep Brother Owen waiting!" she shouted as she entered the principal's office.

"I'm coming!" he snapped as he started to turn away from the display case. Just then PJ noticed that someone had written words in the dust at the bottom of the case. Kneeling down and cupping his hands on the glass to avoid the glare of the hallway lighting, he was able to read *The Lions – RCXC – 2004.*

"C'mon, PJ!" Taylor shouted again from the principal's doorway.

PJ jumped to his feet, slapped his hands together, and dashed the rest of the hallway to Owen's office.

"Hello, my good friend," Owen greeted PJ in a very calm, soothing tone. Brother Owen had been principal at RC for the last ten years. During this time he had handled many difficult situations, including the near closure of the school due to lack of enrollment. Owen handled his affairs with grace and composure, but along with the composure came a no-nonsense seriousness that helped get the school back on its feet. Quietly, calmly, Brother Owen cut through the everyday bullshit to get things done.

"Hello, Brother," PJ replied.

"And how was the first day of practice?" Owen inquired with a smirk.

"Well, we only had three kids turn out," PJ said, shaking his head.

"Andrew, Rod and Teddy."

"Yep, those were the three!"

"All good kids."

"Good kids?" PJ chuckled. "I understand that two of them only showed up because they had detention!"

"Well, actually, PJ…" Owen said, pausing. "I trumped up the charges and gave Teddy and Rod detention, so I could let them off the hook if they went to cross country practice."

"Oh, Brother Owen, I can't believe you!" Taylor laughed.

"Hey, those kids are great athletes. I've seen them run around during gym class. You wait and see. They're popular and I'm sure they'll attract a few others to the team."

"Yeah, misery loves company," PJ quipped. "I hope you're right. I'd like to have a full team for the year."

"I have another idea as well," Owen said as he reached for the public address microphone. "Carmine Nicastro, please report to the principal's office," Brother Owen's voice bellowed throughout the school. "I want to offer you some help. Carmine has been a gym teacher and track coach here for the last two years. He coaches the sprinters, I believe."

"But cross country is for distance runners."

"I know, I know, PJ. That's why we have you! But Carmine is well liked by many in the student body. I think he can help you recruit a few people."

Just then the door to the office flew open, and in walked a college-aged kid who obviously lifted weights. This kid was ripped. "You rang?" wisecracked Carmine as he looked up to see the three standing near Brother Owen's desk. "Oh, I'm sorry. I didn't know you had visitors."

"That's quite all right!" Brother Owen said. "I want you to meet your new boss – that is, one of many. This is Taylor's husband, PJ. He's the new cross country coach."

"Hey, great! Nice to meet you," Carmine declared with youthful exuberance as he reached out his hand to greet PJ. "Brother Owen told me I should con some kids into running cross country this year. Maybe we could fill their heads with things like 'the runner's high is great when it happens' or 'the course is lined with hot-looking chicks.'"

PJ laughed briefly and then added, "Or how about 'a free vomit bag with every uniform?'" Both PJ and Carmine chuckled before PJ's demeanor changed, and he added, "Or how about 'this year we'll return to glory and win the state championship?'"

PJ waited for Carmine's response. Would it be what he wanted? Carmine's eyes met PJ's, and for a moment the silence was deafening. Taylor had seen PJ do this before. He was testing Carmine to see if this was going to be a two-man coaching team. It was a decisive moment.

"Screw the state championship," Carmine said, breaking the silence. I want to make it to the Nationals. But first we have to get past the Easterns. And while we're at it, we'll see if we can help a certain post-collegiate runner with his weight training so he can redeem himself against Sayed," he added playfully.

PJ smiled and looked at Taylor and Brother Owen. "Okay, he'll do!" he said.

"Great!" replied Brother Owen. "You two have a lot of work to do!"

"Let me tell you about the two sorry bastards I caught spray-painting the side of the equipment shed today," Carmine told PJ as they turned to leave Brother Owen's office. "The little shits were quaking in their boots. I told them to run cross country and I might forget about telling their parents."

"Nice," said PJ. To Brother Owen, he said, "Thanks, Bro."

"*De nada*," replied the principal.

"Actually," Carmine continued as they entered the hallway. "I, uh… well…I conned Rod and Teddy into convincing the two sophomores to spray-paint the side of the shed. I was going to paint it anyway."

"Do you mean…" PJ said as he started to laugh.

"Exactly! I set the two new kids up," Carmine roared.

"What if they can't run?" PJ asked in disbelief.

"Don't worry. They'll run. I know them. They have heart," Carmine responded with a serious look on his face. "Their names are Matt and Nick. They're good kids. If they weren't, I…"

"'I' what?" PJ asked.

"I wouldn't have set them up!" laughed Carmine.

"You're frickin' awesome," PJ replied.

"C'mon, let me show you the weight room and then we can head over to the park for the 3:30 practice," Carmine said, as he led PJ into the gymnasium.

Chapter 13

The Meeting

As PJ and Carmine roared down 7th Avenue toward the park in Carmine's red Thunderbird, air whistled through a tear in the convertible's roof.

"So, do you think they'll show up?" PJ asked.

"They better or they're dead meat!" Carmine exclaimed, then added, "They'll show. Have faith."

As they circled the park on their way to the meeting point at the stadium, they noticed a group of Latino runners in their mid-fifties or early sixties.

"Competition?" Carmine wisecracked, peering over his sunglasses at PJ.

"For you maybe," PJ snapped back.

Just then, PJ noticed the same group of seven runners he had seen after practice yesterday. They were striding along the outer perimeter of the park.

"I knew they wouldn't let us down," PJ declared as he nodded in the direction of the stadium parking lot. "Oh…uh…yes, this is good," he said, turning his gaze in the same direction.

"There they are," Carmine boasted. "You have Teddy, Rod, Andrew, Mike – without the wheelbarrow – Matt Shipp, and Nick Garvey. And hey! Look at that. It's Vladimir Manasee!"

PJ surveyed the group, and Vladimir jumped out at him – not because he was the only African American in the bunch, but because he was stretching. PJ believed in warming up well before a race or a workout. It was obvious that Vladimir knew the importance of this as well.

"Hello gentlemen," PJ said as he approached the group.

"So let me guess," said Teddy, "Carmine's going to be your ass kick…err, I mean enforcer this year, eh, Coach?" He winked at Carmine.

"Don't worry, Teddy," Carmine interrupted. "I won't use these guns on you guys." He put his hands behind his head and flexed his biceps.

Teddy laughed and high-fived Carmine. The two obviously had a strong friendship and deep respect for each other. Carmine shook all the other kids' hands as well and introduced the newcomers to PJ.

"This is Matt Shipp, a freshman," Carmine said as he motioned for the boy to come closer.

PJ shook Matt's hand and said, "Nice to meet you. Have you ever run before?"

"Nope, except for gym class and rec league soccer."

"Well, soccer's pretty good as far as running goes. How come you're not playing?" PJ inquired.

Matt chuckled. "Because it's a friggin' commie sport!"

PJ smiled and turned his attention to Nick Garvey. "Hi, you must be Nick."

"Uh-huh," answered Nick, a quiet kid from Rozelle Park. He worked during the summer at the local supermarket where PJ shopped. On one occasion PJ had remarked to Taylor as to how serious the kid stacking the shelf was, as they watched him meticulously place the cans with the labels facing all in the same direction. PJ knew the type – nervous at first, not wanting to fail, the type of kid who needed to be nurtured until their self-confidence kicked in. Once it did, look out. An overachiever was born.

"And who do we have here?" PJ asked as he turned to Vlad. He was lean and muscular, obviously an athlete.

"Vladimir Manasee, Coach, but most people call me Vlad," he answered. "I heard you might need a seventh runner."

"Really? From who?"

"Not sure. My dad took the message off our answering machine."

"Well, I'm glad you came. This is the first time we've had a full team in many years," PJ replied. "I'm glad you're all here. It's a great start for a program that's apparently been hurting for quite some time."

"What are we going to do today, Coach?" asked Rod as he started to stretch.

PJ thought for a moment, because he hadn't really put together a workout strategy. By this time of the summer, most good high school runners would've increased their mileage to about fifty to seventy miles per week. This was known as building a good distance base, which made the runner more efficient and laid the groundwork for more intense workouts and races once the season began. Unfortunately, most of these kids could barely handle twenty-five miles per week right now.

"What to do?" PJ mumbled, knowing that all eyes were on him. "What do you think your competition is doing?" he asked with a grin.

"I have a friend at Cranford who's running about forty-five miles per week right now," answered Andrew.

"Forty-five! What?!" exclaimed Matt.

"That's not enough," PJ replied. "Most good runners are in the sixty to seventy range and starting to throw in some threshold runs and long intervals. And also some fartleks."

"Did you say 'fart lick?'" Teddy asked with a grin.

"He said *fartlek*," Vlad answered. "It's a Swedish word that means *speed play*."

PJ's head snapped around, and he gazed in amazement at Vlad. "Where did you learn that?"

Vlad looked up from the ground where he lay doing a hurdler's stretch. "In middle school I ran for the Stillwater Bears, a youth cross country program out of Sussex County. We used to do a lot of fartlekking."

Thank you, Laura and Gurn Gordon, PJ thought to himself. "Well then, you'll lead us into today's workout," he said as he sat down to stretch the tightness out of his legs.

As the team stretched, PJ noticed the comradery amongst the seven kids. This was a nice bunch. They joked with each other but also showed respect for each other's feelings. For the first time, PJ started to think that this might be fun – even if they got massacred this year.

Just then, from a wooded area behind them, came a group of about twenty high school runners moving so fast they looked like they were sprinting as they passed PJ's team, coming within five feet of them.

"Who's that?" PJ asked.

"That would be Westfield," Mike answered. "They always have a big team. Last year they won the Counties and were ranked in the Top 10 in the state."

"Well, they must be mistaken," PJ said as he leaned forward and touched his toes.

"What do you mean, 'mistaken?'" Teddy asked curiously.

PJ let go of his toes, slowly raised his head, and turned and looked in the direction in which the Westfield team was running. "Mistaken if they think they're going to win the Counties again." The boys looked at each other and smiled. "And mistaken if they think they can outrun us. Gentlemen, today is the first day of RC's return to glory.

Vlad, whaddya say you set the tone for today's workout?"

"Will do," Vlad answered as he jumped to his feet. "Which way should we go?" he asked his teammates.

"Let's go get Westfield," Nick interjected, much to the surprise of everyone else.

"Okay then, we go the same direction as Westfield."

PJ turned around, a serious look in his eyes. "Actually, I heard Nick say, *Let's go get Westfield.*"

"That's right. I heard it too," Teddy joined in.

"Easy mile warm-up, followed by a break into a fartlek. When we catch Westfield, follow my lead," PJ said, and he broke into a trot.

Chapter 14

Glimmer

By now, Westfield was 600 meters in front of them as they circled the outer perimeter of the park. PJ thought that such a large team had to have some slower runners, and that they surely could not maintain the pace they were running when they passed the RC team. Most likely they were showing their best stuff when they passed.

Vladimir had pushed the pace right from the first step. "Let's ease into this, Vlad, and get loose before we start pushing," PJ said.

"Okay, Coach, I'll slow up if I'm too fast for you," Vlad replied with a playful smile.

Andrew, Teddy and Rod all looked at each other and smiled as well, thinking of the whooping PJ had unloaded on them the day before.

"Vlad?" Andrew started.

"Yeah, Andrew? Do you need me to slow down further?" Vlad teased.

"Uh, no, nothing. Never mind," Andrew replied, glancing at Teddy and Rod with a look that said, *Today is your day to go to school, Vlad.*

As PJ and the team progressed through the first mile, he noticed that every time he got within three inches of taking the lead, Vlad would pick up the pace a little.

"So, Vlad, is the three-inch rule in effect?" PJ asked.

"Oh, you noticed," Vlad replied.

"What's the three-inch rule?" Andrew asked.

"It says if you come within three inches of passing me, I'm going to pick it up and put a hurt on you," Vlad answered Andrew with a wink.

Andrew did not reply. Instead he looked at PJ, who was looking across at him. "That's the attitude," Andrew told Vlad.

PJ smiled. *These guys have a great rapport*, he thought, then declared to the seven, "Ten minutes in."

"First acceleration?" Vlad asked.

"It's up to you. However you feel."

They were just beginning to climb a small hill leading to the main entrance of the park. Vlad leaned into the hill and smoothly picked up the pace. Like a swarm of bees, Andrew, Rod, Teddy and Mike surrounded him in a tight pack. Matt and Nick followed closely behind, with PJ and Carmine bringing up the rear.

"Hey, stud, I just want to let you know something," Carmine huffed.

"What's that?" PJ asked.

"I'm a sprinter. This stuff…is going to…kill me."

"Then why are you back here? You should be in the front!" PJ joked.

"Yeah, right!" Carmine gasped, then suddenly exploding into a full sprint. His speed was amazing! "Coming through!" he shouted as he passed the pack of runners.

Approximately a hundred yards later, the group eased up to end their first speed interval. A few moments later they caught Carmine, who smiled at them. Looking at PJ, he said, "23.2 seconds for the 200-meter dash. I still have it!"

"I'm impressed," PJ replied.

"Yeah, but this distance stuff is for the birds. I'll see you at the end of practice to drive you back to your car," Carmine said, turning to take a different route through the park.

"Okay, get in a few easy miles and I'll meet up with you at the track," PJ shouted back.

As the group rounded the east end of Warinanco Park, a slight downhill approached, and PJ decided to hang back a little to check out his runners' forms. "Okay, Vlad, why don't you pick it up again and take us through the downhill at a decent clip – but don't sprint," he suggested.

Vlad nodded and started to accelerate, followed closely by his six teammates. Vlad and Andrew had a perfect downhill stride. Their knees remained low, keeping their bodies airborne the minimum amount of time. The more time a runner was in the air, the more deceleration occurred. Also, the more a runner was in the air, the more energy they wasted pushing up and not forward. And the more likely they were to get injured.

As they neared the bottom of the hill, PJ told the group to continue at this pace for another two minutes. PJ was eyeing the group of Westfield runners, and he noticed the RC bunch had gained a little on them. PJ checked his watch briefly and then started to count the number of steps Andrew took in a minute. 177…178…179…180. Perfect. 180 steps per minute was the perfect cadence in the eyes of most who studied the physiology of running.

"Yo, guys, I think we're gaining on Big Blue," Teddy blurted as they passed the cricket field.

"We closed the gap to just one minute and ten seconds," Nick said from the rear. All six of his teammates turned and stared at him briefly. "What!?" he responded.

PJ was expecting to hear one of Nick's teammates make a wisecrack. Instead, he heard something that made his heart pump a little harder. "Are you sure of that time, Nick?" Rod said as Andrew and Mike looked back to see his response.

"Yes, I checked the time when they passed the beginning of the cricket field," Nick answered methodically.

"Coach?" Rod started.

"What's that?" PJ answered.

"Do you think we can catch Westfield before they circle the park one more time?" Rod asked.

PJ considered the question. The perimeter of the park was 2.1 miles. The Westfield kids were probably running a 6:45 to a 7:15 pace. If they were going to catch them, they would have to run around a 6:00 to 6:15 pace, assuming Westfield didn't pick it up when they saw them coming.

"I don't know. They're moving, and it's only our second practice," PJ replied. "Besides, we set out to fartlek, not—"

"I can't think of anything better than speed-playing our way past Westfield," said Mike, who had been quiet to this point, but now looked strong, almost ferocious. He was more muscular than the other guys, and his crewcut made him look military.

"What have we got to lose, Coach?" said Teddy.

"I don't know. We might lose Matt or Nick, for starters," PJ said, looking back to the two freshmen bringing up the rear. "How do you two feel?" he called back to them.

"Good," they answered, though their faces read *tired*.

"Let's slow this interval down, guys," said PJ after seeing Matt's and Nick's faces. Just as the front runners started to slow, however, Nick and Matt strode past the group and never let up.

"I think they're going for them!" Teddy said.

"Hey! These lads are badass this year!" said Rod.

"Alright, guys, this is the deal," PJ started. "We go after Westfield, but Matt and Nick set the pace."

The group began to accelerate again and quickly chased down the two freshmen.

"Nick and Matt, your goal is to get us even with Westfield," PJ said.

"Okay," Nick answered, "but they're going to pick it up as soon as they see us closing."

"Don't worry about that," PJ reassured the two. "Just get us into contact with them. That's the goal."

For the next nine minutes nobody talked, and a rhythm set in as PJ studied the seven. Nick led the bunch most of the time, and when he seemed to slow, Andrew, Rod, or Teddy would get next to him to urge him on.

They were within twenty seconds of Westfield as they reached the main entrance to the park. They had another mile to go before they reached the track.

"6:20 for that last mile," PJ said.

"They know we're coming!" Nick said, sounding tired. He was sweating profusely, as was Matt, who had fallen back about ten yards.

"You did what you needed to do!" PJ said to Nick. "Andrew, what's that voice in your head saying?" he asked in a low voice as he ran stride to stride next to him. Andrew didn't answer.

"Andrew, what's—" PJ started to repeat himself when suddenly Andrew shortened his stride and increased his cadence. The hair rose on PJ's neck as he noticed Mike, Teddy, Rod, and Vlad making the same adjustment. They were going for it.

Rod looked back at the fading Matt and Nick, held up his right hand, and gave the two a thumbs-up. Then he turned back and refocused on the task at hand...Westfield.

PJ took off with the group but stayed in the rear. Andrew and Teddy were leading the pack of five runners as they passed the public pool and ran toward the cricket field. PJ noticed that the Westfield runners seemed to have picked up the pace as well.

Vlad closed on the lead runners with PJ in tow. "Let's push the uphill after the cricket field and catch Big Blue!" Vlad urged the group.

The bunch was tiring, though, PJ realized, thinking that this probably wouldn't be a smart thing to do because there was another 1,200 meters after the uphill before the finish line.

"It might be better to shorten our strides and hold this pace until we get to the top of the hill," PJ said, trying not to breathe too heavily. "Don't go nuts. Don't drive the arms too much. And let's make a big move after that."

Andrew nodded his head and led the bunch across the remainder of the cricket field to the foot of the hill. As they headed into the hill, the five of them leaned into it and shortened their strides.

"Beautiful, guys. Quick steps up the hill," PJ urged as he neared the front of the pack.

As they crested the hill, Mike came up alongside PJ and Andrew. Then Rod, Teddy and Vlad equaled the feat. RC was running five abreast – and at a sub-6:20 pace!

Teddy snickered noticeably as a Westfield runner turned and looked back at the quickly approaching bunch. The runner's eyes widened when he saw them coming, and he turned and informed his Big Blue teammates.

"Gentlemen, it's time for a spankin'," PJ said in a low voice.

Andrew responded first, once again shortening his stride and increasing his cadence. Teddy and Rod broke next, followed by Vlad and Mike. Mike was struggling, and it was beginning to show on his face. His shoulders were tightening up, and his arms were beginning to rise and swing a little less gracefully. "Stay with it, Mike," PJ urged from behind.

The first RC runner to infiltrate the Westfield pack was Andrew. The RC bunch had formed a single file and were passing the hard-driving Westfield team on the right-hand side of the trail. They were now about 200 meters from the stadium entrance, and the path was only ten feet wide at this point.

Suddenly, the lead group of Westfield runners spread out elbow to elbow, completely across the path in front of Andrew, blocking Andrew as he caught the lead bunch. On the left side of the trail were rose bushes, and on the right side was a park ranger's car. Andrew looked back over his right shoulder to Teddy, who grinned.

Suddenly Andrew let out a burst of speed and veered toward the right-hand side of the group. Teddy went with him, and then – to the surprise of the entire Westfield team (and one park ranger) – the pair leapt into the air, each placing one foot onto the hood of the ranger's car, and hurtled themselves past the lead Westfield runners.

Just then, Rod let out a wild yell. "Coming through!"

PJ watched as the lead Westfield runners went after Andrew and Teddy. They were obviously a good team with a number of strong-looking runners. They deftly chased the duo, and behind this bunch charged a weary Rod, Mike and Vlad.

PJ moved up next to Vlad and Mike and said, "Come on, guys! One lap. Let's give 'em hell!" Then he took off with the three RC runners in tow.

Andrew was now on the track, going toe-to-toe with the lead Westfield runner, while Teddy had fallen back about ten yards. Just then

PJ saw Andrew's arms start to drive even harder, like they were banging drums hanging on either side of his body. He was going into a full sprint, as was PJ, who was closing on the lead Westfield runner himself.

As they rounded the last turn, PJ started to decelerate to the finish line. Andrew crossed in first, PJ second, and together they watched Teddy come across in third with the lead Westfield runner.

As both Andrew and Teddy bent over and put their hands on their knees to recover, PJ grabbed them and pulled them into a jog. "Never let them see you bend over like that," he said. "I want us to look unbeatable, and bending over gives the impression that we're tired."

"But Coach, we *are* tired," Teddy said.

"I know, but this is my number one rule. No bending over. We run. We do our best. We don't show weakness. Got it?"

"Yes," the two answered almost simultaneously.

Teddy and Andrew turned around and returned to greet Rod, Vlad and Mike at the finish line, quickly urging the others to jog and not bend over. They broke into a jog across the track's infield and cheered on the final efforts of the two freshmen runners. Matt and Nick finished together, greeted immediately by their teammates who kept them from bending over.

PJ jogged up to the bunch and said, "Let's go."

Together they walked over to the Westfield guys that were congregating near the end of the straightaway.

"Nice running, you guys," PJ said as RC jogged past.

"What team are you from?" the lead Westfield runner said with a huff as the RC bunch started to jog away.

"Rozelle," said PJ.

"Rozelle Park?" the Westfield runner shouted back.

PJ responded with a thumbs-up but didn't look back.

"But, Coach," Andrew started, "we're not—"

"I know," PJ answered, "but let's keep RC off their radar for now. We haven't proven ourselves."

The Westfield team had started running earlier, totaling about seven or eight miles, with RC running only four. But deep down, PJ was ecstatic. It was unheard of for a team to run like this during their first week of practice. There was something special about this bunch. They had heart – though they still had a lot of work to do.

Thirteen Westfield runners finished in front of Mike, Vlad and Rod. Twenty-one had finished in front of the two freshmen, Matt and Nick. This team had no depth, but they had guts and emotion. PJ just had to figure out how to use this to their advantage.

Chapter 15

Christmas in August 5K

The next week of practice went fairly smoothly. PJ showed up each day to meet the group and take them through a ritual of stretching, followed by running and finishing with stride outs. He didn't push them through any speed work, just focusing on distance.

PJ continued to run his own workouts – which he laid out in advance – later in the evening after the team dispersed. He was training for the USATF Open 10,000-meter XC championship in early December, and he was determined to try to take out Sayed.

Sayed was known for surging multiple times during a race, and he had a good kick. PJ's workouts were designed to help him withstand the surging. He wasn't worried about the kick. He knew he could kick as well. On one occasion he had entered a road race at Swartswood State Park and almost outkicked one of the greatest kickers of all times, Marcello O'Sullivan, the Irish-Italian runner who ran over 100 sub-four-minute miles in his career.

It was a hot August day, and the Bears Running Club of North Jersey was holding their annual "Christmas in August 5K" to raise money for their youth running program, the Stillwater Bears. The race was held during the week the Bears held their youth running camp, and the kids attending the camp gathered and worked the evening race. To their delight, Marcello came each year, won the race, and signed autographs as he mingled with the young runners.

Gurn and Laura Gordan, the race organizers, always did a great job of bringing talent to their events. One of the local stars they attracted each year was a runner named Gary Rosencrantz, who ran a great race each year but only placed second. Gary managed a number of running stores throughout New Jersey known as The Running Corps, and he was very generous to the club.

Gary had great speed and was a good kicker himself, but each year Marcello would distance himself from Gary during the first two miles of the race, leaving Gary no reason to kick. This particular year was different, though. Gary challenged Marcello to run with him until the last quarter mile of the race and then see who had the better kick. Marcello, a true competitor, agreed.

Watching this challenge unfold were two other competitors. One was the unknown, PJ Irwin, a runner who had recently moved to the area. The other was the national ten-mile champion, Mike Tikitok, who was to be the honorary starter for the event.

Tikitok was one of the greatest high school runners in New Jersey history, and every year he gave a talk on what it was like to be an elite high school runner in New Jersey. He would tell the kids how he got thrown off the team a number of times because he didn't run the slow workouts his coach was telling him to do. He knew he had to run harder to be great, and it worked. The kids loved Tikitok because he was just a big kid himself. By the end of his talk, he would have the entire group of kids laughing at some jokes and comical stories.

On this particular day, camp had ended its daily session at noon, and by one o'clock Tikitok and Gurn were a mile into a hard fourteen-mile run. By three, Tikitok was into his third Sam Adams, which he liked to refer to as "cocktails."

By five o'clock, the Gordans and the kids from camp were setting up for the race, which would kick off at 6:30 p.m. Tikitok, the honorary starter, strolled around carrying a sixteen-ounce red plastic sports bottle, mingling with the kids and sipping "cocktails" from his sports bottle. All the while, he was careful to keep the contents of the bottle concealed from his young, adoring fans. PJ observed the spectacle and could tell from Tikitok's swagger that this was not his first "cocktail" of the day. In fact, by a quarter till six, it was rumored that this was Tikitok's fifth Sam Adams.

It was around this time that Doug Petty, one of the kids attending camp, was having a conversation with Tikitok, who had just finished telling Doug that he always "carried a coin with him when he ran" because he wanted to be ready if he "met the ferryman." Tikitok had a degree in classic literature and was referring to the fabled ferryman who took the recently departed across the river Styx to the afterworld, if they made a payment.

Anyway, as Doug thought about the significance of what he had just heard, Tikitok gazed past the boy toward Marcello, who was warming up. "Doug," Tikitok started, "this is really awesome, being able to come here and run with the great Marcello O'Sullivan."

Doug smiled as Tikitok showed that childlike quality that he possessed.

"I can't believe I'm just going to be the starter today. I'd like to be able to run in this race with Marcello," Tikitok continued as he looked down at the khaki shorts and sandals he was wearing.

Doug looked down and saw Tikitok's sandals and then noticed that Tikitok was spying his own worn-out Nike Pegasuses. They were vintage Pegasuses and very well worn, with holes in the toes and heels showing wear on their outer edges. Doug, like most runners, had retired them from service and wore them now only as a recreational shoe.

"Doug, wiggle your toes!" Tikitok said. Doug smiled and obliged, his big toe popping out through the hole in the right shoe. He pulled it back inside.

"What size shoes are you wearing?" Tikitok asked.

Doug's heart raced a little because he knew where Tikitok was going with this. "Nine and a half. Why?"

"They'll do. Can I borrow them?"

Doug smiled as he kicked off the shoes and handed them to Tikitok. He gave the boy his sandals and then hurriedly put the shoes on. "These feel pretty good!" he declared as he wiggled his toes, exposing his big toe through the hole in the front of the shoe. By now a group of fans had gathered and were observing the footwear exchange.

"Here's a pair of shorts you can run in, Mike," said a member of the gathering crowd as he handed Tikitok a pair of black Sub4s.

Tikitok grabbed the shorts and went behind a nearby van. Moments later he emerged, looking more like a runner and less like a race starter.

Gurn approached and said, "Okay, guys, what's going on?"

"Gurn, I have to run. Marcello's here. What a treat!" Tikitok replied with childlike enthusiasm.

Gurn smiled. This was right up his alley. Getting a "tipsy" Tikitok into a race with Marcello and Gary was the type of "sandlot" running event that he believed in. He was a runner in the sincerest form of the word, and often referred to running as his form of recovery. He had a tough day job as a child psychologist for a state child welfare agency. While some of New Jersey's working class were worrying about a late financial report or the latest supply-chain fiasco, Gurn was out there trying to rescue kids from abusive environments. On many days, he would find himself driving home with his heart pounding, wanting to scream at the top of his lungs. At these times he would pull his Pathfinder over at the side of Route 80 and go for a run.

Gurn turned away from Tikitok and grinned at his wife, Laura, who had just approached the group. Laura was just like Gurn – except she was dead sexy with long blonde hair and a nicely tanned body. She too was an extreme runner.

"What's going on, Gurn?" Laura said, giggling slightly.

"Mike is friggin' incredible. He wants to race!" Gurn said, shaking his head.

"Do you think he can win?" Laura asked, her eyes widening.

"I-I…don't think he can find the starting line!" Gurn laughed, walking off to continue setting up for the race.

Laura turned and noticed PJ observing the situation. "This ought to be interesting," she said sarcastically to PJ.

"Who is he?" PJ asked, watching Tikitok list to the left as he did his warm-up strides.

Laura briefly explained who Tikitok was and listed some of his achievements. "Who are you?" she asked when she was finished.

"I'm PJ Irwin. I just moved to the area," he answered. "Can he possibly race in the condition he's in?"

"I don't know," Laura said, giggling again, as she moved closer to PJ. "Rumor has it he had a minor heart attack during the last mile of the New York Marathon a couple years ago. He still managed to run under 2:20!"

PJ stared over his shoulder at the striding Tikitok. He was beginning to sweat, and he was still struggling to run in a straight line.

"Well, this *should* be interesting," PJ said.

"Our races always are!" Laura exclaimed as she returned to work. "Make sure you come to our Beach Blast 5K in December. If you wear a bathing suit, your entry is free."

PJ watched as Laura walked away in her "Mrs. Santa" miniskirt outfit and thought, *I'll definitely have to make that race.*

As 6:30 p.m. drew nearer, the runners approached the starting line near the bathhouse at the edge of Swartswood Lake. The final warm-up rituals were interesting to observe. Gary was doing some serious strides and stretching approximately forty yards in front of the starting line. He had stripped down to his black and gold "Running Corps" racing singlet and shorts. His friendly demeanor had transformed into a very serious, competitive look. He appeared determined.

Marcello was jogging off to the left in the parking lot with his niece and nephew. Although he smiled and joked with them, every once in a while he glanced over at Gary. He wasn't nervous, which he obviously wanted Gary to know, but Gary was avoiding the eye contact.

Tikitok was stretching at the rear of the crowd congregating near the starting line. He was sweating profusely and appeared to be in a trance. Every now and then he lost his balance as he stretched. It was also evident to PJ that Tikitok warmed up in a low-key manner, avoiding Gary and Marcello completely.

Gurn grabbed the megaphone and gave the pre-race instructions to the crowd of 300 or so with the lovely Laura at his side.

PJ was standing about ten rows back in the crowd of runners while Rosie Depp, one of the youth runners attending the camp, sang the national anthem.

"How about a hand for Rosie!" Gurn cheered as the crowd gave a round of applause to the thirteen-year-old.

PJ watched someone give the girl a hug, and then he felt a hand on his elbow. It was Tikitok, and he was inching forward through the crowd toward the starting line. Tikitok looked at PJ as he squeezed past him and said, "Come with me. We're on a mission from God!"

PJ laughed and followed Tikitok until they were in the first row at the far outside of the pack. Gary and Marcello were on the opposite side and appeared oblivious to Tikitok's presence.

"Imagine coming from behind and beating Marcello with a wild kick," Tikitok whispered to PJ. "It would be awesome, wouldn't it?"

Tikitok was visualizing, the way he had done all his life. It was no wonder he studied the classics in college. While some runners visualized the technical aspects of their race – when to surge, when to relax, when to kick – Tikitok visualized his race as an epic saga, often referring to a recurring dream he had of riding a white stallion into battle. He would single-handedly defeat his foes against great odds.

"Give 'em hell," PJ said to Tikitok as he reached out his hand.

"Thanks," Mike answered, shaking PJ's hand. "What's your name?"

"PJ Irwin."

"Okay, PJ, let's push through this one," Tikitok said as the starter raised the gun into the air.

Bang!

Immediately Gary took the lead, followed closely by two of the local college runners, Miquel Printz and Chad Jewell. At the 800-meter mark the lead pack remained the same, with Marcello in fourth. PJ was running in twelfth place, next to an ailing Tikitok, whose breathing was already labored and who seemed to be all over the course.

The 5K course consisted of two loops around the park's campground. The first 800 meters of each loop were in the open, followed by 1,200 meters in the woods.

As they entered the woods, PJ decided to pick up the pace to stay in contact with the leaders. He briefly looked back at Tikitok, whose face was pale, his eyes partially closed. *He's done,* PJ thought to himself.

Shortly after entering the woods, PJ hit the first of two minor uphills on the course. He shortened his stride a bit to maintain his momentum on the uphill, and reduce the wear and tear on his legs. He wanted them to be there for him later in the race.

5:15...5:16...5:17... the timekeeper at the mile marker read off the split as PJ passed. He was coasting and he knew it. PJ was a seasoned veteran, and he had learned the hard way not to lose a race in the first mile. If you wanted to win, you had to be able to run negative splits – your second half of the race had to be faster than the first. PJ was gaining on the leaders with only about six seconds separating them.

As they completed a hairpin turn shortly after the mile mark, PJ could see the expression on Gary's face. Gary took a brief look behind him and noticed that Marcello had moved into second place. Gary looked determined to work his game plan: *don't piss off Marcello, and then try to outkick him in the end.*

Marcello was the consummate professional, smiling and waving to a few spectators on the side of the trail as he stalked Gary. As Marcello passed PJ going in the opposite direction, their eyes met for a moment. Marcello smiled and said, "Way to go, Mike!"

PJ looked back and could see the pale Tikitok struggling through the course – struggling, but not giving in. As PJ exited the hairpin turn, he got a better view of Tikitok. Mike was pale and sweating, his eyes barely open, but his form was there. And the stagger was gone. *He can't possibly be sobering up!* he thought to himself.

As the leaders approached the end of the first loop, Gary and Marcello were running comfortably together, going past the halfway point in 8:10. PJ went by in fifth place in 8:18, closely trailing Printz and Jewell. Gurn and Laura cheered wildly for the runners as they passed. PJ could see Gurn's eyes grow wide as Tikitok completed the first loop in 8:25. "You're friggin' awesome, Mike!" Gurn yelled from behind his Santa wig and beard.

PJ was now pondering strategy. If he moved too early on Gary and Marcello, it would make them go early and he'd have no chance. He needed to get close enough to go with them for the last quarter mile.

Gradually he accelerated through the flat open 800 meters before entering the woods a second time.

Just then, from behind, he heard a voice. It was Tikitok. "They're going to see us at the turn," Tikitok said as he pulled up next to PJ and started to press the pace a little.

He was right. As soon as Marcello and Gary completed the hairpin turn, they would get a good look at Tikitok and PJ, and they would make their assessment. Surely Marcello wouldn't care, but Gary may decide to push the pace a little earlier to avoid getting beat by Tikitok and the unknown, PJ. "Any advice?" PJ asked Tikitok, who seemed to be in total control now.

"Yeah. When they see us, look tired."

PJ nodded and smiled. *Very cunning*, he thought. Tikitok wanted to be in the race when the lead runners hit the last 400 meters.

As Marcello and Gary made the turn at the 2.5-mile mark, they both looked over at PJ and Tikitok. PJ grimaced and squinted while making a grunting noise. He raised his shoulders a little to appear as if he was struggling.

Tikitok, on the other hand, pointed to the leaders and said, "I'm coming for you bastards!" and surged forward.

You son of a bitch! PJ thought as he went after Tikitok. *You awesome, cool, son of a b—,* he thought again as he moved up next to Tikitok. "Atta boy," Tikitok said as they ran stride for stride toward the 400-meter mark.

PJ's adrenaline was flowing, and he felt the runner's high kicking in. This was going to be an awesome finish. With 500 meters to go, PJ and Tikitok caught Marcello. Gary was pulling away a little. "Good day, lads," Marcello said as the two passed him.

Tikitok grinned and shook his head, looking over at PJ. "I think we're dead meat."

PJ was thinking the same thing. Marcello didn't even look tired. With 400 meters to go, PJ started to kick wildly. When he caught Gary, he thought briefly that he might win. But then Gary reacted, shortening his stride for a few steps and increasing his leg turnover. In no time he had put ten feet between him and PJ. Just then Tikitok flew past PJ, followed by Marcello. "Don't quit!" Marcello said as he passed.

PJ shifted gears one more time and started to drive his arms wildly. He caught the four runners one last time, but with 150 meters to go he could no longer hang on. All he could do was watch through watery eyes as the trio dueled to the very end. Marcello took the lead with 100 meters to go and finished in 15:45. Gary crossed in second in 15:46, and Tikitok finished in 15:47. A rigor mortis–riddled PJ staggered across in 15:58.

As PJ exited the chute at the end of the finish line, he looked for Tikitok to thank him. To his surprise, he found Tikitok standing waist-deep in Swartswood Lake, talking to a couple of surprised lifeguards. Apparently, he skipped the chute and ran directly into the lake after finishing the race.

PJ smiled and returned to his vehicle to change. Along the way he passed the kid who had loaned his shoes to Tikitok. "Did he take them off before he jumped in the lake?" PJ asked.

"Nope!" the boy answered.

Later at the awards ceremony, Tikitok took the certificate for a free pair of running shoes he had won and gave it to the kid to make up for ruining his shoes. This race had made him a hero to at least one little boy. As for PJ, this race had made him even hungrier to win the Open XC 10K Championship in December.

Chapter 16

Ministry of Silly Walks

School started on September 3rd, which was to be a special day for the team. PJ was holding his first cross country team registration meeting, hoping a few more runners would come out. He had written the team's workout for the day on a sheet of paper and hung it up on the side of a locker. The existing team was to do an easy forty minutes of running today.

The meeting was to be held in the school library, located between the gym and the cafeteria. PJ arrived early and on his way to the library, he passed a small board displaying the various school records for cross country and track and field. As competitive as he was, PJ couldn't pass up the opportunity to compare his own high school bests to those on the board. He had a high school 5K best time of 15:50. His best mile time came during his senior year when he ran 4:18 at his state outdoor championship meet. He also ran a 1:56 half-mile leg at the Penn Relays in 1978.

PJ's eyes slowly scanned the board, noting each distance, time and date. When his eyes came upon the cross country time, they opened wide. There, neatly engraved in the plastic one-by-three-inch slot, was *Warinanco 5K Course – 14:59 – James Ciabin – 1974.*

Incredible! he thought. But then again, PJ knew every course was different, and the Warinanco course had been changed many times over the years. It may have been a short course in 1974.

PJ continued to scan the board until he reached another significant mark, this one making the hairs on the back of his neck stand on end. *880 Yard Run – 1:49.52 – Joel Savage – 1969.*

"Holy crap!" he muttered to himself.

"Checking out the mile record?" PJ heard a voice behind him say. It was Carmine exiting the gym on his way to the library.

"No, the 880 record," PJ answered, surveying the board, looking for the mile record.

"Savage was one heck of a runner," Carmine answered. "Actually, back in 1969 to 1971, RC had seven runners that could all run the half mile in under two minutes. In fact, four of them could run under 1:54."

"Really? That's pretty uncommon to have that many good runners," PJ said as his eyes locked onto the mile record. He shook his head as he read the inscription. *Mile Run – 4:11.12 – Joel Savage – 1969.*

"Gag was the athletic director and coach back then," Carmine said. "He made it a rule that anyone planning on competing in a winter or spring sport had to run cross country. Their cross country teams always had 100 or more boys on them! The competition was fierce, and often the better athletes would stick with track and field instead of going out for basketball or baseball."

"So, Carmine," PJ started, "do you think we'll get a hundred boys to come out for the team today?"

"Let's look inside and see how many are here so far," Carmine replied sarcastically.

As they approached the library door, PJ crossed his fingers before the two coaches stopped and looked into the library. At first it appeared to be empty except for the librarian, Mrs. Jung, but then PJ heard a hum from the other side of the door. As he peered inside and looked around the room, he noticed a girl in a motorized wheelchair crossing the library floor. She picked up a book on Irish culture from a pedestal on top of a display table. Then she turned and said something to someone off to the side of the room. Just then, a boy came from the fiction section and approached the girl. He took the book from her and read a passage she obviously wanted him to read. When he finished, they both started laughing, and he bent over and gave her a hug.

"Who's that?" PJ asked.

"Oh, that's Kathleen Murphy and her brother Kevin," Carmine said. "They're great kids, more like best friends than brother and sister."

"What do you mean?" PJ asked.

"Well, they hang out together, and Kevin really helps Kathleen cope with her illness."

"What's wrong with her?" PJ asked.

"She has PLS. It's like Lou Gehrig's disease but hits younger people. It's not fatal, but its effect on the nervous system is devastating," Carmine said as Kathleen turned and saw the two of them looking through the door at her. "They always go to the library at the end of the day to wait until their bus shows up to take them home," he added.

Kathleen waved at Carmine through the window. Carmine waved back, opened the door, and the pair entered.

"How are you, Kathleen?" Carmine said as he approached the strawberry-blonde sophomore.

"I'm fine, Carmine, and you?" she said with a smile.

PJ noticed that her speech pattern was slightly impaired by the PLS. He also noticed her eyes floating up and down, checking him out for a moment.

"Kathleen, this is our new cross country coach, PJ Irwin," Carmine said.

"Nice to meet you," PJ said as he glanced across the room at her brother.

"Nice to meet ya," Kathleen said, starting to blush. "Hey, Kevin!" she hollered across the library. "Come over here a minute."

Kevin Murphy was a strong, muscular kid. As he turned and started toward the trio, PJ noticed his huge, friendly smile. He was wearing a pair of torn blue jeans and a black POW-MIA T-shirt. Just then, Kevin broke into a comedic stride. He was imitating Monty Python's "Ministry of Silly Walks" skit.

"Perfect!" Carmine laughed as Kevin realized there were visitors. "I think we found another runner for the team," Carmine added.

"Not me – no way!" Kevin said, still smiling. "I couldn't run a mile if it was off a cliff!"

"Oh shush!" laughed Kathleen. "He run's everywhere…to the store, to his friend's house—"

"To the toilet!" Kevin interrupted and darted toward the hallway where the men's room was located.

"Kevin would be a great runner, but…" Kathleen said as she looked at the ground.

"But what?" Carmine asked.

"But me!" she spoke softly, her voice cracking. "I know he won't do it because he feels he needs to be with me after school. I'm glad he stays with me. He's my best friend. But…I-I feel like these are his best days and I'm robbing him of them."

"I've got an idea," PJ said, grabbing a chair and sitting directly in front of Kathleen. She looked up at PJ briefly, and then toward Carmine. "Kathleen, I could use a team manager to record times during the workouts and races."

"Kevin wouldn't want to do that," she replied. "Ever since he had Reye's syndrome as a kid, he's had trouble with detail work. You know, timing, details, things like that."

PJ smiled broadly and glanced over at Carmine. "I'm not talking about him. I want you!"

Kathleen went silent for a few moments as PJ turned toward the library windows overlooking the track and soccer field.

"Okay, I'll do it. But first, I want to do something about your hair!"

PJ whirled around, his mouth hanging open.

"Coach, if you want to attract kids, you have to look a little more 'with it.' I see a little Ray Liotta in you. He's just standing behind the big Ray Romano in you."

PJ could only laugh. For the first time in his life, he was speechless. He liked this little girl. She was tough, straightforward, witty, and probably the first person he had come across (other than Taylor) who could take anything he dished out.

A hundred students did not show up for the first team registration meeting. However, of the two who did, one of them was special – a hundredfold!

"I'll talk to my brother. Don't worry – he's in!" Kathleen said, giving them a wink.

Chapter 17

Get Out in Front of the Garbage

Taylor entered the library at about a quarter after five and found PJ and Carmine in deep discussion. PJ had prepared a list of team members:

Andrew Cartolano – Senior

Teddy Dohne – Senior

Mike Kinney – Senior

Rod O'Leary – Senior

Vlad Manasee – Sophomore

Matt Shipp – Freshman

Nick Garvey – Freshman

Kevin Murphy – Senior

Kathleen Murphy – Sophomore (Team Manager)

As Taylor approached the table where the two coaches were working, PJ slid the sheet with the names on it in her direction. "Here's who we have so far," he said, looking at his reflection in a glass case next to his chair. "And I need to do something with my hair!" he added.

Carmine snickered as Taylor glanced up for a moment from the list to observe PJ playing with his locks.

"Right. That'll be the day, when you 'do something' with your hair." She rolled her eyes and looked back at the list.

"Do I really look like Ray Romano?"

Taylor smiled, and without looking up from the list, she answered, "Kind of, I guess. I see you've met Kathleen."

PJ snapped the list from her and said, "That's right. And she thinks I look like Ray Liotta!"

"I know. I just heard her talking to her friends while she was waiting for her ride home," Taylor chuckled.

PJ looked up at the clock. "Wow, it's getting late. I have to get out for my run."

As he ran across the school's parking lot to begin, he passed Andrew, Teddy and Rod finishing theirs. "How ya feeling?" he said as the boys approached.

"Good," they shouted almost in unison.

"Any new recruits?" Teddy asked.

"Yep," PJ said, turning to continue his run. "I'm late. I've got to get my run in before it gets dark." PJ was hoping to avoid the question of how many recruits.

"How many signed up?" Andrew asked.

PJ stopped, turned, and answered while continuing to walk backwards away from the trio. "We have a full team...and a team manager!"

"Who's the manager?" Rod asked.

"Kathleen...uh, Murphy, I believe."

Andrew's eyes widened. "Did her brother sign up?"

"It was a package deal!" PJ answered with a smile.

"Excellent!" the trio exclaimed.

"Why? Is he good?" PJ asked.

"I don't know, but he's the funniest kid in school. This is going to be a fun season."

"I'll see you guys tomorrow. Do your sit-ups and push-ups," PJ said, speeding off toward Warinanco Park to get in a twelve-miler.

The run over to the park from the school was about a mile and a half. Once at the park, PJ had a selection of trails and roadways that he could run. Of course, he had the cross country course at the park as well.

As PJ exited the school parking lot, he crossed over a wooden footbridge and turned right onto 9th Avenue in Rozelle. He darted across the street so that he could run against traffic, something all smart runners did because it let them see the car – and maybe even get a good description of it – before it ran them over.

PJ ran past a few kids selling lemonade as he made a left onto Locust Street and started to ascend a small hill leading up to 5th Avenue. Almost without thinking, PJ accelerated up the hill. *Never waste a hill,* he thought as he increased his leg turnover.

PJ's high school coach used to drive this into his head. He had attended Norris Hills High School and was coached by the legendary Jim Rod, who came from a great family of runners, himself a four-minute miler. He had coached numerous teams, including PJ's, to New Jersey state cross country titles.

Rod had a second saying that had also stuck with PJ throughout the years. *Get out in front of the garbage!* he would tell his runners in the pre-race pep talks. PJ loved that expression. Even today, twenty-five years later, it still made him smile as he thought about it.

PJ made a right onto 5th Avenue and headed north toward the park. The street was lined with beautiful Victorian homes, most built around the turn of the century. PJ's favorite was a gray one with the name *Wischusen* on the mailbox. It had a large oak tree in the front yard, and the grounds were impeccably landscaped. PJ would sometimes run across the end of the lawn because the grass was so plush that the cushioning made his legs feel better. Today, however, he had to stay on the sidewalk because new windows were being installed at the house, and the installers had lined up the windows on the lawn bordering the sidewalk.

As PJ ran past the windows, he took the opportunity to check out his form. While he checked out his arm carry and stride, he thought he saw someone running on the other side of the street. Quickly he turned and looked, but there was only a small child on a bicycle watching him run past.

He made it to the park in nine minutes and twenty seconds – exactly the pace he wanted to run, as it equated to somewhere around 6:10 per mile. As he entered the park, he decided to run the trail that went around the outer perimeter.

A few moments later PJ noticed a group of runners about 150 meters in front of him. They appeared to be college age, but he wasn't quite sure. It didn't matter, though, because tonight they were dinner.

PJ was a competitor, and whenever he came upon a group such as this, something came over him. That voice in his head would challenge him. At first, the voice would simply urge him to catch them. If they tried to go with PJ, well, then the voice would get downright nasty, sometimes telling PJ to throw in surges to "test their fortitude." On other days, it would push him for just a gradual acceleration until the victims gave in. One time while on a business trip in Carlsbad, California, PJ was running with a guy who claimed to be an ultramarathoner. PJ decided to simply keep running until the guy stopped. The ultra runner ran forty-one miles that day. PJ ran forty-three!

Surges on hills could be the flavor of the day today, PJ thought as he began to chase this group of seven runners. *At a 6:10 pace I should be able to make up the distance in about a mile. Let's see…that means I'll pass them just as we hit the uphill at the Linden Road entrance to the park. Perfect; surges on hills, an uphill spanking…you know, when I visualize, it's almost frightening!*

PJ was feeling good. His steps were light and efficient, his breathing unlabored. He loved days like this. They were the reward for all those days of running sick, running in bad weather, running at midnight. Days like today made the sacrifices worthwhile.

As PJ approached the skating rink, he checked his watch and did the math. (Most distance runners developed a knack for math, especially marathoners. They checked their watches as they passed the mile marks and then did the math to figure out their pace and their projected finishing times.) PJ's pace was holding at 6:10. He still felt great, but it didn't look like he was catching the group of seven runners in front of him. It was hard to tell with all the turns between him and them. He would know better in a couple minutes. He looked at his watch when they passed the large evergreen tree near the skating rink. He passed it some twenty-six seconds later.

PJ checked his watch again as the group passed the foul pole on the softball field. He would check the watch again when he passed the pole himself. *Let's see,* he thought to himself, *if they're your typical college jocks, I should close the gap to, say, fifteen seconds by the time I get to the pole. Let's see…* PJ approached the pole and looked down at his watch. *Twenty-six seconds. Shit,*

I didn't gain anything on them. These guys are moving pretty good. Great, let me shift gears.

PJ gradually picked up the pace as he passed the Linden Road entrance to the park, then continued to soar around the park's perimeter. He had checked his watch at Linden Road and then again at the public pool, knowing the distance between the two was 800 meters, as it was a well-known place to do 800-meter repeats. Two minutes and fifty seconds was the elapsed time. PJ was now running at a 5:40 mile pace. *I'm flying,* he thought as he assessed his form. *Now, let's get back to the job at hand.*

He noticed the pack of seven passing the water fountain by the park ranger station. PJ glanced at his watch again and continued to push toward the water fountain. *24...25...26! Damn, no ground gained – not an inch!* PJ thought as he double-checked his watch. *These guys are good! Who are they? Can they keep it up? Can I catch them? Who are they?*

On the next lap around the park, PJ dropped below a 5:20 pace and gained a little, but only for a short time. When he neared the runners, he noticed how they glided effortlessly through the rolling hills of the park, their strides almost perfectly aligned. Another thing he noticed was that they changed leads in a very orderly way. They weren't racing each other – they were sharing the lead, encouraging the trailing runner to move up and take the lead. And they never looked back! To them, PJ didn't even exist. Or so he thought.

By the fourth loop around the park, PJ had fallen another thirty seconds back. He wasn't going to catch them. For a moment he considered running the opposite way, just so that he could find out who they were. But he had discipline, and completing the run was more important to him. So at the end of the fourth lap, PJ exited the park onto 3rd Avenue and headed back to the school. Along the way he tapered off his pace and focused on recovering and relaxing.

I hope they're there tomorrow, he thought. *I'd like another crack at them. Hell! I'd like to train with them!* he thought as the school came into view.

Chapter 18

Remember the Alamo

_____

The next two days were distance days for the runners. Kevin Murphy showed up as planned and suffered through the latter parts of the distance runs, but he finished them. Kathleen cheered him on each day, and he gratefully acknowledged her on each occasion. Kathleen recorded the boys' splits and reviewed them with the team at the end of each practice. PJ appreciated the way they listened without goofing off as she went through the information.

"Tomorrow's Saturday," PJ said to the group of runners as they gathered near the cross country starting line to do sit-ups and push-ups. "You're all doing very well, but at some point we have to go anaerobic. We're going to do some harder interval work tomorrow."

"Oh, joy of joys!" Teddy murmured, making Vladimir snicker.

"Vlad, did you want to say something?" PJ asked.

"No, it's just that Ted likes to sleep in on Saturday mornings," Vlad answered.

"Teddy, we'll wait for you," PJ teased.

"Vlad's the one who'll be late," Teddy quipped. "Have you ever watched him get dressed after practice?"

Nobody said anything for a bit, and then Andrew opened his mouth. "You're the only one who watches people get dressed after practice," he joked as he jumped to his feet.

"I'm gonna kick your—" Teddy said, taking off after Andrew.

PJ and the others laughed as he watched the two dash in and out of the wooded area bordering the course. Andrew had the best of Teddy, until he had to stop. Then Teddy took his revenge. He tackled Andrew and in one quick move flipped him onto his back and straddled his body, sitting on him.

"Pink belly!" Teddy yelled as he pulled up Andrew's shirt. Over the course of the next minute or so, Teddy repeatedly slapped Andrew's stomach until the skin glowed red. When he was finished, Teddy helped Andrew to his feet, and they both laughed while they walked back to the group.

"Tomorrow, 9 a.m., we meet at the track," PJ added as he turned toward his car.

About to begin his own workout, he wondered if he would have anyone to run with. As he changed into his training flats, he debated whether to run a tempo run or long intervals this evening. Either way, he would try to reach about 85 percent of his maximum heart rate, which would boost the oxygen delivery to his muscles. He liked to think of training at this pace as "oxygen loading," which referred to the body's increased ability to absorb oxygen into the blood. The more oxygen in the blood, the better the krebs cycle and the more ATP (the basic unit of energy used to fuel the body) produced.

As he leaned against his car and stretched his Achilles, he closed his eyes and visualized his muscles becoming loose and relaxed. He was a great believer in visualization, a loose form of self-hypnosis.

PJ opened his eyes to find his vision slightly blurred. When it cleared, he noticed a group of runners out on the cross country course. As they neared the parking lot, he sensed they were looking directly at him. When they reached the road separating the track from the course, they turned right and headed for the starting line of the course. They slowed for a moment, and then one of them waved at PJ.

PJ waved back and took off in a brisk jog toward them. He was feeling loose as the adrenaline began to flow. It was hammer time, although they didn't know it.

"Hi, do you mind if I run with you?" PJ said as he approached the group.

"No, not at all!" replied the closest runner. "We thought you might want to, based on the way you were chasing us last night!" he added with a grin. "My name's Dan, and these are my running buddies," he added as he extended his hand.

PJ reached out and shook Dan's hand, noticing that Dan was wearing a pair of vintage Nike LDV 1000s with a wedge-shaped heel, one of the first pair of waffle-soled shoes Nike ever produced. PJ thought about the recent resurgence in the market for retro shoes. People were paying top dollar for shoes that hadn't been state of the art since the '70s. PJ thought this was silly because the materials had improved so much since then. As PJ shook hands with the rest of the group, he noticed they were all wearing retro shoes.

"Do you like my Arthur Lydiards?" one of the runners asked.

PJ's eyes widened as he looked down at the runner's shoes. He had heard there was a Lydiard brand at one time but had never seen a pair. They seemed very lightweight.

"Very nice," PJ said, starting to jog. The group joined in.

"What do you plan on running tonight, Coach?" Dan asked.

"I was going to do an interval workout – 800-meter repeats in about 2:25 to 2:30 each," PJ answered. "But I'm willing do whatever you guys want to do if 800s are too much," he added.

"We were thinking of 1,200s going through the 800 in 2:25," Dan said while some of the others behind him grinned and nodded their heads.

PJ knew what was going on. They had just one-upped him. They were going to run 50 percent farther on each interval and at the same pace as PJ. PJ knew he could do this workout; but for how long, he wasn't sure.

"I like to keep my recoveries short – around two minutes!" PJ quipped.

"We usually stick to sixty to ninety seconds," came a voice from the back of the pack.

Turning to see who it was, PJ noticed that all seven runners were grinning at him, and they all wore that confident, smug look. They would definitely lose at poker because their expressions disguised nothing. They were holding a great hand, and they were about to deal him one hell of a workout.

"Well, from the looks on your faces," PJ started, "I can see this is going to be an interesting workout." Then he added, "Painful, too," as he broke into the first 1,200-meter interval.

Approximately one-third of the way into the first interval, two of the runners took the lead, running stride for stride like machines. Their arms swung ever so slightly front and back, and they floated along effortlessly, as did the other five. PJ focused on his own form, not wanting to exhibit any weakness or flaw. Toward the end of the first interval, he struggled a little with controlling his breathing. He did not want to be panting when he finished.

"Three minutes and forty-three seconds," Dan said as he crossed the line, stride for stride with PJ.

PJ broke into a jog and started to collect himself, preparing for the next interval. *There's no way I can do more than five of these at this pace with just a ninety-second recovery!* he thought. *I wonder how many they plan on doing...*

"One down and nine to go," Dan said as PJ turned to look at him. Dan high-fived the runner next to him as they regrouped during the jog.

"You take the next one, Dave," Dan said to the runner next to him while wiping his sweat with the faded T-shirt he was wearing. The front of the shirt, which was obviously well worn, bore a picture of a Snickers bar.

"Okay," Dave replied. Glancing over at Dan, he added, "Hey, you're not blowing your nose in your favorite shirt, are you?"

"Nope, just got some sweat in my eyes, and I don't think it's my own," Dan replied with a grin.

"Dan's a Snickers bar fanatic," Dave said as he moved to PJ's other side. "I've seen him take in three or four at a time."

"I'm partial to Milky Ways," PJ said.

Dan turned briefly to face PJ and smiled. "Milky Ways are okay, but Snickers...mmm-mmm. There just isn't anything better."

As they prepared to start the next 1,200-meter interval, Dan reminded the group of runners to try to stay together and to help each other out.

"We'll each lead one interval until the last one, and then it's every man for himself!"

Dan turned to face the start of the next interval. "Take it, Dave," Dan said as he started to run and simultaneously pressed the start button on his watch.

PJ took off also, deciding to run this one at the back of the pack.

"Stay with it, Coach," came a voice from the far end of the group.

PJ glanced over in the direction from which the words of encouragement came, noticing the shortest runner of the bunch. He had dirty-blond hair and wore a Villanova University shirt. He was muscular, built like a V, and had perfect form. He looked like a running machine. Without turning his head, he shifted his eyes to look over at PJ and then refocused in front of him again.

Dave, meanwhile, lead the trio around the 600-meter pole and downhill toward the "flower garden," an area in the park in which an octagon-shaped garden existed, bordered by protective evergreen shrubs.

"Stay with me!" Dave commanded as he entered the last 400 meters of the interval, which were uphill from the "rose garden" and around the back of another famous landmark known as "the Alamo." The Alamo was an elevated garden in the middle of the park bordered by a large cement wall. Steps on either end allowed access to the interior of the fort-like structure. During cross country season, hordes of race fans battled for a prime position inside the Alamo. From there, nearly the entire race could be observed with very little obstruction. The 1,200-meter and 4,000-meter marks of the high school cross country course were directly in front of the Alamo.

As the group neared the Alamo, PJ noticed something. They were pulling together. The runners in the back pushed a little harder, and they seemed to pack tighter together.

"That's the way!" Dave said as he decelerated to a jog.

"Nice run, Coach," Dan said as he high-fived the muscular kid who had urged PJ on in the middle of the interval.

"Thanks," PJ said, trying to regain his breath. He extended his hand to the kid that urged him on and said, "Thanks for pushing me."

"No problem. My name's Rob O'Mally."

"I'm PJ Irwin," PJ said, shaking his hand. At that point, the others joined in the greetings.

"Hi, Coach, my name's Evan Brand," said an unassuming kid with shoulder-length, dark hair.

"And I'm Mark," came a voice from behind, "Mark Hills."

"Nice to meet you, Mark," PJ replied as he turned and extended his hand to the blond-haired kid in the Adidas shirt that paced the last interval.

"David Santos."

"Hi, David. Nice job pacing that last one," PJ said, responding to the kid's introduction.

"My pleasure," Dave answered with a grin.

"I'm Bill Bahsman," came a voice from behind PJ.

Whirling around, PJ saw a lanky kid with platinum-blonde hair wearing a Cho-Pat strap on each leg just below the knee cap. PJ knew that these straps helped the kneecap move in the appropriate groove or alignment.

"The chicks love them!" Bahsman said, having observed PJ studying the straps.

PJ smiled as he looked past Bahsman toward the only runner of the seven that he had not met yet.

"His name's Pete," Dan said under his breath to PJ. "He's very focused. Almost to a flaw."

PJ observed as Pete jogged in place, shaking his arms out, trying to relax them. His eyes were closed. There was something familiar about this kid, but PJ could not pinpoint it.

"Pete, are you up for this one?" Dan asked as he checked his watch. "We go off in thirty seconds."

Pete looked at Dan and then PJ and nodded, before going back to his routine of jogging in place.

As the final thirty seconds of the rest period came to an end, Pete jogged toward the line, and the other six runners rallied around him with an unusual sense of urgency. In no time, PJ knew why. As PJ desperately tried to stay with the pack, Pete, the new leader, was redefining the workout.

They went past the 400-meter mark in sixty-nine seconds and rounded the 600-meter pole in one minute forty-four seconds. As they raced past the flower garden, PJ noticed how strong the group looked. Not only were they moving, but they were all stride for stride, closely packed, and showing no sign of slowing. They raced up the final hill by the Alamo and finished in 3:27! They had just run a sub 4:40 mile pace for their third 1,200-meter interval.

As PJ reached the end of the interval, Dan held out his hand and high-fived him. "Nice running, Coach."

PJ felt awkward being called "Coach" by these guys. They were far superior to him; plus, PJ never told them he was a coach.

"Thanks," PJ gasped. He could no longer hide it. He was tired.

"We should have warned you. Pete likes to train at a 4:40 mile pace," Dan explained. "His goal is to run a 5K at this pace."

PJ stood there, bent over, his hands on his knees, and did the math in his head as he fought to recover. *A 4:40 mile pace would result in a 14:20 5K time!* PJ grimaced at the thought.

Struggling through the remainder of the workout, PJ was impressed by the way these guys pushed and encouraged each other. The tightly packed finish at the end of each 1,200-meter interval was awe-inspiring.

As PJ warmed down with the bunch, they jogged together toward his car, where he stopped and grabbed his sweatpants from the hood. "Thanks for working out with me," he said as he stepped into the pants.

"Yeah, thanks," came the reply from the group as they turned to walk away.

Just then, Pete turned back toward PJ and asked, "Same time tomorrow, Coach?"

PJ laughed and said, "Yeah, that sounds like a plan."

As the seven runners jogged out of the park onto West Jersey Street, PJ finished dressing, then hopped into the car and drove to the same exit, making a left onto West Jersey Street himself. Driving toward downtown Rozelle, he realized that he must have driven right past the group of runners and not noticed them. Either that, or they must live in the apartment complex bordering the park at the exit onto West Jersey Street.

About thirty minutes later, PJ arrived home. As he drove up the driveway, he noticed Taylor playing with David and Nike in the front yard. Taylor waved and turned to throw a Frisbee for Nike to catch. Nike, on the other hand, took off and ran straight toward PJ. As he stepped out of the car, Nike jumped up and greeted him by putting his two front paws on his shoulders. "Down, Nike!" he shouted through intermittent laughter.

"Daddy, watch how fast I can run!" exclaimed David from the other side of the yard. He ran briskly from the front porch to the broken-down stable that bordered the yard.

"Great job!" PJ yelled as David came to a stop.

"How was practice?" Taylor asked.

"They did an easy distance run today. They're looking a little stronger, but we have a ways to go," PJ replied. "They go anaerobic tomorrow!"

"Speed work – gotta love it," Taylor said with a grin as she picked up a set of roller skates from the lawn and headed in to get dinner on the table.

"That's right!" PJ chuckled, turning to follow Taylor inside.

Taylor was a natural athlete and learned quickly. She ran a few races in her early twenties, but she became a purely recreational runner in her later years. When it came to training, she was smart and learned fast. Many nights she would sit down and graph PJ's workout log, resting heart rates, and race times. She often recommended adjustments to PJ's training, and he learned to follow her advice. When PJ purchased an intermittent altitude training unit, it was Taylor who figured out how to use it.

Dinner consisted of mashed potatoes, chicken and Brussels sprouts, PJ's favorite. After dinner, he read the mail and then, because Taylor was a huge Johnny Depp fan, he sat down and watched a rerun of *21 Jump Street*. He nodded off early and wound up sleeping on the couch most of the night.

Chapter 19

800s

Before practice, PJ stopped for a hard roll and coffee at the Village Bakery, famous for their secret baking process. As PJ took his first bite of the roll, a voice came from behind him.

"I bet you can't eat just one!" said Augie Bernstein, the proprietor. When Augie was in high school, he played football on the same team as a kid named Rosie Grier, who went on to become a famous football player. Augie followed his mother's wishes, took over the bakery, and was proud of the family business he inherited. He had been a good boy and was now an even better man. He supported the local charities and schools, and never had a harsh word for anyone. "I hear you're coaching the cross country team at RC this year," he added.

"Yes, it's just something temporary until I find a real job," PJ said.

Augie peered sternly at PJ over his glasses. "That is a real job! Kids need nurturing more than ever nowadays. There are traps everywhere."

"I know, you're right. It's a tremendous responsibility," PJ countered, hoping to stop the conversation there. He didn't feel like having to justify himself. He had been asked to coach since he had the time, and he had agreed to one season. By January, he'd be an engineer again. There were enough juveniles to last a lifetime in the industry; he didn't need to increase the agony by getting into coaching kids.

"Darn right it is," Augie said, handing PJ a photo album full of pictures of him and Rosie Grier playing on their high school team. "Notice how Rosie's missing his blocks, but I'm making every one of mine," Augie said proudly.

PJ fumbled through the pages while sipping his coffee. Damned if he wasn't right – Augie was outperforming the great Rosie Grier in every photo.

"But Mom needed me to take over the bakery, so here I am!" Augie half-bragged, half-lamented. PJ heard a tinge of sadness in Augie's comment and watched as the little old man cleaned the top of one of the pastry counters. PJ turned and headed toward the exit.

"I find it thrilling to take dough and make my creations out of it," Augie said. "I love making something out of nothing!"

"Have a nice day," PJ said with a smile as he opened the door.

Augie peered briefly over his glasses and then returned to cleaning the bakery counters.

When PJ arrived at the track, the entire team was already there, stretching and talking about the party they had been to the night before.

"I made it on time," Vlad called out to PJ as he approached.

"You didn't sleep here, did you?" PJ replied jokingly.

"Nope. I got up early, ate a light breakfast, and here I am."

"Are you kidding?!" exclaimed Teddy from behind Vlad. "Your mom drove up, went around to your side of the car, opened the door, and dragged your ass out! You didn't wake up until you were halfway across the parking lot!"

"Hey Teddy, I'm going to…" Vlad said, grabbing Teddy in a headlock.

"Alright, guys, it's too early for this," PJ said as he motioned the team toward the track. Together they broke into an easy jog, and PJ went to work describing the goals for the day.

"Guys, today we're going to do 800-meter repeats. I want to start out at three minutes and work the time down to 2:20. You'll have a two-minute recovery between each one. I want you to jog it, not walk it."

"How many 800s will we be doing?" asked Andrew.

"Eight," answered PJ, breaking into a brief stride out to see how his legs felt.

As the group jogged a few more laps on the track, PJ took in bits and pieces of the varied conversations taking place among his runners.

Nick and Matt were discussing their latest video game scores, each one accusing the other of lying. Teddy, Mike and Rod were debating how well the Giants were going to do this year. Kevin was in the middle of a Monty Python routine for the benefit of everyone. Andrew, unlike the others, was quietly running right next to PJ. As they circled the track, PJ noticed Andrew shaking out his arms every once in a while. He appeared to be really focused on the job at hand – loosening up.

PJ thought about the workout he had experienced the night before with the runners he'd met. He was in awe at how they ran as a pack before, during and after the workout. He loved how they encouraged each other and brought out the best in each other as they ran the intervals, each one getting harder and harder. He remembered how Dan, the runner wearing the vintage Snickers T-shirt, rallied the runners and had kind, encouraging words for each one of them after every interval. They were truly a tight bunch, a "team" by every definition.

PJ stopped and turned around to view his team as they completed their jog, and his blood began to boil. Matt, Vlad and Nick were walking around the track a half lap back. Directly in front of him were Rod and Teddy, mocking Mike's haircut. It was obviously bothering Mike, but he tried not to let it show. Andrew and Murphy were already sitting on the ground, stretching, when PJ's eyes landed on them.

PJ sighed and started to write the runners' names on his clipboard. He carefully made eight columns next to the names so that he could record their interval times. *These guys aren't a team,* PJ thought. *I need a kid like Dan, the runner I met last night, to set the tone for the others, to be an example.*

PJ glanced out at the track and saw Matt, Vlad and Nick continuing to walk to the finish, which annoyed PJ. *Who am I kidding? I just need to find a real job. These kids' hearts will never be in it. They simply aren't the caliber of the guys I ran with last night – and they never will be!*

"Does anyone want to lead the stretches today?" PJ asked, receiving eight blank stares in response, a few accompanied with eye-rolling and at least one muffled laugh. "Very well then, I'll lead 'em," he said impatiently.

In no time he had guided the boys through a series of stretches designed to loosen up their legs, arms and backs, so that they would be less likely to hurt themselves during the workout. A few of the stretches resulted in whining and groaning, which PJ ignored and moved on.

Andrew and Kevin seemed to be the most serious of the bunch. They stretched nearly in unison and didn't speak a word. They seemed focused – or maybe, PJ thought ruefully, they were just daydreaming about other things.

"Okay, guys, let's get to the starting line," PJ said. Matt, Vlad and Nick were slow getting to the line; the others stood there, waiting for them. PJ glanced up from his clipboard and noticed their slow stroll toward the starting line. Then he glanced toward the kids on the line.

"Okay, guys, ready…go!" PJ rushed his starting commands to accentuate the trio's lateness.

It was a chaotic start to the workout. Nick and Matt took off from their locations on the infield and tried frantically to catch the others. Vlad, on the other hand, widened his eyes and approached PJ.

"I wasn't ready!" he exclaimed.

PJ gave him a stern look and said, "That's okay. Just join the rest of the team when you are."

Vlad seemed confused. He had obviously been expecting PJ to tell him to "catch the others" or "start now" or something similar. Instead, PJ basically told him to do whatever he wanted and caught him off guard. Vlad now seemed to be struggling with the freedom to decide. He could run now and simply trail the pack, he could wait until they finished a lap and then join them, or he could wait a little longer and start his workout with the second 800-meter interval.

PJ observed Vlad watch the others run and noticed Vlad looking at PJ every once in a while, almost as if he was waiting for PJ to tell him what to do. PJ restrained himself from saying anything to Vlad. Instead, he studied the boys as they circled the track and prepared to write down their 400-meter splits. The boys were very spread out, with Andrew and Teddy leading the pack.

As the lead runners completed their first lap, PJ yelled out the times. "Ninety-three, ninety-four, ninety-six. Pick it up," he added as he watched the sixty-meter-long string of runners round the first turn of the second lap.

Just then he noticed Andrew glance back toward Teddy and Kevin. Immediately, the two trailing runners surged until all three were side by side going into the last turn. As they approached the finish line, PJ checked the times – 3:01 flat for the first three runners. The remaining four crossed the line in 3:06 to 3:12.

As they crossed the line, PJ assessed how they looked. None of the boys appeared particularly tired, which was good because they still had seven more intervals to go.

"Let's jog the recovery, not walk it!" PJ shouted to the kids. The boys broke into a jog, and Vlad joined them in preparation for the next interval.

"Wow, I'm not even tired," Vlad joked with the others as they jogged their recovery. Nick and Matt looked in his direction but didn't say anything.

As they approached the start of their second interval, PJ reminded the group that he wanted to see negative splits with each 800-meter interval being faster than the previous one.

"Vlad, why don't you take this one since you bailed on the first one," Rod said tersely.

Vlad looked at the rest of the runners and found them all staring back at him. "Sure, I'll take it," he said. "I just hope you chumps can stay with me!" he added, looking over at PJ. "Let's get this party started!" He motioned to PJ to start the next interval.

"Okay…go," PJ said, and Vlad led the runners into the first turn.

The mood during this interval was in sharp contrast to the first. All eight runners went through the first 200 meters in thirty-three seconds and the 400 meters in sixty-eight. PJ watched as the group raced recklessly around the track, slowing tremendously during the second lap, tying up because of the excessively quick first 200 meters. He grimaced as he watched them struggle during the last 100 meters, their form falling completely apart. They came across the line not as a pack, but resembling more a long line of zombies, collapsing to their knees as they finished the interval. Vlad, Andrew and Teddy crossed the line in 2:37. The rest of the group were strung out, crossing between 2:40 and 3:01. They were all visibly tired. Rod, Vlad, Matt and Nick were all bent over, their hands on their knees, as they tried to catch their breath.

"Guys, don't bend over and put your hands on your knees!" PJ shouted. "It makes you look tired, weak. Being a competitor means not revealing your weakness, not showing the competition you're tired. I want others to think we're invincible!"

The boys straightened up and started to walk. "C'mon, guys, let's jog," said Andrew.

PJ glanced at Andrew as he broke into a jog, with Teddy, Rod and Mike, the upperclassmen on the team, immediately joining him. In a few moments, the entire team was jogging their recovery. They weren't tightly packed, but they were jogging.

As they approached the starting line, PJ reminded them that each interval had to be faster than the previous one. He also pointed out that they didn't run negative splits on the last one. Their first lap was simply too fast. Everyone looked at Vlad.

"Hey, I'm sorry, guys. I forgot what our instructions were," Vlad said.

"Teddy, you up for this one?" Andrew asked.

"Sure thing, boss," Teddy said as he moved toward the starting line.

"Okay, guys, we run this like a pack. Got it? Teddy leads," Andrew instructed.

The team nodded, almost in unison.

"I'm targeting 2:50 to 2:55," Teddy said.

"Okay, ten seconds and then we start," PJ said.

As he reset his watch, PJ surveyed the scene as the boys readied themselves for the start of the third interval. It was quiet, and the second row of runners were lining up noticeably closer to the first row this time. Andrew joined the underclassmen – Nick, Matt and Vlad – in the second row.

"Ready…go!" PJ shouted, and the team took off.

Teddy broke to the front, and the pack fell in just off his shoulder and behind him. As they entered the first turn, Rod stumbled when his foot landed on the crease where the grass infield met the track. Almost immediately, Kevin reached out and grabbed Rod's arm to keep him from falling. Rod recovered, nodded toward Kevin, and the pack pushed on.

Teddy brought them through the first lap. "Nice job! Eighty-four seconds!" PJ yelled at the tightly packed group.

As they went into the third turn, PJ noticed Nick and Matt falling off pace a little. Andrew was right behind them, and the three fell about five yards behind the lead group. As they entered the back straightaway, Andrew moved up alongside Matt and Nick, and he patted Nick on the back. "Go for another gear," he said to them.

PJ watched as the trio gradually gained on the lead pack of runners. As they entered the last straightaway, PJ watched as the runners approached him. With about seventy meters to go, PJ's eyes widened as he saw Nick, Matt, Vlad and Andrew move outside and become even with the four lead runners. They were running eight abreast, not struggling, and their form looked good. They seemed to have this one under control.

"2:48!" PJ shouted as they crossed the line in unison.

A few moments later they were jogging, and PJ watched as Andrew high-fived Nick and Matt. Andrew reminded him of Dan, the runner he had met the previous evening. He was respected by the kids around him and had leadership qualities.

PJ remembered his first conversation with Andrew when the boy revealed that he heard voices when he raced in grammar school. He remembered how he described that feeling of "letting himself (the voice) down" when he gave in and folded during races. It was obvious that Andrew was becoming a team leader.

As practice continued, the pack became tighter and tighter. PJ dropped the total number of intervals to six; he didn't want to run them into the ground with speed work at this point in the season. At the end of the sixth interval, he told the bunch to do an easy two-mile warm-down around the park. They immediately broke into a jog and headed toward the entrance to the trail leading around the park.

Suddenly, they slowed and turned toward the track. "You coming, Vlad?" Andrew yelled to Vlad who was still standing on the track.

PJ whirled around to see Vlad standing on the starting line, slightly crouched, his head down, as if he was getting ready for another 800.

"Well, Coach, how much more recovery do I have?" Vlad asked without facing PJ.

"You're done, Vlad. It's time for the warm-down," PJ answered as he approached the boy.

Vlad's head turned slowly, but he remained poised to start another interval. "I've only done five, Coach. I've got one more to do."

PJ stared at Vlad and for the first time noticed an intensity in his eyes.

Vlad stared for a moment and then added, "Got your watch ready?"

PJ quickly grabbed for his watch as Vlad turned his head and peered into the first turn.

"Okay, Vlad," PJ said, fumbling with the reset button. Vlad glanced down at the ground for a moment and then blessed himself.

"Ready…go!" PJ shouted.

As Vlad took off into the turn, the rest of the team jogged to various locations around the perimeter of the track.

"No prisoners, Vlad! Take no prisoners!" shouted Mike.

"Go, Yift!" shouted Andrew as Vlad passed the 200 in thirty-five seconds.

"Go, *Yift?*" asked PJ as Andrew laughed and looked at him.

"Yeah, Myrus Yifter. Vlad's father said he raced against him a long time ago. Yifter was a great African distance runner."

"Yeah, I remember seeing him run." PJ chuckled as he grabbed for his watch. "Seventy seconds," PJ shouted as Vlad went through the 400 meters.

"His dad thinks Vlad has Yifter's form," Andrew added.

PJ studied the lone runner as he raced past his cheering teammates. *He has a nice, quick stride*, PJ thought, and then he noticed the similarity.

Vlad held his arms a little on the high side, and his singlet was a little too large, causing it to slide off his shoulder – a Yifter trademark.

"You know, no one was really sure how old Yifter was," PJ said to Andrew.

"Well, Coach, we're not really sure how old Vlad is either!" Andrew replied.

Vladimir came through the 600-meter mark in 1:45. As he entered the final turn, his leg turnover seemed to quicken. PJ wondered how much he had left. His teammates, now lining the final straightway, cheered wildly.

"Run, you SOB!" shouted Teddy as Vlad bore down with fifty meters to go.

"2:12, 2:13, 2:14!" shouted PJ as Vlad crossed the line.

PJ and the team watched Vlad decelerate. He was gasping and in obvious pain. He stopped, staggered a few feet, then started to bend over to put his hands on his knees and catch his breath. *Come on, Vlad. Don't stop. Don't bend over. Don't show the weakness,* PJ thought.

Vlad continued to slowly move forward. He coughed and spit...and then it happened. He straightened up and broke into a slow jog. *Yes!* PJ cheered to himself.

Vlad jogged to the end of the straightaway, regaining his composure. He turned and jogged back toward PJ and the rest of the team. "Piece of cake!" he said as he approached the group.

"Two miles...easy now," PJ said as he recorded Vlad's time on his clipboard.

As the group strode off into the trails, PJ made his way back to his car. The team's first dual meet was only ten days away. It was a scrimmage against Union Catholic Academy, a school from the next town over. They had been fourth in the county the previous year, and most of their runners had returned.

He made a quick phone call to the other school's coach to confirm the meet, and then he started to stretch in preparation for his own workout, which would begin after the boys went home.

Chapter 20

The Bowl at Holmdel Park

The week leading up to RC's first dual meet went by quickly. It wasn't so much that the team was running so well that the workouts went by quickly. It had more to do with PJ's own workouts over the last week and a half with his new running partners.

Over the last seven days, Dan and the six other runners pushed PJ through a series of distance and hill runs. PJ loved the intensity of the workouts and the training-related dialogue they shared.

PJ's new training partners loved to hear the stories PJ told of the kids he was coaching at RC. One evening, David Santos, the runner that always wore an Adidas shirt, suggested a nice interval workout for the high school kids that PJ decided to use the following day. It was a ladder workout consisting of intervals of 1,000 meters, then 3,000, 5,000, 3,000 and back to 1,000, all at tempo pace with three minutes of recovery between each one.

When he put them through Santos' recommended workout, the kids loved it. They were getting noticeably stronger. In fact, PJ was feeling a little guilty because over the last week his team had responded so well to workouts based on feedback and advice from his new running partners, and not something that PJ had come up with on his own!

It was now Tuesday evening, and PJ was stretching when his seven buddies showed up to run.

"How's it going, Coach?" Dan Hutchens said as the group approached PJ.

PJ laughed. "Fine. I'm a little tight, though."

"That's okay, we're going easy tonight," said Pete, the most serious of the runners, as he touched his toes and stretched his calves. "How's the team doing?"

"Pretty good," PJ answered. "Not great, but getting there."

"They'll need to be better than 'pretty good' if they're going to beat BCA," Mark interjected.

PJ looked over at Mark, the quietest of the bunch. "BCA?" he inquired.

"Yeah, they have a string of 300-something dual meet victories without a loss. They must have fifty to seventy-five kids turn out each year on the first day of summer practice. By the time November hits, they're beating everyone," Pete Bailey added.

"They train on the hills over in Holmdel Park," Pete said as he went into the hurdler stretch on the ground next to PJ's car. "Holmdel is the premiere course in New Jersey, the home of all the key championship races – the States, the Meet of Champions. The course consists of an opening 600 meters that's across a slightly upwardly sloping grassy field. Then for the next 400 meters, you hit a roller coaster-like stretch consisting of four short hills."

"Those little hills beat the hell out of your legs!" Dan added as the other six nodded in unison.

"After that, you have about one mile of flat running on mixed cinder trails and dirt road until you hit 'the bowl,'" Pete said, and the others started to groan.

"The bowl?" PJ asked, laughing at the sight of seven groaning runners.

"Yeah, the bowl," Dan said, taking over relaying the details since Pete had just laid down and put his legs back over his head. "The bowl's roughly a 400-meter section of the course where you run about 200 meters in a gradual downhill, followed by 200 meters flat, then a very steep uphill section of about 100 meters. The last five meters of this section are very steep. They make your thighs burn!"

"I've eaten cinder on that course many a time!" said Pete as he sprung to his feet. "The final mile and a quarter is much easier, though.

Most people are hurting so much by the time they exit the bowl, they just want to get the race over with."

"My kids have done some hill work here at Warinanco Park," PJ replied. "I have them doing hill repeats out to the 600-meter pole." He noticed then how his running buddies just looked at each other for a moment. "What?" he said through nervous laughter.

"Your kids are in trouble, Coach," Pete said as he did one final set of Achilles stretches.

"Why's that?"

"Because the hills here just don't cut it. You need longer, tougher grades."

PJ didn't have to be told this. He had scoured the area for hills within running distance from the school, but just couldn't find anything better than the first 600 meters at Warinanco. He said as much to Pete.

"Yeah, that's a problem," Dan replied, jumping to his feet and getting the group started into their evening run, which was quiet and civil. Nobody pushed the pace, and PJ mentally retraced all the streets and trails he had investigated in search of some better hills. As the eight runners approached PJ's car at the end of the run, they stopped and started to stretch lightly.

"Coach," Pete said without looking up as he sat with his legs crossed. "A great hill to run on is Diamond Hill Road in Murray Hill. It's about a twenty-minute drive from here. The hill's the perfect grade and about a mile long."

"That's too far to run to, don't you think?" replied PJ.

"Yeah, you wouldn't run there," answered Pete. "I recommend having the kids do double workouts three days a week for about two weeks. The morning workout would be hill runs on Diamond Hill Road. You could take the school's bus or van there."

"I don't know if I can get use of the bus, and I doubt the kids will come in early," PJ quipped.

"It can't hurt to try," Pete added.

PJ stretched quietly and thought about the suggestion, once again thankful for his new running companions. Their suggestions always seemed so focused and correct. He knew that hill work would be the key to the team's success, and was beginning to feel guilty for not coming up with the idea of using the school's bus on his own. It simply never dawned on him.

"You know what, Pete? I'm going to try it. You guys haven't been wrong yet!" PJ said and then closed his eyes and leaned over into the hurdler's position to stretch.

Pete and the others looked quietly at each other and nodded. It was as if Pete's suggestion had been made and shared by all of them, and they all took satisfaction in the fact that PJ was going to follow through on it. These seven runners were more than just training partners for PJ – much more – and PJ was about to learn how much!

Chapter 21

One Big Family

———————————

"I'm sorry, PJ," said Brother Owen. "The school has one bus and one van. The bus is used in the mornings by the hockey team since it's the only time they can get ice time. The van…well, the van has a blown transmission and we can't afford to fix it right now."

PJ and Carmine sat quietly as Brother Owen went through a brief list of the school's current debts, until Carmine said, "The heck with the hockey team, Brother!" Carmine shook his head. "They always get them the best of everything – uniforms, equipment. We hardly cost the school anything!"

"Now, Carmine, I appreciate what you're saying," Brother Owen said, peering over his glasses at him, "but their parents are active in fundraising for the team. They pay for the ice time and uniforms themselves." He paused, then looked at PJ. "I'm sorry, PJ. You could have the van if it was working – no problem. But we simply have to control costs."

"I understand, Brother," PJ replied. "Thanks for your time anyway." He got up to leave.

"Kevin Murphy won't be at the race today," Brother Owen said as PJ turned toward the door. "His sister Kathleen wasn't doing well, and he stayed home to help care for her."

PJ looked at the floor for a moment and then at Brother Owen. "How bad is she?"

"She's deteriorated quite a bit over the last year. PLS moves at different rates with different people. You simply can't tell. The Murphys are salt of the earth and they'll get through this. Kevin, God bless him, has been like a rock through it all. I make sure he gets the freedom he needs to be there for Kathleen and the family. I ask that you be just as gracious."

"I will, Brother. He's one of my runners, and she's the team manager. That makes them family. I see how they care for each other." He paused and decided to try to lighten the mood by adding, "And besides, Kathleen thinks I look like Ray Liotta!"

Brother Owen shook his head and laughed as PJ and Carmine left his office.

Chapter 22

UCA Dual Meet

Union Catholic Academy showed up with two school busloads of kids in slick, royal-blue uniforms with matching nylon sweatsuits. They went through their warm-up jog and stretches in unison, their captain barking out instructions and the team responding like well-trained soldiers. PJ watched, impressed by their discipline.

At 3:45 p.m., with the race scheduled to begin at 4:00, Mike Rocha, the coach of Union Catholic Academy, walked over to PJ with the race official in tow.

"Hi, PJ, nice to meet you." His greeting was friendly, but he looked impatient. "Where's your team?" he asked as he surveyed the course.

Carmine and PJ looked at each other and grinned. "We were just wondering that ourselves," PJ answered with a laugh.

"Well, I'm busy this evening. We're going to have to start this scrimmage with or without your team at four o'clock sharp," Rocha snapped back.

"I'm sorry, Mike," PJ replied. "I wasn't being a wise guy. They're just getting in a few easy miles before the race. They'll be here."

"Well, okay then," Rocha replied as he reached out and shook PJ's hand.

Rocha returned to his team, but the official remained, staring at PJ without speaking for a few moments. "Coach, do you even have a team?" he asked. "RC hasn't fielded one in years!"

PJ fought back the "up yours" he wanted to throw at the official, and instead looked over the official's shoulder to see the Union Catholic

Academy team stripping down and approaching the starting line. They were going to start without the RC team being there.

Just then PJ saw movement from the wooded area between the starting line and the skating rink. PJ knew the Union Catholic Academy team would be tough, so he decided to have the RC team simply train through this race. He asked the team to do two easy miles followed by one hard mile before the race. He didn't want them to have much rest between the mile and the start of the race. At the end of the race, PJ wanted his team to continue on with an additional hard mile followed by two easy ones.

The Union Catholic Academy team was lining up on the starting line as the RC runners came into view. All their disciplined drill calling, stretch counting, and coordinated stride outs seemed to pale in comparison to the sight of the seven ragtag RC runners rapidly approaching, having finished their hard one-mile segment. They approached as a fast-moving pack, running stride for stride.

And they were silent.

PJ had asked them to visualize during the hard mile and to continue to visualize their race plan until the gun sounded. He wanted them to plan their attacks and rehearse how they would respond when their bodies felt tired late in the race.

Parents and spectators from both schools watched as the RC team reached the starting line. The race official chastised the RC runners for nearly missing the race, and some of the Union Catholic Academy kids snickered. The RC runners remained stoic and silent through it all as they toed the line, waiting for the start.

When the official turned and walked out into the field to start the race, the pack of RC runners gently tapped fists together and crouched slightly, awaiting the gun. As the official raised the gun, Andrew glanced over at PJ and grinned.

"Runners set!" shouted the official. *Bang!* And they were off.

"Did you see Andrew?" Carmine asked PJ as they jogged to the 800-meter mark.

"He looked ready, didn't he?!" PJ replied, watching the wave of runners heading out toward the 600-meter pole.

The RC runners were in the thick of it, running as a tight pack among the top twenty runners. As they approached the 800-meter point, Andrew, Teddy, Mike and Rod were running together with the lead five runners from Union Catholic Academy. The underclassmen – Vlad, Matt and Nick – were about three seconds back.

"2:40!" PJ shouted at Andrew. Andrew's eyes met PJ's, and he nodded in acknowledgement.

Carmine and PJ sprinted toward the left-field foul pole on the larger baseball field. This was the mile mark, and if they hurried, they could give Andrew and the bunch their mile times.

"5:10!" shouted PJ to Andrew as he raced stride for stride with the lead UC runner. Mike, Teddy, and Rod went by the mile in 5:14, surrounded by five UC runners. Nick gained on the lead runners and passed the mile in 5:20.

"Nice job, Nick!" PJ shouted at Nick as the coach raced toward the flower garden to meet the lead runners before they headed out around the lake.

As PJ ran, he noticed a surge from Andrew. This was no gradual increase in pace either. Andrew shifted gears and pushed the hill up to the 600 pole! By the time he reached PJ, he was fifty meters in front of the second-place runner.

PJ stepped close to where Andrew was running and whispered as he passed, "Listen to that voice…you won't fail it today!"

Andrew went by in a flash. His breathing was perfect, and PJ saw the spring in his step.

"He's on fire!" Carmine said between gasps, having finally caught up with PJ.

"Let's hope he's there at the end!" PJ said, concerned, then yelled, "Atta boy!" to Mike and Teddy as they moved into second and third place.

"Okay, so we're running first, second, third, tenth, and thirteenth. That's twenty-nine points," PJ said as he tried to determine which team had a lower score based on their first five runners and, as such, was winning the race at this point.

"That leaves them with fourth, fifth, sixth, seventh, and eighth. That's a total of 30 points!" Carmine added. "We're winning!"

PJ remained quiet because he could see Mike and Teddy's faces. They were entering the twilight zone. Their form was beginning to break down, and their breathing was labored. Rod was panting as he went by, and PJ knew the remainder of the race would be difficult. To make things worse, the UC team was running like a pack, and their first seven runners looked comfortable.

"Go now!" a UC runner shouted to the pack running behind Teddy and Mike. PJ could only watch as the pack of UC runners put on a mid-race surge. Within about a minute they had caught Teddy and Mike, both of whom were doing their best to stay with them.

Andrew zipped alongside the bike path that bordered the lake and passed the two-mile mark in 10:40. He was now about 100 meters ahead of the second-place runner.

"10:40, Andrew! Just hold this pace, you're running great!" PJ shouted.

Once again, Andrew nodded toward PJ.

"Put it to them Ted, Mike!" Carmine shouted as the next pack of runners passed the two-mile mark. Teddy and Mike responded and surged to the front of the pack.

Meanwhile, PJ darted across the field to catch Andrew as he turned and started heading up the first of the final two hills. PJ's eyes widened as he watched Andrew shorten his stride and increase his leg turnover.

"Pushhhhhh! Puuusssshhhhhhhh!!!" PJ yelled to Andrew. With each step, Andrew looked more and more like a future champion.

As Mike and Teddy reached the sweeping turn at the end of the soccer field, they saw Andrew running up the hill they would soon face themselves.

"Damn! Look at Andrew!" Teddy said through labored breaths.

"You ready?" Mike gasped.

Teddy looked over at Mike and nodded, then they shortened their stride and increased their leg turnover. PJ had just started running toward the finish line when he noticed Mike and Teddy's move. He immediately turned around and raced up the hill, cheering wildly.

"Pusssssshhhhh! Puuuusssssshhh!" he yelled, his voice cracking.

Andrew was now at the top of the last hill and making a left-hand turn to run down the bike trail next to the road that encircled the park. After he left the bike path, he had about 300 meters to go across grass to the finish line.

PJ and Carmine reached the finish line as Andrew rounded the final tree and streaked toward them. PJ noticed an older gentleman with a notebook and stopwatch at the finish line. The small crowd of parents and spectators that had accumulated applauded as Andrew raced through the finish line.

"16:10! Nice job, Andrew!" PJ shouted as Andrew headed out onto the course for the extra hard mile without slowing down.

"Looks like he simply can't get enough of it," a voice said from behind PJ.

Turning, PJ saw the older gentleman with the notebook and stopwatch smiling at him. "I'm having them run through this race as part of their training," PJ replied in a low tone as he approached the gentlemen. He didn't want to sound cocky – or let anyone else know how he was preparing his team.

"Yeah, this early in the season, it's a challenge to keep the distance up when you have dual meets during the week and invitationals and championships on the weekends," the older gentleman replied.

"Well, you're obviously no stranger to this sport." PJ smiled as he held out his hand. "I'm PJ Irwin, the new coach at RC."

"I know who you are, PJ. I remember when you raced McNab in the Meet of Champions in…I believe 1978. I'm Grant Edwins with *The Ledger*." The old man reciprocated and shook PJ's hand. "I've been covering cross country and track for various newspapers in New Jersey for nearly forty-eight years."

"Way to go, guys!" cheered the Union Catholic Academy coach as three of their runners crossed the finish line at 16:45. Immediately behind them were the second and third RC runners, Mike and Teddy.

PJ surveyed the last section of the course and saw two Union Catholic Academy runners in a close battle with Nick and Matt. As they turned the last corner, Nick surged to the lead of the pack while Matt visibly struggled to stay with the UC runners. As they crossed the line, the order was Nick, both UCA runners, and Matt. The UCA runners surged through the finish to the wild cheering of their coach and fans.

"That's the way to win!" the UCA coach yelled to his runners.

And while the win went to UCA, the more knowledgeable in the crowd of spectators couldn't help but notice that, as the blue-uniformed runners were crossing the line and stopping, bending over, and lying on the ground, the green-shirted RC runners were heading out without stopping, logging additional hard mileage.

"Way to go, Matt!" PJ shouted to Matt as he headed out for the final hard mile. Despite the fatigue, Matt smiled, shortened his stride a bit, and increased his leg turnover.

As the rest of the RC runners finished the race and headed out onto the course for an additional hard mile, PJ couldn't help but notice that the frenzy of the victory celebration had quieted down.

"Nice race," PJ congratulated the UCA coach and team as they huddled nearby for a post-race congratulatory talk.

"Yes, congrats to your team as well," the coach replied.

PJ noticed a number of the UCA kids watching the RC runners put in their additional mileage. As he turned to walk away, he heard the UCA coach tell his team to get in a two-mile warm-down.

"You don't expect us to run it as hard as those RC guys, do you?" one of the UCA runners asked.

"No, that's nuts," the coach replied.

PJ simply smiled to himself and kept walking. As he neared the grassy area where the RC runners had left their gear, Grant approached him. "Coach, do you mind answering a few more questions?" he asked as he flipped open his notepad.

"No, shoot."

"Where did you coach before RC?"

"Nowhere," PJ said with a smile.

"So how did you land the coaching job at RC?"

"Well, I got laid off at my real job; and my wife, who happens to work at the school, got pissed off when I started to redecorate the house while she was at work," PJ laughed as he answered.

Grant smiled as he made notes in shorthand. "How well do you expect the team to do this year?"

PJ stood silent for a while, and then as he looked over Grant's shoulder and saw his team finishing their warm-down, he said, "I'm not sure. We haven't had a full team in a number of years—"

"Eight to be exact," Grant said without looking up from his steno pad.

"But this group of kids has a lot of heart and I think they can run with anyone," PJ said, loud enough for the boys to hear. "My coaching style will test their limits. In fact, already today, I've been criticized for having them run too many miles. But if you're only running forty to fifty miles per week and plan to cut back toward the end of the season, what do you do? Cut back to twenty-five miles per week and have them running three to four miles per day?" PJ said with disbelief in his voice. "I simply can't comprehend this!"

Grant smiled as he looked up and closed his notepad, signifying the end of the interview. "I agree with you 100 percent, Coach," he said. "You remind me of the fellow that coached at RC in the '70s."

"Hey, do you want the kids' names for your article?" PJ asked before Grant could leave.

"No, I already have them all," Grant answered as he headed toward his car. Then he stopped and turned toward PJ, motioning for him to come closer. "Coach," he said in a hushed tone, "your guys are going to get massacred at Holmdel if you don't start doing some serious hill work."

"I have plans to take them to Diamond Hill Road for hill repeats," PJ replied.

"Good idea, I know the place," Grant responded. "Years ago, that used to be a popular training spot for teams such as yours."

Grant left him then, and PJ started to brainstorm how he could get the kids to Diamond Hill Road. He needed to get the van repaired, but how?

Chapter 23

I Know This Guy

As the last RC runner boarded the bus with Coach Carmine, PJ waved goodbye at them and started to stretch in preparation for his evening workout. Tonight, he was going to do seven one-mile repeats at a 10K pace with his seven training buddies. Sitting in the butterfly stretch position, he heard footsteps on the cinders behind him and turned in time to see Dan Hutchens jogging up behind him.

"Nice Snickers shirt," said PJ jokingly, as if Dan hadn't worn that same shirt for every run since they met.

"Don't you know it!" Dan responded gleefully. "Coach, I've been thinking about your broken bus problem, and I think I have a solution."

"Please, I'm all ears. We lost a close one today and I know I have to get the kids to do quality hill work," PJ said as he closed his eyes and got into the hurdlers stretch.

Dan sat down beside him and started to stretch as well. "Coach, I know this guy who has an auto repair shop in Rozelle," Dan continued. "I think he might fix the van for you very cheaply – maybe for free. He's an old acquaintance of mine," he added, glancing off into the distance.

PJ studied Dan for a moment, noticing the far-off look on the runner's face. They passed a few silent moments between them, the only noise a car radio playing in the distance.

"Everything okay, Dan?" PJ asked as he resumed stretching.

"Uh-huh," he answered without looking at PJ. "I thought I recognized that song I heard coming from that car over there."

The two sat silently, listening to the faint melody floating across the parking lot a bit longer, until the moment was broken by the clamor of footsteps behind them.

"Hey Dan, Coach," came a voice from among the six runners approaching.

"Sorry we're late," Bill Bahsman said, stopping next to PJ.

"No problem," PJ said with a smile. "Me and your buddy Dan were just listening to some music and stretching. He had a great idea, that I should stop by…by, uh…" PJ stumbled momentarily. "Dan, what's the name of the guy I'm supposed to contact to fix the van?"

Dan's eyes met the eyes of his six buddies for a moment and then fixed on Pete's. "Bailey's Garage, on Chestnut Street. He's a great guy. I'm sure he'll help you out. Isn't that right, guys?"

"Yeah, he's one of a kind," David Santos responded as he grabbed Pete and put him in a playful headlock. It was almost as if he was trying to take his attention away from the conversation.

"Wrestling! Hey, I want part of that!" Dan shouted as he jumped to his feet and tackled the two runners. In a moment, all seven of PJ's running partners were on top of Pete, pulling his shirt over his head and giving him a pink belly.

Jeez, PJ thought, *these guys are just like the clowns I coach, only older*, then he said out loud, "Okay, guys, if we're going to run, I gotta get started soon." PJ leapt to his feet.

Moments later the group was striding out of the parking lot onto the road that circled the park, a relatively flat 1.8-mile loop, perfect for a pre-workout warm-up. As they ran, the group talked among themselves, mixing their accounts of the day's experiences with running lore; which, while supposedly true, showed the signs of embellishment often present in stories shared on the run.

"Hey, Coach, did we ever tell you about Harry Spooner?" Rob O'Malley asked. The other runners started to laugh when they heard the question.

"No, who was he?" PJ answered, still amused at the way these guys referred to him as "Coach."

"Harry Spooner was this fictitious character we made up in high school," Rob continued. "When we got in trouble, we'd always blame things on him. It became almost a game to us. One day, the principal actually made an announcement over the loudspeaker system, asking Harry Spooner to report to his office!"

"I almost pissed myself that day," Dan remarked.

"Yeah, me too," David added.

"Anyway, we had a runner on our team named Joe Mount. He was a sweet but gullible guy who we loved to tease. A great kid, but a target for almost every practical joke. Anyway, Joe had these very stylish glasses that he always wore – he could barely see without them. One day, while we were all taking a post-workout shower, Joe blurted out that he would love to meet this Harry Spooner kid who was always getting in trouble. The rest of us looked at each other in disbelief, because we never realized that Joe didn't know Harry was fictitious. Anyway, I noticed that Joe was standing there with his head and face completely covered with lather while his glasses were sitting on the shower ledge nearby. I grabbed his glasses and positioned them over my 'manhood.'"

"It kind of looked like Jimmy Durante with a beard," Rob said jokingly. "Don't you agree, guys?"

"Uh, I don't think we were watching that closely. Finish the story," Mark Hills urged.

Rob continued, "So there I stood with his glasses positioned over my peter and I said, 'Hey Joe, here he is now, that Harry Spooner kid!' Joe started to rinse the water off his head, saying, 'Where? Where? I gotta see this guy!' And as he finished getting the water out of his eyes and started to move toward the ledge to find his glasses, I said, 'Right here,' and pointed toward my work of art. Not only did he call me every name in the book, he wouldn't put his glasses back on when I gave them back to him. The next week, he showed up with a new set of glasses."

PJ shook his head as the story came to an end, and his attention transferred to the track in front of them. "Are you guys ready for this?" PJ asked, accelerating into the first of the seven one-mile repeats.

"I've been ready for decades," came the muffled response from Pete, who had been quiet throughout the warm-up.

Chapter 24

The Awakening

The next day, PJ left for school a little earlier than normal. Practice was not until three, but PJ was going to stop by Bailey's garage. He had concluded that he could afford up to about $400 toward the van repair. However, he hoped that Dan was right, and that Mr. Bailey would fix the van for free.

At a little after one, PJ turned onto Chestnut Street and drove north toward the center of Rozelle, passing the Jack in the Box and the bank. He crossed over 7th Avenue and soon came upon Bailey's Auto Repair, a typical oil-laden garage. Cars were strewn all over the front yard in various states of repair. Oil drums and a stack of used tires bordered the north side of the three-bay garage. The south side of the garage joined an old salt box, a colonial house with an eagle on the front door. To the right of the front porch was a holly bush, to the left an azalea. The roof of the house was showing signs of wear, and the gutter was hanging off toward the rear of the home.

PJ parked his car near the stack of tires and walked toward the first of the three bay doors. As he approached, he peered into the dark garage bay. The sun was bright, so it took his eyes a moment to adjust to the dark bay. PJ stood still for a few moments after entering the bay door.

"Anybody home?" PJ called into the darkness of the shop. There was no answer. "Mr. Bailey?" he tried again.

"Hold on, dammit, I'm coming," a monotone voice answered from deep in the back of the shop.

PJ surveyed the room as his eyes focused. There was an old Chevy Malibu on the center lift. Along the rear wall was a countertop that ran the length of the three bays. The countertop was cluttered with batteries, alternators, hubcaps, and numerous cans of oil.

Just then, PJ saw a large figure emerge from behind the Malibu. "Yeah, I'm Hugh Bailey. What can I do for you?" the figure asked in a voice that was neither lively nor friendly.

PJ was taken back by Mr. Bailey's appearance. He was huge, approximately six feet tall, and he must have weighed nearly 300 pounds. He was wearing black pants with a black T-shirt. The monotony of the outfit was broken only by the portion of Mr. Bailey's stomach that emerged from beneath his shirt near his belt line. There was grease on his stomach, and a small hole above a breast pocket that contained a pack of cigarettes.

"I'm pretty busy these days," Mr. Bailey said as he looked past PJ toward the street while pulling his cigarettes from his pocket. "You may want to try the Getty station up the street."

"Mr. Bailey, I'm PJ Irwin, the cross country coach over at RC, and I—"

"Who the hell did you say you were?" Mr. Bailey growled as his eyes darted back to meet PJ's.

PJ was startled. *Wasn't he listening?* Even more startling than his words was the intensity in Mr. Bailey's eyes. As PJ stared at him, he thought he saw a lightning bolt jump out of Bailey's left eye, then he realized it must have been the reflection from a car passing by outside. Looking down, PJ noticed that both of Mr. Bailey's hands were clenched, his forearm muscles looking like a boxer's just before the knockout punch.

PJ took a half step back and answered, "I'm the cross country coach over at RC. My name—"

"Don't let the door hit you in the ass on the way out!" Bailey grunted through tight lips that clenched a Marlboro. He was breathing heavy as he pointed toward the street and stared at PJ. It was clear that he wanted him to leave.

As PJ turned away, Bailey did likewise and receded into the back of the garage where he had been working. PJ walked slowly toward the exit, eyes cast down, trying to figure out what just happened. As he approached the bay door, he bumped into a man in a pin-striped suit just entering the building.

"So, is he going to fix the van?" came a familiar voice.

Surprised, PJ looked up and saw Dan Hutchens, minus his ever-present Snickers shirt. "What are you doing here?" PJ asked.

"I work nearby and was returning from lunch when I thought I saw you walking into the garage," Dan answered. "I thought I'd see if you were able to get anything out of the ol' bulldog."

"Well," PJ said with a grin, "your bulldog buddy told me to hit the road and that's pretty much what I intend to do."

"Did you tell him who you were?" Dan asked.

"Yeah, I think that's what pissed him off!" PJ shook his head. "So, if you don't mind, I'm leaving."

"Hold on, hold on," Dan said, chuckling. "Let's try one last time."

"I don't think he's going to listen."

"Here's what I want you to do. Did you ever hear of this guy Jumbo Elliot?"

"You mean the former track coach at Villanova? He's dead, isn't he?"

"Yes, he's dead, but before he died, he made Villanova one of the greatest track programs of all time. He was consistently producing one great distance runner after another. People like Marty Liquori, Sydney Maree and Eamonn Coghlin, to name a few."

"Yeah, so?"

"Well, I was told that he was a philanthropist of sorts. He owned a successful construction company, and rumor has it that he personally donated quite a bit to the school and the team. Without people like him, programs struggle."

"I still don't know where you're going with this," PJ said, growing impatient.

"Tell Mr. Bailey that Jumbo Elliot would have bent over backwards for you."

"You must think I'm a friggin' idiot," PJ said as he walked out of the building. "There's no way that Bailey will know who Jumbo Elliot was or appreciate the significance of what you're saying!"

Dan grabbed PJ's arm and twisted him so that they were face-to-face. "Listen, you want your kids running hills, don't you?"

"Of course, but—"

"Well then, do it!" Dan urged again. "I'm pretty sure he won't be able to catch you if he starts to go after you! Besides, I'll be right behind you."

PJ stared at Dan, then shrugged his shoulders and turned back toward the garage. *I can't believe I'm doing this. Bailey couldn't care less about Jumbo or this school! I just can't friggin' believe—*

PJ stopped suddenly in mid-thought. Mr. Bailey stood in the doorway, his arms folded, a stern look on his face. "I thought I told you to leave!" he barked, stepping toward PJ.

I can't believe I'm doing this! PJ thought again.

Just as Bailey put his hands out in front of him to give PJ a shove, PJ blurted out, "Jumbo Elliot would have bent over backwards to help me!" Then PJ shut his eyes and readied himself for the first blow.

The silence was deafening. PJ opened one eye to find Mr. Bailey standing directly in front of him, his hands on his head. His eyes were tightly closed, as if he was battling a headache or some type of inner pain. As PJ watched, Mr. Bailey's eyes slowly opened, and a bead of sweat ran from his forehead down the side of his nose. His face flushed, and his outstretched hand trembled as he shook his forefinger at PJ.

"Oh yeah?" Bailey started. Through a broken voice, he continued, "Well, Jumbo Elliot's dead now, just like my son…who died in a bus accident on the way to the Eastern Cross Country Championship twenty years ago."

Bailey fought for his composure, while PJ tried to comprehend what he had just heard. "His death tore us apart. I blame the school for it. My wife blamed me for it. I could have driven him that day, but I didn't!" With that, Mr. Bailey started walking toward the house adjacent to the garage. "Come with me, Coach."

123

PJ turned toward Dan, who was nowhere to be found. *'I'll be right behind you.' Yeah right, Dan,* PJ thought.

"Come on, Coach," Mr. Bailey said again, without looking back at PJ.

PJ quietly walked behind Mr. Bailey, studying the imposing figure as they made their way to the house. Bailey walked with his head slightly tilted to one side. He quickly traversed the four steps leading up to the front porch, then briefly glanced behind him to check on PJ.

"Watch the bricks on the second step. A few of them are loose," Bailey warned.

The brown front door to the Bailey house was old and worn, the paint having oxidized and appearing grayish. Upon entering the house, PJ was greeted by a musty odor. The house was dark and somewhat gloomy. Dark wood trimmed doors and windows. The white linen curtains were turning a dark yellow. The television was a black-and-white Zenith; it had a knob for changing channels.

"Well, what do you think of the place?" Mr. Bailey asked as he stopped in the center of the dining room.

"It's...uh, nice. I like the woodwork, and—"

"Listen, Coach, don't bullshit a bullshitter," Bailey interrupted him as he made his way into the kitchen. "This place is a disaster. My wife was the one who took care of things." He reached into the refrigerator and pulled out two bottles of spring water.

PJ took the water without saying a word. He looked over Bailey's shoulder and saw a "God Bless This Kitchen" plaque hanging over the stove.

"My wife and I split up a few years after my son died," Bailey said, resuming the conversation as he headed past PJ into the dining room again. "They were really close, and she simply couldn't deal with it. She blamed me for not driving him that day and wouldn't let me forget it. I was suffering too, but she simply couldn't get control of herself."

Not knowing what to say, PJ looked at the floor as Bailey glanced at him.

"She tried to kill herself, twice," Bailey uttered as he wiped his eyes.

"She eventually entered an institution, got some help, and left me a few months later. I haven't seen her in fifteen years."

PJ watched as Bailey paused at the bottom of the stairway leading to the second floor.

"I've worn black every day since he died, a sign of mourning," Bailey continued as he wrestled for composure. "I don't live my life anymore. I just exist. I want to..." Bailey stopped and shook his head, as if he wasn't in full agreement with what he was about to say. "Come with me, Coach. I have something to show you," Bailey said, starting to climb the stairs.

PJ followed Mr. Bailey up the steps to the landing at the top. Directly in front of them was the bathroom. Off to the right was a large bedroom, apparently the master. Bailey turned left and stopped momentarily in front of a closed door. He reached out and gently traced over the impression of a winged foot that had been carved into the door. He sighed.

"He carved that into the door. This was his room," Bailey said quietly. "I haven't been in here in twenty years." He slowly turned the knob and pushed the door open.

The two men stood outside the room, greeted by rays of sunlight that shown in through the bedroom window. Dust floated in the air, illuminated by the sunlight.

"My wife and I couldn't find the strength to clean up the room after he died," Bailey said sadly. "Everywhere you turn in there is some reminder of him."

PJ looked through the doorway into the room, noticing pictures of Jim Ryun and Peter Snell on the wall to the left. A bookcase and desk occupied the right-hand side of the room. The bed was a simple cot with a dark-green blanket folded on top of it.

As PJ scanned the length of the bed, he noticed something at the end that caught his eye. "Hey, I remember wearing a pair of these," he exclaimed as he stepped into the room and then stopped abruptly.

"It's okay, Coach. You go right ahead. I'll just wait here if you don't mind," Mr. Bailey offered.

PJ knelt down next to the bed and picked up a pair of Nike LDV

1000 running shoes. "These were the first shoes to have the wedge-heel design," PJ said, his voice sounding like he had just discovered a treasure.

"Oh, uh, really? That's nice," Bailey answered, sounding uninterested.

"Yeah, today most shoes have this wedge design. It was revolutionary. And what do we have here?" he continued as he reached under the bed, pulling out a fluorescent green and black pair of Adidas spikes and a single yellow and green Nike Oregon waffle racer. "This model of spikes was known as the 'spider,'" PJ said with a smile. "I had a pair of these in college."

"Pete preferred to wear the waffles for cross country," Bailey said. "They only recovered the one waffle from the crash scene. They were Pete's favorite racing shoe."

PJ stared at the lone Oregon waffle for a moment and laughed. "Funny thing, my dog just stole one of these from a runner at the park a few weeks ago. He ran off into the woods and when I got home, he was sitting on the porch with the shoe in his mouth. It was like he was bringing me a gift. Funny thing…crazy dog…"

"I love dogs. They're like angels," Bailey answered, beginning to warm up to PJ.

As PJ laid the shoes on the bed, he turned and noticed a picture on the wall next to the doorway. PJ studied the picture for a few moments. It was an eight-by-ten of a high school runner crossing the finish line with a time of 4:11.8 above it. *There's something familiar about this runner*, PJ thought, as he moved closer to get a better look.

PJ suddenly felt a chill on the back of his neck. He had seen this kid somewhere before…but where? He stood there, the chill taking over his body, as if a cool breeze had passed by him. Then suddenly, it hit him.

When PJ suffered the concussion at running camp, he had that dream that he caused a bus accident. As he struggled to recall the dream, he vaguely remembered lying on the ground next to a dying boy that was bleeding from where his ear had been. The boy said he was "here to win the Easterns!" This was the boy, he was sure of it.

PJ staggered backwards slowly until he touched the bed. As he pointed to the picture, he stammered, "Who's...who's the miler in that picture?"

Bailey tucked his head into the room and looked at the wall. "That's him. Peter, my son."

PJ simply stared motionless at the wall.

Mr. Bailey entered the room. "Twenty years is too long to have not looked at that picture. Are you okay, Coach? You don't look so good."

PJ looked at Bailey and then back at the picture. "Uh, yeah, I'll be fine. Just my mind playing games with me."

PJ glanced over at the left-footed Oregon waffle lying next to the bed. He thought hard for a moment. *Did Nike bring home the right-footed or left-footed shoe?*

Mr. Bailey walked over to the bookcase and grabbed a yearbook off the shelf. He opened it, brought it to PJ, and then stopped suddenly. "Wrong year," Bailey mumbled, returning to the bookcase and grabbing a different yearbook. "This is the one I wanted to show you," Bailey said as he sat down on the bed.

PJ took the book. It was open to a picture of the entire cross country team standing in front of the bleachers at RC.

"We lost all seven of them that day. They were great kids," Mr. Bailey said, his voice breaking as he stared off into the distance. "My son's right there in the middle."

PJ studied the picture and the inscription below it. "Varsity Cross Country Team – Dan Hutchens, David Santos, Rob O'Mally, Evan Brand, Mark Hills, Bill Bahsman, Pete Bailey."

Once again, a chill surrounded PJ as his gaze locked onto this black-and-white picture of a group of boys who never got their chance.

"They were a phenomenal bunch," Bailey interjected as PJ sat there motionless. "Four of them had mile times below four minutes and twenty-five seconds. They set the distance medley record at the Penn Relays."

Reaching out to take the book back from PJ, Bailey noticed that PJ's grip on it had grown tight enough that his knuckles were turning white. "Coach, do you mind? I'd like to go back downstairs. I can only take this room in small doses."

PJ's gaze remained fixed on the team picture. *Those names...those faces. I know them.*

"What's that on the front of that kid's shirt?" PJ asked as he pointed toward the kid on the leftmost side of the picture.

Bailey leaned over, squinting as he surveyed the picture. "Oh," he said with a chuckle, "that's Dan Hutchens. He loved Snickers candy bars. That's the Snickers logo on his shirt."

PJ pulled the book closer and stared intently at the faces in the picture. "Son of a bitch," he mumbled to himself. *I do know this bunch,* he thought as the hair stood up on the back of his neck.

Bailey peeled the book away from PJ and placed it back on the bookcase, then he stood there with his back to PJ for a moment. PJ noticed Bailey bow his head momentarily, as if in prayer. When Bailey turned around, his eyes were watery.

"I'll head over to the school and take a look at the van tonight, but I can't guarantee anything," Bailey said, breaking the silence.

PJ looked up. "Oh...uh, thanks."

Still coming to grips with what he had just seen, PJ rose slowly from the bed. He felt nauseous, and his legs felt weak. He slowly made his way down the steps, followed closely by Bailey. Neither of the two spoke as they made their way onto the front porch. PJ descended the steps and walked slowly down the front walk. The warmth of the sun began to fight off the chill that had set in while he had been in Pete Bailey's room.

He turned to say thanks to Bailey, only to find the man sitting motionless on the porch, his head hanging down. PJ couldn't help but feel guilty for invading Bailey's privacy. He couldn't imagine the painful memories he must have stirred up. *What do you say after having done such a thing?* he thought. *Thank you? Hardly.*

"Mr. Bailey?" PJ said from the front walk, but Bailey simply sat with his head down.

Before PJ spoke again, Bailey made a sweeping motion with his hand, as if to say, *Please go. I've had enough.*

PJ turned and walked slowly to his car. He looked back over his shoulder a few times, but Bailey didn't move. PJ got into the car and took one last look at Bailey before turning the ignition. Bailey rose slowly and walked back into the house.

Looking at the clock on the car radio, he noticed it was 2:50 p.m. Practice would begin in ten minutes.

Chapter 25

Our Hero, Kevin

As PJ pulled into the school parking lot, the team was already loosening up on the track. The warm-up routine was becoming just that – routine. They would jog, then stretch, and follow that with some strides. As PJ crossed the bridge across the creek that ran though the school property, the boys jumped to their feet and started to do some strides.

They're almost ready to rock and roll," came a voice from PJ's right. He turned and saw Kathleen Murphy sitting near the fence bordering the track. Her wheelchair was next to her, and she had her books arranged around her.

"How are you feeling, Kathleen?" PJ asked. Her mere presence brought a smile to his face.

"Much better now. Last week was rough. My medicine wasn't right," she said, shrugging her shoulders and rolling her eyes.

"We were worried."

"Ahh, I'm fine now. Besides, Kevin was with me and he kept me laughing the whole time."

"He has that effect on people," PJ laughed as he looked toward the striding runners. There was Kevin, skipping, making the others laugh.

Kathleen followed PJ's eyes, and she shook her head. "My brother – what a goof!"

As PJ walked toward the runners, Vlad was the first to greet him. "I hear it's going to be an easy day."

Still wrestling with what had happened at Bailey's garage, PJ stared at the group for a moment. "Well, Vlad, it's going to be kind of a moderate day. I'm hoping to start doing some real hill work next week, so I'd like to tone the workouts down a little. That way you guys can go into it with fresh legs."

The runners listened intently. They seemed focused, awaiting instruction, and ready to perform.

"Today will be an eight-mile run with the middle being at tempo pace. I want you to do the Mother Seton route," PJ explained.

"Will we be adding on the Rahway Park Loop?" Nick asked.

"Yes. I want you to go out at a 7:30 pace until you reach Mother Seton High School. Then I want you to drop it down to about a six-minute pace until you exit the park. That'll be about three miles at tempo pace." The runners continued to stretch while they listened. "I expect you to be back at the track in fifty-six minutes. I'll be here waiting for you," PJ said before turning and walking toward the track exit. "C'mon guys, let's get this one over with."

A few hurdler's stretches later and they were off. Andrew and Rod led the team out of the parking lot and onto Raritan Road, the rest of the pack tightly bunched behind them. When they reached the Rozelle Shopping Center and the road became a little busier, they went single file. They crossed the intersection at Wood Avenue and continued up Raritan Road to Winfield Park. Along the way they passed Springfield Road where legendary runner and high school coach Jim Rod had lived as a child. It was also the two-mile mark, and Andrew checked his watch to make sure they were on target. "Fifteen flat," Andrew uttered as he darted around a garbage can left on the sidewalk.

They continued out Raritan Road until they reached the JB Williams factory in Clark. They made a left onto Westfield Avenue and headed toward Mother Seton. As they passed under the Garden State Parkway underpass, Teddy let out a yell. He loved the way it echoed, and he always yelled when he reached this point of the run. Rod and Andrew added their versions to his.

The first intersection after the underpass was Amsterdam Road. The group made a left onto it, knowing that the pickup was about to begin. Andrew readied the troops. "We pick it up at the red house." No one responded. It was time to focus.

For most runners, a change in pace started with a change in stride length – usually a brief shortening of the stride, followed by a gradual pickup in leg turnover rate, then finally a gradual increase in stride length. PJ had taught them this technique and urged them to think about it whenever they were changing pace. From PJ's point of view, it was a good way to take their minds off the fact that they were challenging themselves to run faster.

The group crested the hill on Amsterdam and were heading toward the entrance of the park when Kevin noticed two people having what appeared to be an argument. "Hey, what the hell is going on over there?" Kevin said as he motioned toward the scene.

Andrew looked over and saw a woman clutching a baby carriage with one hand while her other arm was outstretched, clutching her purse. Also clutching the purse was some guy in torn jeans and an old sweatshirt. He was frantically pulling at the purse and beating on the woman's head to get it away from her.

"Hey! Leave her alone!" Kevin yelled as he took off for the couple.

The woman released the purse and fell to the ground, and the guy took off running with the purse. Kevin chased the guy into the park, and the rest of the team chased Kevin. They were heading toward a tall fence, and they figured they had this guy trapped.

Suddenly, like a gazelle, the loser jumped up and started to scale the fence. Just as he hoisted himself over the top, Kevin yelled and leaped over the fence, virtually in a single bound. He landed on the other side, directly on top of the purse snatcher.

"Give me the damn purse!" Kevin growled as he wrestled with the guy.

The criminal handed it over and ran away. Kevin cut his lip during the scuffle, but otherwise he walked away unscathed.

The rest of the team congratulated Kevin as he scaled the fence again, rejoining the group.

"You okay?" Nick asked.

"Yeah," Kevin replied. "Is the woman okay?"

"She seemed okay," Nick answered as he turned and noticed a cop car approaching. "I think this is her now."

The cop car screeched to a halt, and the team walked over to the car. The woman was in the back seat, and the officer was helping her out as the boys walked up.

Kevin handed the purse over to the woman. "Are you okay?" he asked her.

Through broken English she replied, "Thank you very much."

The boys watched nervously as Kevin gave the police his information. Moments later a second police car rolled up with the purse snatcher in it. Kevin and the woman both identified him, and he was arrested.

Finally, the lead cop said they were done and that the boys could leave. In no time they were up to full stride and circling the perimeter of Rahway Park. Andrew checked his watch. They were down to a six-minute pace.

"We're only an hour late," Andrew chuckled as they headed into the homestretch of the run.

Meanwhile, PJ was pacing back and forth across the parking lot because they weren't back yet. He wanted to leave and get over to the park to talk to that strange group of runners who looked exactly like the kids in the pictures at Bailey's house. He was irritated. He wanted answers, and he didn't want to wait for these kids. *Screw them*, he thought, deciding to leave. *They're probably doing something irresponsible again. I'll straighten them out tomorrow.*

PJ went to the library to find Kathleen Murphy. "Hey, kiddo, I have to hit the road. Will you be okay?" PJ whispered across the library.

Kathleen looked up from her books, gave him a thumbs-up, and went back to her schoolwork.

PJ left through the rear entrance to the school where his car was parked. Moments later he was headed over to Warinanco Park for a meeting with…well, he wasn't sure with whom.

Chapter 26

Destiny

As he pulled into the parking lot, PJ could see the seven of them standing close together, near the track, not stretching, just talking.

PJ stepped slowly from his car. His legs felt a little rubbery, like they did the time he ran his first and only triathlon. He hadn't liked the feeling and vowed never to do another.

As he locked his car door, he caught his reflection in the window. For a moment, he thought of getting back in the car and leaving. As he stared, he noticed his hair gently blowing in the wind. He shut his eyes, enjoying the moment as the cool breeze passed. He felt the wind go through his hair, and he knew what he had to do.

It was ninety-seven steps from the car to their warm-up area, and PJ felt every one of them today. His legs continued to feel weak, trembling more the closer he got to the group.

There were no appropriate words for their greeting tonight. PJ could only stare at them as he stood facing the group. He gazed into the seven sets of eyes, the fourteen pupils, and they stared back…without blinking, without movement. They just stared.

"Are you Peter Bailey?" PJ asked as he motioned toward the runner.

"Yes sir, I am," came the reply.

"And you? Are you Dan Hutchens?" PJ pointed to the runner.

"Hey, you're good," snickered Hutchens as the rest of the group chuckled lightly.

"Well, what the hell do you want me to do?" PJ snapped back. "You guys aren't real! You're dead! You're friggin' dead!"

"Hey, Santos, that means '*mucho muerto*' for you!" Rob O'Mally teased.

"Gotcha! *Yo soy mucho* dead!" David Santos answered. "*Por que?*" he added.

"Yeah, like you don't know why," quipped Rob. "You're the numbskull who threw the spike wrench at Bahsman!"

"Hey, Bahsman should've caught it!" David shouted back.

"Hey, wait a damn minute. I didn't even know it was coming." Bill Bahsman jumped to his feet and lunged for David.

Dan and Pete grabbed Bill as PJ simply stared and looked confused.

"You've been blaming me for the accident for years!" Bill shouted.

"Relax, Bill," Dan said calmly. "Dave is only kidding."

"Yeah, sorry about that, Bill," David added, walking up and putting his arm around Bill's shoulder.

Bill looked at the ground and started to weep. As the group of runners quietly gathered around him to comfort him, Dan looked over his shoulder at PJ and then whispered something into Pete's ear. Pete nodded, broke away from the group, and walked over to PJ.

"It's rough for us," he started. "We've been dead for nearly twenty years, and it's different than we imagined. It's lonely, frustrating," he added as he looked back at his tight-knit bunch of friends.

"At first, we didn't know what was going on. We thought we survived the crash. But when the rescue squad showed up, they simply walked around us. They didn't hear our voices. It was like they were ignoring us when we told them we were okay. We told them they didn't have to climb down the side of the hill bordering the Hudson River. After all, we'd all managed to climb up the embankment to the side of the road where the bus went through the guardrail.

"We shouted to the rescuers that the bus was empty, that we were all accounted for and the body of the driver was only a few feet from the side of the road. But they went down anyway."

"So, what happened?" PJ asked as the rest of the boys came closer.

"They started pulling out the bodies," Dan said, fighting back tears. "We were dead."

"So why are you here?" PJ asked.

"Good question. We don't know," Pete answered. "For the last twenty years we've been wandering around Union County, watching and visiting our families and our friends, trying to communicate—"

"The key word is *trying*!" Bill interrupted. "Twenty damn years trying, wandering, wondering…"

"And running!" Pete added with an upbeat tone. "It's what we do to find peace." He paused before speaking slowly to PJ, obviously intent on ensuring he heard every word. "Coach, you're the only person in the last twenty years who's been able to see or communicate with us."

PJ stood silently gazing into the eyes of the seven before him. For the first time, PJ noticed a sadness, a loneliness in their eyes. "Why do you think I can see you?" he asked.

"We're wondering the same thing," Pete answered.

"I…I don't know what to say."

"Neither do we," Dan interjected. "But there must be a reason. This has to end," he added, his voice strained.

"Yesterday I ate dinner with my mom and dad, but they never knew I was there," David chimed in. "I watched my mom cry as she looked at the picture of me in the china closet in our dining room. I hugged her, but it didn't help. She didn't know I was there."

"I had the same thing happen to me last week," Evan Brand said. "My sister, Jana, cries at least once a day."

"And my father, he wishes he was dead." Pete turned and looked again at PJ, exposing the tears that had formed in his eyes. "My father wanders through life wishing he was dead! I can't bear to see him this way, but I can't escape it! He wanders through life wishing he was dead…and I wander through death wishing I was either alive or dead. Just not wandering!"

"Somehow, Coach, you've got to help us," Pete said.

PJ nodded, but he had no idea what to do. As he watched the boys console each other, he repeated everything he had just heard over again in his mind, and the same question kept coming back to him: *What can I do?*

"I feel weak," PJ said as he moved toward his car. "My legs feel a little wobbly."

"Like you saw a ghost?" David wisecracked.

"Seven of them," PJ chuckled.

"There's only one thing to do when the legs feel wobbly," Dan shouted as he smacked his hands together.

"A two-mile warm-up followed by a five-mile tempo run?" Rob said matter-of-factly.

"Exactly! You in, Coach?" Dan said.

All eyes were on PJ when he turned and said, "Uh...yeah, I suppose so." He walked numbly back to the boys.

Moments later the group gently broke into an easy pace for the next two miles around the park's perimeter. They were silent during the warm-up, speaking only when they increased the pace at the start of the tempo portion of the run.

PJ ran behind them, observing the seven runners. They looked like thoroughbreds as they gracefully ran around the park. PJ noticed how perfect their form was. They glided as they ran; they didn't bounce. All their motion was in the forward direction, no up and down. There was no wasted motion, no side-to-side in their arm-carry either. They were perfect. Well-coached, no doubt.

PJ's legs recovered enough to allow him to run the next five miles at a 5:45 pace. Actually, PJ would normally run a tempo run such as this when he felt a little tired or wobbly, and one of two things would happen during the two-mile warm-up: he would recover and have a productive workout, or he would fold before he started the tempo section. Today he was happy that he made it through the tempo. The final mile was more of a warm-down for the group.

"You know, Coach," Pete Bailey started as they glided gently through the last mile, "in life, there was only one constant for me. It was running.

It never mattered what type of crap happened during the day, I could always count on my appointment with the road."

PJ smiled. "I know exactly what you mean, Pete. I can remember planning out my workday and then going to work and accomplishing nothing I'd planned. It would be one surprise after another. But when the day was over, I regained control and did my run. I did *my* run, on *my* course, at *my* pace, for as long as I wanted to."

The two looked at each other and smiled.

PJ chuckled and said, "You know, when it got really bad at work, I'd run at lunchtime. Afterwards, I used to love sitting there in afternoon meetings with sweat still running down my face with some fat SOB on our management team staring at me like I was from another planet – or moving away from me because I reeked. Even though half of them smelled like cigarettes, had yellow teeth, and couldn't take the stairs to the fourth floor without taking a break."

PJ paused for a moment and then continued, "I always scheduled my meetings for the fourth-floor conference room and then pasted out-of-order signs on the elevator. Did it for two years without anybody catching on."

The boys laughed at PJ's story as they came to the end of their run.

"Gentlemen," PJ said hesitantly, "I really don't know how I can help you, but I'll do whatever I can."

"Thanks, Coach," they replied.

PJ took a deep breath and watched the boys jog off toward the track. *But what can I do?* he wondered.

Chapter 27

Crossing Over

As PJ drove home, he still couldn't believe what had happened. He thought he would wake up at any moment and realize it was just a dream.

As he turned off Park Avenue onto Linden Road, raindrops started peppering his windshield. A few moments later a steady rain was falling, and the wet streets reflected the headlights of the rat race heading home from work.

PJ stopped briefly for a coffee at a Quik Check and got back into his car. He sipped the elixir and took in the "earned sensation" that was a combination of endorphins and caffeine. Sitting and listening to cars passing by on the rain-slicked road, PJ noticed how their tires "sighed" in the rain, as if even the vehicles would rather be somewhere else. PJ himself sighed and thought of how these boys would like to be somewhere else as well.

When he thought of them, the word "ghosts" came to mind, which made him uncomfortable. "Ghosts" didn't seem like the right word for them. They seemed so full of life, so beyond death. *You become a ghost after you finish your life here on Earth,* PJ thought. *Ghosts are part of the "afterlife."*

PJ started up the car again and continued home, pulling to a stop in his driveway. Taylor opened the front door and watched as he walked up the front path.

"You look dead," she joked.

PJ didn't laugh. "No, I'm just a little tired."

"Well, how was your day?" she asked.

"Same ol' stuff," he mumbled as he walked into his den and turned on his computer.

"I saved dinner for you."

"I'm not that hungry," PJ answered, turning to look into Taylor's eyes.

"Are you okay?"

"Yeah, just a little tired. I need to do a little research on...uh, race strategies tonight. Boring stuff, you know."

"Yeah, yeah, I know," Taylor answered as she headed off toward the living room. "I have a show to watch tonight anyway."

PJ turned back to the computer in time to see the last of the desktop icons loading on the screen. He opened a browser and in no time was busy surfing the web for answers.

Searching "Rozelle Catholic" and "accident" and "cross country team," he found nothing. He also tried each runner's name but came up empty-handed. He entered "ghosts," "spirits" and "*séance*" *and got thousands of hits*; but after searching for hours, he didn't come away with any ideas.

He looked down at his watch and noticed it was eleven thirty. Taylor must have gone to bed. He went to shut down his computer by pressing the "start" and then "shutdown" icons on the screen. The computer prompted him, "Are you sure you want to shut down?" He answered, "Yes."

As the computer started the shutdown process, PJ left the den and walked into the bedroom. "Are you asleep?" PJ whispered in Taylor's direction.

"No," she responded from her side of the bed. "I just shut off the TV. The show I was watching had a two-hour special tonight and it just finished."

"Oh, I see," PJ said, sliding into bed next to her. "What show was that?" he asked as he leaned over to kiss her.

"*Crossing Over*," Taylor said as she pressed her lips against his and started to reach her hand behind his head, letting out a sexy little moan.

PJ pushed back abruptly. "I'm sorry, hon. I forgot something." He jumped out of bed and hurried back to the den.

The computer screen was still displaying the "Are you sure you want to shut down the computer" prompt. PJ shook his head. *I thought I told this thing to shut down.* Regardless, he was glad it didn't because he wanted to do one more search. He frantically logged back on and pulled up a search engine.

This time he searched for "spirits," "afterlife" and "crossing over." A single article came up. It was by a Peruvian paranormal expert named Heide Aliaga. The article indicated that she had been consulted in some unsolved murder cases. She had also been involved in what were termed "ghost whisperer" situations, where she was apparently hired by homeowners to rid their places of ghosts and apparitions.

As PJ read on, he learned that in most cases she claimed the ghosts had some sort of "unfinished business" here on Earth at the time they passed. She attributed her successes to being able to complete the business for the apparition, whatever it was.

The desk chair squeaked as PJ leaned back and stretched his arms out over his head. *What unfinished business could a group of high school students have?* he wondered. *And why did all seven of them have unfinished business? Surely one of them would have crossed over?*

Chapter 28

There's *Our* Press

It was 5:30 a.m. when the first light broke through the bedroom window, warming Taylor's cheek enough to cause a stir. Still in a haze, she reached over and felt for PJ. His spot on the bed was cold, and she rose to survey the situation.

Moments later she quietly strolled down the hall and noticed a light on in the den. The door creaked as she gently opened it and found PJ asleep at the computer. Putting her face next to his ear, she whispered, "You're going to be late."

"Whaa…uhh," PJ groaned as he opened his eyes, the light from his computer monitor irritating them – never mind the backache he had from sleeping in the desk chair.

"I'll get some breakfast ready for the two of us," Taylor said. She kissed him and headed for the kitchen.

"Great," PJ groaned as he put his head down on the desktop to catch a few more winks.

Just then, PJ noticed something and looked up at the computer monitor. He must have hit the mouse or keyboard as he laid his head on the desk, because the screensaver was gone. Instead, he saw the local *New Jersey Online* webpage. He briefly surveyed it and then decided to get up to take a shower. As he turned toward the door, he took one more look back at the screen and noticed the local "Happenings" section, the part of the website that usually contained information on local music and entertainment. It also listed the various speakers lined up to present at the local library and literary club.

PJ clicked on the "Happenings" icon and brought up the calendar of events. As he surveyed the list, he noticed Heide Aliaga's name. She was scheduled to appear at the library two days from now to hawk her latest book, *Voices from Beyond*. Maybe she could help him, he thought, noting the time for the presentation.

"Get a move on, buster!" hissed Taylor as she passed by the den.

"I'm moving, I'm moving," PJ replied. He leapt to his feet and headed for the bathroom to shower, shave and be on his way. Later, as Taylor showered, PJ wolfed down the French toast she had prepared. He took one final sip of his coffee and headed out the door.

In no time, PJ was driving down Raritan Road toward RC, where he would complete a few meet entry forms and prepare the workout for the day. The boys were getting stronger and would soon be entering the next mesocycle of training, geared to increase their anaerobic thresholds. Mixing speed work with the dual meet schedule would be the challenge for the next four weeks. Today's schedule would be repeat 800s, finishing each with an uphill surge. They would start out at a three-minute pace and work down to 2:20 by the last one.

The team gathered at 2:45 p.m. to jog over to Warinanco Park, arriving at the site near the lake where PJ had measured out an 800-meter loop. The boys stretched as PJ and Kathleen Murphy prepared the log sheets to record the interval times.

"You look a little tired, Coach," Kathleen said.

"Didn't sleep too well last night, Kathleen," he replied as he filled in the clipboard, figuring she must've noticed the redness in his eyes.

"Wife problems?"

PJ laughed and tapped the clipboard on Kathleen's head. "No, not wife problems, young lady!"

"Drat!" Kathleen replied jokingly.

"Okay, guys, I'm not happy that you decided to screw off during the tempo run around Rahway Park yesterday. I waited here for you for nearly seventy minutes and you still weren't back. I come here every day hoping to make runners out of you guys. I expect you to meet me halfway."

"Coach—" Matt started.

"Not now, Matt. I want to make my point. We're here to train, *you* and *me*. I expect you guys to do the workout I assign to you! Got it?"

"Yes," the group answered.

"You guys are improving, but you're not good enough to sacrifice even one workout! Got it?"

"But Coach—" Vlad started.

"Quiet, Vlad," PJ interrupted again as he pulled a newspaper from his bag. "Listen, guys, in two days we go up against Westfield and Cranford in a tri meet. In today's paper there was an article about the race. Let me read it to you. Here's the headline: 'Westfield faces off against powerful Cranford team in cross country showdown!'"

PJ paused and looked briefly at his team before continuing. "'On Thursday, returning Group 4 Champion Westfield puts their unbeaten streak on the line as they face a rejuvenated Cranford squad at Warinanco Park.'" PJ looked again at his men then kept reading. "'Westfield returns with six runners from last year's varsity squad to defend itself against a Cranford team predicted to be in the top 10 at the Meet of Champions this year. Cranford's number one runner, Mitch O'Donnell, placed 12th in the national championships last year in San Diego and is considered a favorite to win the meet this year. The rest of the Cranford squad are juniors and seniors, all with times below 17:05 on the Warinanco course. As we head into the championship portion of the season, this dual meet should be a preview of what lies in store for later in the season.'" PJ glanced up at the team one more time.

Teddy stood there with his mouth wide open. "Hey, wait a minute! That's not a dual meet on Wednesday!" he blurted out.

"Exactly!" PJ said as he shook his head. "We can't be screwing around, guys. We have no reputation! People don't even know we exist!"

Rod walked up, grabbed the paper from PJ's hands, and ruffled through it for a few moments before handing it back to PJ. "There, Coach. There's our press! You should read more than the sports section." He chuckled as he turned and looked at his teammates behind him.

PJ scanned page 2 until his eyes came across the article Rod wanted him to see. "'RC Runner stops purse snatching,'" PJ read aloud as the team started to high-five each other.

"Coach, we took a little detour during that run, but we still did the whole workout!" Andrew added. PJ looked at him, and Andrew smiled and nodded. "You should've seen Kevin. He looked like Houston McTear running after the guy."

"Actually, I think he looked like Skeets Nehemiah when he hurdled the fence!" Mike said, doing an exaggerated hurdler's stretch.

"My big brother's a hero!" Kathleen said, reaching from her wheelchair and putting Kevin in a headlock as he sat stretching on the ground next to her.

PJ finished reading the article, all the while feeling a little stupid about the tongue-lashing he had started to give his team. "Well, Kevin, nice job!" PJ said, shaking Kevin's hand. "I guess I owe you guys an apology." PJ laughed. "I tell you what, I was going to make you guys do sixteen 800-meter repeats today as punishment. But instead, I'll reward you and only have you do eight." The team groaned good-naturedly.

"Guys," PJ continued, "today I want you to run the first 400 meters at a moderate pace, then pick it up during the last 400 meters, which will be on that slight uphill near the Alamo." He directed their attention to the workout at hand. "I want you to focus your attention on the hill. Don't let it beat you! When you finish each interval, I don't want to see anyone stopping and bending over and putting their hands on their knees. I want you to recover while jogging. We'll start out at three minutes for the first one and work down to 2:20 for the last one."

The boys splashed through puddles on the wet field as they started their first interval. The starting point was located at the two-mile mark of the cross country course. The half-mile section PJ had chosen was known for being a swamp on wet days because the field didn't drain well. The boys ran as a pack through the first 400 meters.

"Ninety-three, pick it up!" PJ yelled as they turned for the final 400 meters up the hill to the Alamo. Andrew and Mike paced the group up the hill, and PJ noticed how they all seemed to match each other's strides.

"2:59, 3:00, 3:01," PJ called out the times as they finished their first interval. "Okay, guys, you have one minute and thirty seconds to recover," he said as he watched Kathleen record the times for the first 800.

They did the next two 800s in 2:55 and 2:50. PJ was enthused as he watched his runners share the lead and hit the exact times he was looking for. More importantly, they looked strong. The distance training and conditioning had paid off, and they were able to train at the caliber he had hoped for.

"2:45," PJ shouted as Andrew crossed the finished line just slightly in front of the rest of the team on the fourth repeat.

Turning, PJ saw Nick and Matt bend over to recover with their hands on their knees. "Damn it, guys! Use the jog to recover! Don't let them know you're tired by bending over and holding yourselves up by your knees. Gather around!"

Once the team was surrounding him, PJ said, "Listen, guys, we didn't even make the newspaper today! When we show up for the race on Thursday, we may not win, but we'll at least let them know we were there!" Andrew looked up at PJ and nodded. "Andrew, on Thursday, Mitch O'Donnell goes down!" Mike patted Andrew on the back without saying a word.

"And down goes Westfield!" PJ added. "And down goes Cranford! No more hard runs before the race. On Thursday, we let the cat out of the bag. The Lions will be released from their cages!"

PJ checked his watch. "Okay, now I want four more under 2:40. Push each other. Think about passing Cranford and Westfield on this hill on Thursday." The eight stood silent as they waited to start the fifth 800 repeat. "Go!" he shouted, and the boys broke into the interval.

Andrew trailed the pack as Nick led them through the first 400 in seventy-eight seconds. Andrew picked it up during the final 400 and pulled the runners with him. The tight pack crossed the finish line in 2:34. Andrew grabbed Nick's arm as he started to bend over, and Nick corrected himself and got into a jog with the team.

"I'll take the next one," Rod said as they jogged toward the starting area. He had been quiet up until now.

"Run it like an Irishman," PJ coaxed Rod. The coach knew his runner was proud of his heritage.

Looking out toward the road, PJ noticed a group of runners approaching the lake. They wore blue and gold. Cranford.

"That's O'Donnell, with the curly brown hair," Rod said to Andrew as the group came close to the RC bunch. Andrew watched as O'Donnell led the group past the starting point of the 800 meters.

"You'll start in thirty seconds," PJ said, getting the team's attention again.

Andrew stared at the group of runners in blue and gold as they continued with their run. "Hearing voices in your head, Andrew"? PJ teased. Andrew said nothing, but simply circled the RC team while he jogged to stay loose.

"Okay, guys, to the start." PJ ushered in the next 800-meter repeat. "Go!" he shouted and watched the team break into full stride.

Andrew was noticeably pushing the pace of this sixth interval. "Hey, Andrew, I thought I had this one," Rod said as he matched Andrew stride for stride.

"Sorry, Rod, I got carried away for a minute," Andrew replied.

"Bullshit, you want to catch O'Donnell, don't you?"

"Yep, but it's yours."

"Goddamnit. You owe me for this." PJ watched as Rod shifted gears and brought the group through the 400 in seventy-one seconds. As they raced up the hill for the final 400 meters, they caught the Cranford team. O'Donnell must have seen the group coming, because he picked up the pace long enough to hold off Rod and Andrew. He never looked back.

"2:06!" yelled PJ. Andrew and Rod looked over in disbelief as they approached PJ, who saw O'Donnell look back when PJ announced the time.

"Are you serious, Coach?" Rod asked.

"Nah, I was just screwing around with that show-off," PJ said with a smirk. "It was actually 2:21.3."

They ran the next two 800s in 2:20 and 2:16, the pack staying together for all of them. PJ was so happy with the results that he bought them all Slurpees on their way back to school. He had heard this was a tradition amongst the high school runners from North Jersey who liked to post their workouts on the local running website, Runstat.com.

As best as he could tell, someone with the username "JerryGrote" used to buy his team Slurpees after running Sunday long runs on River Road in Bedminster. Before he knew it, kids from neighboring schools were showing up for the runs – or the Slurpees. He was never sure which.

Chapter 29

A Cure for MS

The workouts for the next two days were easier distance runs. Tomorrow was race day; and for the first time, PJ was not going to have his team run hard immediately before the race. So far they had run three and had a record of one win and two losses.

After the high schoolers showered and went home, PJ went to the park and ran a workout with the "spirits," as he liked to think of them. He said nothing of the visit he was going to make to meet Heide Aliaga later that evening.

As PJ changed back into his street clothes next to his car, Dan Hutchens approached while the others stretched near the track. "Coach, do you have a minute?" Dan asked.

"Sure, what's up?" PJ answered, turning to face the apparition.

"I don't know what it means, but we…uh, ghosts can kind of sense things, you know?"

"No, you're the ghost, but I'll take your word for it. What's up?"

"Well, when we're not running with you, we're not always together. We kind of roam around your world."

"Yeah, and so?"

"Well, most of the time I have no control over where I go. Lately, I keep ending up in Manhattan."

"Not a bad place – great nightlife!" PJ joked. But Dan wasn't laughing. He seemed confused.

"For some reason I end up in the apartment of this woman. She's your age, Coach, maybe a little older. Her name's Martha. She seems very sad. I'm not sure why, but I do know one thing – she's destined to change the world."

"What do you mean?" PJ asked.

"She lives alone, and she has MS. She was a very successful venture capitalist until she came down with the disease. The stress of the job made the MS worsen to the point where she had to give it up."

"And where do I fit in?" PJ asked.

"Coach, she's heading up a group dedicated to researching the human genome to look for MS markers that could lead to a cure for the disease. I just want to encourage her not to give up the fight. I met her father a number of years ago. He's so proud of her. He asked me to tell her so. He asked me to tell her that he loved her and knew that she'd have an impact on the world – a tremendous one!"

"What kind of impact?" PJ asked as he studied the boy's expression.

"She's destined to find a cure for MS," Dan said.

PJ just stared at Dan for a moment. "Well, she's heading up the research team! Good for her."

"Yeah, but you don't understand. Something's wrong. She's not right… Anyway, her name's Martha Crowner. Here's her address." PJ took the paper with her address written on it and placed it in the visor of his car. "Thanks, Coach," Dan said.

"I'll do what I can, Dan," PJ said, and he turned his thoughts to Heide Aliaga. It was 6:50 p.m. He had ten minutes to get to the presentation at the library.

Chapter 30

Unfinished Business

Heide Aliaga smiled at PJ and pointed to an open seat as he entered the lecture hall at the library. She was a short, rotund woman, with her hair tightly drawn back into a bun. She spoke softly to the crowd of thirty or so that had shown up for the evening. Most had copies of her new book and were there to see a celebrity and get an autograph.

Following Heide's lecture, PJ waited at the rear of the room while Heide talked to the remaining few fans. When she reached down to pick up her purse and the rest of her belongings, PJ approached her. "Ms. Aliaga," PJ said.

The woman jumped. "Oh, I'm sorry. I didn't know you were there," Heide replied. "You startled me."

Hmm, you can see ghosts, but you couldn't see me standing in the rear of the room, PJ thought to himself.

"So, I see you haven't purchased my book yet," Heide teased. "That's okay. I'll help you with your ghost issue anyway."

PJ's eyes widened. "How did you know I had a—"

"Why else would you be here, Mr. Irwin?"

"It's just that—" PJ started. "Hey, wait a minute! How did you know my name?" Heide chuckled and pointed to his shirt where "Coach Irwin" was embroidered on it. "Oh yeah," he laughed, "I forgot about that."

"So, tell me what's on your mind," Heide said as she sat down at a table in the back of the lecture room.

Taking a seat across from her, PJ explained about the ghosts, the dream with the bus accident, Pete Bailey's father, and other things that he thought might be related. Heide listened with her eyes closed as PJ described the torment the ghosts were going through, how they wanted to cross over but couldn't.

"You know there's unfinished business that's preventing them from crossing over." Heide opened her eyes and stared over her glasses at PJ.

"Okay, but what is it?" PJ asked.

"You'll have to figure it out," Heide replied. "Have you asked them what bothers them?"

"No, but one mentioned a woman in Manhattan," PJ added.

Heide closed her eyes for a moment and then smiled at PJ.

"What?" he asked.

"There is more than unfinished business. The name 'Dan' comes to mind, and he's close to this woman," she answered.

How did she know it was Dan who mentioned the woman named Martha? PJ wondered.

"Dan loves this woman and is concerned about her well-being. That's all that's coming to me. He wants you to talk to her." Heide's smile faded into a look of concern. "You need to speak with her."

"Yes, that's what Dan said," PJ replied. "I will, after the race on Thursday."

Heide picked up her bag and said, "Well, good day…and buy my book next time."

"I will, thank you!" PJ replied.

Chapter 31

The Tri-Meet

By the time Thursday arrived, Kathleen Murphy had created a stir amongst the student body. She had organized an impromptu pep rally in the cafeteria at lunchtime, when she locked herself in the principal's office and used the school's public-address system to announce the arrival of the new RC cross country squad. As she craftily read from the notes she pulled together during the week, she gradually brought the student body to their feet when she announced the names of the runners.

At first the team was a little embarrassed; but as Kathleen went on, more and more students took the time to wish the team members luck, and some even said they would go to the meet!

In a flash it was three o'clock, and PJ was already on the bus when the team exited the school to take the trip to the park. "Are we ready, Coach?" asked Phil Cappria, the school's bus driver, his smile lighting a spark in PJ.

"You bet, Phil!" PJ answered, giving him a thumbs-up. He watched as the runners boarded the bus and Phil wished each kid good luck. He knew all their names and was probably the best cheerleader RC had ever had.

After Mike and Carmine boarded the bus, Phil looked at PJ and asked, "That's all of them, correct?"

PJ quickly surveyed the group and said, "No, we have one more, Kevin Murphy."

"He's beside the bus," Andrew said as he and Nick exited. PJ looked out one of the windows and saw Kevin and Kathleen reaching for the handicap entrance mechanism.

PJ started to get up to go help, but Phil put his hand across the aisle. "No, Coach, they got this."

The trio of runners helped Kathleen ride the mechanism up onto the bus, all four of them pretending to be swashbucklers boarding a pirate vessel. It was kind of comical – and beautiful – as the boys made this activity fun for Kathleen. For a moment, PJ completely forgot about the race.

When the bus roared out of the parking lot a minute later, the silence was so thick PJ could have cut it with a knife. It worried him a little. He hoped he hadn't put too much pressure on the team to perform today. While they had been improving at a rapid clip, he didn't expect them to win. He just wanted to set high standards for them. If they could beat Cranford, he would be very happy. Westfield, on the other hand, seemed unbeatable.

In no time, the bus had travelled down Third Avenue and turned into the stadium parking lot at Warinanco Park. It pulled up and came to a halt at the far turn of the track.

"Everyone, before you grab your stuff and head to the starting line area, I have a few things to say," PJ said as he looked at his clipboard where he had jotted down a few notes. "I've been tough on you guys the past few weeks with the double workouts, hill work, and running hard runs through races." Teddy looked over at Nick , and they both rolled their eyes. "But this week we entered a new cycle of training," he added, "and I even gave you an easy day yesterday to recover from the interval work we did this week." He noticed Andrew and Rod staring motionless at him.

"I don't know what to expect today. Cranford and Westfield are two of the top-rated teams in the state, and they're going to take it to each other since the conference ranking is on the line today."

"In my opinion, Westfield should easily beat Cranford today," Matt chimed in.

"That could be, Matt, but I want to make sure we don't get caught up in that war," PJ advised. "O'Donnell's going to take it out hard for Cranford, hoping the entire top five of the Westfield team go with him. Westfield likes to run up front. O'Donnell's team is weaker, but

O'Donnell has enough in him to take the sting out of Westfield's top five, maybe giving the Cranford team the chance to compete against a tired Westfield team later in the race." Andrew, Nick and Mike nodded as they listened.

"I don't want you guys going out hard with O'Donnell. I want you running as a pack behind the first pack of runners. Let them pound on each other up front as you run on those fresh legs in the back, waiting for your moment. To be honest, I don't know what to expect from you guys now that you have fresh legs. If we can be in a pack near the front third of the race at the end, then we might be able to disrupt the scoring and beat one of these teams with a surge at the end. Any questions?"

"I have a question, Coach," Kevin said from the rear of the bus.

"What's that?" PJ asked with a smile. He never knew what Kevin would say.

"How's comes me legs feels so goooood?" Kevin said comically. "I feel as happy as a jaybird and as peppy as a minstrel!" he added as he danced up the middle aisle of the bus and turned to face his teammates. "Guys – and gals," he started as he acknowledged his sister, "do you feel it? Do you feel fast today?"

"Yes," came the unorganized response from the rest of the team.

"Do you feel like a lion?" he added.

"Yes," came a louder, more unified answer.

"Are we here to race?" he added emphatically.

"Yes!" came the response.

"Then let's go out there and let them know we're here by stinking up the porta-johns before they get to use them," Kevin said. Turning to PJ, he said, "There you go, Coach. That's how you get them energized."

PJ stood motionless as he watched Kevin exit the bus, then he turned and looked at Kathleen and the rest of the team.

Kathleen rolled her eyes and said, "Sometimes I wish I could disown him."

The rest of the team gathered their belongings, exited the bus, and started their trek toward the starting line. Kevin and Mike helped

Kathleen exit the bus, and took turns helping her with her wheelchair as they walked through the track parking lot, crossing the interior park road and then the field to the starting line.

The team set up their tent and laid down their belongings on the left side of the starting line, close to first base on the softball field. The right-field foul line served as the starting line for cross country races.

"Hi, Coach," came a voice from behind PJ. It was Grant Edwins.

"Hi, Mr. Edwins," PJ said, extending his hand to the seasoned sportswriter. "Here today to see Cranford and Westfield go at each other?" he asked in an effort to take the focus off his team.

"It should be interesting," Grant replied as he looked toward the other two teams that had just arrived. They were setting up their tents and taking their places on the field near the starting line. "I understand you've been doing doubles, thanks to the courtesy of Mr. Bailey. I heard he fixed the school van for you."

PJ was surprised that someone outside the school would know about this. "Yes, he contributed his services toward fixing the transmission. I highly recommend him."

"He's a great guy. I'm glad to see he still has such tight ties to the team," Grant said, watching the RC squad venture off into a jog. "His son, Pete, ran for RC years ago."

"I know," PJ replied in a somber tone. "Mr. Bailey filled me in on the team back then."

"Well, I'm glad to see Mr. Bailey back at it. He had a really tough go of it," Grant said, jotting something on his notepad. "Will Bailey be here today?" Grant asked.

"No, I don't think so. He told me he isn't really into the sport anymore," PJ answered, noticing the Cranford and Westfield coaches approaching.

"I understand," Grant said, turning to the approaching pair.

"Hey, hey, Grant," called Clark Walters, the Westfield coach.

"This must be a big event if you're covering it," added Cranford's Bill McNair, the shorter of the two. "Thanks for coming out. We expect quite a duel between us and Walters' team."

"Let me introduce you to Coach Irwin from RC," Grant interrupted.

"Hi, Coach," McNair said as he shook his hand.

"Nice to meet you, Coach," said the stately Walters. "I hear you have RC on a resurgence," he added, nodding to the RC team that had just returned from a jog and were stretching within earshot.

PJ looked over and noticed Andrew and Nick eavesdropping as they stretched. "Yes, we have a nice group of kids, and they've been working hard," PJ remarked.

"Just the fact that you're fielding a full team is quite an achievement!" McNair added. "To be honest, we didn't expect you to show up today. The last few years RC didn't show." Andrew grimaced a little at that remark as he did his hurdler's stretch.

As the coaches continued to chat, the race starter and official approached. He went through the timing and rules for the day to make sure all three coaches were aligned. Then the official gave them their starting line assignments: Westfield would start on the left end of the line, RC would be grouped in the middle, and Cranford would be grouped on the right.

"Do you think you could put Cranford in the middle position and move RC out to the far right," McNair interjected, "so that we can be closer to the competition? That would also keep us from burying the RC kids from the start and demoralizing them."

Walters looked stunned by the aggressive comment and glanced at PJ, who stood silently and didn't show any reaction to the comment. Inside, he was stewing. *What a thing for a coach to say within earshot of my team,* PJ thought, glancing over at them. Nearly all of them were staring at him. They must have heard that last exchange. PJ saw Kathleen flip the bird toward the Cranford coach and turn away in disgust.

"Coach, you okay with that switch?" the official asked.

PJ took a moment and then answered, "Nope. I want my guys to experience the burial in preparation for the larger state meet next week. Keep us in the middle. Good luck, coaches, nice meeting you." He turned away and walked toward his team as they jumped to their feet.

"Who's that guy think he is?" Andrew asked PJ as the team gathered around them.

"He meant no harm," PJ answered, gathering the group for some final instructions. "Those two coaches are focused on each other. We're not on their radar screen. When the Cranford coach suggested having his team switch with us, it was his way of telling the Westfield coach that the Cranford team was here and ready for a race. Let's stick to our 'run as a pack' strategy and see what we have at the end. If we can push over the last 800 meters, we might get to one of these teams, most likely Cranford."

Andrew and Nick whispered something to each other as PJ finished speaking, then Andrew announced, "Come on, guys. Let's do some long stride outs." The two stared at PJ for a few moments as the rest of the team headed for the starting line. Carmine caught the stare – and then the grin on PJ's face as he stared back at them.

As Andrew and Nick turned to join the team doing stride outs, Carmine asked PJ, "What the hell was that stare all about?"

"Something's up, Carmine," PJ answered. "They were just dissed by that coach and they're figuring out how to respond."

"Well, what do you think?" Carmine asked. "Do you need to pump them up?"

"No, let's let this one play out on its own," PJ said with a smirk. "This is in their hands now."

At the end of the seventh stride, Andrew huddled up the team as they came to a rest. "Okay, guys, change in plans," he started. "I'm sure you all heard that they wanted to protect little RC from the embarrassment of being buried by these two so-called powerhouses at the start of the race." He looked at them, and they nodded in agreement. "Do you feel as good as I do today?"

"Yes," they responded in unison.

"Then let's take it to them, right from the start."

"But Irwin wants us to run as a pack, doesn't he?" Matt questioned.

"We will," Andrew said, "but closer to the front – right in the thick of it from the beginning. After we get through the first mile, me and Nick are going to press O'Donnell."

"Press O'Donnell?" remarked Nick, surprised.

"Yup, we can do it if we help each other out," said Andrew. "And Kevin, Matt, Rob, Vlad and Teddy won't be far behind us as a pack. You five need to hang with Westfield's top five so we can outscore them. Whad'ya think?"

"Let's bring it to them," Rod replied. "They won't expect it!"

"Okay, guys, hands in," Andrew said. The huddle tightened, and he led them in prayer.

At the end of the prayer, Kevin Murphy gripped the hands tighter and said, "Who are we?"

"Lions!" they answered.

"And this is our course!" Kevin added. "This is where the lions roam! Now let's go after our prey!"

"Runners to the starting line!" shouted the official.

The team broke huddle and jogged back to the starting line. As the teams stripped off their sweats, PJ and Carmine started for the Alamo flower garden, where they would give the team their 800-meter splits.

PJ looked back at the team as they nervously waited for the start. The official walked about forty meters out in front of the starting line and fumbled for the megaphone mic. While the Westfield and Cranford runners put their heads down, preparing for the start of the race, Andrew noticed that the official had pulled out an old-school starter's pistol, which he was raising to the sky.

"Eyes up!" Andrew urged his team, keeping his voice low. "He's using a pistol. Look for the flash."

Every runner on the RC team locked his gaze on the nozzle of the starter's pistol. A few weeks earlier, PJ demonstrated how a runner on the starting line will see the flash at the muzzle a full tenth of a second before they hear the shot. PJ smiled when he saw the RC eyes locked on the gun. *Way to go, guys*, he thought as he readied to start his watch.

"Runners set," shouted the official. *Bang!* went the starter's pistol.

PJ knew it was hard to describe the moment when the gun went off from the runner's point of view. A runner was focused, tense, twitching, and in close contact with the runner next to them. The ground was uneven, and the runner wanted to run straight to avoid a collision with the person next to them, especially if they were on the same team. Elbows flew, and the runner tried to gauge their leg turnover to be fast enough not to get buried in the crowd, yet under control so as not to get winded too early.

The RC runners seemed to have a full step on the other teams as they came off the line. "Smart runners, PJ," said Grant, standing beside him. PJ smiled and walked calmly to the 800-meter mark.

"PJ, look," Carmine exclaimed. "What the heck are they doing?" PJ turned to see the entire RC team about ten yards in front of the rest of the field of runners. Amongst them was one runner in gold and blue – O'Donnell. They were flying across the field and getting ready to circle the Rose Garden before heading to the Alamo.

PJ noticed Coach McNair of Cranford standing next to him and grinning. "I wanted O'Donnell to burn out Westfield's top runners, not your entire team, Coach," McNair said. "You might want to tell them to hold back a little."

PJ just watched as the wave of green encircled O'Donnell as they rounded the Rose Garden and headed toward the spectators and coaches at the Alamo. "2:10, 2:11, 2:12," Carmine yelled as the group of RC runners and O'Donnell passed the 800-meter mark.

"Okay, Andrew, Nick, keep it under control," PJ yelled, noticing a maniacal grin on Nick's face. "Run as a pack! Help each other out!" he shouted to the rest of the team as they passed.

"Jeez," said Carmine as he and PJ took off in a mad, straight-line dash toward the mile mark.

PJ said nothing as he ran next to Carmine. He surveyed the race as it was unfolding. A large, tight pack of Westfield and Cranford runners were about three seconds behind the RC team and O'Donnell. As they looped past the starting line and headed for the mile mark, PJ saw O'Donnell surge into the lead.

Nick looked over at Andrew. The two shifted gears and quickly got alongside O'Donnell, who appeared a little frazzled to have not one, but two runners alongside him.

PJ stood with Carmine at the mile mark. His game plan of having his pack run just off the leaders until the two-and-a-half-mile mark was not going to happen. His team had extended themselves early, and PJ wrestled with what to tell his runners as they passed him at the mile.

Carmine shouted the mile times. "4:26, 4:27!" PJ saw the looks on Andrew's and Nick's faces as they shared the lead with O'Donnell. Their strides were in perfect unison, their arm carry efficient. All three runners leaned forward into an uphill shortly after the mile mark.

"Way to go, guys!" PJ shouted to the next group of five runners who were all from RC. Vlad gave the "six-shooter" signal to Carmine as they passed.

"Stay focused, Vlad!" Carmine yelled. "What the hell is he giving me the six-shooter for?" Carmine laughed, looking at PJ.

"They look incredibly strong," PJ said as he started to jog toward the end of the lake and the two-mile mark. "I believe he's telling us that the five of them are executing as planned...as a pack."

"Yeah, but way too fast, way too early, don't you think?"

I don't know.... I just don't know, PJ thought. "No, they know what they're doing," he said to Carmine as they slowed to a stop near the two-mile mark.

"Now make your move, gentlemen!" came the thundering roar of Westfield's Clark Walters. "I told them to hang loose while O'Donnell burned himself out, to make their move once they got to the lake," Walters shouted to Grant, who was frantically taking notes for his article.

PJ watched the runners make their way around the lake toward the two-mile mark. The blue swarm of Westfield runners had caught up to the RC pack. O'Donnell was still slightly in the lead, but his arms were flailing a bit, and he seemed to be tiring. Andrew and Nick still looked strong as they paced off O'Donnell – who was wavering, which was unusual this early in the race.

What PJ and the other coaches didn't see as the runners ran the three-quarters of a mile around the wooded perimeter of the lake was the thirty-second intervals that Nick and Andrew were putting in while trading the lead with each other. Each time one of them took the lead, O'Donnell tried to stay with the leader. Eventually the two RC runners backed off the pace and let O'Donnell take them into the two-mile mark, but by this time O'Donnell was broken. The real threat now was the Westfield pack, which was methodically gaining on the leaders.

PJ looked at Carmine just before the group hit the two-mile mark. "You give them their splits. I'll meet you near the finish," he said, taking off toward the hill at the bottom of the Alamo.

"9:18, 9:19…way to go, Andrew and Nick!" Carmine shouted.

PJ situated himself at the two-and-a-quarter mark at the bottom of the next hill the runners would have to climb. There were no other coaches at this location, probably because PJ was the only one fast enough to get there in time.

As Andrew and Nick approached, PJ got as close to them as possible and said, "Okay, guys, risk it. Go for another gear. It'll be there. Break this race wide open! At the top of the hill, the trailing runners won't be able to see you as you turn into the trees. Take a look back at the race behind you and then surge and commit to a big finish!"

Andrew and Nick responded to PJ and adjusted their leg turnovers as they ascended the hill. Their gap began to increase, and PJ was banking on one last emotional kick to get them to the finish line first. *My legs are burning, and my arms are like lead weights,* Nick thought as he crested the hill.

"C'mon, Nick," Andrew gasped as they headed toward the turn at the tree line. But Andrew was fighting with his breathing and looking for that little extra, that little bit more. He was fighting for every inch, hoping for that miracle. And then he remembered PJ's instructions. *Look back at the race as you turn into the trees.*

Andrew and Nick made the left turn at the first tree of the line that would lead them to the finish. Andrew's eyes widened as he saw Vlad smiling and leading a group of five RC runners about twenty yards behind them. O'Donnell was just behind this group, surrounded by a group of three Westfield runners.

"Look!" Andrew said to Nick, motioning at the trailing pack. The sight of the pack of RC runners right behind them gave Andrew and Nick enough confidence to try for one more surge. They could risk laying it on the line because there were five more RC guys behind them who would help their team's score.

Nick moved first as he surged on the tangent along a curve in the bike path that was part of the course. Andrew tucked in behind him, thinking, *Atta boy, Nick, we got this.*

Andrew's mind went back for a moment to those days when he raced as a youth at Brundage Park. To that voice that used to urge him on. That voice that would vanish when he folded during the races. He wasn't going to fold today. He could feel the endorphins kicking in. Too bad his childhood friend, the voice, had faded away some time ago. The voice would be proud of what he was about to do.

As they neared the three-mile mark, Nick's gait began to waver. "Great job, Nick," Andrew said as he strode up next to him.

"You got it?" Nick gasped through tired lips.

"We got it. One more gear," he urged while pressing forward.

PJ stood next to Grant at the starting line as he watched the two lead RC runners emerge from the tree line onto the final straightaway. He could see them digging down, deep down, as they ran side-by-side to the finish. Other spectators ran toward the edge of the final straightaway and cheered them on. "Run, RC!" Grant yelled, dropping his clipboard and jumping up and down.

PJ fumbled for his watch and barely managed to get the time for the two runners as they broke through the finish tape together.

15:12.

As they decelerated in the finish chute, Andrew and Nick clung to each other and walked toward the exit. *Don't bend over!* they each thought as they struggled to recover.

The official at the end of the chute smiled and handed Andrew two popsicle sticks with the numbers 1 and 2 written on them. "I couldn't tell who won," she laughed, moving the boys out of the chute so she could give the next runner, Vlad, the stick with number 3 on it.

PJ watched as sticks 4 through 7 were given to Rod, Teddy, Matt and

Kevin. O'Donnell held off the surge by the Westfield top five at the end, as did Mike, who crossed in a dead tie with O'Donnell. The RC runners gathered at the end of the chute and looked over at a stunned PJ. "We're going for a warm-down," Matt shouted to him.

"Okay...uh...yeah, that's a good idea," the flabbergasted coach answered.

"Congratulations, Coach," said Kathleen from behind him. "I got all their times." She moved her wheelchair toward him and handed him a clipboard.

"Thanks," PJ said. "Still trying to come to grips with what just happened."

"Isn't it called a 'shutout' when you get the first five runners across the line?" Kathleen asked with a big smile.

"Yes, it is," they heard from behind them. The voice belonged to Laura Gordon, who was covering the race for the *Sussex County Swamp Rat*, a running newsletter that covered major running events in New Jersey. Laura was also one of the founders and coordinators of the Xtreme Running Camp that PJ had attended earlier in the year.

"Your team's made remarkable progress, PJ," Laura said through a smile that would stop a clock. Laura loved the sport of running, and had qualified for the Olympic trials years ago. Unfortunately for her, while out on a winter training run, she was struck by a kid driving a jeep with a snowplow blade on the front of it. She nearly died, but managed to get back to walking on a treadmill while still in the hospital with a fractured skull. Three months later she ran a 2:50 marathon with the scars still healing. From that point on, she focused on her journalism career, running a personal fitness business, and producing one of the best running camps on the East Coast – oh, and perfecting one of the best strawberry jams anyone would ever taste!

"Thanks," PJ answered her. "I'm still stunned. I honestly didn't expect this. We didn't execute as planned."

PJ watched as Laura feverishly took notes. She stopped and took a sip of lemonade from a bottle she was carrying. As she wiped her lips, she continued, "So did they win because they didn't follow your plan?"

PJ saw her grin. "Maybe," he answered.

"Let's try that one again," Laura coached PJ. "So, do you think they took a huge risk and that's what great runners do to have 'breakthrough' performances?"

"Uhh, yeah, that'll read much better!" PJ chuckled.

"See you at the Meet of Champions, Coach," Laura said, picking up her bag and taking off for the parking lot. PJ watched as she hopped into her Mach 1 Mustang and screeched out of the lot.

"Congratulations, Coach," Walters said as he held out his hand. "You took us by surprise."

"Thanks," PJ replied.

"Good luck next week in the Parochial B State Championship. We'll see you at the Meet of Champions."

"Okay, see you then."

"Great job," Walters said to the RC team as they approached at the end of their warm-down.

"Thanks, Coach," Nick said, answering for the team.

"When we meet at the Meet of Champions," Walters said, "I'll have my top five runners back with me. They couldn't come because they had SAT testing today. Anyway, good luck!"

PJ was not going to let that last comment affect the high of this team's first major win. "Whaddya say? Pizza's on me tonight!" he exclaimed to a loud roar.

By 5:30 p.m., the team was seated behind the antique booths at Spirito's in Elizabeth, a classic New Jersey pizza joint, complete with servers with big New Jersey hair and tough, no-nonsense attitudes.

While they dined, PJ took in the traditional New Jersey scene, complete with "fuhgedaboutitz" and "pru-shoot." Kevin Murphy took center stage during the meal. It was his time to shine as he brought the team to uncontrollable laughter over and over again. Each kid on this team had their purpose, PJ realized. Kevin was good at dialing in the team to the correct emotional level, no matter what the situation. PJ laughed and cheered him on as they celebrated the team's coming of age.

Chapter 32

PJ vs Sayed – The Tune Up

The next week passed quickly. The workouts were shorter, with fewer but sharper intervals. PJ was bringing the team into its prime by changing the workload and intensity. Soon the peak would be in, and PJ was excited to see how the team responded.

The Parochial B State Championship was run at Warinanco Park, a competition for the smaller parochial schools. RC had no problem placing four men in the top five of the championship event. A young runner from Bergen Catholic, Kenneth Byrnes, won the race, with RC taking the next four spots. Mike placed second overall; Andrew and Nick sat this one out to allow their legs to recover. Both had been complaining of shin splints for a few weeks, and PJ wanted them sharp for the Meet of Champions. He knew the team would win the Parochial B Championship without using them. RC was simply too deep in talent.

The day after winning the Parochial B Championship was an easy distance day for the team; and since it was Sunday, they met and ran on their own. For PJ, however, this was no easy day. He was going to settle the score with Umar Sayed at the USA XC Open Championship in Newark, New Jersey. This race was a fundraiser for the Newark Engineering College, and it had built up quite a reputation over the years for attracting post-collegiate athletes from around the world.

As PJ read about the event and the host college, he noticed that last year the college had been moved to Division I under the leadership of a new coach, Alphonso Adalbert, a former Olympian from Mexico who had coached at Steven's Preparatory School for a number of years. Like Irwin, Adalbert had taken a bunch of unknown runners and molded them into a competitive Division I team. His "we never turn away a walk-on" approach led to some unexpected finds, even though it tried the patience of the college's athletics office. But it worked. He took his men's team, consisting of Roy Davies, Brian McClue, Gabe Camby, Matt Morno, Derrick Essell, Will Farrell and Andy Shenada, to the regional finals where they placed third. The prior year they had placed eighteenth!

On the women's side of things, his coaching techniques took more than four minutes off Evelina Merut's 22:25 high school best 5K, getting her down to 17:22! Three freshman—Kelly Rain, Cassy DeCritstini and Lalanna Hill-Grover—followed Ewelina's improvements with their own attempts at the college's record books.

Adalbert's strongest habit was the use of his post-collegiate athletes as coaching assistants. Sayed was one of these assistants, having run for Adalbert at Stephens Prep. This year Sayed and former Newark College standouts Blake Unger, Freddy Smith, and the 1996 women's distance squad of Breanne Hollenstein, Megan Higglesworth, Catherine Conlon, Vannessa Lopez and Amanda Huffin, were all "on the payroll," assisting with team practices and putting on events such as the 5K open championship to help support the school. But today's volunteer group would be without one member, Umar Sayed, because he was prepared to run – and most likely win – the event. This would undoubtedly be a big feather in the college's cap, because Sayed would donate the prize money back to the school.

PJ warmed up as he had done thousands of times before. He felt good, and his mind was on the task at hand as he walked down High Street to the starting line.

PJ noticed a redheaded runner from South Africa, and a group of three with Colombian colors on their shirts. On the back of one of the shirts was the name "Ruiz." This was no doubt Frank Ruiz, who had just won the famed "Foulmouth Road Race," the race that started out as a joke, making light of a more famous race of a similar name. Spectators were encouraged to line the last 200 meters of the course and verbally bash the runners as they finished. Somehow the event caught on. It was well managed and promoted, and the purse and level of competition had risen significantly. The race was five miles long, and Ruiz broke the course record this year when he ran it in 22:53. Sayed placed second to Ruiz, but only after making a wrong turn and losing precious time. Today, Sayed's focus would be Ruiz.

PJ started in the second line of runners. In total, the race had over 5,000 entrants, which was just too many for a 5K. As a result, runners such as Ruiz, Sayed and PJ were given special numbers that allowed them to start in the front of the pack.

After the initial sprint, PJ settled in at the end of the first group of runners. At the front of the group was Ruiz, followed closely by Sayed, who was determined not to take the lead and make a wrong turn. PJ hung back with Antoine Latinsacs, an American from western New Jersey, and Dean Sholtz, the owner of a chain of running stores and a very competitive local runner. Just behind this trio were the Sherrier twins, Justin and Jeremy, two former Pope James standouts.

Sayed pushed Ruiz early, and the two went through the mile in 4:12. PJ, Sholtz and Latinsacs went through in 4:20, with the Sherrier twins in tow at 4:22. This pace was fast, and PJ was beginning to think all seven of the frontrunners went out too hard. Lurking a few seconds behind them all was a strong-looking group that contained Rufino Mendosa and Jerry Livessee, both New Jersey natives and fierce competitors known for their kicks.

No sooner had PJ started to think that the group had gone out too hard than the Sherrier twins surged past PJ and moved in front of Latinsacs and Sholtz. They looked strong and comfortable as they glided down Frehlinghausen Avenue wearing their Jersey Shore-based running club's colors.

Latinsacs was wearing the colors of a new club in the area. His blue and black shirt had a logo that read RACING NJ. Sholtz wore an orange singlet bearing the name of his running shoes store. Sayed opted to wear the Newark Engineering College singlet, which earned him great applause as he ran through the streets surrounding the college. PJ wore a simple Xtreme Running Camp T-shirt that he cut the sleeves off of. He felt briefly outclassed – until he shifted gears and got up alongside the Sherrier twins.

No sooner had he started to match strides with the Sherriers than he saw Latinsacs on his immediate left. As they leaned into the left turn onto

Broad Street, Latinsacs was pushed into the front of the group and was now only one second off the lead shared by Ruiz and Sayed. PJ moved up next to Latinsacs, and the two evened up with the leaders as they started up the hill on High Street.

Ruiz was breathing hard, and Sayed could sense his fatigue, so he decided to break Ruiz with one final surge. The seven runners were only 600 meters from the finish in front of Weston Hall. With about 500 meters to go, the Sherrier twins made a move that surprised everyone. Justin looked a little stronger and edged out in front of Jeremy.

Ruiz began to fall back, as did Latinsacs and Sayed. PJ felt he had one more gear left, and when he hit the three-mile mark, he increased his leg turnover and took the lead from the Sherriers. The finish line was about 100 meters in front of him as he drove his arms and tried to get every last ounce of momentum out of them.

With about fifty yards to go, PJ heard steps next to him. He looked to his right and there was Latinsacs, who had conserved a little on the uphill and was now calling on his kick. With twenty meters to go, PJ could see that Latinsacs had just shifted into another gear. He could only watch the back of Latinsacs' RACING NJ singlet as he crossed the finish line, beating PJ by less than a second in 13:32.

Latinsacs turned around and nodded at PJ. "Nice race," he said as began his recuperation.

Later, as PJ warmed down with Latinsacs and the Sherrier twins, they all discussed the upcoming "unofficial" Olympic trials 5,000-meter qualifier that would be held in December.

To be invited to a trials qualifier, a runner had to run this event. Based on his performance today, PJ realized he was ready.

Chapter 33

He Heard You

Later that afternoon, PJ hopped on a Northeast Regional train to Manhattan to meet with Martha Crowner. He was not travelling alone; alongside him sat Dan Hutchens (although PJ was the only one that could see him), who was repeating the dream he kept having where he woke up in Martha Crowner's apartment. It was comical to watch PJ shoo people away from sitting on Dan during the train ride, but eventually they made it to Penn Station and were soon walking up to Central Park.

PJ sensed Dan was not telling him something about this visit, and PJ had to figure out how to introduce himself to this woman, which was weird. He had no reason to be there, and she didn't know him from Adam. The best plan he could come up with was to listen to Dan, who said he knew she had a habit of eating alone at the Lunar Deli near 76th Street every Sunday. This bothered PJ. How could she be a stranger if Dan knew her eating habits?

PJ arrived at the deli at six that evening and took a seat on a bench outside in front of the restaurant. At six fifteen, Dan coughed to get PJ's attention and nodded toward a woman coming up the sidewalk. She was no old woman as Dan had led PJ to believe; she was probably no more than forty, though she did use a cane to balance herself as she walked. Her limp was barely noticeable.

When she approached the door, PJ jumped up to hold it for her. As he opened it, he hit her cane and knocked it over. His plan was to pick it up and give it to her and somehow suggest they eat dinner together.

"Thank you," she said as she grabbed the cane from PJ and whisked herself inside the building.

PJ stood there looking at Dan. Neither of them had a backup plan. Eventually, PJ stepped inside.

"I'm sorry, Martha," said a man behind the counter, "all the counter spaces are full. We only have one table for two, but it's reserved for the Irwin party."

PJ turned and looked at Dan, who had a smug grin on his face. "That would be us, sir, thank you," PJ said, nodding to Martha. When she started to ask PJ who he was, he said, "Martha, it's okay. A friend sent me to speak with you. Dinner will be on me."

Martha was a confident, successful woman and already quite wealthy. She didn't need someone to buy her dinner. But when she looked at PJ, a good feeling came over her, and that was something she had been missing for quite a while. Martha's MS had been getting the better of her recently. She had made hundreds of millions of dollars as an investment banker, and eventually the stress of the job fueled episodes of MS-related issues. Her balance was off, and she had recently started using a cane to stabilize herself. Her spirits were so low that depression was beginning to set in, and her thoughts were going to dark places.

"Well, what the hell. I know half the people in here," she said to PJ as she started toward the table at the rear of the room. PJ followed, as did Dan, although no one noticed Dan. He was a spirit, after all.

"My name is PJ Irwin, Martha – do you go by Martha?" PJ asked.

"Martha's fine," the brunette said with a slight laugh. "And who's the friend who sent you to speak with me?"

PJ looked up at Dan, who was sitting on top of a hutch next to their table. PJ was hesitant about how to answer. "Tell her it was someone she knew when she lived in Rozelle as a kid," Dan suggested.

PJ stared for a moment at Dan. *Hmm, this is new information. He didn't share this with me before. I wonder where this is going...* "Let's see if you can guess," PJ said, looking up at Dan again.

Dan groaned. "You don't want to go that way, PJ, trust me. Just ask her how she's doing, how she's feeling."

"On second thought, don't guess," PJ said. "If you don't mind, before I tell you who it is, he wanted me to ask you how you're doing. How are you feeling?"

"Oh, so it's a 'he,'" she said as she started to think about who it could be. "I'm doing quite well now. I'm fully recovered."

"Okay, that's good to hear," PJ replied as he glanced at Dan, who was now leaning toward them.

"Ask her if she's talking about the MS or the divorce," Dan prompted.

PJ looked at Dan for a moment. This seemed to be getting a little personal, but he asked the question.

"My heart was crushed when he left me for her," Martha responded. "But I've moved on, and I believe I've fallen in love with this wonderful musician!" she added, realizing she knew nothing about the man sharing her table and ordering a garlic shrimp appetizer. "Make that two," she said to the server, then looking across the table at PJ. "So who did you say you were?"

"Tell her who you are, Coach," Dan called over to PJ, as he jumped off the hutch to take a seat in an empty chair a waiter had taken out of service and put next to Martha.

"My name's PJ, and I'm a coach at Rozelle Catholic High School."

Martha's face went blank and her skin paled for a few moments before she spoke. "And why are you here, Coach?" Martha said with a stern look on her face.

"Careful, Coach, you don't want to scare her," Dan said, reaching for her trembling hand. "She's my sister, and she's losing her battle with MS. I'm by her side every night, but she doesn't know it. Last week she was reading literature on suicide methods and even wrote a suicide note. It's on her stereo cabinet," he added with tears welling in his eyes.

PJ noticed Martha's hand stopped trembling when Dan touched it. He didn't know what to say as Martha stared at her hand as well.

"My touch helps her…keeps her calm during the dark moments. But I won't be here to soothe her if I cross over," Dan lamented.

PJ thought for a moment, then he looked at Dan and then at Martha. "Martha, please don't make a scene. I'll tell you who sent me, but you have to swear you won't say I'm crazy."

Martha looked up a PJ. "Who sent you?"

"Your brother, Dan," PJ whispered and waited for her reaction.

Martha grabbed for her cane. "Okay, you nutcase. I'm—"

"Tell her I'm here," Dan said.

"He's here, right next to you in that chair," PJ whispered, motioning for her not to leave.

"Tell her I have to speak with her," Dan shouted at PJ.

"He has to speak with you! Please, I'm just a normal guy, a middleman for him. For some reason he can communicate with me," PJ said, beginning to plead with her. "Listen, I'm not thrilled with this either, but just give me a chance and I'll be gone before you know it."

PJ watched as Martha sat back in her chair and took a sip of her water. "Okay, go ahead. Make your case," she said.

"I first came in contact with your brother about ten weeks ago. I met him while running in Warinanco Park," PJ said.

"He loved to run," she quipped and rolled her eyes.

"He was wearing a Snickers bar T-shirt," he added.

Martha straightened up when he mentioned the candy bar shirt. "You know, he probably would've dated more if he would've just worn a different shirt once in a while!" she said, realizing this guy knew a little something about her late brother. "Okay, so you know my brother ran. You know he wore an ugly shirt. Why are you here? Are you trying to make some money off me? Rob me? Do you think I'm an easy mark? Because let me tell you—"

"Martha, no, no, that's not it. He's brought me here to speak with you, but that's all I know," PJ said as he looked at Dan.

Martha tracked PJ's gaze. "Is he really here?" she asked as she looked at the empty chair.

Dan looked at his sister and then kissed her on her cheek.

Martha blushed and touched her face. Her eyes widened as she looked at PJ.

"He just kissed your cheek," PJ said with a smile.

Martha still wasn't sure what she believed, but she welcomed the positive image of this and decided to go with the flow. "Okay, since he's here, what did he want to say?"

"Tell her I miss her," Dan told PJ.

"He said he misses you," PJ conveyed to Martha.

"Tell him I miss him too," she replied, sounding skeptical.

Dan grew frustrated when he saw the skepticism. He wanted to make some ground on this conversation, so he told PJ to ask her about the note on her stereo turntable.

PJ paused for a moment and then followed through. "Your brother's asking about the note you have hidden on your stereo turntable."

Martha froze for a moment, knowing there was no way anyone could know about that...not anyone. Her eyes welled up, and her hand began to shake again. Once again, Dan took hold of her hand, and it calmed her down.

"Tell her she can't...wait, ask her about the work she's currently doing," Dan suggested to PJ.

"He wants me to ask about the work you're currently doing," PJ told Martha.

Martha gathered her composure, and through teary eyes she told PJ that she used to be a venture capitalist and that all she did now was fund a research grant at Harvard's medical school, where she had people mapping the human genome and trying to find ways to understand MS. "I'm not a scientist, but they do invite me to presentations once in a while to keep me informed on their progress," she explained.

"And how are they doing?"

Martha shook her head and fumbled for a tissue. PJ could see the despair in her eyes. "I don't see any progress. And every day I can see my situation deteriorating more and more. There's no hope for me," she said as she wept quietly, trying not to draw attention to herself.

"Tell her that her team should continue down the KN-498 pathway, and that it will eventually lead to a marker and a cure," Dan blurted out.

"What?" PJ said to Dan as the server placed their cocktails in front of them. "KN – what was it?"

"KN-498?" Martha asked PJ as he stared at Dan.

PJ looked at Dan, who nodded. "Yes, KN-498 … whatever that means. Dan said that it will eventually lead to a cure for MS."

"Tell her in her lifetime," Dan replied, as if speaking directly to Martha.

"In your lifetime, Martha," PJ said. "But you have to drive the program or it will fall apart," he added as he looked up at Dan for approval. Dan gave him a thumbs-up, and PJ relaxed a little.

"In my lifetime," she said. "Wow, that would be something. How does he know this?"

PJ looked at Dan. Dan paused for a moment, then snapped his fingers and said, "Tell her I have friends in really high places."

PJ laughed and said, "He has friends in high places. Also, Martha, even if he couldn't foretell this – which I honestly believe he can – he'll never be able to cross over if he believes you're going to give up on life and kill yourself. He's been holding your hand for nearly twenty years and he won't leave you if you need him. He loves you so much."

"Is he headed to heaven?" she asked.

"I believe he would be if he crossed. He seems like a wonderful soul," PJ answered, sounding more like a mystic of some sort.

"If it means he'll go to heaven, I'll do it," she declared. "Hmm, KN-498 … that was the pathway I was interested in."

"Can I take your order now?" the server asked as he looked at Martha.

Martha looked across at PJ and winked. "Filet of sole sounds like it would hit the spot right now."

"And for you, sir?"

"I'll take the same, with angel food cake for dessert," he added.

"You have my word, PJ," she whispered. "You hear that, Dan?" she shouted loud enough for the neighboring tables to hear.

Dan laughed and gave her a hug.

"He heard you," PJ laughed, and he toasted the two.

Chapter 34

Runner's Hell

The Meet of Champions was just one week away, and RC was now on the radar screen of most teams that had qualified. For most coaches, participating in the Meet of Champions meant an opportunity for their teams to be heavily scouted by local college coaches. As a result, most adjusted their schedules to allow their runners to race on fresh legs.

For PJ, the goal went well beyond the exposure to college coaches. This race was the New Jersey qualifier for the Eastern Championships to be held on November 20th. Based on the discussion he had with Heide Aliaga, this race could be the "unfinished business" that Dan and the other spirits had to go through to be allowed to cross over – the burden that would be lifted from their shoulders and set them free. PJ wasn't sure how this would play out at the Easterns or whether this was the answer at all. He promised to do everything he could to help them cross over, though, and this was one of the avenues he would go down. To do this, his team would have to place in the top three in the New Jersey Meet of Champions.

Monday was a light workout day that consisted of a fartlek run to help the legs recover. Tuesday was a seven-mile day with a two-mile tempo thrown into the middle of it. The team was unusually quiet on these two days, and PJ wanted to stir things up a little during the Wednesday speed workout. He also wanted to drive the message home that the runners they picked off at the end of a race during the last 200 meters counted, so he wanted them to be prepared to dig down deep at the end of the race. He knew that if you dug, most of the time you would find something there.

"Okay, gentlemen," PJ announced as he met the team at trackside. "Before you start to warm up, I need to have these eight orange traffic cones placed in the correct positions along the inside perimeter of the track."

Vlad reached down and picked up the entire stack of cones, and PJ stopped him. "No, Vlad, I want each of you to take one cone. I'll stand here at the starting line and tell you each where to place yours. We're going to place them only along the inside perimeter of the first 200 yards of track. This is the portion of the lap we'll be running."

Vlad dropped all but one of the cones, and the rest of his teammates each grabbed one and started to walk the first 200 meters of the track. "Okay, Vlad, you stop and put your cone down right there and stand next to it," PJ yelled as the team started to walk around the beginning of the first turn. "The rest of you, keep walking."

As they neared the second point, PJ shouted, "Nick, drop your cone there and stand with it! The rest of you, keep walking." Nick stopped next while the rest of the team continued around the track. About twenty-five meters later, PJ asked Andrew to stop and put his cone down. He continued on, asking each of the remaining runners to put their cones down at twenty-five-meter intervals.

When the runners started to head back to him, PJ said, "Whoa, whoa! Get back with your cones!" The runners went back to their cones and stood there staring at PJ, who stood at the starting line and surveyed the scene without saying a word.

"Coach—" Vlad started to speak until he saw PJ wave his hand in a gesture indicating he wanted them to be quiet.

Vlad and his teammates remained silent for the next two minutes until PJ finally said, "Okay, Nick, move your cone five inches up the curve." Nick responded to the request.

"Now, Andrew, move your cone about two inches down the track toward Nick." Andrew followed through on the command.

PJ looked in Matt's direction and said, "Hey, Matt, put some grass under the right side of your cone so it looks more perfectly vertical." Andrew and Nick rolled their eyes at each other as Matt followed through on PJ's request.

PJ fought the urge to lock eyes with Andrew and Nick because he didn't want to laugh. For the next twenty minutes PJ had his runners make final, miniscule adjustments to the cones that bordered on ridiculous. He struggled against the urge to laugh every time a runner groaned after he made a request to make a minor adjustment to the cones. It was clearly driving them nuts.

Finally, PJ exclaimed, "Okay, perfect, get your warm-up started. We're doing twenty-five 200-meter repeats today, with a short recovery across the track. You'll be running at Saturday's race pace, which should be around thirty-seven seconds over 200 meters."

PJ focused on setting up his log sheet to record the times as the runners went through the workout. Meanwhile the team jogged around the track, throwing in some stride outs every so often to stretch their legs.

"A little obsessive with the cone placements, doncha think, Coach?" Kevin remarked as he jogged past PJ.

"All for good reason," PJ answered without looking up from his clipboard. "Those cones are critical to this workout."

Once the team was loose, they approached the starting line to begin the speed work. "Are you serious about doing twenty-five of these, Coach?" Vlad asked.

"Dead serious."

"What's with the cones?" Nick asked.

"You'll see. Be patient," PJ answered smugly. "Just hit thirty-seven seconds for each of these 200s. That's all I ask."

The team nodded and approached the line. No sooner had the last runner edged up to the line than PJ gave the start command. In a flash they were off, and PJ watched as the first runner hit the end of the first 200 in 36.5 seconds, with Vlad, the last runner, coming in at thirty-nine seconds.

"C'mon, Vlad, stick with the leaders," PJ said encouragingly as the team took the shortcut across the field to return to the starting line.

Vlad was a tremendous athlete, but he required a lot of encouragement on some days. By the end of the tenth 200-meter repeat, PJ could see that this was one of those days. Vlad had not done a single repeat in thirty-seven seconds, and he was as slow as forty-one seconds by the tenth. In fact, while Andrew and Nick were managing to hit thirty-seven seconds, the others were stringing out and just going through the workout.

"Come on, guys, let's put some life into this workout and hit the times," PJ urged the team. "You gotta love this stuff!" he added in a sarcastic manner.

"Twenty-five 200-meter repeats isn't a very exciting workout," Vlad exclaimed as he led the group into the eleventh repeat and then immediately fell to the rear of the pack.

PJ grinned to himself when he heard Vlad's comment. "You're not excited about this?" he asked as the group jogged back to start the twelfth repeat.

"Not in the least," Vlad replied, his sentiment supported by a multitude of groans from the other runners. They liked running on the courses and in the woods much better than speed work on a hot track. PJ didn't want to bring his team to the course today, because he wanted to lay low and out of sight of the other teams.

"Okay, just don't disturb any of the cones," PJ said as the group started their twelfth repeat.

Screw these stupid cones, Vlad thought to himself.

By the end of the twentieth repeat, Andrew and Nick were still hitting the times, but the other six had all drifted back and were hitting forty seconds, with Vlad now hitting forty-two.

"You guys have five left. Push through this workout," PJ cheered the team on. "You didn't disturb any of the cones on that last one, did you?" he added.

The runners looked at PJ and indicated they hadn't, but they all had curious looks on their faces. They were primed, but PJ avoided eye contact because it wasn't time to reveal the meaning behind the cones.

The twenty-first through twenty-fourth repeats went much the same way as the last fifteen. Andrew and Nick were up front with the rest of the team trailing, and Vlad continued to take the rear.

After each repeat, PJ made it a point to ask if the cones had been disturbed; and each time he asked, he made it seem like he was a little more concerned. As the group headed across the field after the twenty-fourth repeat to begin their final interval, PJ asked about the cones one more time. This time, the question pushed Vlad past his breaking point.

"What the hell is it with those cones?" Vlad exclaimed as he turned and looked at PJ. "You made us take so much time setting them up, and then you keep asking us if we disturbed them! What use were they?"

"What use were what?" PJ replied with a puzzled look on his face.

"What use were the cones?" Vlad shouted back as he shook his head.

"What cones?" PJ asked, his puzzled look giving way to a grin.

"Those cones!" Vlad barked, pointing toward the cones bordering the track.

PJ squinted his eyes as he shielded them from the sun and scanned the perimeter of the track. "There may have been eight cones out there at one time," PJ said, "but right now you have one final 200-meter interval to run. You've completed twenty-four repeats and you're suffering. You have little minions and demons poking at your legs, arms, heart and soul, because they know the hell you're in, and they also know that those orange things are the eight gates of hell and they don't want you to leave."

PJ scanned the eight runners' expressions, and he knew he had their attention. He found their trigger and was about to pull it. "Gentlemen, those gates will close every 4.6 seconds in sequence, starting with the closest one first. On this last interval you don't want to get caught on the wrong side of a gate when you hear it close. You'll be in runner's hell forever!" He closed his eyes and solemnly shook his head. "When the gate closes, it sounds like this—BOOM!" He reset his watch for the final interval.

The runners looked at each other, rolled their eyes, and stepped up to the line. "Okay, guys, ready…go!" PJ shouted, starting his watch.

He watched the group approach the first cone, with Vlad once again bringing up the rear. Just as Vlad reached the cone, PJ shouted "BOOM!" about as loud as he possibly could. It startled Vlad, whose eyes darted toward PJ. Vlad had a look of panic on his face and immediately increased his leg turnover. In virtually no time, he passed Matt, who was the next runner in front of him.

When Matt passed the second cone in last place, PJ yelled "BOOM!" again, and Matt realized he was last and almost caught on the wrong side of the gate, so he increased his leg turnover as well.

PJ proceeded to yell "BOOM!" every time the last runner in the group passed a cone. Each time, the "BOOM!" motivated that last runner to pick it up. By the time the group was on the final straightaway, the runners were in a very tight pack, spanning the width of the track. Nobody wanted to be last, and every "BOOM!" sparked life into their legs.

It was nearly a dead heat as all the runners crossed the line within inches of each other. PJ clicked his stopwatch and looked down at the time. It read 25.2 seconds, which was twelve seconds faster than the target. PJ grinned, wrote down the time, and watched as the runners regrouped and high-fived each other.

"Okay, guys, well done. Now get your sweats on and warm down," PJ instructed.

As the team jogged around the track during their warm-down, PJ could hear them talking about that last interval. They were energized, and they all seemed to be proud of what they had just done.

As they came to the end of their warm down, Teddy asked PJ, "What was our time for that last 200?"

PJ looked at all the faces staring at him and said, "25.1."

"Holy crap!" said Vlad. "That might have been my fastest 200 ever!"

"What's your takeaway?" PJ asked the group.

"None of us want to get caught in runners' hell!" Andrew said while changing his shoes.

"Exactly!" PJ chuckled. "But even more importantly, even when you think you're done, exhausted, and can't give any more, there's always something left. You just need to reach down and find the last ounce of strength and bring it to the surface. It's there…it's always there!"

PJ added one more point. "Gentlemen, runners' hell is when you lose and say, 'I could've…I should've…I would've! It's too late then. There may never be a next time, and you live with that regret forever. This Saturday, let's not get caught in runners' hell."

Chapter 35

The Meet of Champions

PJ woke up early on Saturday morning and got a quick fartlek in before joining his team at school for the bus ride over to Holmdel Park. Every year on this day, the top three teams and the top ten individuals for the various school districts around New Jersey converged on this park in the central farmlands, to determine the best cross country runners and teams in the state. This year, BCA was once again the clear favorite with the other teams, including RC, vying for a top-five position. The top three teams and the top five individual performers would progress to the Eastern Championships, which was PJ's goal. RC had some unfinished business that had started twenty years earlier at the Easterns.

The bus ride down the Garden State Parkway was uneventful, and the bus passed through the Exit 114 toll at approximately 7:30 a.m. Moments later the bus entered the park and stopped next to the stable near the starting line. PJ gathered his belongings and exited the bus into the crisp fall air. The conditions were perfect for racing today.

PJ walked to the check-in area and picked up his team's entry packet, which contained bib numbers, pins and race-day instructions. As PJ turned to leave the check-in area, he saw Grant Edwins interviewing Tim Hallorin, the coach of the heavily favored BCA team. Grant winked at PJ and went on with his interview. Meanwhile, PJ headed back to the bus where the team had gathered at the team tent.

"C'mon, guys, let's set up over near the finish line," PJ instructed, heading for the other side of the park road near the entrance. He wanted to avoid the other teams as much as possible. During the final minutes of the bus ride, he had noticed another entrance to the park that was off the beaten trail. He was going to have his guys warm up there to avoid pre-race distractions.

As the team broke into a warm-up jog, PJ said, "Guys, we're going to jog down Longstreet Road and make a right onto Roberts Road. I noticed a trailhead entrance about 100 meters from there that leads to a secluded area where only the greatest runners are allowed to go."

Rod grinned, acknowledging what PJ had implied, and led the runners to the trailhead. PJ noticed the deafening silence that surrounded the team as they stepped over the chain that blocked access to the trail.

"How's everyone feeling?" PJ asked as they resumed their warm-up on the trail.

"Ready," said Nick, breaking into a stride and starting to put a little distance between him and the group.

"Good," said a few of the others who followed Nick in his stride out.

Their typical warm-up would consist of an easy jog, followed by accelerations to stretch the legs out. Then the team would do a mix of dynamic and static stretching. At the end of the warm-up, the team would do a couple 400- to 800-meter tempo-paced intervals to get their hearts pumping. PJ observed Andrew and Nick leading the team through the array of pre-race preparations. It was amazing how they had gone from a bunch of cutups to contenders in just one season.

PJ and the team returned to the bus about fifteen minutes before race time. As they put on their racing shoes and bib numbers, PJ reminded them to run as a group and push through the first mile with a vengeance. The second mile had "the bowl," the quarter-mile downhill followed by a steep – but fairly short – uphill section. While the bowl was the most talked-about portion of this historic course, most races were won during the initial mile, so it was important to be in the race from the beginning. He also reminded them that the last mile of the course was nearly all flat and downhill, probably the easiest last mile of any course in New Jersey. "No matter how sore your legs are when you reach the top of the bowl," he told his runners, "have faith. You'll rebound over the last mile!"

As they walked toward the starting line, PJ looked toward Andrew, who appeared to be totally focused and in the zone. "Let's go! Time to let them know we're here," Andrew said to his team as he broke into a stride off the finish line. PJ watched as the seven runners (Kevin Murphy was out with a sore hamstring) started their stride outs. RC's starting position was right between St. Joe's and BCA. Two powerhouses!

"Five minutes until race time," came the call from the starter, Wayne Lebwink.

PJ looked at the team as they gathered around him for one last word of advice. He put his hand out in front of him, and the team put theirs on top of his. For a moment PJ just surveyed their expressions. They looked stoic, ready for battle.

"Remember, be up front with the leaders as a pack during the first mile and a quarter," PJ started, all eyes on him. "And most important of all, when you near the top of the bowl and those demons are poking at your legs and arms and souls, just say to yourself, 'Stay in the game, stay in the game, stay in the game,' and you'll be there…in the game! Good luck!"

Teddy led the team in a quick prayer, and they got onto the starting line. Meanwhile, PJ reset his watch and broke into a run to get into position on the roadway at the top of the first hill about 700 meters into the race.

When the gun went off, PJ started his stopwatch. He looked out toward the pack of runners as they crossed the grassy field leading to the first steep hill. Leading the race were three runners in blue uniforms from BCA, followed by a large group of about twenty-five runners. The RC team was buried in this bunch.

BCA's coach ran stride for stride with PJ as they made their way down the park roadway to catch the runners near the mile mark. "Who do you think will win the individual title?" Hallorin asked PJ as they came to a stop.

"Your lead guy looks good," PJ answered. "What's his name?"

"Frank Kuser," answered Hallorin. "But I think one of those Cranford kids, Amitronni or O'Donnell, could steal it. They've been tough lately." PJ remembered O'Donnell from their tri meet with Westfield, but Amitronni was a recent transfer to the school.

The first two runners to appear as they emerged from the wooded trail were wearing the blue of BCA. "Way to go, gentlemen!" Hallorin yelled as his eyes widened in surprise.

The next group of runners consisted of three additional blue shirts and seven green ones! The entire RC team had placed themselves into the top twelve of the race. "Go, RC!" PJ yelled.

Hallorin looked over at PJ and then back at the front pack. "Watch the RC, guys!" he yelled. "They're here to race!"

"Here we go, Teddy," Andrew said as they picked up the pace on the flat leading up to the mile mark. Teddy responded with Vlad, Nick and Rod in tow. Andrew caught the lead runners as they approached the mile marker.

"4:38," came the call from the timer at the mile mark as Andrew, Teddy and the two runners from BCA came through.

"4:42," was the next read as Nick, Vlad and Rod came through in a tight pack. Not far behind were Mike and Matt, surrounded by a sea of blue and gold shirts. O'Donnell and Amitronni from Cranford were in gold. The blue shirts were a mix of Westfield and BCA runners.

As the second group neared, Hallorin realized the blue shirts were not just from BCA, and he struggled to do the math to see if his team was winning. They were, but not by much. His fifth through seventh runners were mixed in with Westfield's and behind RC's. "Let's go, Tommy, Ed, Kip! Get up with RC in green!" he yelled frantically as the runners passed by.

As he watched his runners head toward the bowl, PJ heard around him the banter of coaches and spectators. More than one was asking who the "team in green" was. This made him smile. He hoped his team could hear this as well.

PJ continued toward the exit of the bowl to watch the lead runners emerge. Once again, two blue-shirted runners came into view as they crested the top of the bowl. Immediately behind them were Andrew, Teddy and the Cranford runners, O'Donnell and Amitronni. And then, to nearly everyone's surprise, came a pack of ten runners – three BCA, four RC, and three from Cranford. This was a three-team race! Somehow, Cranford had positioned themselves into contention as BCA and RC battled for the lead. Westfield was in fourth place; however, their fifth man was well back, and they most likely had no chance to win.

"Stay in the game!" PJ reminded his runners as they crested the hill at the end of the bowl.

Stay in the game, Andrew thought to himself as he focused on the runners in blue ahead of him.

Stay in the game, Teddy thought to himself as he hung with Andrew and felt the pace increasing.

Vlad could feel Nick and Rod on either side of him as they accelerated down the straightaway leading toward the two-mile mark. "Stay in the game," Vlad said to his teammates as O'Donnell and Amitronni drew even with them.

"Fight off the gold and blue shirts!" PJ yelled to the trio as they passed. He started his long run down the park road toward the finish area, buzzing through the crowd of spectators and coaches trying to do the same thing. They were no match for PJ, though, as he ran down the last hill to the grassy field that made up the last 200 meters of the course. Soon the leaders would emerge from the woods and sprint to the finish. PJ stood silently staring toward the trailhead from which the runners would emerge.

"Here they come!" came a yell from a course official. PJ's eyes widened when he saw the two lead runners emerge from the woods. It was Teddy and Andrew, followed by the two BCA runners.

"Push! Push!" PJ yelled from the sidelines.

Andrew responded with a final surge and pushed past Teddy during the last fifty meters. "Push, Teddy!" Andrew cheered as the two raced to victory.

BCA had the next two runners, followed by Cranford's Amitronni and O'Donnell, then another BCA runner, then Vlad, Nick, two BCA runners, and Rod. The next two runners were all from BCA.

PJ added up the scores in his head. RC took first, second, seventh, eighth, and eleventh, for a total of twenty-nine points. BCA took third, fourth, ninth, tenth, and twelfth, for a total of thirty-eight. If Cranford had not taken fifth and sixth, RC would have lost to BCA.

Regardless of the score, PJ had kept his commitment to the "other" RC team. RC had qualified for the Easterns. *The real question now,* he thought to himself, *is will they cross over at the Easterns? Does RC just have to show up, or do they have to win? What if anything had to happen? Would the Easterns be the answer?* PJ wondered. In one week, the answer would be clear.

During the warm-down following the Meet of Champions, PJ and the boys revisited the secluded part of the park where they did their warm-up. They ran through the shady trails and relived not just the race but the whole year as they worked the aches out of their legs.

As the group ran through a heavily wooded section of the park, they noticed what appeared to be a homeless person camped out deep in the woods. The gentleman nodded as the group ran past his home, which was made out of a tarp and an old refrigerator box.

PJ nodded back and said hi as he passed the man. There was a sadness in the exchange. "You guys ran great today!" shouted the man as they passed.

"Thank you," the group of boys replied as they continued. PJ's heart filled with joy, because he realized at that moment that, despite this man's downtrodden situation, somehow he managed to take in the race.

As PJ turned and looked behind him at the gentleman, he noticed he was wearing a pair of Nike LDVs. Those were serious shoes. *Running's a sport for everyone*, PJ thought as the group continued with their warm-down.

Chapter 36

Grant's Article

Saturday, November 20th started off like most Saturdays did for PJ. The alarm clock went off at 5:30 a.m., and PJ rolled over and knocked it off the table onto the floor. He lay in bed for a few more minutes, thinking about the season and today's Eastern States Championship race. RC's first-place finish in the New Jersey Meet of Champions had earned them one last trip to Warinanco. One last opportunity to run the course that now seemed so familiar to his team – or, for today, his *teams*.

Because today was more than just a race. Today, seven of his runners would make the trip that everyone must make one day. They would make that "river crossing" for which every traveler should bring a coin for the ferryman. More importantly, for seven of the runners, this was a trip delayed for twenty years. For them it would be their final mile, the bell lap.

PJ sat up in bed and squinted as he looked out the bedroom window into the yard. The wind gave life to a pile of leaves that had not been picked up. PJ watched as the leaves danced in a vortex from one side of the yard to the other, the mix of yellow, orange and red resulting in a strange but warm glow coming through the window.

He slipped into his shorts and Gel-Kayanos, and before long he was heading down the driveway toward the trail entrance into the woods covering Baldpate Mountain. As he ran, he reviewed the things he had to do to get ready for the race. Gatorade had to be put into the cooler, the race cards had to be completed, and the tent had to be put into the car. He'd have to get to the park by 9:00 a.m. in order to complete all the pre-race activities. PJ decided to run only four miles this morning to accommodate the busy schedule.

About nine minutes into the run, he came to a clearing where an abandoned farmhouse stood next to a small pond. He took a dirt trail off to the side that led to an open field at the top of Baldpate Mountain. As he neared the open field, he watched as the tall grass rippled with the wind, looking like a greenish-brown ocean.

He slowed as he neared the elevation marker that designated this spot as the highest in the county. He came to a stop next to the single oak tree in the middle of the field, and took in the view of the valley and the Delaware River below. He had been to this spot many times before. It was a very personal place for him, as he often came to this place to recover from those hectic days everyone had now and then. This was where he came to think, to recover, to regroup. If running was his religion, then this place was his church.

PJ closed his eyes for a moment and prayed. *Father, please guide them home. Take them home with you.* PJ listened to the whispering of the wind through the leaves.

Dad, I haven't thought of you in a while, he thought, *but I know you're here. I feel you in the wind. You flow past me and I feel you. I hope I've done things right by these boys. I just wish I knew for sure that RC winning this race would bring closure to the boys and help them cross. I hope I can get these "lions" to a peaceful place. I hope my team can come through and win for their teammates of twenty years ago.*

He listened for a reply, a sign, but the only thing he heard was the whispering wind. As he listened, the whispers grew louder. The wind was picking up. He should head back soon to the house. As he turned toward the dirt path leading back home, he noticed that the wind had grown louder. At times it sounded like the roar of a crowd, and at other times it sounded like the distant roar of a lion. He smiled as he realized that what he was hearing could be the sign he was looking for – the crowd roaring as the lions roared to victory!

Thanks, Dad! he thought, and broke into his return run.

"There's French toast on the stove," Taylor yelled from the bedroom as PJ came in through the front door.

PJ loved French toast. He made an abrupt turn and headed for the kitchen. He covered the toast with salt and gulped down the first slice in one bite. As he ate, he thumbed through the morning newspaper. He stopped chewing as his eyes fell upon the headline at the top of the sports section: "Where the Lions Roam – RC Going for XC Title Today."

Grant Edwins had written nearly a full page about the RC team's season and the race today. PJ stopped eating and continued to read the article. "For the first time in nearly two decades, Rozelle Catholic high school has a team competing for the coveted Eastern States Champion title, having already claimed the New Jersey State Championship." He went on to mention how hard the boys from RC had worked over the summer, and the training tactics PJ used that were reminiscent of the teams fielded by RC twenty years earlier. The hard pre-race mileage, the hill work, and the double workouts were all part of the repertoire that made those earlier teams great. PJ smiled as he sipped his coffee and continued to read.

"This team reminds me of the greatest of all the RC teams, the one taken from us the morning of the Eastern States Championship in 1984. They were such nice young men, taken from this world way before their time, all honor students with a multitude of quirks and personalities, each with a story never fully developed, never fully heard. And even though time can heal most wounds, there are some who will never forget this loss – their parents, families, and closest friends. For them I have written this article; because no matter how hard today's RC team has trained for themselves and Coach Irwin, today they run a race long overdue. They run to bring home a victory that's been too long in coming. They run to bring a happy ending to a tragic story that started over twenty years ago.

"The team captain was Pete Bailey back then. Pete was a senior with a scholarship offer from Villanova. He also had one of the highest grade point averages in the school. Pete's dad still runs the garage on Chestnut Street where his son used to work during the summer. In fact, the entire team used to work there during the summers to earn spending money. Their summer group runs used to begin and end at the garage. I interviewed Pete once and asked him what he wanted to do for a career. Without any hesitation he replied that he wanted to become a doctor and work for the Peace Corps. He wanted to dedicate his life to helping others.

"Pete's dreams – along with the other boys' – were cut short by a drunk driver on that fateful morning in 1984. The accident occurred on the Cross Bronx Expressway as the team headed to Van Cortland Park to run in the Easterns Championship. It was there that the El Camino racing along at 110 mph smashed head-on into the RC van. Their lives were over in an instant. That's all it took! (Moms and dads, I hope you're reading this and taking notice. Love your children today, for tomorrow they may be gone!)

"Rather than write about how these boys died, I want to write about how they lived and who they were. I want to give them a voice and let their parents know that we have not forgotten them. I never will.

"Dan Hutchens was another lost on that fateful day. Dan's true love was wrestling, but he used cross country as a means of getting in shape. His 5K PR was 15:23, and during his junior year outdoor season, he ran a 4:19 mile. All this, and he was an even better wrestler. He won three consecutive state championships before his senior year even started!

"Dan was also on his way to being the valedictorian at RC. He never received less than an A in any subject. I remember the stories his friends told at his funeral about how he gave unselfishly of himself to others. As I recall, he worked at a local gas station and was often helping motorists with directions and car problems, and he never accepted payment in return.

"And I remember the Snickers addiction! Dan loved Snickers candy bars. He had this old Snickers shirt that he wore to every race, and his locker usually held a treasure chest full of Snickers bars, which he gladly shared with his teammates (and an old reporter on one occasion).

"Without doubt, Dan would have become a writer. His way of relaxing before a race was to read poetry. (If I remember correctly, he liked the works of Robert Frost.) Such talent, warmth and beauty, all snatched away from this world in a single moment. To some, their deaths at the hands of a drunk driver made them a statistic. In reality, they were so much more.

"David Santos and Evan Kite were best friends. They were always together, whether it was practicing the French horn or being the first to cross the finish line during a 5K dual meet. Santos wanted to be a meteorologist, while Kite was interested in business. Santos was really into mapping, and provided course maps to the New Jersey State Athletic Commission for use at their meets. Santos was planning to attend the University of Wyoming after graduation. His father and uncle were talented runners in their day for RC.

"Kite was interested in attending Trenton State College. His younger sister, Jana, took up running the day he died, and became one of the first American female marathoners to run faster than two hours and forty minutes.

"Rob O'Mally was the youngest of five boys who all attended RC. His brothers Mark and Jack became two of the greatest running coaches in New Jersey history. Jack still coaches to this day, and has a track meet in North Jersey named after him. Rob's father was a real fan of running. One day, when I interviewed Rob after he won the Union County XC Championship, he told me how his father would whistle loudly when it was time for him to make his move. He went on to reflect on how, during solo runs in the park, that whistle seemed to live in the area of the lake, and he often found himself picking it up a bit, even though he didn't have to. I asked him why he thought this was, and he replied, 'I respect my dad!'

"Rob wanted to be an educator. He wanted to give back to the community, he once told me. Imagine that! An educator who might be interested in fostering the development of parental respect! How many students were denied the opportunity to learn under Rob O'Mally? Let's see, a typical career might last 45 years. Maybe, on average, a teacher would have 200 students per year. That means about 9,000 lives were denied his influence! Drunk drivers, your impact is widespread!

"I remember Bill Bahsman's eulogy was given by his best friend, Bambi. Holding back tears, she spoke of his warmth and quiet nature. She recalled the first time she saw him run with cho-pat straps on each leg to prevent knee pain. She said he looked like a marionette! I recall how she turned serious at that point and said, 'But he ran like the wind. His form was deceptive. He looked like he wasn't moving too quickly, but he could cover ground.'

"Bahsman wanted to be a chemical engineer, and he would have been a good one. He was environmentally conscious and wanted to work in an industry where his influence would keep the environment safe. He worked during the summer at the now-defunct Union Carbide. He always hoped to one day work there as an engineer. I can't help but think if more people like Bill worked for companies like Union Carbide, we would have fewer Bhopal-like disasters. (A week after the team perished in the bus accident, an explosion at a Union Carbide facility in Bhopal, India, released methyl isocyanate, a toxic material, resulting in the deaths of over 2,000 people.) More people like Bill and fewer drunk drivers; what a wonderful world this would be.

"Mark Hills wanted to be a cadet at West Point and serve our country, and he was well on his way. He had earned a 1550 on his SATs and had a recommendation from his local senator. I interviewed Mark when he was athlete of the week and found he had a deep love for our country. He volunteered often to help the various local service organizations. He was an Eagle Scout, the second in his family. His dad was the first.

"In closing, while I do have a few years under my belt as far as covering cross country races at Warinanco Park, I'll see the course in a different light today. As hundreds of fans and competitors make their way around the course, I'll be there to see the lions.

"As I recall, this place is sacred. It's the place where the lions roam!"

PJ stared silently at the paper for a few moments, then he felt a hand on his shoulder. It was Taylor.

"I'm so proud of you," she whispered in his ear. "The big cats are waiting for you!"

He grabbed her hand for a moment, then got up and walked out of the kitchen, never looking back. She wasn't supposed to see the tears.

Chapter 37

Chains Forged in Life

———————————

Albert Santos woke up in a heavy sweat at 6:00 a.m. He rushed to the kitchen and pulled a bottle of water from the fridge, leaned against the kitchen wall, closed his eyes, and gulped down the water. This made him sweat even more, and he could feel his heart racing in his chest. The dream that had haunted him last night had finally won and forced him to wake up, but he remembered every second of it.

Hugh Bailey, Peter Bailey's father, was in the dream. He came to their house to make sure they were going to the race today. It was the Easterns, and Peter needed him. But Hugh was wearing chains like Jacob Marley! He looked like hell, like the weight of the world was on his shoulders. Bailey's voice strained as he begged for forgiveness for David's death. His face was contorted and strained and deathly pale. He said his alcoholism was a disease, and he would have been there if he was a better man. He threw himself on the floor and crawled toward Santos, begging for forgiveness.

"I would trade my life for theirs if I could, but I can't!" Bailey cried as his ragged fingers grabbed hold of Santos' foot.

He looked up at Santos and stared; he was in agony. Bailey was decaying right there in front of him, and it was horrifying. Santos tried to back away, but he couldn't. He was powerless. Bailey's chains clattered while he thrashed about on the floor in front of Santos.

"Please, help me!" Bailey groaned as he melted into a slump of decaying, oozing flesh.

Santos closed his eyes and prayed. "Dear God, why? I can't forgive him. Not him. Never!"

Albert Santos was a religious man, and for the last twenty years he had been torn between his hatred for Hugh Bailey and his religious upbringing, in which forgiveness was a virtue. Never talking to Hugh Bailey was about the best he could do, as far as forgiveness went. Albert could not forgive Hugh Bailey for not driving the bus that day, for assigning the task to a rookie driver instead.

"Dad, it wasn't his fault!"

He heard a faint, familiar voice. It was David's! He opened his eyes and saw only the crumpled mass of what used to be Hugh Bailey oozing in front of him. He glanced past the mass toward the front door, which was slowly coming to a close, as if someone had just left the house.

Albert ran for the door and flung it open, surveying the street for any sign of an intruder or David...or anyone. There was no one in sight. As he turned to walk back into the house, he noticed a reflection in the glass on the front door. It was David, standing behind him. "Come to my race today!" he heard David say.

Albert swung around, but again he found no one. When he turned back and looked at the glass door, he saw only himself in the reflection.

It was at this point that he awakened.

Albert took another sip of the cool water without opening his eyes. His body responded with a cool sweat. He felt a hand touch his, and he opened his eyes. Standing next to him was Ann Marie, his wife of thirty-nine years. "Are you okay?" she asked.

"Uh...yeah, I, uh, had a nightmare. It must have been something I ate. I'm so thirsty."

Ann Marie stared at him for a few moments, as if she had something to say. "Yes...probably something you ate." She moved closer and hugged him.

"You're trembling!" Albert said as he put his arms around her.

"Did your nightmare involve Mr. Bailey and David?" Ann Marie whispered, staring at the wall, still embracing her husband.

"Yes," Albert replied, and Ann Marie clenched him tighter.

So what could it mean, Al? I had the same dream! she thought to herself. "I miss him so much," she said out loud, her voice thick with tears. "We should go to the race today."

"We will, we will," Albert said, comforting her. "I have some unfinished business I need to take care of."

Chapter 38

Reunited

PJ arrived at the park at 9:00 a.m. sharp and parked his car near the flower garden by the 600-meter pole. As he was walking the course toward the baseball field bleachers where his team and the few RC spectators normally gathered, an older Latino runner in a green-and-white-striped running singlet greeted him.

"Hello, Coach," the man said as he made his way around the 600-meter pole.

"Hi," PJ replied as he looked for a good spot to set up the team tent. *It's windy today,* he thought. *Better set it up near the bleachers on the first-base side of the baseball field.* As he approached the location, a handful of students from RC came running over.

"Need a hand with that, Coach?" yelled Kathleen Murphy. She was sitting in her wheelchair behind the bleachers.

"Hi, Kathleen. Yes, I could use some help. I always seem to screw it up!" PJ laughed and gave her his clipboard and a pen.

"Good luck today," Kathleen replied as she grabbed his hand and squeezed it.

"Thanks, Kathleen, I think we're ready," he said, then turned and saw the group of Kathleen's friends busy setting up the tent. He decided they didn't need him and turned back to Kathleen. Handing her the blank race cards, he barked, "You know what to do with these!"

"Yes sir!" Kathleen replied as she grabbed them and fumbled for the pen to start filling them out.

"Are you Coach Irwin?" came a voice from behind PJ. He turned around and saw an older couple standing arm in arm behind him.

"Well, it depends. Is he in trouble?" PJ joked.

"No. Our son ran for RC many years ago, and we thought we'd come down to see the race today," the stocky gentleman answered.

"Well, thank you for your support," PJ said, extending his hand. "I'm Coach Irwin."

"I'm Dan Hutchens," the man said. "My son—"

"Ran for RC in the early '80s," PJ interrupted as he looked over the gentleman's shoulder toward his wife. She seemed distant, nervous, as she surveyed the park. She seemed to be looking for something. "I read about him in the paper this morning," PJ added.

"This is my wife, Clare," Daniel Hutchens Sr. added.

"Hello, Clare," PJ said, stepping forward to shake her hand. She was trembling.

"Hello," she replied, pulling away and taking hold of her husband's arm.

"You're welcome to camp out with us near the team tent today," PJ urged as he pointed toward the partially assembled monstrosity surrounded by a group of teenagers.

"Oh, that would be nice," Clare replied.

"Clare Hutchens!" someone yelled from the center of the baseball diamond. A thin, dark-haired woman started to run toward Clare, and in a moment they were embracing.

The woman had been walking with an Asian man across the diamond before she ran to hug Clare. When the man reached them, he held his hand out to Dan Hutchens and said, "Dan, how are you and Clare doing? It's been too long."

Dan turned and looked at PJ, who was standing next to him, and said, "Coach Irwin, this is Linda and Kevin Kite. Their son Evan ran with my son."

"Oh yes, his sister was the sub-three-hour marathoner," PJ said, shaking hands with Kevin, whose grip was strong from all his years as a chiropractor and massage therapist.

"Coach, I wanted to thank you for what you said to Martha," Dan Hutchens interrupted. "We were so worried about her. She was becoming reclusive, but whatever you told her gave her the strength she needed to not only deal with the MS, but wage war against it!"

"I'm glad to hear that," PJ said as he watched Mrs. Kite and Mrs. Hutchens wipe tears from each other's eyes. In the distance, he noticed Grant Edwins approaching him. He was walking with two other couples, and PJ could tell he was bringing them toward him. "Excuse me," he said, going to meet Grant.

"Mr. Edwins, thank you for the nice article today," PJ said, holding out his hand to greet him.

"It was a wonderful article, wasn't it?" said the woman standing next to Grant with a proud smile. "You must be Coach Irwin," she added as she stuck out her hand. "I'm Ellen O'Mally, and this is my husband, John, and our friends the Hills, Joan and Tom."

"Yes, I recognize the names from our record board at school, as well as from Mr. Edwins' article this morning," PJ said.

"Yes, isn't he a dream!" Ellen giggled as she hugged Grant, whose eyes revealed he was loving the attention.

"I'm so happy you came to the race today. The team's really pumped and the extra cheering could put us over the top," PJ said as he turned and pointed to the others. "I believe they may be friends of yours?"

"Clare!" yelled Joan Hills, as the four excused themselves to greet the other parents from the class of '84, leaving PJ alone with Grant Edwins.

"Mr. Edwins, I must thank you again for that nice article. It put things in perspective for me."

"Don't mention it, PJ," Edwins answered. "I'm not sure why I wrote it. It sort of just came to me."

"I guess it gave their parents the strength to come out and see a race and support us."

"I guess it did. Or maybe they need to see the race as closure, a healing process."

"Whatever it is, you got them to come – and look at them," PJ said. The parents in the group were laughing and talking. "Who would've thought that they'd be able to smile here, of all places?"

"Let's hope you guys win," Grant said, winking at PJ.

PJ's stomach did a flip-flop. "Yes, let's hope we win."

Tom and Sherry Bahsman stepped from their SUV at a quarter till ten. "Come on, Tom!" Sherry said as she headed for the starting line. "It's over here."

Tom Bahsman was an ex-country singer who had written and produced a handful of songs and a number of commercial jingles between 1965 and 1984, but he hadn't touched his guitar since the day his son Bill died. The Bahsmans were getting to the park a little later than Sherry would have liked, because Tom had the sudden urge to play his guitar that morning. It took him nearly an hour to find it in the fire trap known as the attic at their house; but he did, and he played it for her while they drove to the park.

He finished with a Jackson Browne song called "For a Dancer." His eyes welled as he sang, "Don't let the uncertainty turn you around… go out and make a joyful sound." He thought of all the music he had failed to write since his son's death, and knew he had some healing and catching up to do. Today would be the first day for that. After all, last night he heard his son's voice tell him there were important songs that are yet unwritten – that, and that he should come to the race today!

As the group of parents gathered around Sherry and Tom, Sherry pulled Joan Hills close and said, "Did you have the dream too?" Joan simply stared at her without answering, and the rest of the group all focused on Joan. Sherry surveyed the others and said, "Okay, people, no need to answer. I see it in your eyes."

Joan looked at her husband and asked, "You too, Tom?"

"Yes, Joan."

"I had a dream too," said Dan Hutchens as he looked at Ellen O'Mally.

"I think we all did!" Ellen remarked. "What does it mean?"

The group stood there silent as PJ approached. "So how's everyone doing?" he asked, noticing the fan base had grown larger.

"Well, Coach," Ellen O'Mally started, "it appears we all had similar drea—"

"What Ellen's trying to say," interrupted her husband, "is that we all felt it was time to come out and see RC win this race!"

"Yes, exactly," Tom Bahsman said as he shook PJ's hand. "We're the Bahsmans, Tom and Sherry."

"Nice to meet you both," PJ said. "Here's a course map for you, so you'll know where the race goes." PJ excused himself then and trotted off to meet his team, who had just arrived with Carmine on the school bus.

"Ellen, do you want him to think we're nuts?" John O'Mally blurted out in front of the others.

They stood silent for a moment until Ellen told her husband, "Oh, shush!" Then the group broke out in laughter because they remembered that was the same thing she used to say back in the early '80s, during arguments with her husband.

Chapter 39

Embrace the Wind

The RC bus pulled in right beside the one belonging to the BCA team, who were busy unloading their gear. The RC boys jumped off their bus and headed toward PJ.

"You guys look ready," PJ said.

"We feel ready," Teddy answered as he rolled his eyes toward the BCA team and smiled.

"Okay, guys, we have about an hour, and I'd like you to get in an easy jog and then meet by the bleachers to review strategy before the race."

"Okay, Coach," Andrew said as he picked up the pace in order to drop off his bag near the team tent. The other runners followed Andrew's lead, and in a few moments they were all heading out onto the course for a relaxed warm-up.

PJ looked nervously around the park for signs of his *other* team, but they were nowhere to be seen. The weather looked threatening, the early morning sun continuing to give way to overcast skies, and the wind was beginning to pick up.

PJ watched as the contingents from St. Joe's, Cranford, Westfield, Kittatinny, Old Bridge and Hopewell Valley streamed past, to set up their camps and start their warm-up routines. He turned and noticed the race timers, Racing NJ, struggling to secure the results display board to keep it from being blown down by the wind.

At 9:30 a.m., the RC runners returned to do some final stretching and get some last-minute instructions from PJ before heading over to the starting line. He gave each one their number and pins, and they put them on – along with their racing spikes – as they continued to stretch.

"This wind's going to kick my ass today!" exclaimed Nick.

"Tell me about it!" Matt chimed in. "I was standing still when it hit me head-on. I hate that feeling."

"Yeah, that and the feeling that you can't breathe when it blows directly into your face," Rod lamented, shaking his head and looking concerned.

"Ah crap, I got dirt in my eyes from that gust at the end of our warm-up," added Teddy. "I can't run when it's like this. My eyes dry up."

Andrew, Mike and Kevin said nothing, but the looks on their face said it all to PJ. They were also concerned about the wind and race-day conditions.

PJ didn't like to see the breakdown in confidence occurring right before his eyes. This group of overachievers that had come from out of nowhere and was ready to claim the East Coast Championship was showing a weak link. They had worked so hard to get there, overcome so much, devoted themselves to a workload that other sports view as punishment. They had transformed themselves into champions. They were one race away – one important race away – and their spirit was about to break. *Their tremendous spirit,* PJ thought to himself.

"Okay, knuckleheads, gather 'round," PJ barked, taking a seat on the bottom bench of the bleachers, filled mostly now with parents of RC runners present and past.

PJ heard a giggle from behind him as the boys huddled around him and directly in front of the bench. Taylor and David had just arrived, and David got a kick out of his use of "knucklehead." PJ held out his hand and guided David to sit with the team in front of him. A number of parents seated on the bleachers smiled and positioned themselves so they could eavesdrop on the pep talk PJ was about to give.

"I'm so proud of you guys," he started off. "A few months ago we weren't even expected to field a team – and we certainly weren't on anybody's radar to make it to the state championship. But with the hard work you put in, we managed to win it!"

PJ looked beyond the group toward the starting line, as other teams began to congregate there. The wind was gusting, and a few runners were chasing their bib numbers across the field in front of the line.

"But now, gentlemen, I want to tell you the truth of the matter. It wasn't just the hard work that got you here. It was your *spirit!* Your incredible spirit! And I'm proud to have been exposed to it. It made me a better coach. A better man."

The boys continued to stretch but were beginning to take note of what he was saying.

"I have to ask you guys now, though, if you understand what I mean by *your incredible spirit!* Do you understand the concept of your spirit?" Andrew looked up at PJ. "Andrew, do you know?"

"It's who we are," he answered as the others looked at him.

"And it's who you've decided to be," PJ added. "Your spirit is developed as you go through life. It comes from those who have gone before us and influenced us."

PJ looked back over his shoulder at the parents of the seven boys that never had the chance to run this race and saw that they were listening to his words. He gave them a slight nod and turned back to the team.

"Your spirit comes from those who have influenced you in life. You adopt certain qualities, traits and principles from these people and make them your own. And together, what you adopt becomes *yours, your spirit, YOU!* It may have been a parent or a teacher or a relative who influenced you. Or it may have been a friend you respected and wanted to be more like. Or it could've even been a coach! It's most likely that your spirit's a combination of the *best of* a number of these people. And it's because of your spirit that we're state champions and here today! Your spirit, above all, is what got you through the twice-a-day workouts, the hill repeats, the additional fast mile following those early dual meet races!"

Nick held up his fist, and Teddy tapped it with his.

"It was your spirit that got us here. Do you know that in the teachings and passages of many religions, the concept or presence of the *spirit* is communicated in a form that's more real – more physical – so that it can be understood and felt? For instance, in Catholicism, Judaism, and even with the American Indians, the *spirit* is described as a wind, a breeze, a breath. Andrew, what do you say when someone sneezes?"

Andrew looked up. "Uh, God bless you?"

"That's right. We say that because the belief was that when you sneeze, you exhaust all the breath you have—all of it completely—and this is the only time the body is without spirit. So saying 'God bless you' protects you from 'evil' until your breath or 'spirit' returns."

PJ looked down solemnly and continued. "I never met my father. He died in the war shortly after I was born. But I've felt his spirit on windy days, so I've come to love windy days. I'd rather run on a windy day than any other day, because it's in the wind that I find my strength, my answers – my answers for those times when I'm searching, or puzzled, or feeling lost." PJ looked at Andrew and said, "When those voices are in my head, asking questions or taunting me. When I wish my father was nearby to give encouragement or help me through a difficult time."

PJ paused and then carefully went on. "I'll purposely go out on a windy day to feel the wind in my hair. I imagine my father is there, running his fingers though my hair, telling me *everything's alright* and assuring me that he's proud of me and what I've become. I felt him this morning as I ran through Baldpate Mountain. He's with me. His *spirit* lives within me. I know it."

PJ looked up and noticed he had every runner's attention. They were understanding every word.

"So today, don't fear the wind. Embrace it. For it should remind you of the *spirit*…and of all those people who have impacted you in your lifetime. I don't really care how fast you run today. What I do care about is that you represent the people who have made you who you are. That you run with their courage, their intelligence, their *spirit* in your hearts. I hope you'll take the time to dedicate your race to them today, that you'll imagine them running with you, stride for stride, breath for breath, and that you'll enjoy this fleeting moment known as the Easterns Championship."

"Final call! All runners, please report to the starting line," announced the starting-line official.

"Hands in, guys," PJ said, and the team reached in and held each

206

other's hands. "When you get to the starting line, feel the wind and remember those who have made you the fine men you are. Dedicate your race to them. And one other thing – take a moment to look directly into the direction the wind is coming from. Face it. You shouldn't fear it. Your spirit is there. As the great Bob Dylan said, it's where your answers can be found...*blowing in the wind*! Good luck."

Taylor noticed that David's eyes darted toward his father's when he heard the Bob Dylan quote. He knew he'd heard it before, but he couldn't recall that it had been written on the bathroom wall at the truck stop on the route to the running camp.

PJ watched from his knees as his team trotted toward the starting line. They looked focused and ready to run. The wind was now their friend.

Clare Hutchens watched as the coach gathered his clipboard and stopwatch from the grass in front of him and rose to his feet. She was impressed with the way PJ shared his feelings with the boys, and how he communicated the concept of the spirit. It was poetic, the kind of stuff her son Dan would've loved. She wasn't sure why she was there, but for a moment she could hear Dan in PJ's words. When the wind picked up slightly and took hold of PJ's hair, making it flow, Clare noticed and was reminded of his message to the boys: *take a moment to look directly into the direction the wind is coming from...it's where your answers can be found!*

Turning her head to the north to look *into the direction the wind was coming from*, she faced a lovely wooded area just behind the starting line. The trees were so beautiful as they swayed slightly in the wind, with the remaining leaves reflecting the sunlight starting to peek through the clouds. She felt the wind in her own hair and imagined Dan there with her. She could feel him. Then she closed her eyes and remembered his favorite poem by Robert Frost, and the words just flowed from her. "The woods are lovely, dark and deep ..." she said as her husband turned and kissed her softly on the back of her neck, "...but I have miles to go, and promises to keep," she continued. "Miles to go, and promises to keep..." she said again as a tear escaped her shut eyes.

As Clare opened her eyes and again focused on the wooded area, she noticed movement near an opening between the trees. The sleek figure of a runner appeared and slowly emerged from the woods. There was something familiar about his stride, and when he stopped momentarily to stretch, she started to tremble. It was her Danny! Her eyes fixed on his, and she could see his smile.

"My God!" Clare said, tightening her grip on her husband's hand. Dan Sr. turned and looked at her and then in the direction she was staring. "It's him," she said.

Mr. Hutchens stood motionless as he tried to understand what he was seeing.

"Do you see him?" Clare asked as she smiled. "He's beautiful!"

Sherry Bahsman was standing next to Clare and heard what she said to Dan. She too looked toward the woods and could see the boy, who turned and gestured toward the woods until a second runner emerged. She knew this boy. It was Bill.

"Tom, you're not going to believe this, but look," she said to her husband as she pointed toward the woods.

Tom's knees nearly buckled as he realized the boy that just emerged from the woods with the strap around his knee was his son, Bill.

As John and Ellen O'Mally reached out to support Tom, they followed his stare toward the woods, and saw three runners in what appeared to be the final phases of loosening up.

"John, doesn't that boy look like our Robby?" Ellen exclaimed, continuing to watch the Irish-looking boy take his stride.

John O'Mally glanced toward the boy and then stood up, letting go of Tom Bahsman, who tumbled to the ground. He turned to his wife with tear-filled eyes and said, "It's Robby!"

Bahsman clambered to his feet again and looked at O'Mally. "Praise God," he said, putting a hand on John's shoulder.

"Are you guys seeing this?" Tom Bahsman said to the Santos, Kites and Hills.

They were.

They stood motionless as their sons emerged from the woods and joined the others in what appeared to be their old warm-up ritual. The boys made their way from the woods toward PJ and the parents. PJ smiled and looked at the parents, who appeared to be frozen in the moment.

"Dan, I have to go hug him," Clare said, starting toward the boy.

Dan grabbed her arm. "No, Clare, not now. They've been waiting twenty years for this moment."

As the boys approached PJ, Pete Bailey called out, "Do you have any last-minute instructions for us, Coach?"

PJ started to speak but stopped as the boys jogged right past him. When he turned, he found them gathered around Mr. Bailey, who had arrived only moments before.

Hugh Bailey looked different today. For one thing, he wasn't wearing black. Instead, he wore a sweat suit and had a stopwatch around his neck. But it was more than that. Something else seemed different. He actually looked somewhat happy, or at least at peace.

"Well, uh…it's been a long time, boys, and I'm not sure what to say," Bailey started. "Maybe I should start with 'I love you.'"

"That's not enough to get us across the line first, is it?" Rob O'Mally joked.

"Years ago, I probably would've agreed with you, but right now, I think it needs to be said," Bailey said warmly. "I made you kids work so hard, and I don't think I ever told you how proud I was of you. Instead, I retreated to the bottle after every workout and spent too much time sleeping it off or moping around with a hangover, when I should've been spending more time showing my love for you. I should've been with you when the accident happened, but I woke up late after a night of heavy drinking. That poor substitute driver was blamed for the crash, but he shouldn't have died – I should have," Bailey said through tear-filled eyes.

"We all loved you, Coach," Dan Hutchens said as the others nodded in agreement.

"And we knew you loved us," David Santos said. "We – and our families – will always be grateful for the short time we had together," he added, looking at his father, Albert.

Albert Santos walked toward Hugh Bailey and hugged him. "My friend," he said, "I was wrong for holding this grudge. I hope you can forgive me."

Bailey fought for composure and answered, "I hope we can be friends."

"Three minutes 'til race time!" came another announcement from the starting-line official.

"Okay, guys!" Coach Bailey sprung to life right before PJ's eyes. "These guys are going to go out hard and you need to be in the race at the 600 pole. These are the cream of the crop. There won't be any novice rabbits out there. If you expect to win, you should be in front. Try to go by the mile in 4:40. You trained for this, and you're capable of doing this. You'll drop most of the race at this pace, and that's quite all right! When you make the turn to go around the lake, I want you to be together, and I want you to surge at this point for about a minute. A *spirit-* …uh, *will*-breaking surge," he said, laughing quietly.

"When you emerge from around the lake at the two-mile mark, you'll hear people saying things like, 'Holy Cow!' and 'They're running too fast!' and 'It's not possible!'" Bailey said matter-of-factly. "I want you to look into these people's eyes and grin. Let them know you're in control of everything you're doing and setting a new standard. Let them know that this race is yours, and that you own this course. This is *where the lions roam*!"

The boys smiled at that.

"When you get to the track, the entire world will be there watching you finish. Run that last lap as if it'll be your last, as if you'll be leaving this place and never coming back!"

The boys looked at PJ and then back to Hugh Bailey.

"And one last thing. I repeat…I love you."

Hugh Bailey stood motionless with his eyes closed for a moment, as the seven spirits gave him a hug and headed off to the starting line. He reopened his eyes and saw PJ slowly approaching him with his clipboard in hand. Bailey quickly surveyed the landscape as if he was searching for something.

"You were the coach?" PJ said in disbelief.

"I was, but that was a long time ago," Bailey added as he again surveyed the park, as if looking for something.

PJ surveyed the park as well, but he had no idea what Bailey was looking for. "Well, your advice seemed pretty on the mark for someone that's been away from it for a while," PJ teased.

"You think so?" Bailey asked. "It's been so long. I wasn't sure what to say. I never really knew what I was doing. I always thought of it as a hobby, something almost anyone could do."

"Well, you sounded like you knew what you were talking about," PJ said as he and Bailey walked toward the starting line.

"You know, you should make sure your runners protect Andrew," Bailey said, resetting his stopwatch.

PJ looked at Bailey for a moment and thought, *Yeah, you don't know what you're doing, do you, Mr. Bailey? What else don't you know?* Hugh Bailey was right, and PJ moved behind his runners to offer some final encouragement.

"Matt and Nick, I want you to help Andrew get out cleanly. You got it?"

Matt and Nick both looked at PJ and nodded with fire in their eyes. They looked at Andrew, who was focusing on the course in front of him. Mike, Rod, Teddy and Nick also noticed Andrew's demeanor. He was focused. He was visualizing. He was hearing that voice again.

Chapter 40

That Voice is Back

The spirit of Pete Bailey moved toward the starting line with the others. He positioned himself right behind Andrew as the other spirits gathered just behind the RC team. Pete leaned forward until his mouth was right next to Andrew's head.

"Andrew," Pete whispered, "I was with you at Brundage when you were in middle school, and I've been by your side ever since."

Andrew heard the voice and looked down at his feet before glancing at his teammates briefly, to see if they were paying any attention to him. He wondered if they had their own voices, if they could hear his...

"You've done everything you needed to do to prepare for this race. All you need to do now is run it," Pete whispered.

Andrew smiled and hopped up and down on his toes for a moment to shake off the nervousness.

"It's nearly race time. Take a nice, long stride out and let everyone know you're here to race!" Pete urged.

Andrew turned to his teammates and grinned. They stared at him, not sure what to make of the look on his face. "Gentlemen, let's let 'em know we're here!" he said, and then he broke into a ferocious 100-meter stride out off the starting line. His teammates followed with the same level of energy. They were showing off. It was part of the game.

Pete Bailey looked at his six teammates and said jokingly, "Well, what are we waiting for?" and he broke into a similar stride out, just as his mortal teammates had done. The rest of the 1984 squad followed his lead.

Both RC teams gathered about eighty meters in front of the line, and Andrew called his teammates into a huddle. The spirits gathered around the perimeter to listen in as well.

"You guys read the paper this morning, didn't you?" They all nodded. "Then you know this isn't just for us today. Their parents are here! Here to see us, to see their sons through us! Got it?" He peered into the eyes of his teammates. "I'm going out hard today, 4:40 pace maybe. I know I can handle it. And if I can't, well, at least the others will know I was here, because if they go with me they'll be hurting. I just figure I can handle the hurt a little better than them."

"I bet you can," Nick agreed.

"Come with me, you guys," Andrew challenged the others. "Let's go for it. Total annihilation. No prisoners. Today we run like lions released from their cages."

"We're with you," Vlad boasted. "I feel ready for this."

"Me too!" said Nick, who had been quiet all morning.

Andrew put his hands up on Teddy's and Nick's shoulders. The others did the same, and the group huddled close. Andrew put his head down and led the group in prayer.

"Dear Lord, today we run not only to give you praise, but to honor our teammates from twenty years ago. Let us represent them well, as true gentlemen, as we go out and kick some ass. Amen!" Andrew was grinning as he looked up to the stares of his six teammates. "I said, 'Amen!'" he exclaimed.

"Amen!" said Mike with a smile.

Pete looked at his teammates, and they were smiling.

"Pete, I do believe they're ready!" Dan said with a smile.

As the RC runners trotted back to the starting line, Pete and the other spirits jogged behind them.

"You know, Pete, I'm not sure what to make of this, but I see this bright light just beyond the starting line," Dan said.

"I see it too," Rob said. "What is it?"

"I'm not sure," Bill replied. "I noticed it earlier this morning, when

I saw my father playing the guitar next to his car. Funny, I haven't seen him play that thing in years! Son of a gun looks like Clint Black with that thing in his hands."

Mark nodded to the group. "I see it now also. It seems to be getting brighter."

As they arrived back at the starting line, they stood directly in front of PJ.

"I see the light also," said David. He looked over at Pete. "I first noticed it as my dad gave your father a hug this morning."

They turned and looked at PJ with puzzled looks on their faces. "What's it mean, Coach?" they asked him.

PJ looked around so as not to draw attention to the fact that he was about to appear to be talking to himself. "Uh, what does *what* mean?" he asked through clenched lips.

"We all see this glorious bright light over there," Dan said, pointing in the direction of the skating rink. PJ looked but saw nothing. "It seems so warm, so bright. It's beautiful. I saw this light once before, the day you returned from talking to my sister. I never told any of you about it."

PJ looked at the spirits with mixed emotions. He knew what it meant. As much as he wanted this moment to come, it didn't seem right. He didn't want to utter the words he was about to say. He looked back over his shoulder toward the bleachers where the parents of the spirits still sat.

Mrs. Hutchens waved and yelled, "Good luck, boys!"

PJ nodded, then turned back to the ghosts. "It's time," he said with a sigh.

"What do you mean?" asked Dan.

"That light you see. You're done here. You need to walk toward it," PJ answered with a smile.

"But what about the race?" David asked.

"Apparently, it was less about the race than it was about your families getting back together," PJ replied. "There must've been some pain that needed to be healed amongst them. It wasn't what you did to them. It was about what they did to themselves that needed to be corrected."

214

The ghosts were wide-eyed – all of them except Pete. "So go toward the light," he urged. "Go now…"

The group started toward the light, but after just a few steps, Dan turned and saw that Pete wasn't with them. "Hold on," he said to the others. He turned and saw Pete staring expressionless at them.

"You coming, Pete?" Dan shouted.

"No," he answered as he turned back toward the starting line.

"No?" shouted Bill. "What do you mean no?"

"I can't!" Pete answered.

There was dead silence for a moment, then Dan said, "What do you mean you can't?"

Pete whirled around. "I can't see the damn light that you guys see!" he shouted at them. "I can't see it! I'm sorry, I just can't!" he cried and fell to his knees.

PJ stood motionless, not knowing what to do. He had no answers for them.

Dan looked back toward the light, then back toward the weeping Pete. He walked up and knelt beside him, putting his hand on his head. "I'm not going without you, Pete. You've been a great friend."

Pete moaned, "Dan, go. Take them with you. You need to go."

"You're right, Pete. We need to go…but not without you."

Pete looked up through teary eyes and saw all his teammates standing around him.

"Not without you," said David.

"We've been through too much together," Evan added.

"You're like my brother," said Mark.

They looked toward PJ for an answer, but he didn't have one.

"You know, Andrew reminds me a lot of my son," came a voice from behind PJ. He turned to see Hugh Bailey approaching. Apparently, Hugh could no longer see the ghosts huddled in front of PJ. "My son was in a similar position in that he was heavily favored to win this race."

"Favored?" repeated PJ.

"Oh yeah, there wasn't a kid on the East Coast that could run with him. Talk about major pieces of work left unfinished. He was ready to leave his signature on this race. It seemed like it was his destiny. It seems like everything in his life was leading up to that race." He turned and walked away, shaking his head and playing with his stopwatch.

Like everything in his life was leading up to that race, PJ repeated the words over in his head. "Dan, Pete, guys, gather yourselves and get to the starting line." PJ rushed through his directions as he noticed the starter heading out to begin the race. "Pete?"

"Yes, Coach?" Pete answered.

"Have you been the voice in Andrew's head all these years?" Pete smiled. "Enough said. Give him his chance to come through for you. Be there with him, every step of the way."

Pete stared at Andrew as he stood silently on the starting line. Then he looked back at PJ and nodded.

As the spirits nestled into the starting line alongside the RC runners, the boys felt a slight breeze flow across their faces. "Do you feel that, guys?" Andrew said as he stared motionless at the starter in front of them. "They're here with us. They're running with us, I know it."

The starter raised his pistol. The RC runners lowered their heads, tapped their neighboring teammates' fists, then looked back at the starter.

Pete leaned toward Andrew and whispered into his ear, "Remember, get out fast – 4:40 for the first mile."

Andrew nodded and thought, *I won't let you down.*

"You never have," Pete whispered back.

Chapter 41

Going Out Hard

Trained to look for the flash of the gun, the RC runners seemed to get off the line faster than any other team. Andrew had the cleanest start of them all, and was clearly in the lead after the first 400 meters.

Carmine, PJ and Hugh Bailey jogged toward the 800-meter mark, all the while watching as the swarm of green shirts moved into the lead.

"Going out kind of hard, aren't they?" asked Hallorin, jogging beside PJ. "Inexperienced runners get a little anxious sometimes, and tend to burn themselves out early in these big meets."

PJ picked it up a little, and Hallorin was unable to keep up with him as they closed on the 800-meter mark and the flower garden nicknamed "the Alamo."

"Do you think Andrew's going a little too fast?" Carmine asked PJ.

PJ looked toward the 600-meter pole and saw the leaders beginning to make their turn around it. PJ counted fourteen green shirts in the lead pack of about twenty-one runners. Six of the remaining seven wore the dark-blue singlets of BCA, and one other wore yellow – O'Donnell from Cranford, no doubt.

"I'd like to see him run the first mile between 4:55 and 5:00 minutes. That way he'll have some gas in the tank after two miles," PJ said, checking his watch as Andrew raced past the 800-meter point of the race.

"2:27!" PJ shouted toward Andrew. "Perfect!"

If I'm going to go by the mile in 4:40, 2:27 is too slow, Andrew thought to himself, picking up the pace.

PJ was a little concerned with the pace the rest of the team was running. All six of his remaining runners went by in under 2:30. They had never gone out this hard before, and as fast as they were running, BCA was already well positioned in the middle of this group.

"I'm nervous," he said to Carmine.

"Me too," Carmine replied.

"They're ready for this, PJ. You need to have faith," said Hugh Bailey before he sprinted ahead toward the mile mark. He looked across the field toward Andrew and wondered if he could get to the mile mark before the boy. He laughed at the thought because he remembered racing Pete to the mile mark on a number of occasions, and on a few of those occasions not getting there in time.

As PJ and Hugh came to a stop at the mile mark, they watched as Andrew ran directly toward them. His leg turnover was great, his arm carry had no wasted movement, and he was flying, opening a gap on the rest of the field.

Then all of a sudden, a second runner stepped into view just off Andrew's shoulder. He stepped out from behind him and pulled up next to him as they both went through the mile mark.

PJ was shocked and checked the time. His watch read 4:39 as they passed the left field foul pole that served as the mile marker. PJ looked over at Hugh, who stood there with his mouth agape. "Atta boy, Pete!" Bailey yelled.

PJ looked over at the duo and saw Pete in his 1984 vintage Nike Oregon Waffles, running stride for stride with Andrew. "That's it, Andrew! 4:39!" he yelled.

The buzz was immediate as PJ yelled the time. The other coaches and parents gathered at the mile mark were amazed, though some were doubtful that Andrew could hang on. A few were bewildered, trying to figure out who Hugh had cheered for, since they were only able to see Andrew.

"4:55...4:57!" PJ yelled as the remaining RC runners passed the mile mark.

Cranford's O'Donnell was with them, but he looked like hell. The

BCA kids were faring much better, running as a pack, a strategy that had brought them much success in the past.

Andrew circled the 600-meter pole a second time and headed for the lake. PJ and Hugh could see Pete right there with him. "Cheer your teammates on," Pete said to Andrew as they rounded the pole and could see the group of runners behind them.

Andrew's eyes locked in on Teddy's for a moment. He gave him the thumbs-up and then focused on the field and lake that lay before him.

Knowing what this meant, Teddy switched gears and surged. Nick, Mike and Rod went with him. The underclassmen, Kevin and Matt, fell off the pace slightly.

Billy Cole, the captain of the BCA team, noticed Teddy's move and sprung into his own surge. The five other BCA runners went with him. They were strong and confident, having already won a major invitational in North Carolina and having earned an invitation to the National Championship meet in San Diego to be held two weeks from now.

Billy Cole was the individual winner at the National Championship last year, and he was undefeated this season. A week earlier he had tied the Holmdel course record. He was on a roll and locked onto Andrew. More importantly, though, Cole was smart. He was a team player, and would run in a manner to bring his team with him to get the team victory. Beating Andrew was only a secondary goal to him.

Teddy wasn't sure if he could hold this pace, but he felt strong at the moment and decided he'd take his shot. He rounded the 600-meter pole and leaned forward for the downhill that followed. He flailed his arms as he ran down the hill, nearly out of control. Mike, Nick and Rod all took the hill in the same manner, on the edge of falling over as PJ had described it during practice.

At the bottom of the hill, Cole surged past Teddy, and the rest of the BCA runners passed Mike, Nick and Rod. At the 2,000-meter mark, it was RC in first, BCA in second, RC in third, and BCA taking up the next five places. If RC didn't respond, they would lose.

As Andrew dodged the roots of a series of maple trees leading to the path that encircled the lake, he waited for a clear patch of ground before attempting to look back and see where his teammates were. When he did look back, he saw that Teddy and Cole were battling it out and were now within five seconds of him. He could also see the wave of dark-blue shirts following Teddy, the second RC runner.

Andrew crossed the bridge and was now running on the other side of the lake. It was quite a sight for the spectators to see two teams so far out in front of the rest of the race.

As Andrew – and Pete – approached the end of the lake where the two-mile mark was, Coach Hallorin yelled, "Come on, BCA! There's no way these guys can hang on at this pace! We have them where we want them!"

Smile at him, Pete said to Andrew. Andrew obliged and gave Coach Hallorin the six-shooter signal as he raced past.

Hallorin turned his back on Andrew and mumbled "wiseass" as the RC runner raced past. He turned back in time to see Teddy run past and wink at him.

"9:28!" PJ yelled to Andrew as he raced past the two-mile mark. "Now pick it up!"

Andrew nodded and visibly changed gears, increasing his leg turnover as he did. Cole and the other BCA runners continued to run as a pack with Teddy.

"Okay, guys, we just hang with this rah-rah boy from RC and we have this race won," Cole said to his teammates as he grinned at Teddy.

As Mike, Nick and Rod passed the two-mile mark, PJ told them they had to put everything on the line. They had to break up the BCA pack, or they would lose.

Mike knew what had to be done. He had to string them out a little, get one or two of their runners to push a little too hard and fall off pace. They were running their race, and they needed to be taken out of their comfort zone.

"Time to ruin their day," Mike told Nick and Rod. They had discussed this strategy a week earlier and knew what to do. For Mike, it would mean a very painful end to this race – sure suicide. For the rest of them, it meant a chance to break into the BCA pack before the race ended.

Mike surged as he ran along the far side of the lake. He moved up on the BCA runners and then surged again, blowing by the group and catching Teddy and Cole. Now RC had three runners in the top four.

"Nice job!" Teddy said to Mike. "Now let's put Cole through the wringer!" He looked over at Cole next to him. Cole grinned and surged in front of the two RC runners. The rest of the BCA pack had already increased their pace and were closing quickly on Teddy, Cole and Mike – maybe too quickly, exactly what Mike was hoping for.

The crowd was in awe of this spectacle. Many had abandoned their own teams to join in the epic chase between the RC and BCA runners. Many thought it might not ever happen again.

Andrew had increased his lead to ten seconds, and was now headed up the first of the two remaining hills on the course. "Never waste a hill," Pete said to Andrew as they raced up the first hill together. The multitude of 800-meter intervals PJ had had them run on this hill prepared Andrew for this surge, for the extra burn in the calves and quads that would occur. It had built in him the ability to change gears again and start to widen his lead on the rest of his team…on the rest of the race.

"Okay, Andrew, from here on in, you're going after Tikitok's course record," Pete suggested. "After we get past the Alamo again, we make the final push! Got it?!"

I got it, Andrew thought to himself.

The course record was 14:38, so Andrew would have to cover the last 1.1 miles in 5:18. This meant he had to average a 4:49 per mile pace. His second mile had already slowed to a 4:48 pace, and that was a flat part of the course. There were two hills in the remaining mile. He did the math and began to doubt.

"You can do it," Pete encouraged Andrew as he ran next to him stride for stride.

I can't. No, not again. I'm sorry. I just…it hurts too— Andrew wrestled with the fatigue, with the thought of letting that voice down one more time.

"You've never let anyone down, Andrew," Pete said as they headed toward the second hill. "Now think just one thought: stay in the game… stay in the game!"

Stay in the game…stay in the game, Andrew repeated over and over to himself as he began his ascent up the second, final hill.

"Stay in the game!" came a yell from a blond spectator in dark sunglasses. Andrew recognized him from his stay at the Xtreme Running Camp. It was Mike Tikitok himself. "Break the record!" Tikitok yelled. "Run like the devil's chasing you and you're doing your best to hang him out to dry!" Tikitok majored in the classics in college and was known for delivering the coolest pep talks.

The second hill was Andrew's finest moment. He shifted gears halfway up and visibly changed his pace again. The spectators could sense the importance of this change, and the mad dash to the finish line was on.

While Andrew ran away with the race, almost lost in the excitement was the fact that Mike's surge had caused the BCA runners to surge prior to the two remaining hills. This boded well for the remaining RC runners – Rod, Nick, Teddy and Matt – who had remained calm and were ready to move in the hills.

Teddy and Cole were battling for second place as they went through the two final hills. It was a dogfight with neither runner giving in to the other. Mike was struggling and fell off pace on the first hill. Four BCA runners passed him, as did Rod, Nick and Matt.

"Come on, Nick, you're our fifth man," PJ yelled as he ran across the field toward the park.

BCA had their fifth man in front of RC's third man as they started to climb the second hill, but they looked weary. Mike's surge took a lot out of them. But would it be enough?

As Matt passed Mike, he patted him on the back. Mike could only muster up a groan; he had fallen back and was now RC's seventh man. Next to Matt – and passing Mike with Matt – were BCA's sixth and seventh men. As Mike ascended the second hill, the team score was RC in first, second, eighth, ninth and tenth. BCA's top five held the third through seventh places. That meant BCA was winning the team race with a total score of twenty-five points compared to RC's thirty.

Mike was struggling, but certainly running a personal record for the course. As he approached the second hill, a tall, thin, graying man in a bandana came yelling across the field. "Way to go, bud!" he yelled as Mike hit the bottom of the hill.

PJ smiled as he looked back at Mike. The man cheering for him was his dad, Ed Kinney; and if anyone could give Mike that extra incentive, Ed could. They were about as close as a dad and son could get. Ed was an adventure race participant, and Mike was his lone support person on many occasions. But today, it was Ed's turn to support Mike.

"Mikey, you're awesome, friggin' awesome!" Ed yelled. "The score's close and you're still a big part of this race!"

Mike looked over at his dad and lowered his head slightly. His stride shortened, and his leg turnover increased.

"Atta boyyyy, Mikey! Now you're cookin' with goosebutter!"

Mike was running stride for stride with Cranford's O'Donnell, each pushing the other, not relenting the lead. O'Donnell had beaten Mike by a full minute in their last race. They were both running PRs as they headed toward the track for one final lap. Both had passed Matt and the sixth and seventh men for BCA. More significantly, they were gaining on Nick as they approached the track.

Andrew broke through the bushes and entered the track to the cheers of the crowd that had gathered and completely circled the track. "Ladies and gentlemen!" the announcer shouted through the PA system. "That's Andrew Cartolano from Rozelle Catholic approaching the start of the final lap!"

It was pandemonium as the coaches and parents checked their watches and Andrew raced to the start of the final lap. "Ladies and gentlemen," the announcer said, "Andrew has to run the final 400 meters in sixty seconds to break Tikitok's record!"

Andrew grimaced at the announcement. He had been running a 4:48 mile pace and now would have to drop to a sub 4:00 pace to break the record. His legs were burning, his field of vision shrinking, and he felt dizzy as he avoided the crowd encroaching at the side of the track.

I...can't...I just... Andrew tried desperately to increase his speed. *Dear God...please...*

"You can do this, Andrew," came the voice he had heard before in other races – at Brundage Park in middle school, at Van Cortlandt Park and Holmdel Park in high school. It was Pete Bailey, and he was right next to Andrew, though only PJ could see him…at least for now.

As they approached the middle of the first turn, Hugh looked at PJ and said, "This is where my son would have started to 'bang the drum.' He'd start driving his arms and break into an all-out kick. If he had to run sixty seconds, he would have!"

PJ was standing at the end of the first turn as the boys came off it, heading into the first straightaway. He could hear Pete's words very clearly as they went by. "Okay, Andrew, let's bang the drum now. It's blood and guts time. Sixty damn seconds. You can do it. Bang the drum… stay in the game…put your signature on this race!"

Andrew's heart raced as the voice cheered him on. He felt the hair on the back of his neck rise as he effectively increased his leg turnover. He had 250 meters to go. His legs were cramping slightly, but they were turning over. He heard his father cheer for him as he entered the last turn. "Come on, Andrew! Look at the first turn!"

Andrew looked off to his left as he raced through the final turn. At the opposite end of the track, he saw BCA's first runner, Cole, coming off the first turn, followed by Teddy. Cole was kicking wildly, and Teddy was sticking with him, almost stride for stride. The cheers from the crowd were deafening. Behind Teddy was a group of four BCA runners and Nick, who had a decent kick. PJ reminded him of it as he came off the first turn. Nick unleashed a furious surge, and it propelled him into fourth place as he raced down the back straightaway. Unfortunately, the next five runners were all BCA, followed by RC's Rod, Cranford's O'Donnell, and Mike from RC.

"Ladies and gentlemen, the team race is very close, with BCA four points in front of RC. But there are bunches of runners on the track, and anything could happen!" the announcer called.

Rod heard the announcement and went after the pack of BCA runners in front of him. As Andrew came off the final turn, he looked to his right as he sprinted down the last straightaway. There was Mike surging past O'Donnell onto the track for the final lap.

Do it, Mike! Andrew thought. And at that very moment, Andrew shifted gears one final time and focused on the clock at the finish line. 14:21. Andrew drove his arms harder. 14:22…14:23…

Hugh watched from twenty yards beyond the finish line, tears welling in his eyes as he watched Andrew come off the last turn. He saw his son right there next to Andrew as they raced together down the last straightaway. As Andrew and the apparition approached the finish line, he saw their arms go up together.

"14:26! A new course record!" came the announcement over the PA system as Andrew struggled to stay on his feet. *Don't bend over. Don't hold my knees!* he thought as he struggled to stay on his feet.

Hugh raced over to Andrew and put his arms around him. "That was a magnificent effort, young man," Hugh said to him. "You reminded me of my son, the way you were banging the drum on the back straightway." *He was right there with me, Mr. Bailey,* Andrew thought, but he could not say the words as he gasped for air.

"Look at this, son!" Hugh said as he turned Andrew to face the finish line. Billy Cole from BCA crossed the line in 14:53, followed by Teddy in 15:04 and Nick in 15:09. Nick held his arms in a victory V as he crossed the line, then quickly lowered them, wrestling to catch his breath. Andrew gave Nick a hug as he got to the end of the chute.

"In third and fourth place, we have two more RC runners, Ted Dohne and Nick Garvey," came the next announcement. "Ladies and gentlemen, the next five runners on the final 200 meters are all BCA runners followed by Rod O'Leary of RC, Mitch O'Donnell of Cranford, and Mike Kinney of RC. It looks like BCA has a slight lead over RC at this point."

Rod made his last move. Coming off the last turn, he managed to pass one of the BCA runners, which put him in ninth place. BCA had crossed in fifth, sixth, seventh and eighth. If O'Donnell finished in tenth and Mike in eleventh, as they were currently running, then it would be a tie between RC and BCA. The sixth man would decide the win.

All eyes looked across the track toward the battle between O'Donnell and Mike. They were running stride for stride as they went into the last turn. Mike faltered slightly, and O'Donnell took the lead at the beginning of the turn. Mike moved outside to try to pass, but O'Donnell gradually moved outside as well, making it harder to move around him. Mike was tiring, and O'Donnell was a tactical runner and a great kicker. "You go, booooyyyyy!" Ed yelled from outside the final turn.

Mike closed his eyes as he exited the final turn. The pain in his legs and back was incredible. He was cramping in his hamstrings, and he knew at any moment it could be over. He tried to pass O'Donnell on the right but ran into O'Donnell's elbow as he was drifting right as well. Rather than back off the pace to try to get around O'Donnell on the other side, Mike relentlessly pushed forward into the elbow O'Donnell was throwing. He looked for a spot, some vantage point to get by, but there was none. PJ watched from just beyond the finish line as O'Donnell continued to force Mike to the outside of the second lane, as they raced down the last fifty meters.

Suddenly O'Donnell started to lean forward in a mad, final dash for the finish. Mike realized something was wrong. They were too far to be leaning yet. Then O'Donnell's head started to go down, and his back kick seemed to be too high. He was falling forward. His arms flailed wildly as he tried to keep from falling. Mike used the opportunity to get around him and crossed the finish line. A fraction of a second later, O'Donnell fell across the line and landed on the back of Mike's legs, sending them both to the ground.

Immediately, Mike got to his knees and then to his feet. He started to walk toward the end of the chute, then looked back and saw O'Donnell lying facedown at the beginning of the chute. Mike turned around and went back, helping O'Donnell to his feet.

"We gave 'em quite a show, didn't we?" Mike said to O'Donnell as he helped him through the chute. O'Donnell nodded and smiled. When they reached the end of the chute, they were greeted by the rest of the RC team.

"Nice race, O'Donnell," Andrew said as he handed the runner a bottle of water.

"Thanks, did you get the record?" O'Donnell asked.

"Yes, I think so."

"Nice!" O'Donnell said, turning to be greeted by his own coach.

PJ raced over to Mike and lifted him into the air with a big bear hug. "You won that race for us!"

"Did we win?" Mike huffed.

"Yeah, Rod and you made great moves, and I have us winning twenty-seven to twenty-eight!"

PJ looked at the group of runners as they huddled together in the infield. Just beyond them stood the other group of RC runners, the spirits. They appeared to be no different from the other runners, and only PJ knew how they had run. Between Andrew and Cole, all seven spirits crossed the line. Hence, they would have shut out the great BCA team – and nearly shut out the RC team!

"Okay, guys, I want you to do a thirty-minute warm-down. You ran great today," PJ said to the new Easterns champions.

"So this was my last high school cross country race," Rod said.

"Maybe not," PJ said. "We may have one more," he added with a smile.

The boys knew what he was referring to – the National Championship in San Diego.

"Let's git 'er done," Andrew said as he headed toward his pile of running gear to change into his training flats.

Chapter 42

A Race Well Run

PJ headed over to the group of spirits and congratulated them on a nice race.

"Where are they, Coach?" PJ turned and saw the ghosts' parents standing in a pack behind him.

"Who would that be?" PJ asked.

"Our sons," Mrs. Hutchens replied. "We saw them on the starting line and during the race, but we don't see them right now."

PJ turned and looked at the ghosts and then looked back at the parents. He didn't say anything at first, but then moved closer to the parents. "They're right here with us. I can see them," PJ explained.

"Are they okay?" Albert Santos asked.

"Yes, they are," PJ said.

"We can see the light, Coach," Dan Hutchens said. "That is, all of us except Pete."

This news did not go over well with PJ. "What's wrong, Coach?" asked Hugh Bailey.

"Well, it appears they've been here, unable to cross over into the afterlife, for the last twenty years."

"Unable to cross over?" Dan Hutchens asked.

"Yes. I…uh, consulted with an expert on the topic, and she said this often happens when there's unfinished business, or a significant burden on the soul that prevents it from crossing."

"Why are you the only one who can see them?" Clare Hutchens asked.

"I don't know," PJ answered. "I just can. The good news is that right now they can see the light, the passage to the afterlife. They *can* cross over now – all of them except for your son, Hugh." Hugh Bailey sighed and looked at the ground.

"Can you tell David I love him?" Ann Santos asked.

"I don't need to," PJ replied. "They can hear you."

David walked over and put his arms around his mom. "I…I can feel him!" Ann said, laughing softly as she fought back tears.

"They're all here and they can hear you. They've seen you suffer over the last twenty years. They want you to heal, to rest easy, to know they're okay."

"What about my Pete?" Hugh Bailey asked. PJ stood silent and looked at Pete. "He needs my help. How can I help him?" Hugh said in a desperate tone.

"Tell him I'm okay," Pete said to PJ. "Tell him I have my friends with me."

"Hugh, he says he's okay, that his friends are with him and they won't leave him."

Pete looked at his ghostly companions and told them, "You guys should go. I can handle myself here for as long as it takes."

"We're *not* leaving you, Pete," the group replied as one.

"Coach, what can we do?" Pete asked.

PJ looked at Hugh and said, "I thought the unfinished business keeping Pete here was not having a chance to win the Easterns. You said you felt it was his destiny. I thought so too. I'm at a loss right now."

"Peter," Hugh said, "I know you can hear me, but I want you to really hear this. I love you."

"Ask him if he loves himself," Pete said to PJ as the other runners moved away, giving PJ, Peter and Hugh some privacy.

"He wants to know if you love yourself."

"Of course I love myself, Pete," Hugh said in a tone of disbelief.

"Then what happened? Why the black clothes? The reclusive behavior? What about Mom? Did he love her?"

"Pete wants to know—"

"No need to ask, PJ. I think I know," Hugh interrupted, then continued, "Pete, I lost the only son I ever had. You were my best friend. The grief was overwhelming. I tried to be strong, but you were everywhere I turned. I saw you in the sunlight, in the shadows, in the faces of everyone I met. I heard your voice echoing everywhere I went."

"But what about Mom? You gave up on her, I saw it!" Pete said as he looked down to hide the tears from PJ.

"And your mom. I loved her so much…to this very day I—" Hugh stopped when he felt a hand on his shoulder.

"To this very day, eh?" came a whisper from behind Hugh. He felt the hair on the back of his neck rise at the sound of the familiar voice.

Pete Bailey felt a calm come over his spirit, and he looked back toward his teammates. Over their shoulders he saw something unusual – a light that was getting brighter, increasing in intensity. It gave off a warm, peaceful glow. His eyes were wide open as he took in the sight.

"Pete," said Bill.

"I see it," said Pete.

"No, Pete, look behind you," Bill said with a huge smile on his face.

Pete turned around slowly to see his father embracing a woman. As Pete moved closer, the couple turned slightly, and Pete could see the woman was his mom.

As they relaxed their embrace, Pete's mom said, "I'm so sorry I was late. Route 95 was at a standstill in Hartford."

"As long as you're here, Eve, that's what matters most," Hugh said as he hugged her once more.

"She's beautiful, isn't she?" Pete said to PJ. PJ smiled and nodded. "Can she hear me? Does she know about us?"

"Why don't you ask her?" PJ replied.

Pete walked up and gently kissed his mom on the cheek. "I feel you, Pete," she said immediately. "I'm sorry I missed the race, but my real reason for coming here was to talk to you."

"Tell her I'm listening, Coach."

"I think she knows you're here," PJ said, smiling at Hugh and Eve.

"Your dad and I had our problems dealing with your death. As we tried to understand why, we found ourselves lashing out at the world – and at each other – in our grief." Pete stood motionless directly in front of her. "Last week, when your father got in touch with me, my heart raced like it did the first day we met." PJ and Pete looked at Hugh, who smiled and blushed slightly.

"We realized we both felt the same way about each other," Eve said as she looked up into Hugh's eyes. "That we both were still very much in love with each other." Eve hugged Hugh and then continued. "He mentioned that this race was coming up and that maybe we should use the occasion to reunite. I wanted this more than ever, so I decided to come...and I'm not ever leaving."

Hugh started to weep, and Eve grabbed his hand tightly. "Hugh, I don't think it's a good time to start crying when I say I'm not leaving," Eve joked.

"I was thinking the same thing," Pete said to PJ.

"So you don't need to worry about us, Pete. We'll take good care of each other," Hugh said. "This is a promise."

Pete looked at PJ and said, "So what now?"

PJ looked in the boy's eyes and said, "It's time for you and your teammates to cross over."

"But what will it be like?" Pete asked as his teammates gathered around him and PJ.

"It will be more wonderful than you can ever imagine," PJ said.

"How do you know?" Dan asked nervously.

"Well, I have faith, and I believe it to be so," PJ replied, not knowing if the answer would be good enough.

The team stood and stared at the light in the near distance. It felt warm, but their uncertainty froze them in place. As they watched the warm glow, they noticed a shadow forming within it. The shadow morphed into the silhouette of a runner standing before them…then a second and third…then five more.

The boys looked at PJ, who was standing there taking in the same sight, not knowing what it meant. When the boys turned back to face the light, the eight silhouettes started to come forward out of the light. As they came closer, PJ noticed that they were built like typical distance runners and that they were wearing yellow and brown shorts and singlets with *WYOMING* written across the front of the shirt. On the shorts was a silhouette of a cowboy riding a horse with a circle with the number 8 in the middle of it.

As they stopped directly in front of the boys, the tallest of the bunch greeted the RC runners. "Hi, my name's Nick."

Pete held out his trembling hand and said, "Hi, I'm Pete."

The two sets of runners simply stared at each other for a few moments. Then Nick looked back at his Wyoming teammates and joked, "Why, they look like they just saw a ghost!"

The group burst out laughing as one of the other runners in a Wyoming shirt said, "Duh. Tell them it takes one to know one."

Nick turned back and shook his head. "Hey, we were sent here to greet you. To be with you as you cross over."

"Kind of like a college recruiter!" one of Nick's teammates joked.

"But who are you guys?" David asked.

"We ran for the University of Wyoming – at least we did up until the week of 9/11," Nick said.

"You mean you were killed in the 9/11 attacks?" Evan asked.

"No, no, we were killed by a drunk driver not far from Laramie." The RC runners looked at each other for a moment. "We crossed immediately. We've been at peace ever since."

"Except that we have no legitimate competition on the other side," came a voice from the rear of the Wyoming bunch.

Nick looked back and laughed. "He's right. We could use a few good runners on the other side. Plus, you're dead. You're done here. You pretty much have no other alternative."

The RC runners looked at each other then back toward their new friends from Wyoming and nodded.

Nick walked out and traced a straight line in the turf in front of them. "Okay, runners, everyone to the starting line."

As the two teams walked up to the starting line, Nick said to PJ, "Coach, would you be today's honorary starter?"

PJ smiled. "Sure." As he got out in front of the group, he surveyed the faces of the RC boys. They looked at peace, with a hint of their game faces on. They were going to be okay.

"Hold on. Time out, wait a second," Pete said, breaking the silence. He walked over to PJ. "I just wanted to thank you again."

"No need to, Pete," PJ replied.

"I have a favor to ask you, PJ."

"What's that?"

"Let my father help you coach. Get him back into it."

PJ looked over Pete's shoulder and saw Hugh in the background. "I will. I promise!" PJ assured him.

"Thanks, Coach," Pete said, then he turned and trotted back to the starting line.

PJ put his hand over the front part of his head to look more like one of the balding race officials that the boys had come to know and love. "Gentlemen, there will be two commands. 'Set'…and then 'Go.'"

"Get out quick, RC," Eve yelled from behind.

"Runners, set!" PJ shouted.

Nick glanced at Pete next to him and gently held out his fist. "Don't be afraid. The place where you're going is beautiful – even better than Holmdel Park." Pete cracked a smile and touched the Wyoming runner's fist.

"Go!" PJ shouted. And they were off. For PJ, watching their silhouettes fade into the light was an incredible sight. He felt a slight breeze blow across his face as they disappeared, and was filled with mixed emotions.

"PJ, are they gone?" Hugh asked.

"Yes, they're where they should be." He sighed with relief.

Hugh, PJ, Eve, and the rest of the parents of the boys who had just crossed over walked quietly back to their cars. They came to a stop near PJ's, and he turned and said, "They were nice boys. You should all be very proud of them."

"We are," said Sherry Bahsman. "And we want to thank you for helping us."

"It was something I guess I was destined to do," PJ replied.

"I bet your father's very proud of you," Sherry added.

"Hmm, maybe..." PJ answered as he thought about whether his father even knew what he had done. "Maybe," he repeated as he shook his head and unlocked his car.

Chapter 43

San Diego Bound

The day following the Easterns Championship, PJ received a phone call from Blake Newberry, the director of the National Championship race in San Diego. Blake congratulated PJ and invited his team to the race. PJ accepted, pending Brother Owen Oakley's approval and the school's financial support.

On Monday morning, PJ drove to the school to meet with Brother Owen. Pulling into the rear driveway, he noticed a white-haired man running slowly around the track. As he parked, he realized it was none other than Brother Owen. PJ crossed the footbridge leading from the school onto the track.

"Congratulations, PJ," Brother Owen called out.

"Thank you, Brother. You deserve much of the credit as well."

"You're too modest," Brother Owen replied as he put his arm around PJ's shoulder and continued to walk with him around the track. "I bet I could run a lot better if I stopped smoking." He chuckled.

"Now why do a thing like that?"

"The archbishop called me late last night, PJ."

"He did? Wow, that's pretty significant, isn't it?"

"Well, uh, *yeah*! It is."

"So what did he want?"

"He offered his congratulations for winning the Easterns," Brother Owen said, stopping and turning toward PJ. "And he offered to pay for you and the team to go to San Diego for the National Championship. I assume his brother, Blake, called and invited you?"

PJ smiled. "Blake? Oh yeah, Blake Newberry. He contacted me last night."

"You know, Blake and the archbishop both ran cross country in New York at Archbishop Malloy High School many years ago."

"I didn't know that."

"Yeah, they love the sport. Both of them still run."

"So I assume we can make arrangements?"

"Of course, but try not to overdo it!" Owen said, patting PJ on the back and turning to start jogging again. As PJ started to walk back toward the school, Brother Owen called out to him once more. "PJ, did you have something you wanted to ask me?"

"No, not anymore," he said with a big grin on his face.

"Then I have a question for you."

"What's that?"

"Will you be back coaching for us next year?"

PJ stared at Owen for a while, then answered, "Let's focus on the Nationals right now."

"Fair enough," Brother Owen replied, turning again toward the track.

PJ watched Owen break into a jog. As he crossed the bridge again and exited the track, PJ thought about the brother's question. PJ knew his finances were dwindling and he probably couldn't afford to simply coach next year. Plus, he promised to get Hugh Bailey back into the sport. He was already thinking of suggesting that Hugh Bailey take over as coach next year.

Chapter 44

Mission Bay

———————————

The next two weeks flew by, and on the day the team departed for San Diego, a light dusting of snow fell on New Jersey.

The night before, PJ visited his mother at the nursing home. It had been his parents' wedding anniversary, and PJ always made sure he visited his mom on that day. She seemed very tired and weak, having had an usually tough day. Despite how weak she appeared, she managed a smile for PJ. She had also obviously pulled out the forty-year-old bottle of French cologne that PJ's dad used to wear and spritzed herself with a small amount of it, something she did every anniversary so that she could remember what he used to smell like. PJ noticed she was wearing it as he kissed her goodnight after she fell asleep.

"I love you, Mom," he whispered in her ear. He detected a smile on her face as he said the words, but she remained sleeping.

For most of the boys on the team, this was their first time on an airplane. The six-hour flight passed quickly, and the transfer from the airport to the Hampton Inn in Mission Bay went smoothly. It was two in the afternoon when they arrived at the hotel, and by three they were at Mission Bay Park to familiarize themselves with the course where they would race tomorrow.

Mission Bay Park was not a typical cross country course composed of woods and trails. It was more like a community park with nicely manicured grass and cement bike paths. It bordered Mission Bay, so there was a nice view of the water.

As PJ and the team jogged along, they discussed tactics and how best to run the course. The turns were tight, and the course was relatively flat with only minor rolling hills. It would be a tight race because the course was narrow, and because they flagged off the lanes, limiting the opening for the runners at a few locations.

A number of other teams were out learning the course as well. PJ noticed two local teams, one from Chino Hills and the other from San Diego. PJ also spied the BCA team and a team from Tyrone, Pennsylvania. In all, twenty-four teams – 168 runners – had been invited.

The ride back to the hotel was a quiet one. The boys were totally focused – so much so, they weren't even talking to each other. PJ took them to a local Italian restaurant for a spaghetti dinner, and then they went back to get some rest.

PJ woke at five the next morning. The race was scheduled to start at ten, and he was to meet the boys at seven for a light breakfast. The boys ate primarily breakfast bars and bagels for breakfast, though PJ and Andrew had some oatmeal. "How'd you sleep last night, Andrew?" he asked.

Andrew looked up with a wide smile and proclaimed, "Like a baby!"

"Excellent," PJ said. "And how about the rest of you guys?"

It was unanimous; they all slept very well, which gave PJ some confidence. The teams in this race were the cream of the crop. This was not the Easterns; it would be a much harder race – and they only won the Easterns by one point.

The ride over to the park was quiet as Hugh Bailey, who seemed very much at peace, drove the rental van. Next to him in the passenger seat was Eve. She decided to come with Hugh, saying it would be like a second honeymoon for her since they spent their first in San Diego. For Hugh, this was no honeymoon; this was the National Championship. But as much as he tried to focus on the race, he managed to smile and nod in agreement whenever Eve brought up the second honeymoon. She was having fun with him. She knew that for today, the race was the most important thing in his life.

The team arrived at the course at eight thirty and found a nice shady place to set up their tent. The crowd was growing. This was definitely going to be the most exciting race the boys had ever run.

Andrew led the boys through a two-mile warm-up, the second mile of which was quick. PJ believed a small amount of fast-paced warm-ups better prepared a runner for the race. If their legs were a little tired at the start of a race, that would help keep them from going out too fast. But then again, with this narrow, flat course, the start was going to be fast no matter what.

By a quarter till ten, the boys were in full uniform and ready to run. Radio-frequency chips (used for accurate timing) were in place on their shoes, and their numbers were neatly pinned to their shirts, front and back, so the race sponsor's name could be seen in whatever photos or film footage was taken.

"Gather around, guys," PJ said. "Listen, I'd be satisfied if you guys simply had fun during this race. The whole goal was just to get here." The boys gave PJ a unified blank stare. "Seriously, I'd be 100 percent satisfied if you just ran and enjoyed the race."

"But Coach," said Ted, "the school paid for us to come here! We kind of owe it to Brother Owen to represent RC well at this race."

"We might attract some runners to RC if we do well here," Rod chimed in. "Hell, we might even field a girls' team next year!" The boys looked at each other and smiled, and the seriousness and maturity with which they were approaching this race impressed PJ.

"Then what should we do here today?" PJ asked. "Andrew, what should we do? What does that voice say?"

Andrew saw that all eyes were on him. He looked down for a moment, then looked at his teammates and answered PJ. "Even if we can't beat them, we should let them know we were here!"

The boys liked his answer, and they high-fived each other. The announcer called all teams to the starting line, and they jogged to their assigned slot, number 12, right in the middle of the line. It was a tough location, one that required a fast start. If you were caught napping, the entire field would close in front of you, and the race would be over before the first quarter mile was finished.

Andrew led the team through a few long stride outs in front of the starting line, then they stopped and huddled, just as they did before every

239

race. The words flowed from Andrew like he had rehearsed them all night.

"Two weeks ago, we completed a chapter for our teammates from 1984. Today, we write this one for ourselves. I'll look back on this day when I'm a parent or a coach and I'll remember all your faces. We waged war together, and I'll always respect the strength and courage you showed. You made me a better runner. We'll always be brothers. Now let's go put Jersey on the map!"

"Any strategy, Andrew? Any advice?" Nick asked.

Andrew looked at them seriously and replied, "Get out fast. We're in the middle of the line."

"Then what?" Nick asked.

"Then run your asses off!" he shouted as he broke into one last stride toward the starting line. The team followed, looking pumped.

PJ and Hugh watched from the sidelines as the team lined up for the start.

The CEO of the company sponsoring the race said a few things to the boys, and then handed the microphone to the race announcer. The starter walked slowly – and dramatically – out into the field in front of the runners. The DJ stopped the music that was playing and readied the selection that would be played loudly as soon as the race started. Every year the selection was a surprise, but it usually got the crowd and the runners going.

"Runners," the announcer bellowed through the PA system, "there will be two commands: 'Runners Set,' then the gun." A pause, then, "Runners...set."

The starter raised his pistol. The RC runners gently tapped their fists together as they stared intently at the muzzle of the pistol. *Look for the flash,* both PJ and Hugh thought to themselves. PJ's eyes widened when he saw the RC runners in motion exactly as the flash went off. They were off the line a fraction of a second before the others, and he knew this would help them tremendously.

Andrew was in fourth place as he passed PJ at the 800-meter point. He went by in 2:15, which was fast, but the course was slightly downhill in the beginning. Mike, Teddy, Rod and Nick were all grouped together in the top twenty runners. Even the underclassmen, Matt and Kevin, were in the top fifty. The team was running well.

As they went through the mile, Andrew was still running in fourth place but was within striking distance. His mile split was 4:38. The leader, a local kid named Sal Nova, went through in 4:33. Sal ran a 4:14 mile last year, setting the school record at Chino Hills and qualifying him to run in the elite high school mile at the Millrose Games last February.

The rest of the heavily favored Chino Hills team was running in a pack with the BCA team. They lost last year to BCA and were totally focusing on them for this race. RC was not even on their radar screen since they were a late qualifier, and the news of their Easterns performance had not been heavily publicized.

"Smile, Andrew!" PJ shouted as the runners approached the halfway point in the race.

"Smile?" Hugh asked PJ. "Is that the best advice you have?"

"Yup!" PJ laughed. "Actually, I noticed that when Andrew's relaxed, his face is relaxed. When he smiles, I honestly think he relaxes and his form improves." Hugh nodded and then turned his attention back to the race.

"Way to go, Teddy, Rod! Stay in the game, Nick – you're the key! Go, Mike!" PJ yelled as the boys ran past. They were running the race of their lives, and were still in the top twenty with half the race to go.

Andrew increased his leg turnover slightly as he approached the two-mile mark. He was winded from the fast start, but he was beginning to breathe better and felt more confident as the race progressed. He passed two runners as he went through the two-mile mark in 9:18. Now he was focusing on Sal Nova. *Stay in the game,* the voice in Andrew's head repeated over and over. *Stay in the game!*

While Andrew hung on to the runner from Chino Hills, Mike made a move of his own and broke into eighth place by the two-mile mark. Teddy and Nick went with him. Rod was running solidly in eighteenth, but he let the others go when they surged.

With a half mile to go, Sal Nova and Andrew were running perfectly next to each other. It was a beautiful sight to see their legs move in unison, matching each other stride for stride.

PJ watched as the two ran past a group of local fans from Chino Hills. "Time to put a hurt on that little boy, Sal," one of them yelled. "No Jersey boy can run with you!" Sal Nova glanced over at Andrew and grinned. Then he shifted gears and pulled out in front of Andrew.

Stay in the game, Andrew thought.

PJ didn't like to see the fans talk trash, but he knew it was part of the game. He rushed toward the next turn on the course, and as the two boys approached, PJ yelled, "That's it, Andrew, you knucklehead! Keep smiling like you know something we don't!"

Andrew didn't hear PJ, but Nova did – and it worried him. He was running as fast as he could…and the kid behind him was smiling? How could this be? *There, that has him guessing,* PJ thought to himself.

Andrew got up next to Sal and looked over at him. Nova knew Andrew was looking at him, but he wouldn't return the stare. Instead, he drove his arms harder and tried to gap Andrew, to no avail. Andrew was in his zone. He was flying, barely feeling the ground under his feet, and he was only a few seconds from unleashing his final kick.

Andrew could see the finish line about 500 meters in front of him. *And now for some good ol' ass-whooping,* Andrew thought, shifting gears one final time and racing for the finish. Sal Nova's legs couldn't respond to Andrew's kick, and as a result he had to settle for a second-place finish.

Andrew raised his hands over his head as he broke the ribbon at the finish line. His time was 14:21, even faster than his time at the Easterns. He decelerated in a controlled manner and turned to watch the others finish as he walked through the chute.

Finishing in fifth was Mike. Two places behind him was Nick. In eleventh place was Teddy, and finishing with a big surge in fourteenth place was Rod. Immediately behind Teddy were the fourth and fifth men for Chino Hills.

"Ladies and gentlemen," came the voice over the PA system, "you don't need to be a math major to see that Rozelle Catholic just won the

National Championship. They came here all the way from New Jersey. Let's give them – and all the runners – a loud round of applause."

Andrew blushed as a number of young kids came up and asked him for an autograph. "The heck with the autograph," he told them. "Let's go for a run together." And off they went, the RC squad and a handful of fans, for a well-deserved victory warm down.

PJ looked at Hugh and said, "Wow. I can't believe it."

"I can," Hugh replied. "They were the best team out there."

"Hugh."

"Yes?"

"I was thinking of handing over the coaching reins to you next year. What do you think?"

"Make me the assistant coach, and you have a deal," Hugh replied with a smile.

"I'm not sure I can support myself on this salary," PJ said. "I'm going to have to get a job."

"Let's talk about this when we get home, PJ."

"Sounds like a plan," PJ replied, heading off to join the boys on their warm-down. "You coming?" he shouted back to Hugh.

"Uh…no, I'm happy just standing right here. Have fun. I'll see you at the awards ceremony."

Chapter 45

The Look of an Eagle

For a national championship, the awards ceremony was fairly simple. The boys received their plaques and medals on a stage near the starting line. Pictures were taken, and the local reporters asked a few questions. At first the reporters seemed to be more interested in the local teams, but eventually they were won over by the RC runners' personalities, interviewing them and enjoying their tough, Jersey approach to racing.

The team had an early morning flight and retired at around eleven that night, after an adequate amount of celebrating with a local girls' team they met at the awards ceremony. PJ hopped into bed at nine, after checking the Internet to see who had won the New Jersey Masters 10K Championship. As he expected, Frank McNab won the Masters division with a time of 30:32. PJ felt he could have run that time if he had run the race.

As he tossed and turned and tried desperately to drift off to sleep, he couldn't shake the excitement of the day – or the entire season, for that matter. He already missed Dan Hutchens and the rest of the '84 team. And he still wondered why. Why was he chosen to be able to see those souls, those spirits? Did any of it really happen? What did it all mean? Surely there was a reason he had been chosen. He had seen enough movies to believe there must be some grand plan, but what was it? Was this simply to end with the National Championship?

PJ's legs twitched a little with nervous energy, an annoying feeling that occurred every once in a while. The tingling feeling in his legs was strong, and he knew he would have to get up and move around a little to get rid of the odd sensation. He jumped out of bed and touched his toes, stretching his calves, then he pulled a Sam Adams from the minibar. *I earned this one,* he thought, popping the lid.

No sooner had he put his lips to the can than there was a knock on the hotel room door. "Hold on," PJ grumbled as he headed toward the door. "If that's you, Andrew, you should be sleeping."

He opened the door, and there was Grant Edwins, still wearing his press badge from the race. "C'mon, PJ, you have a Masters 10K Championship to run in one hour!" Grant said abruptly as he entered the room and grabbed PJ's gym bag off the floor. "Here, grab your running stuff."

"Whoa, whoa, Grant! What's going on here? The race was early this morning in New Jersey. I missed it."

"Oh, you mean the one McNab won, with Roland Price coming in second?"

"Yes, exactly!" PJ laughed.

"That's not the race I'm talking about! Now come on!"

"But..."

"C'mon, PJ, we don't have much time!"

PJ grabbed his bag and opened it, quickly cataloging its contents. *Okay, I got shorts, singlet, Asics Gel Kayanos...I can't race in Kayanos.* PJ turned and looked at Edwins, who was holding something in his left hand.

"Oh, I thought you might need these," Grant said, handing him a pair of maroon Nike Kennedys racing spikes. "Size ten. I hope they fit."

PJ took the shoes from Grant and looked them over. "Perfect, that's my size. How'd you know?"

"Never mind that, we don't have time," Grant replied as he grabbed PJ by the arm and yanked him into the hallway. "We have a limo waiting for us downstairs."

Grant raced down the hallway with the zeal of a college kid, taking the stairs rather than waiting for the elevator. PJ followed closely behind, repeatedly asking where they were headed. A black Lincoln Town Car awaited the two directly in front of the hotel. Once inside, Grant turned to PJ and said, "We're going to San Diego State University. Tonight you're running in the 10,000-meter race."

"Is it a Masters race?" PJ asked, the reality that he was going to race beginning to sink in. He started to knead his thigh muscles in the early stages of what had become a habitual warm-up routine.

"Kind of."

"What do you mean, 'kind of'?"

"You'll see," Grant said, grinning mysteriously at PJ. "You'll see."

Yeah, I'll see! PJ thought to himself as he closed his eyes, leaned back in the seat, and continued to gently massage his legs. As PJ kneaded his calf muscles, his thoughts went back to his morning run on the first day of running camp. That was the morning when he first saw Peter Bailey lying next to him, a flaming bus only a few meters away.

"PJ?" Grant poked PJ in the thigh.

"Yes?" PJ answered, turning groggily to Edwins and opening his eyes. "What?"

"Look there," Edwins said, pointing over PJ's shoulder out the passenger side of the car. PJ spun around and his jaw dropped.

The San Diego State University stadium was off to the right of the car. The parking lot was full, and the stadium was lit up and alive with the noise of a packed house. As they entered the parking lot, PJ noticed the Jumbotron marquee that greeted everyone who entered the stadium.

World Masters Championship tonight!! PJ read the words as they scrolled across the giant display, momentarily stopping to pay attention to key information. *Come see the greatest runners of all time.* PJ continued to read the marquee as the limo driver pulled up close to turnstiles in front of the stadium.

Jesse Owens versus Jim Thorpe in the 100 meters! PJ's jaw dropped as he continued to read the sign. *And a Special 10,000-meter run featuring…* PJ's eyes widened. *Abebe Bikila, Mamo Wolde, Steve Prefontaine…* PJ's mouth began to grow dry. *Paavo Nurmi, Emil Zatopek…* PJ looked over in disbelief at Grant, who was grinning. Those were the names of some of the greatest distance runners in history, though of course they were all dead now.

"Look! Look!" Grant pointed back at the marquee. PJ turned and watched the message change one more time. *...and debuting tonight, from New Jersey, PJ Irwin.*

PJ blinked his eyes, then turned to Edwins and shook his head. "You gotta be kidding me!" PJ said as he laughed. "Mr. Edwins, I don't know what strings you had to pull to pull off this prank, but I have to hand it to you, it's pretty funny. Actually, it's amazing." PJ stared at Grant who just grinned and stared back. "Mr. Edwins?" PJ said, waving his hand in front of Grant's face.

"Put your hand down, PJ, and let's get inside before we run out of time."

"Mr. Edwins, it was a great prank, but I should be back at the hotel with the kids."

Grant turned toward PJ and put his face within inches of the coach's. "This is no prank!"

"Aw, c'mon, those guys are all dead!" PJ snickered.

"So what? Have you cornered the market on who can see ghosts?" Grant said, raising his eyebrows at PJ. "Now c'mon. We'll talk on the way in."

As they raced through the turnstiles and down the causeway into the stadium, Grant filled PJ in. "I saw those boys from 1984 run the Easterns two weeks ago. In fact, I saw them at a few of your practices as well." PJ remained silent as he listened. "The Hutchens boy was a family friend. He approached me after the Easterns and told me that you were going to miss the New Jersey Masters Championship because you had to go to the Nationals with the RC team."

Grant and PJ opened the iron gate at the end of the track. Pushing it open, their eyes widened as they saw the colorful, packed house in front of them. "Dan told me to bring you to this race," he continued. "He said that you were destined to run it; that if you didn't, you'd end your life with unfinished business. You'd end up like they were – stuck between this world and the afterlife when your number was punched." PJ looked at Grant without speaking. "Dan said this would be his way of thanking you."

"What do you think he meant by me having unfinished business?"

"I don't know, PJ. He said one day you'd understand."

"Hey! Nice job with that bunch from New Jersey!" came a voice from the first row of the stadium.

PJ turned and saw an athlete in a green and yellow sweatsuit climbing down onto the track. As the athlete turned, PJ's legs grew weak. He knew who the mustachioed figure was.

"That Andrew kid reminds me of me. I'm Steve—"

"Pr-Prefontaine," PJ stuttered. "I…I know who you are." Prefontaine held out his hand and shook PJ's. PJ stared at his hand for a few moments after Prefontaine released his grip, then he looked up at the legend.

"You know, there are a lot of dirtbag coaches out there who screw kids up. Never mind those who take advantage of kids, or even molest them. I'm talking about those who fail to push their runners. They lump them all into one group and don't put the time in to consider individual needs." PJ just stood there, listening to the greatest American distance runner. "You did a great job with Andrew, as well as all the others. You managed to bring each to their peak potential."

"Thanks," PJ said.

"Although I would've kicked their butts for stopping their workout to chase a purse snatcher! Come on! First things first!" PJ laughed as well and felt at ease with the star. "Hey, I have to warm up right now because we only have about thirty-five minutes left. I suggest you do the same. It's a pretty talented field out there." He winked and then took off into a brisk jog on the outside lane of the track.

PJ started to say, "There's no way I'm going to—"

"PJ, you have to," Grant interrupted. "Remember what Dan said. You'll be caught between two worlds if you don't. It's something you must do for some reason – a reason we may never know, although Dan said you'll understand one day."

"But I'll get lapped," laughed PJ.

"So be it," quipped Grant. "Better to be lapped than to have no chance at your eternal reward."

PJ thought for a moment, then the expression on his face relaxed. "You know, you've got a point there!" he said as he handed his gym bag to Edwins. "I'm going to jog a bit, and I'll come over for the bag in about fifteen or twenty minutes."

"Gotcha," Grant answered. "I'll be right here."

PJ broke into a strider down the back straightaway and then adjusted to a more reasonable 6:45 mile pace. He surveyed the crowd and was in awe of the spectacle before him. He audited how he was feeling—first his legs, then his arms, then his feet. *All systems are go!* he thought.

PJ was pretty sure he could run in the mid-thirty-minute range, but with this field that would most likely put him last. He wasn't sure. As best as he could tell, there appeared to be twenty-five or so runners warming up on the back straightaway and infield. He recognized Abebe and Mamo, but most of the others were strangers to him. He jogged past a group of African runners and two Brazilians.

As he strode across the infield, he saw an Irish runner who gave him a thumbs-up and yelled, "Nice job this year, laddie!" PJ smiled and waved back. Then a group of runners in USA sweatsuits came up alongside PJ and simply ran stride-for-stride with him.

"Wow, I'm among them, but not of them," PJ joked as he ran. The red, white and blue-clad runners laughed and congratulated him on the fine season. As PJ came to the end of his jog, he slowed down, and the USA runners continued past him. He noticed a brief, cool breeze and thought to himself, *I hope that continues. It's a little warm here tonight.*

PJ sat on the infield and stretched until ten minutes before the race, then he donned his maroon Kennedys and finished his warm-up with some dynamic stretching.

"Final call. All 10,000-meter runners to the starting line," came the announcement over the PA system. PJ jogged nervously over. As he waited in the group that formed behind the line, he counted twenty-eight runners, among them eight Americans and six Africans. The rest were an assortment from Europe and South America.

As PJ bent over to touch his toes, he felt a tap on his head. He stood up to find an American standing next to him. "You should watch for Zatopek and Nurmi. They're potent and should be there at the end of the race." PJ nodded and looked at the two runners the American was pointing toward.

"That one there, he's Nurmi. If his head starts bobbing, that means he's feeling fatigued. That's when you want to pass him," the American whispered. "And that's Zatopek. His head's always bobbing, so don't get him mixed up with Nurmi. If Zatopek goes to his watch, that means he's tired – but he's tough. He could stare at that watch all the way to a gold medal!"

PJ started to thank the runner when he was suddenly interrupted by the starter. "Gentlemen, as you are aware," the starter said with a French accent, "there will be two commands: 'Runners, to your marks,' at which time you will move up to the starting line, followed by the gun. Is it clear?"

The mass of runners didn't reply. Instead, they continued to do whatever it was that runners did just before a race. Some jumped on their toes. Others shook their hands at their sides to wake up their arms. And some prayed. PJ did none of this. He was contemplating the quick trot from where he was to the starting line.

Glancing over at the American who had just given him the advice, PJ noticed the runner was wearing a pair of fluorescent-green Adidas spikes. He had seen a similar pair on display at the Armory Track and Field Museum in the 168th Street Armory in New York. The model was known as the "Spider." The runner in the Spiders had tremendous calf muscles, but what worried PJ was how close he was standing to him. He was worried about being boxed in at the start.

Suddenly, the call came. "Runners, to your marks!"

Just as PJ started to inch forward toward the starting line, the runners on either side of him – the American and Emil Zatopek – hit him with their elbows and grabbed the starting line positions. PJ would have to settle for a position behind them on the line. He was pissed, but he also knew he had just been taken to school!

The moment of serenity that existed just before the starter's gun sounded seemed like an eternity as PJ stared at the American in front of him. He noticed a tattoo of a winged foot on his left forearm. *I gotta get me one of those!* he thought.

Bang! The gun went off, transforming a moment of intense stillness into a moment of supreme havoc. PJ raced through the first turn, doing his best to avoid being tripped by one of the other runners. As he came off the turn, he moved to the outside and made a move that put him in seventh place. In front of him were Prefontaine, Nurmi, Zatopek, Wolde, Bikila, and the American in the green Adidas.

Prefontaine pushed the pace early, going through the first lap in sixty seconds. By the end of the second lap, Prefontaine had a ten-yard lead over Wolde and Bikila. Nurmi and Zatopek were about fifteen yards farther back, followed by the American and PJ. He couldn't help but focus on the American's tattoo as they went through the 800 meters in 2:11. *Yup, I definitely gotta get one of those tattoos!* PJ mused to himself before refocusing on the race at hand.

Prefontaine went through the 1,600 meters in 4:23, then slowed during the second 1,600 to a 4:30 pace. Wolde and Bikila raced past Prefontaine during the third 1,600 meters, appearing to be trying to push each other to the limit. Only Prefontaine tried to go with them and match their effort. The others seemed to hang onto the second pack being led by Zatopek and Nurmi.

Stay in the game! PJ thought to himself as he tried to get into a mid-race rhythm. In road racing, a runner could break the monotony by running tangents, or looking ahead on the course, or if in the lead by trying to catch the pace car. In track racing, a runner looked forward to the lap counter each lap, or stuck to other runners, watching them closely, looking for signs of weakness or pending failure, the smallest hint of rigor mortis. A runner would look for their competitors to be shaking out their arms, or stumbling, or wandering out of the lane, or closing a gap…and that was what was happening.

Wolde, Prefontaine and Bikila were being reined in. With six laps to go, all three were passed by Nurmi, Zatopek, the green-shoed American, PJ, and at least four additional runners. PJ felt a tinge of sadness as he prepared to pass Prefontaine.

He wondered why Prefontaine had pushed so hard to go with Wolde and Bikila when he could have held off and probably kicked his way to a top-three finish at least. But then again, he remembered the 1972

Olympics when Prefontaine passed the more seasoned European lead runners three times on the last lap and faded to a fourth place. When asked why he pushed the seasoned runners instead of sitting back and kicking at the very end to a top-three finish, Prefontaine responded with something to the effect of he "didn't come to the Olympics to come in third!" That quote continued to inspire many young runners to this day – and at least one aging New Jerseyan.

PJ surged and caught the American with 2,000 meters – five laps – left in the race. As they entered the first turn, the American surged slightly in front of PJ, and then forced PJ to go outside as he tried to pass. The American's elbow caught PJ with a light blow to the rib cage. Nothing much, but PJ was sure it was a warning shot.

Okay, two can play at that game! PJ thought as he tucked in behind the runner and ran quietly. PJ liked to play this game of cat and mouse when he had been in high school. He would remain quiet and tucked out of sight, allowing the American to think he had gapped PJ, then PJ would annoy him by touching the American's elbow lightly, letting him know he was still there.

As they headed down the back straightaway, PJ tapped the American's elbow and watched for a response. To his surprise, the American smiled at PJ, then he pointed at Nurmi and Zatopek in front of them. Nurmi's head was beginning to bob, and just as PJ noticed it, Zatopek and the American surged past Nurmi before entering the second turn of the twentieth lap. PJ struggled to get around Nurmi in the second lane but eventually prevailed, focusing his next efforts on catching the American. He'd let Zatopek win, but not the guy who elbowed him. As they entered the last 1,600 meters, Zatopek dropped the pace back down to 4:20. The American and PJ were right on his heels, but PJ was beginning to have his doubts.

Stay in the game, damn it! he thought. *Don't let that voice down!* He thought of his mom for a moment, of all the pain she had endured, how brave she was and how much spirit she had – the spirit she bestowed on him. She had twice the spirit of other moms, raising him as both parents would normally. Then it hit him; he was full of this spirit as well. *Let's do this, Mom!* he thought as he focused on the American.

Right at that moment, the American looked back at him and nodded. PJ watched the American surge past Zatopek as he was checking his watch. PJ shifted gears and passed Zatopek as well. The race was on; the question was which American would win. They were three laps from the finish and running stride-for-stride. As they entered the first turn, PJ stayed in the second lane, right on the American's shoulder. He expected to be hit with an elbow, but the blow never came. As they hit the backstretch, PJ accelerated, hoping to pass the American before entering the second turn, but he was held off.

With two laps to go, PJ was stuck on this guy like glue, but he was worried that the guy had a lot left in him. Coming off the first turn, PJ got right next to the American on the outside, gently using his left elbow to try to get around him. The American lightly pushed the elbow away and, for a moment, held it between his thumb and forefinger. "Are you ready for this!" the American said, his breathing labored.

"The question is, are you!" PJ winced back.

The American looked over at PJ and nodded approvingly. "Then let's have at it!" he said and shifted gears, catching PJ off-guard and moving into the lead.

PJ suddenly admired this guy. He reminded him of himself – in your face, ready for any challenge – but that was where it ended, because PJ was wearing armor that took the form of a singlet, shorts, and maroon Nike Kennedys. His coat of arms took the form of a number pinned to his chest. It was time to wage war!

As he came off the second turn and approached the start of the bell lap, PJ began to close on the American. Just as he caught him, a gust of wind stirred in the stadium. The runners pushed through the first turn, battling each other and the headwind that had developed on the back straightaway.

PJ moved outside to pass the American, but the American strayed toward the outside, blocking him. As he did, PJ noticed the drafting effect the body in front of him had on the headwind. PJ decided to hold off and wait for the final straightaway. He would try to draft off the American and save his strength for one final 110-meter kick. He knew the American would be wary of this and would try to avoid allowing PJ to draft off him, moving side-to-side to keep PJ in the headwind.

But the American did not move. He stayed in lane one, with PJ drafting perfectly off his back. In fact, it almost appeared that, at a couple points, the American motioned with his right hand to keep PJ in the best location.

They entered the last turn, and the American started to drive his arms furiously. PJ felt the pace increase again and knew it was time to respond. *Time to go animal!* he thought.

Halfway through the last turn, PJ shifted gears one last time. He was going to take this kick to the finish line or die trying! And like most kickers will tell you, shortly after you start your kick you know if it's there. It's a feeling you get, a feeling like you can fly. You're on your toes, you're springy, and your arms are strong and moving front to back with little effort. Your eyes begin to tear up, and you don't hurt anymore. You've pushed through. You've crossed over…

Crossed over! he thought as he surged past the American with fifty meters to go. The American evened up with him with thirty meters to go. He wasn't giving in, and neither was PJ. Twenty-five meters to go and they were exchanging glancing elbows, both runners fatigued, dizzy, cramping. Each one reaching out, reaching down inside, looking for that extra inch. At this point it was a game of inches. The preceding 9,980 meters meant nothing. Each runner began to lunge, straining to break the tape, closing their eyes with just twenty feet left, because there was no way they could inadvertently change direction now. They were both leaning forward, both past the point where they could right themselves. They would both be bloodied from the impact with the Tartan track. The only question was who would have the gold around their neck in the end.

PJ crashed to the ground and tumbled one complete rotation before coming to a rest at the foot of the lap counter. The American also crashed to the ground, taking out a judge who was standing in the wrong spot. PJ lay face-down on the track and looked briefly over at the other runner, who was on all fours. The American looked back and crawled toward him.

PJ was too tired to move and simply remained face-down on the ground. The American crawled next to him and put his hand on his shoulder, his head down near PJ's. He whispered in PJ's ear. "You know what? Your father just saw you win tonight."

PJ was too exhausted to move. He reached his hand up and felt the American take it. "C'mon, man, I believe you told your runners not to bend over and hold your hands on your knees after a race. I believe you said it was a sign of weakness!" the American said to PJ as he lay there motionless. "C'mon. I'm proud of you. Let's take a victory lap." He stood up and pulled PJ to his feet.

PJ wobbled for the first fifty meters of the victory lap, supported by the American and one of the race officials. PJ didn't speak until he was halfway around the stadium. At that point, he did something he had never done before. He waved to the packed stadium, and the crowd erupted in applause. Finally, PJ looked at the runner next to him and said, "Nice race."

The American smiled back and said, "You too," and pointed up at the results on the overhead monitor. PJ had finished first with a time of 27:48.

"I didn't think I had a shot at winning," PJ laughed.

"I knew you'd win," the American replied. "You had the look of an eagle in your eyes."

PJ looked briefly at the runner next to him. "Listen," he said, "that was a great race! I'm going to top it off with a nice cold beer somewhere. You interested?"

The American was looking into the stands as if he was searching for someone. "Nah, I, uh…I can't."

"Are you sure?"

The American pulled his attention from the stadium seats back to PJ. "I'm sorry, PJ. I'd love to. But, you see, my sweetheart and I had a parting of ways a number of years ago. She used to come to all my races before we were separated. Well, anyway, I saw her tonight in the seats, watching me, cheering me on like old times. I have to do what's in my heart. I need to be with her. You understand?"

PJ saw an innocence in this runner as he went back to surveying the stadium seats. "Yeah, sure, I understand," he said as he held out his hand. "It was an honor to have raced you."

"Hey, one last thing," the American said, looking back at PJ. "You're a good coach. Don't stop. Some of the kids you'll coach will change the world, make it a better place. Maybe prevent a war or two. You know what I mean?"

PJ nodded. "I understand. Thanks."

The American smiled at PJ one last time and then turned and jogged over toward the stands. PJ watched as he walked slowly along the front of the stands until he noticed someone, waved, and then hopped over the railing and jogged toward an exit. PJ watched as a woman emerged and hugged the runner. They walked out through the tunnel together.

"Nifty race, PJ," Grant said from behind him.

PJ turned. "Are you going to write an article about it?"

"Are you kidding? People would think I'm nuts!" Grant laughed. "Now come on, let's get ourselves back to the hotel."

"Hey, wait!" PJ turned, wanting to yell up into the stadium seats to ask the American, *Do you know where my father is?* But it was too late. The American had vanished.

"Are you okay?" Grant asked.

PJ turned around and replied sadly, "Yeah, uh…I'm fine."

Chapter 46

Going Home

PJ woke up at five thirty the next morning and was checked out of the hotel by six, as were the RC runners, Carmine, and the Baileys. They stopped at McDonald's on the way to the airport and picked up a sack of McMuffins and hash browns. By eight thirty, the team and coaches were on Continental Flight 342 to Newark, due to arrive at five that afternoon.

PJ had called ahead to Brother Owen, suggesting that it might be nice to have the boys' parents greet them at the airport with a victory celebration of some sort. Brother Owen said the plans were already in the works.

As the plane touched down and taxied to Gate C-78, PJ peered through the terminal windows, looking for signs of a crowd. Closing in on the gate, PJ could see a gathering of people through the window who appeared to be holding some type of banner. He also saw balloons, but he kept it all to himself as the plane came to a stop. He thought the surprise would be good for the kids, who happened to sleep most of the way.

"Ladies and gentlemen," came an announcement over the plane's PA system. "At this point we ask that you remain seated. Today, we have a team of runners from Rozelle Catholic on board. They just won the National Championship, so in honor of their win, we would like to have them disembark first. While we're at it, how about giving them a round of applause?"

PJ and the rest of the team grabbed their belongings and headed toward the exit amidst mild applause...and a few cat calls. PJ ushered the team past him so that he would be the last of the bunch to emerge from the jetway ramp.

He was almost giddy as he waited for the cheers from the friends and family members that had gathered at the gate, and he watched as the team emerged from the jetway into the arms of friends and family members, some of them holding congratulatory banners and balloons. Other than that, though, the reception was somewhat subdued.

I'll have to talk to Brother Owen and teach him how to work up a crowd, PJ thought as he looked around for Taylor and David, who were standing off to the side of the group, close to the check-in counter. PJ walked past the parents, noticing that he was being watched as he approached Taylor.

"Hey, David! Hon!" PJ said putting his arms around Taylor and hugging her. "Don't these people even know how to celebrate?" he whispered in her ear, waiting for Taylor to respond in kind or at least giggle, but there was no response. Catching his reflection in a shop window across from them, he could see that the entire bunch of parents were looking at him and Taylor. He tried to pull back from Taylor, but she continued to cling to him tightly – very tightly! She was trembling as well.

"You okay?" he asked. Taylor grabbed his hand, walked over to a seat in the waiting area, and sat down. PJ sat down next to her. "What's wrong?" he asked.

Taylor looked up at him, her mascara smeared, a single tear running down her left cheek. "Your mother...she's an angel now," she said, gripping both his hands and leaning into his chest.

PJ put his head down onto Taylor's as he held her. He was numb. He had known the day was quickly approaching, but it still hurt like hell. Eyes were still on him, and he didn't want to break down in front of the team. Then he felt David's hand on his shoulder. "Grammy's an angel, Daddy. Isn't that cool?"

PJ fought the tears, hard, and smiled back at David. He put his left arm around him and said, "Yeah, that's very cool."

On the way home from the airport, PJ lay in the back of the Tahoe, saying his back was sore from the flight. The truth was that he wanted to be alone with his thoughts, and he didn't want Taylor or David to see the tears. As Taylor headed south on the New Jersey Turnpike, PJ watched the clouds pass by through the rear windows. He brought his arms up and folded them across his forehead, sobbing that he had not been with Rose when she died. *She left this world alone. That's not the way it should've been,* he thought.

"Daddy?" PJ looked up and saw David peeking over the top of the passenger seat. He had his Tickle Me Elmo doll in his hand and was dangling it over the seat back. "Take my Elmo. He'll make you happy again."

PJ gazed into the two blue eyes looking down at him and then smiled, reaching up to take the doll. He held it to his chest, and in a few moments dozed off to sleep.

David looked back at PJ and then at Taylor. "Mommy, Daddy's sleeping with my Elmo."

Taylor looked back at PJ through the rearview mirror. A tear rolled down her face as she reached over and patted David on the head, whispering, "You're a good boy, David."

He nodded in agreement and was soon sleeping himself.

Chapter 47

The Attic

Rose O'Kane Irwin was laid to rest five days after the National Championship. The wake was in the typical Irish style, complete with whiskey and storytelling. PJ was somewhat removed from the whole thing, the realization that he no longer had living parents hitting him hard. Despite her age, there were moments when Rose could still inspire PJ. He never could put his finger on it, but after his visits to the nursing home during the last year, he always felt renewed, like he had just spent time with a very close friend. Now that friend was gone, and all that remained was the small house on Grove Street that still contained the few items that Rose had gathered during her lifetime, the house he would soon have to sell. He felt guilty about it, but he couldn't afford to keep it.

PJ decided to do as much work on the house as possible during the short break between cross country season and indoor track. It was late December, but the weather was still quite warm, allowing PJ to paint the shutters before moving inside to inventory and clean things up. Spending much of the Christmas holidays cleaning Rose's place, PJ donated the living room furniture to a local shelter and gave Rose's clothes (except for her wedding gown, which he brought home to store in his attic) to the Salvation Army.

Up in Rose's attic he found an old chest that was locked. The key was missing, but he was able to pry the latch open with a screwdriver. With the chest open before him, his eyes widened. There, lying on top of everything else, was a flag folded in a triangle – no doubt the flag given to Rose at his father's funeral. Holding it in his hands, PJ noticed a smudge on one of the white stripes, so he moved over to the attic window so that he could examine the flag better. A tear formed in his eyes as he realized the smudge was in the shape of two lips – a leftover from a final farewell kiss Rose had given his dad.

PJ sat back and held the flag to his face. It smelled musty and old and felt rough against his face. He wondered if the soldier who had presented it to his mom ever knew his dad, and if that soldier could still be alive. Maybe he could find him and learn about his father from him, the father he never knew, never got to know, and now with his mom gone would certainly never get to know.

PJ cursed the fact that he spent the last several years focusing on his career and not on his family. He should have spent more time talking to his mom. He could have learned so much more from her. At an early age he made a foolish decision not to bring up his father because he thought it upset his mother. Moreover, he always wondered how his dad could've enlisted while his mom was pregnant. Surely his father didn't care enough for him, since he was able to leave him behind and go to Vietnam.

Wondering about him now, though, was a waste of time, because his only link to him was gone. PJ pulled the flag away from his eyes and looked at the chest. The sun shining across the attic reflected off something metallic inside it. PJ walked over and found that the metal object was a button on one of his father's dress uniforms.

Pulling the uniform out of the chest, PJ held it up against himself. *Almost my size,* he thought. Then his eyes fell upon a smaller wooden box buried underneath the uniform. PJ lifted the box out of the chest and sat down to open it. Inside was a pile of letters tied with a red ribbon. He slid one of the letters gently from the pile and looked at the envelope. It was addressed to his mom from his dad and was from an Army post office.

PJ opened the letter and started to read.

Dear Rose,

It's only been one month and already my heart aches with an emptiness that only you can heal. I should have taken Canada more seriously, but I knew that someday I would have to face one of my children and I wanted to be able to say I played a part in creating the America they live in.

PJ blinked his eyes against the heat of the attic to keep his focus on what he was reading.

But now I question my choice. This is a bad situation over here. I'd be lying if I said I wasn't scared, but I'm determined to return to you. To once again see the stars reflected in your eyes as we dance in the moonlight.

PJ stopped and folded the letter. This was meant for his mom, and with his mom it would stay. These words were some of the last his dad ever said to Rose, and while he could read them, they were meant for her eyes only.

Noticing that a number of the letters in the box were addressed to his father from his mom but had never been mailed, PJ knew just what he should do with them. He carried them downstairs and placed them in his car, then he locked up the old place, deciding he would come back and finish cleaning the house tomorrow. For now he had to go for an evening run…a very important evening run.

Chapter 48

Windy Baldpate

"Hey, hon. Get much done today?" Taylor greeted PJ as he whisked open the screen door and hurried past her.

"Uh, a good bit," he answered.

"Clean the attic?"

"Yeah, partway, but it started to get late and I wanted to go for a run."

"Okay, well, I'm fixing your favorite tonight, slum-goo!"

PJ grinned as he darted up the steps to his bedroom where his Asics awaited him. He loved "slum-goo," which most people knew as Beefaroni, but it would have to wait until he returned. He had just enough time to get this run in before evening fell. Time enough for one final act of love for his mom.

PJ whisked past Taylor and headed out into the garage. A few moments later he came out carrying a small spade and an old backpack that he used to run with when he was in marathon-training mode. Removing the wooden box from the car, he stuffed it into the backpack. It hung out slightly, but it should suffice for the two-mile run up to Baldpate Mountain. PJ was headed to the spot where he used to go to be with his dad. To that windy place where he felt his dad's fingers flow through his hair. To that place where he heard the lions roar in answer to a prayer.

He would take these letters to his dad, burying them there in a wooden time capsule of sorts, so that his father might have a chance to read the letters he never received. He would help bring his parents together. He needed to do it. He wasn't with Rose when she died, and he needed to make amends, if only in his own mind. She couldn't be alone, not like those seven runners were. She needed to be with her husband, and PJ prayed that this act would make it so.

He raced through the woods like a man driven, clenching the spade in his right hand as he hurdled a fallen tree and came to the final clearing he had to cross, which he often referred to as "his Kenya." A few moments later he came to a stop at the old lone oak tree at the top of Baldpate Mountain, and took in the beautiful scenery. Feeling a slight breeze across his face, he thought, *Hi, Dad. I brought you a gift. I'm going to leave it here with you.*

Just then the backpack strap broke, and the pack fell, the wooden box crashing to the ground. Half the letters fell out and scattered in the grass. As PJ bent over to pick up the letters, a gust of wind blew a handful of them across the field. PJ laughed and raced after them. As he neared each letter, he gracefully bent over and picked it up, barely breaking his stride.

When he came to the last letter, the wind stopped and PJ stopped running. He put his foot on the letter so it would not blow away again, and sorted through the bunch he picked up. They were all letters from his dad to his mom. Picking up the letter trapped beneath his foot, he noticed that this one had never been opened. He turned it around, and his eyes widened when he saw it was addressed to him.

His hair stood up on his neck as he realized that this letter had been written to him by the dad he never knew. His hands trembled as he gently tore open the edge of the envelope. He wiped his sweaty hand on his shorts and then gently removed the handwritten letter from the envelope. His lips formed each word as he read the letter, alone, at the top of Baldpate Mountain.

To my son, Paul,

Mom surprised me last month when she told me she had given birth to a beautiful baby boy. You'd think I'd have been smart enough to realize that the weight gain I saw on her was due to more than her appetite for fast food! Had I known you were on the way, I may have made a different decision about Vietnam.

PJ shook his head, realizing his father never deserted him. He simply didn't know Rose was going to have a baby. He read on.

I can't say this war is right or wrong, but I can tell you one thing, it's bad. I've lost many a friend in the short time I've been here. What worries me more is that I don't see the end on the horizon. They keep asking for reinforcements, because they don't expect us to survive very long out here in the field.

I'm not afraid to die, though, especially in service to my country. What I am afraid of is that we may never meet. The hope that one day we will is what keeps me going. I think about that day I can put my hand on your shoulder and tell you how proud of you I am. I know I'll be proud of you.

Your mom sent me a picture of you and I can already see that you have "the look of an eagle in your eyes." You're a winner in my book, and I want you to know that I'll be with you through thick and thin, even if only in spirit. And when the time comes for you to run your bell lap, I'll be there with you, stride for stride.

Have no fear.

Always,

Dad

PJ stared at the letter for a few moments, thinking that some of the words sounded strangely familiar. *The look of an eagle in your eyes,* he repeated to himself before folding the letter and walking back to the wooden box lying near the oak tree.

As he bent over to pick up the box, he noticed that a board that had divided the bottom half of the box from the letters in the upper half had popped open. He grabbed the board and pried it from the box. PJ's heart raced as he stared at what he had just uncovered – a weathered pair of lime-green Adidas Spider racing spikes. They looked exactly like the pair the American runner wore in the 10,000-meter race he had just won, the American who had pushed him through the final mile of the race. The American who was with him, stride for stride, during the bell lap.

Stride for stride during the bell lap! PJ thought as he frantically reopened the letter he had just read. *And when the time comes for you to run your bell lap, I'll be there with you, stride for stride.* PJ read the words over again, remembering that this runner had told him he had the "look of an eagle in his eyes" as well. That was where he had heard those words before.

PJ refolded the letter and tried to reinsert it into its envelope. As he did, it hung up on something. PJ looked into the envelope and noticed something blocking the way. He stuck his finger in and pulled out a small photograph. A man with a huge smile on his face was wearing Army fatigues and a helmet. His shirtsleeves were rolled up, exposing what appeared to be a tattoo on his left forearm. As he examined the picture closer, PJ fell to his knees. The tattoo was of a winged foot, just like the American runner had.

It was true. The runner had been his dad.

Thank you, Lord, for letting me meet him, PJ prayed silently. *And thank you for getting them together again. I know the woman waiting for my father at the stadium was my mother. I also understand why I needed to be at that race. I saw them together. I know they're at peace. Thank you.*

PJ buried the wooden box containing the letters right beneath the oak tree on Baldpate Mountain. But he kept the picture of his father.

Chapter 49

Nicole

The annual cross country banquet was held on January 10th in the school cafeteria. It was catered by a local Italian eatery, with a menu consisting of spaghetti, meatballs, salad, bread, and tons of desserts. All the runners and their friends were dressed in their Sunday best. Their parents attended as well, and they mingled and bragged about how proud they were of their kids. Many special guests also showed up for the ceremonies, including alumni, officials, the mayor, and the archbishop himself.

Immediately after dinner, Brother Owen welcomed everyone, remarking on how proud he was of the boys and PJ. He said what they had achieved was unheard of in a coach's first year at the helm – winning not just a state championship, but a national one too. When Brother Owen invited PJ to come back and coach the following year, a round of applause filled the auditorium.

Noticing how quiet PJ was during Brother Owen's remarks, Taylor whispered to him, "What's the matter?"

"It's just that I…we can't afford for me to continue coaching. I have to get a real job," PJ whispered back to her.

She could see the sadness in his eyes, but she knew he was right. They were nearly tapped out, and he had a couple job offers pending.

The rest of the evening consisted of awards presentations from the underclassmen to the graduating seniors, awards for the most stellar performances, and a slideshow full of pictures taken during the year. One of the last presentations was made by Andrew, who presented a running singlet signed by the team to PJ.

"Coach, we just wanted to make sure you never forget us and what we accomplished this year," Andrew said, his voice strained as he fought off tears. "I'm graduating and heading off to West Point. While I expect to be transformed into a soldier there, I know I became a warrior here. I'll always remember you, my teammates, and my accomplishments here at RC." PJ watched Andrew as he spoke with a youthful eloquence. "And as you prepare for next year, Coach, I have one last question for you." He smiled at PJ.

"And what's that?"

"What does that voice in your head say?"

PJ felt Andrew stare at him as if the boy knew he would not be returning to coach next year, as if Andrew could hear the conversation taking place in PJ's mind. It was as if he could hear PJ's struggle to decide between doing what he loved to do and what would provide financial stability for his family.

PJ walked slowly to the podium as the crowd rose and gave him a standing ovation. His heart raced, and he could feel his palms sweating as he reached into his pocket for some notes he made earlier in the evening. Stopping at the podium, PJ looked out at the team in the first row. As the applause stopped and the audience sat down, the boys remained standing.

"Thank you very much for the kind words, Andrew," PJ began. "And thank you all for the wonderful evening and season. We were all part of this miracle." He paused. "*Miracle*. There's a word you don't hear much nowadays." He shoved his notes back into his pants. He wouldn't need them. He could hear the voice in his head speaking to him.

"But we experienced a miracle this year! In July, I had three names on the team roster, none of whom had ever run in a championship race. Hell, we didn't even field a team in the last five years. Cross country was just a club sport because we couldn't get seven runners to come out for it. Fortunately for the school, Brother Owen has had a vision for this school, one that started with reenergizing the student body and increasing student participation in sports and extracurricular activities."

Archbishop Newberry looked over at Brother Owen and nodded in appreciation. Brother Owen blushed and continued to listen intently to PJ.

"What I didn't realize when I took this job was the journey I was about to make, a journey that started twenty years ago with a group of boys who were destined to win the Easterns Championship. A group that had the same dreams and visions that the eight boys before you have right now – to continue to grow, to make their marks on the world, to have children perhaps, and to leave a legacy that their children will be proud to inherit.

"I heard after the Easterns win that the boys dedicated the race to their predecessors from 1984. You know, there's this bond among distance runners that's natural, instinctive. It's not learned. It's inherited. When they toed the line at the Easterns, I saw fourteen boys on the line. I saw Pete Bailey whispering into Andrew's ear…" Andrew's eyes darted toward PJ as he said this. "I know these boys felt their teammates' presence as they stood there on the line. A cool breeze, maybe?" He looked at the boys standing in the front row. They were smiling and nodding.

"And at that moment, the race took on a new meaning. It was now a matter of eight runners being called upon to finish what their late teammates had started. To recapture the spirit that is RC and set the tone for years to come. To return to the glory of what once was and put in motion RC's second coming."

PJ paused for a moment while a number of alumni and students applauded. He also gathered himself for the news he was about to deliver, that he would not be around to coach again next year.

As he surveyed the audience, he noticed a group of seven or eight girls coming from the rear bleachers toward the stage. They stopped at the foot of the steps and whispered into Brother Owen's ear for a moment. He smiled and looked at PJ, shrugging his shoulders. Two of the girls ascended the stairs at the right side of the stage and walked toward PJ.

"Hello, can I help you?" PJ joked.

The darker-haired of the two girls handed PJ a manila envelope and a gift-wrapped box, and then she spoke into the microphone. "Coach Irwin, my name is Katie Conlon, and I'm in ninth grade. I represent the newly formed Rozelle Catholic varsity girls' cross country team. In the manila envelope we just handed you is our team roster. We hope that next year we can be state champions, just like the boys' team."

PJ stared at the list of names and grinned at the decorative artwork doodled across it. Stepping up to the microphone, however, his heart was heavy, because he was about to deliver the message that he would not be returning.

"Go ahead and open your present," the other girl giggled.

PJ glanced over his shoulder and saw the girl with the light-brown hair gesturing for PJ to open the present, so he placed the box on the podium and opened it. Inside was a jacket with "Head Coach" printed on the back. On the front was the RC logo with "Lady Lions Cross Country" written beneath it. PJ didn't know what to say. His mouth went dry as he approached the microphone.

As he passed the brown-haired girl on his way to the podium, she grabbed his hand and said, "Coach Irwin, my name's Nicole and I'd like to help you make the Lady Lions national champions!"

PJ nodded and smiled politely as he thanked her and prepared to deliver one final message into the microphone.

"First off, let's give these two girls a round of applause," PJ said as he searched for the best possible way to deliver the bad news.

The applause was intermittent, and PJ looked out toward Taylor, who had a strange look on her face, as if she didn't understand what he was saying. He checked the microphone to make sure it was turned on. "Is this working?" he asked.

"It's working, Coach," said Nicole, the brown-haired girl, with a grin.

PJ glanced at Katie Conlon, who was looking in Nicole's direction, then back at PJ. "It's working, Coach," Katie said with a confused look on her face.

PJ approached the mic and motioned for both girls to join him at the podium. He put his arms around their shoulders. "I'd like to have Nicole and Nancy stand beside me as I announce—"

PJ noticed a few people giggling in the audience as he proceeded to speak, which caught him off guard. He glanced at Katie, who still had a puzzled look on her face, and then at Nicole. "Nicole, what are they laughing at?" he asked. Nicole simply smiled and shrugged her shoulders. He looked at Katie. "And you? Do you know?" Katie looked past him for a moment, then behind him. She wiggled her pointer finger at him, as if she wanted to whisper something in his ear.

PJ bent over, and Katie asked, "Who's Nicole? I'm the only one up here with you."

At that moment, PJ looked over at Nicole. She gently placed her forefinger to her lips, winked at him, and said, "I'm lost. Pete Bailey said you might be able to help me find my way."

Author's Note

Life is stranger than fiction sometimes, even more so when it parallels it. Let me explain.

My father was an engineer for a large pharmaceutical company and often traveled as part of his job. He had a habit of purchasing souvenir stickers containing the names of the various places he visited, which eventually covered an old suitcase he had. My mom, on the other hand, never even got a driver's license.

In 1972, I was twelve years old (the middle of five children) when my parents had to make a tough decision. My mom was dying of cancer and had less than a year to live. She was about to start her last series of cancer treatments, designed to simply try to extend her life a few months, which would result in her being in the hospital more than at home.

They had one window of opportunity to spend some final moments together. One night in early June, as they prepared for bed, my father asked my mom if she had any unfulfilled dreams. She said she wanted to live long enough to see my cousin Gregory ordained a priest. For a few moments they sat there in silence, both knowing it was doubtful this would happen, since it would be a year until he was ordained.

Then my mom looked down at the old suitcase next to the bed, smiled, and said, "And I always wanted to see a few of those places you have decorated all over that suitcase."

The next morning my father got up early and went out on an errand, returning later in the afternoon in a "new" used 1966 Cadillac DeVille convertible sedan. It was beautiful – red with a white convertible top – a Polish limousine! When Dad walked through the door, his face was lit up with a tremendous smile. It had been a long time since we had last seen him like that. A few moments later, he was sitting at our dining room table with that old suitcase and a collection of maps. When Mom asked him what he was doing, he said he was planning out the trip, then he asked her which places she wanted to visit the most. She giggled, sat down next to him, and started to make her selections.

By late June, my father sent my little brother and me to live with my aunt Mary in Reading, Pennsylvania, while he and Mom went on their journey. I had a sense that what was going on with my mother's health was serious, but I was in denial. Fortunately for me, my aunt was a nice Catholic woman with ten children. Three of them – Chucky, Jonathan and Lisa – were close to my age and were great at taking my mind off the things going on with my mom. (By the way, my mom's name was Rose, just like PJ's.)

Later that summer, everyone focused their attention on the Olympics. My older brother, who was living at home, was a great runner for Roselle Catholic (on which the fictitious "Rozelle Catholic" is based) during their heyday in the late '60s and early '70s. He ran in the Penn Relays and on some of their winning relay teams under Coach Deniz Kanach.

My father was an avid runner as well. Daily runs were a habit for him well before the running boom hit America, before Lycra and performance apparel hit the shelves. He often completed twenty-mile runs in his khaki work pants on cold winter days! The neighbors thought he was nuts, and when I caught wind of this, I was a little embarrassed by some of the things they said about him. In addition, having running in common with my brother made their relationship a tight one. They were often away together at races, running together, or on some occasions traveling to purchase a pair of Tiger Montreals or Arthur Lydiard racing flats, being sold by an entrepreneur out of a garage behind a funeral home in Massachusetts.

As their relationship tightened, I became very close with my mom, who got me involved in baseball when I was in grammar school. While my brother poured on the miles, I focused on pitching and hitting.

My cousins in Reading were neither baseball players nor runners. They liked to fish and play golf with their dad, Adolf, a roly-poly guy with a great sense of humor – and a great ability to know what to say to a twelve-year-old boy about to lose his mother.

During the opening ceremonies of the Olympics, my uncle asked me to watch the games with him. He told me about this guy Mark Spitz and what an incredible swimmer he was. I remember how exciting it was, cheering him on as he won medal after medal. And, as a young American, I was proud to be from the same nation.

During the day, we would go to the Sleepy Hollow Swim Club, which was about three miles from my uncle's house, and pretend we were Spitz as we raced across the pool. When my uncle couldn't drive us there, we would often ride our bikes – usually with me having to ride on the handlebars of my cousin Chuck's bike.

My uncle helped me understand what was going on as terrorists interrupted those Olympic games. At one point he tried to explain how the schedule changes (due to the attacks) would impact the distance races, allowing some runners like Lasse Viren to recover for an extra day or so before having to run his second race of the games. He described how terrifying it must have been for the younger athletes like Steve Prefontaine. At this point in my life, I didn't know who these athletes were. If they didn't wear a Yankees or Mets uniform, I just didn't care. It wasn't exciting for me.

That all changed the day I sat in my uncle's living room with my cousins, and we cheered wildly as we watched young Steve Prefontaine surge to the lead three times during the last lap of the 5,000-meter race. I was upset when he faded toward the end, but my uncle explained that he ran a courageous race.

A couple days later I sat down with my uncle to watch this race called "the marathon." As the runners ran through the streets of Munich, an American named Frank Shorter moved to the front of the pack. My uncle described how grueling it is to run a marathon, how you have to be fit and mentally tough. Then he looked at me and said, "Tough, like your father."

There was something about the way he looked at me over the rim of his glasses as he said those words that impacted me, something I feel to this day. I remember thinking of my mom that night and being conscious of my self-denial that I was going to lose her. I remember thinking how tough it must have been on my father, and how his running probably helped him prepare to face the challenges associated with her illness and losing her.

At the swim club the next day, while my cousins continued to play "Mark Spitz," I found my thoughts moving back to the day before and that guy named Shorter. It was so cool watching him bang out one mile after another. He looked graceful as he gradually pulled away from the others, and it was exciting as he approached the Olympic stadium during the final mile of the marathon. I remembered the announcers pointing out that he could hear the crowd inside the stadium cheering as he approached, and watching him run triumphantly through the last lap on the track inside the stadium. This was a life-defining moment for me. I could feel his joy, his energy. I now understood why my father and brother ran.

When it came time to return home from the swim club that day, I told my cousins that I wanted to try to run the three miles home. A few moments later I sprinted out of the parking lot, quickly learning the virtues of pacing myself as I had to run and walk the rest of the way. To this day, I remember arriving at the Bingaman Street Bridge, imagining entering the Olympic stadium as I crossed it. I threw my hands over my head and made the "V" for victory sign as I reached the other side, and then I walked the three blocks from there to my aunt's house, imagining myself signing autographs for fans the whole way. That day I became a runner.

I became a man a little over a year later, when my mom died a few weeks after attending my cousin's ordination. She had made it. (And my father decided to retire the old suitcase at that point.)

When my son was in middle school, he received a flyer for a youth cross country race at Warinanco Park. He had never run a race before, and I had given up running about fifteen years earlier due to Morton's neuroma, which basically results in a nerve becoming inflamed and then enveloped in scar tissue. The nerve is in the forefoot, and it gets pinched every time the foot bends near the toes. It got so bad that I couldn't press the gas pedal in my car. I avoided surgery, but noninvasive treatment just didn't work. As a result, my mileage (and enthusiasm) dropped until I completely gave up running. At the time my son received the flyer, I weighed about 250 pounds, and my health was very poor.

My son ran the race and came in thirty-first. Because the top thirty qualified to move forward to the USATF youth state championships, he was disappointed and it showed. The following year, rather than play summer baseball, he decided he would do a little running and attend a running camp. (I was relieved because it meant I didn't have to do the Little League thing anymore.)

I searched the Internet and came across a number of camps located in Vermont, Pennsylvania, New York and New Jersey. Deciding to give the one in New Jersey a shot, I called them. (I never realized the impact this phone call would have on my life!) The camp was called the Extreme Running Camp and was located in Newton, New Jersey. The man that answered the phone was Guy Gordon. He explained that it was the first year for the camp, but that he had been spearheading a youth running program for a number of years. He described his plans for the camp and what my son could expect. It sounded like it would be a fun time.

Both my son and daughter attended the camp. For my daughter, it was more of a social thing, but she enjoyed the running as well on many days. Since the camp was a commuter camp and far from our home, my wife and I decided to camp at Swartswood State Park where the camp took place, thinking we would just hang out and swim while the kids ran their workouts. We never had a chance, not with Guy around. He got us involved and, more remarkably, got me running again. By the end of the week, Guy and I realized we had some close ties in life: we ran in high school around the same time, and he had been coached by a man who started out his career at my high school, Roselle Catholic.

A few months after the camp, David went to the AAU National Championships with Guy's team, the Stillwater Bears. He had spent the fall racing at Brundage Park with the team and made many friends in the group. And, like so many Guy has coached, he became a very good runner.

At the National Championships, Guy's motto was, "They worked hard to get here. Let's let them have as much fun as possible." And they did! The race was in Ames, Iowa, and they played and raced their hearts out, making memories they will never forget.

A couple days later, Guy called and asked me if I would run on a Masters 4x800-meter relay team. I laughed at first, thinking he was kidding. He wasn't. So I did my best to get a couple speed workouts in, and brought my svelte 220 pounds of middle-distance runner to Fairleigh Dickinson University for the meet. Guy approached the race the same way he approached all his races: he was fun-loving up until race time, then you could see the seriousness in his eyes.

Well, as it turns out, the team of Guy Gordon, Bill Bosman, Chucky Jewel and me won the Masters division race that day. More importantly, I think Guy's true goal was met – he got me interested in racing again. And I've been at it ever since.

I took up road racing that spring and found myself plodding through a series of 5K and 10K races. I was very slow, running twenty-three- to twenty-five-minute 5Ks, but I was having fun running with Guy's adult running club, the Bears.

One of the weird things that happened when I took up road racing was that I found myself running alongside the same individual at almost every race I entered. He didn't look much like a runner, and he was very noisy, coughing and clearing his throat the whole time he ran. I found this very annoying; I would go to these races to run in some beautiful setting, and there he would be, coughing his way right beside me.

Then it got worse. This fellow was very popular among the other runners, and he would talk to almost everyone. He loved running and raced multiple races on the weekends. I tried to steer clear of him because…well, because I was an ass. I didn't want to be near him because he didn't look like a competitive runner. He was "different," and I had no time for "different." Hell, I was a sub-twenty-five-minute five-miler at one point. This guy had no right being next to me in a race!

I kept training and eventually became fast enough that listening to the "hacker" running beside me became a thing of the past. Then one day Guy invited me to a Bears Christmas party at Big Poppa's, a pizza parlor in Stillwater, New Jersey. My wife and I went, and many good runners and parents of the youth club members were there. After mingling with the other members, my wife and I sat down at one of the tables. Moments later, *he* came over and sat down next to us. The "hacker," who loved to talk to everyone, was going to sit right across from us at the very same table.

"This guy's going to drive us nuts!" I whispered to my wife. She smiled politely and introduced herself to him while I groaned silently to myself.

(Now remember how I started this piece, "Life can be stranger than fiction.")

My wife asked the hacker what the book was he was carrying. He said it was a photo album containing pictures from his favorite races. He placed it on the table and said he wanted to tell us about a few of them. I groaned – this time it might have been noticeable.

The hacker opened the album to the first page and looked up at me without saying a word. He just stared at me, so I decided to look down at the first picture so I wouldn't have to look at him. The image seemed familiar, but I wasn't sure why. I studied it for a few moments, finally asking him what race it was. He told me it was the starting location of a trail he ran in Pennsylvania, just outside Reading. I looked down at the picture again, and my eyes filled with tears as I realized why the place in the picture seemed familiar.

It was the Sleepy Hollow Swim Club, the place where I spent my time while my mom and dad were touring the country in that red and white Cadillac. It was the starting point of my first run, the run I took the day after Frank Shorter won the Olympic marathon. It was in that place where I am 100 percent sure I took my first steps toward becoming a runner.

The memories flooded back, and I excused myself from the table, going outside and struggling for my composure. I felt sad; not because of the memories, but because I had never bothered to even get the hacker's name! To this day, I'm sure his intervention in my life was heaven sent. I went back inside and reintroduced myself to the hacker, and we became friends from that day forward. I stop to greet him at every race and cheer him on whenever I get a chance. In fact, he has gone through a physical change, as did I, and he looks like a runner now.

But there were other, even stranger events that took place while I was busy (or not so busy) writing this book, that in the end leave me believing I was destined to complete it. I'm not sure if it will ever get published, or if another soul will ever read it, but I honestly feel that I was meant to write this story. Let me share a few of these "coincidences" with you.

I started to pen this book on September 17, 2001, the week following 9/11, when I found myself thinking of my son and daughter and how I was responsible for bringing them into this world. I was worried about the world they were inheriting. For the first couple of years, I only wrote the book while I was traveling. It was a way of killing time.

In 2006, my son and I made the trek to the University of Wyoming, the school he had selected to attend to study meteorology. The University of Wyoming was an NCAA Division I school with very competitive cross country and track and field teams. During our visit to the University of Wyoming, my son visited Coach Cole, the cross country coach, and the two of them hit it off.

David walked on to the program and competed for the cross country and track and field teams. This was totally unexpected and made getting acclimated to the university much easier.

During that first trip, we came across a memorial near the university fieldhouse. My legs went numb when I learned that this memorial was in memory of the eight runners from the University of Wyoming (Cowboys) who were killed by a drunk driver. I had to sit down when I realized that the accident occurred on September 16, 2001 – the day before I started writing the book! Like many people, I didn't know about this sad event, because the events of 9/11 had filled the news during that time. But I'd like to believe there was a connection between this event, my son selecting the University of Wyoming, and me writing this book.

In tribute to those boys, I decided to have them appear and help the RC runners "cross over." They were obviously a close-knit group, traveling to Fort Collins together, the way they had done so many times. My son has experienced the same type of bonding with his teammates at the University of Wyoming (as well as at Hopewell Valley High School). I think this is not uncommon amongst running teams. The workouts are so grueling that you gain a mutual respect for each other, and a camaraderie develops.

In 2007, I ran in an 8K road race honoring the eight members of the Wyoming team. It's held every year in September and is a simple, beautiful event. At each kilometer marker the name of one of the fallen eight is displayed, and I found myself saying a short prayer as I ran past each one. Later that same day, I drove to Fort Collins and came across a memorial to the runners at the site of the accident. It's located about eighteen miles south of Laramie on US 287. The memorial consists of eight sets of running shoes draped over a wooden "tree" at the side of the road. It is simple, thoughtful and beautiful. As a kid growing up on the east coast, I used to wonder if I'd ever see the place where cowboys roamed. I now believe that I've visited this place!

And finally, there was Nicole, who I met while I was an assistant coach at Roselle Catholic. Through Nicole I learned that it's worth taking the time to ask your friends, "How are you?" and then to really listen to the answer.

In closing, I just want to say something to my father, Ted Siuta. I heard, felt and understood every word you ever said to me when I was growing up, and I feel I have succeeded in life (thus far) because of you! I hope I've become at least half the father to my own kids that you were to me. If I have, then I'm ready to cross over when the time comes – but not right now. I have a few more *miles to go before I sleep.*